GINA CONKLE

For a Scot's Heart Only

A Scottish Treasures Novel

AVONBOOKS

An Imprint of HarperCollinsPublishers

FOR A SCOT'S HEART ONLY. Copyright © 2023 by Gina Conkle. All rights reserved. Printed in the United States of America. No part of this book may be used or reproduced in any manner whatsoever without written permission except in the case of brief quotations embodied in critical articles and reviews. For information, address HarperCollins Publishers, 195 Broadway, New York, NY 10007.

First Avon Books mass market printing: April 2023

Print Edition ISBN: 978-0-06-299901-6
Digital Edition ISBN: 978-0-06-299897-2

Cover design by Amy Halperin
Cover illustration by Gene Mollica & Sasha Almazan, GS Cover Design Studio

Avon, Avon & logo, and Avon Books & logo are registered trademarks of HarperCollins Publishers in the United States of America and other countries.

HarperCollins is a registered trademark of HarperCollins Publishers in the United States of America and other countries.

FIRST EDITION

23 24 25 26 27   BVGM   10 9 8 7 6 5 4 3 2 1

She cocked her head, perusing him through her lashes. "And in this imaginary assignation, did we agree to meet here? Or did I pay handsomely for you?"

His laugh had a primal quality. "You paid, and we had no regrets."

She worked her fan, loose curls teasing her hot skin. They were teetering on an impossible precipice.

"Once a woman procures a room of her own, how does she go about inviting a gentleman to join her?" she asked.

"She informs him directly."

"An interesting approach." She shrugged, indifferent, but it was an act, and they both knew it. "Where's the mystery? The seduction?"

His was a sea wolf's smile. And she, the morsel he wanted.

"Forthrightness *is* seductive—in the right measure."

She contemplated that. "Are you suggesting that men prefer to be the hunters? And women, their prey?"

"It is the rules of nature, Miss Fletcher."

She touched her fan to his chest and whispered, "Sometimes nature likes to be played with."

Mr. West sucked in a fast breath.

"I wonder, if deep down, sir, you wish to be played with."

Also by Gina Conkle

Scottish Treasures Series
THE SCOT WHO LOVED ME
A SCOT IS NOT ENOUGH

MEET THE EARL AT MIDNIGHT
THE LADY MEETS HER MATCH
THE LORD MEETS HIS LADY
MEET A ROGUE AT MIDNIGHT
MEET MY LOVE AT MIDNIGHT

NORSE JEWEL
TO FIND A VIKING TREASURE
TO STEAL A VIKING BRIDE
KEPT BY THE VIKING
HER VIKING WARRIOR

For Brian

For a Scot's
Heart Only

Prologue

Scotland, 1738

*M*en were the problem—or rather, one French-
man and the kiss he stole from her mother on the
deck of a ship. Mary witnessed their kiss through
dark hair buffeted by chilly wind. A dutiful daughter, patience was her virtue. Every time her mother
returned, Mary would wrap herself in wool and wait
for her on Leith's shore. Their reunion was always
the same—a loving embrace clouded in rosewater
while her mother's soft curls feathered her cheek.

Eyes shut, she'd hoard the tenderness.

"You look exactly the way I did when I was fifteen,"
her mother would whisper in her ear.

"Except you are prettier," she'd whisper back, wishing this would be enough.

It never was.

"Will you stay home awhile, Mama?" Her question would burst with hope and brightness. There'd
be a gentle touch to her chin and enigmatic gray
eyes, so like her own, chided her.

"My dear, sweet girl, let us not waste a splendid day on such things."

Indeed, they never did. Mary quietly stuffed emotions into a neat box and took joy where she could. On that particular morning, they'd linked arms and strolled through Leith, discussing her mother's latest journey, this time to Niderville pottery works, its factory leased by a Frenchwoman.

"So delightful, Madame Andre," her mother had trilled. "As a woman of business, she rules her fate. Remember that, Mary."

Beautiful and restless, her mother had already forgotten the gentleman on the ship.

But his kiss had not forgotten her.

A month later her mother's fair cheeks were sallow and her black hair lank and greasy. Entombed in a richly appointed bed, she was fragile. No man attended her save an old physic, Dr. Ross, holding a handkerchief over his nose. Understandable. Urine and sweat perfumed the air. The examination done, he dropped the handkerchief into the bedside brazier. Mary watched delicate flames lick the pristine cloth. *What a waste.* Dr. Ross could've used the handkerchief on his next visit.

Her mother's fevered stare followed him. "What . . . ails me?"

The physic rummaged through his medicine case, the bottles *clinking* softly.

"You have the French fever, madame."

"But—how?"

"Have you visited France of late?"

"Yes, Lorraine," she rasped. "But the fever—I thought it was . . . finished."

Dr. Ross sighed heavily. "In Paris, yes. However,

there are reports the sickness lingers in provincial towns." He set an amber vial on the bedside table. "Take this for your discomfort."

Candlelight glinted on a near-empty bottle.

"Won't she need more than that?" Mary asked from her corner of the room.

Hooded eyes etched with age and gloom met hers. "No."

Dr. Ross locked his wooden case, the brass *click* a confusing noise. So cold, so final. Like a certain end. Mary worried a seam on her stomacher, this stygian nightmare growing. She'd read about the sickness last year, the details vague. Mouth sores, terrible sweats. The malady took half the afflicted. For the other half, recovery was agonizing. Yet, Dr. Ross wasn't issuing further advisements.

"Now may I climb on the bed and hug Mama?" was the childish whisper beside her.

Her sister, Margaret, not yet five years old, waited on the bench, her legs swinging idly.

"Later," Mary said, stroking Margaret's ink-dark hair. "First, we must tend her, you and I, and when Dr. Ross returns, he will proclaim you an angel for healing Mama."

"I will not return," he said.

Mary rushed forward. "I don't understand."

Reed thin, Dr. Ross towered over her, his bony fingers flexing on the case's handle.

"The air in here is tainted. You, too, should leave. Take your sister and find lodgings elsewhere."

"But my mother—"

"Will soon be dead."

She dropped her scented kerchief, its weight too much.

No . . . this couldn't be. Not her mother.

"Surely, there's something you can do," she said, frantic.

"There isn't."

From the bed, a coughing fit seized her mother. Mary grabbed the physic's sleeve, her fingernails scoring pressed wool.

"I cannot leave her."

"What about little Margaret?" he hissed. "Do you care naught for her? Because we both know no one will look after her should you die."

Arguments were building, another plea to convince the good doctor to stay, but his demeanor flattened. A soulless withdrawal. She let go of him, truth knifing her. For too long, Dr. Ross had carried the burden of Fletcher family secrets. Her mother's peccadilloes, her father's indifference, the minute burns on her fingers—the ordered chaos of her life.

She didn't know any different. But that life, her life, was crashing into pieces.

Shadows carving his cheeks, Dr. Ross collected his hat. "I must alert the Royal Infirmary. And we all must pray this plague does not leave this room."

A plague?

She slumped against the bedpost, trying to breathe. Dr. Ross exited the room, plush carpet muffling his footsteps. Her throat clogged. The room spun. Dark paneled walls loomed, heavy and stifling in the windowless chamber.

This nightmare was real.

A small body folding into her petticoats stopped her collapse. She looked down.

Blue eyes, saucer big, beseeched her. "I'm frightened."

Mary dropped on shaky knees and drew her sister into a desperate hug.

"Shhhh. Don't worry. I'll take care of you."

Confident words, yet a tear wanted out. She squeezed it back and inhaled Margaret's sweet, soapy cleanness. Sapped to the bone, Mary held on. Childish exhales touching her ear began to unwind the tightness inside her. The two souls she loved most in this world were in this room. She *would* save them.

"Be a dear," she said, pulling away. "And go dress your doll in that pretty blue gown we made together."

Small, trusting hands cupped her cheeks.

"May I show Mama my stitchwork?"

"Yes." She kissed Margaret's forehead. "Off with you now."

Her little sister scampered away, taking the last scrap of joy with her. Mary tucked a messy lock behind her ear. She pushed off the floor, her mind reeling. How could she save her mother *and* her sister? Another doctor, perhaps. There was talk of a promising new physic on Drummond Street.

"I know . . . what you're . . . thinking," her mother rasped. "It's . . . useless."

Mary faced the bed, resolve firming her joints.

"Then you know I cannot leave you."

"You must. For—for . . . your sister's sake."

She leaned in with a fierce, "I can take care of both of you."

A curdled noise startled her. It was her mother's mournful laugh.

"Isn't that . . . what you've . . . always done?"

"Then let me—"

"No! Your duty is . . . to Margaret." Her mother's face crumpled. "She is better off . . . with you."

Hot tears pricked Mary's eyes, agony rising with them. Her mother's defeat. A family lost. Their slow demise finally met. An ache spread behind her breastbone, more truth coming with it.

A choice must be made.

Her sister. Or her mother.

She wavered as if the ground wanted to swallow her in one bite—part of her wished it would.

"You can . . . do this," her mother said.

Could she?

At the tender age of ten, a midwife had set a newborn slick with blood and afterbirth in her arms. Her heart brimming with love, she'd bathed and swaddled Margaret. But love wasn't enough. The babe couldn't knit their family together. Barely two months later her mother had embarked on a journey to the Baltics. Another adventure, she'd called it. The following year her father and her half brother took up residence above her father's shop, while the women remained in Mary King's Close off High Street.

Mary had endured the brunt of this new arrangement. Grumbling neighbors; the wet nurse who'd lived with them, frowning her disapproval. It didn't matter. Little Margaret was deeply, deeply loved.

But the same brazier that shined on Margaret's birth lit her mother's sunken eyes.

"Go to your father. Tell him . . . about this fever," her mother said. "And tomorrow . . . arrange for an escort to—to Arisaig."

"You are sending me away?" Mary's voice pitched painfully.

"To Clanranald MacDonald. My kin—they will . . . look after . . . you."

Mary cuffed her watery chin. "What about you?"

Eyes the shade of a storm-tossed loch scolded gently.

"Mary . . ."

"No, Mama!" she wailed. "Don't make me leave you."

But her mother was already gasping instructions. In the kitchen there were silver coins in the Niderville soup tureen. They were hers to keep. For her future and Margaret's. At the bottom of her mother's traveling chest was a false bottom. She should hide the money there, and when the time was right, use it.

The orders given, her mother's head fell onto the pillow.

"Dear Mary . . . you are blessed with—a—a keen mind. Use the money and . . . make a new life . . . God willing."

Her heart banged, raw and aggrieved. Why would God steal her mother? The one person who understood her? Her father, an eccentric silversmith, was kind when he thought of her, but for him, the sun rose and set on her half brother, the fruit of his first marriage. His eldest daughter was from his second wife, the fair lass from Clanranald MacDonald. His youngest daughter? Her paternal line was debatable. The silversmith claimed his willful wife was a blight on his reputation, but she was Mary's bright morning star. She'd encouraged her eldest daughter to expand her mind and use her talents and never let a man diminish her worth.

And now she was dying.

"Be . . . smart," her mother said. "Do not let . . . men turn your head as . . . they have . . . turned mine."

"I won't."

Her mother's dry lips cracked a smile. "Such a . . .

good girl. You look . . . like me . . . when I was fifteen."

Mary stood tall, her heart and soul crumbling. "Ach a-mhàin gu bheil thu nas fheàrr." *Except you were prettier*, she said in Scots Gaelic.

Her mother's eyelids sagged over a weakening smile. Tears bathed Mary's face, bringing an awful awakening. Of aching loss and the years she'd strived to please. To be a diligent, responsible girl. Her posture, her manners, her speech—always impeccable.

But love wasn't enough.

It never was.

Chapter One

London, October 1753

To prepare for an evening in a brothel, the adventurous spinster must strike a balance with the rouge on her cheeks. Too much and men would assume she was a harlot. Too little and men would assume she was a charwoman masquerading in silks. Add a touch of confidence and the blend was just right.

Self-assurance, as it turned out, was the best cosmetic—a trait Mary Fletcher owned.

Velvet slipping off her shoulders, she passed her cloak to an attendant and waded into a sea of excess. Of men feasting their eyes on half-dressed women posing on plinths. Of giggling nymphs playing in a fountain, and a red-headed Venus couched in a papier mâché shell. Pink, of course. In the middle of it all, women in gossamer Greek-styled gowns swirled around a harpist, the opulence fascinating. Almost dreamlike.

Mary skimmed her collarbone, her fingertips

tracing its structured line. Beside her, Cecelia Mac-Donald, her partner for the evening's mayhem, snapped open a fan.

"Well, what do you think?"

Mary tried for an insouciant, "Not much, I'm afraid."

Cecelia snorted delicately.

"I don't believe you."

Cecelia was right to doubt her, but Mary wasn't about to spill her soul. She smoothed white silk panniers, her best, though an odd choice given their environs. Soft green vines and spring flowers had been painted on the fabric. Her gown was more daytime luncheon than nighttime debauchery, save two pink crescents rising from her bodice.

She whisked her fan strategically over them.

"If you must know, I noticed the organizer of this evening's entertainment mixed their mythologies. A deplorable job, in my opinion."

"Whatever do you mean?" Cecelia asked.

"Nymphs are mainly Greek, and Venus is definitely Roman. Hence, the mixed mythologies."

Hazel eyes sparkled within a green silk mask. "Your first time in a brothel, and *that's* what comes to mind?"

Her mind? She couldn't claim control of it, not with sensual currents dusting her skin. From the glorious high ceilings to the gilt-trimmed mirrors, everything glimmered. She couldn't *not* stare.

Mary wetted her lips. "My second thought was how did they get a fountain to work in a ballroom?"

Cecelia giggled. "Men are not here for lessons in engineering."

"And we are not here to discuss my impressions of Madame Bedwell's establishment."

Here was Maison Bedwell, an expensive brothel in King's Square—Soho Square to the fashionable, as it had recently been renamed. The house was an elegant, sizable brick structure designed by Sir Christopher Wren. Somewhere under the palatial roof, a secret society was known to meet. A group so clandestine, they took names such as Lady Pink and Lord Blue to hide their identities, even from each other. But not all of them were Jacobites, a fact Mary and Cecelia had learned from a recent find—a coded ledger that came into their hands. One of the society's members had the last of the Lost Treasure of Arkaig. Gold livres, support the French sent seven years ago to Bonnie Prince Charlie and his rebels.

A treasure which had disappeared.

For that reason alone, Mary found herself in this luxuriant den of iniquity. Highlanders wanted their money back.

She and Cecelia belonged to a Scottish league sworn to find it. Four long years they'd hunted for the treasure. This past summer they'd taken the first of it from the Countess of Denton. The league was hungry for more. To protect her identity, Mary wore a mask, though it was more precaution than necessity. As proprietor of Fletcher's House of Corsets and Stays, she didn't swim in the same social waters as the men in attendance. She sold her goods to their housekeepers and governesses, not their wives and daughters.

But tonight she was a shark in silks. A huntress.

A touch to her elbow and Cecelia beckoned, "Come with me."

They returned to the entry hall where loudmouthed lordlings were dropping coins into the attendant's white-gloved palm as they crossed the threshold.

Despite the ruckus, Cecelia lowered her voice. "I will investigate abovestairs."

"Where Madame Bedwell's nymphs ply their trade," Mary said archly.

Cecelia ignored that conversational bait and nudged her chin at a wide hallway off the entry.

"Meanwhile, you will investigate the gaming room. An hour should suffice, after which we'll meet here."

Mary flicked her fan with an indolent wrist. Tonight was their first foray in the brothel, and they were here for one reason only—to see what they might find. Down the passage, double doors had been flung wide. Tobacco's sweet, dark aroma and deep male laughter floated past them. A bastion of masculinity there.

"Why am I investigating the gaming room?" she asked, casual. "I don't gamble."

"Nor do you have sex."

A flush tinged Mary's cheeks. "I'm not an innocent."

Cecelia pinned her with a knowing look.

"When was the last time you even kissed a man?"

She bristled. "That's irrelevant."

Five years was the whisper in her head. Five long years.

A fan dangling from her wrist, Cecelia was in the act of retying her mask. "You'd be agog if you went abovestairs, and we both know it."

Mary's gaze wandered to the gaming room. Cecelia had a point. Every nerve in her body crackled, hot and alive, simply from being in a brothel. If she went abovestairs, she'd probably combust.

"Tonight is for observation only," Cecelia said. "Look for anything that hints at Jacobite sympathies."

"That's all? It doesn't sound very difficult."

"It shouldn't be. All you have to do is smile, be friendly, and listen—as one does in the company of men. I call it the art of paying attention."

"Our four years in London, and *that's* how you've gathered information?"

Cecelia rolled her shoulder like a woman born to flirt. "Men want to talk to a beautiful woman, which means they'll be desperate to talk to you."

Mary pinched her lips. Prettiness was Cecelia's calling card. For Mary, it was a bother and the subject, a matter of contention. Commentary on a woman's power often ensued, specifically, Mary refusing to use hers—a silly argument as far as she was concerned.

"I also have friends in interesting places," Cecelia said, smiling.

"Your paid spies."

"Indeed, they are paid. But never forget, beauty is as valuable as any coin. Only you decide how to spend it."

To which Mary huffed. Poised and pale, Cecelia fixed a pin in her hair, the corners of her mouth curving kindly as though she understood a woman's hidden fears and, at the tender age of twenty-five, was already miles ahead.

"Be safe, Mary."

"Always."

Theirs was a gentle parting. Mary stowed her fan in her petticoat pocket, a harmless accoutrement, while a treasonous coin nestled deep in Cecelia's pocket. Showing it guaranteed admittance to the secret society who gathered in Maison Bedwell; when and where they met inside the brothel was the mystery. Cecelia would probably uncover it tonight.

Mary watched her take the grand staircase, elegant and unhurried, the hem of her green silk sacque gown dragging behind her. Wet-skirted harlots in flimsy attire climbed the same stairs with amiable men in tow.

A wealth of secrets must live in Madame Bedwell's home. *Smile, be friendly, and listen*, and she would find them. Was subterfuge really that easy?

Laughter leached from the gaming room, shades of lust coming with it. Two footmen in pink-and-white livery headed toward that hallway with serving trays tucked under their arms. One with auburn hair, broad shoulders, and a lovely smile slowed his step to wink at her.

A soft exhale passed her lips. She smiled back.

Had she acquired a taste for adventure?

She idly stroked the high curve of her breast. Perhaps she had. The gaming room was wide open. Only a certain kind of woman would pass through those doors.

For one night she would be that woman.

Chapter Two

Like a moth to a flame, she strode into Madame Bedwell's gaming room. A pretty blonde in black silk ruled a green baize table. Faro, by the look. Her slender fingers shuffled cards while men crowded her table with fistfuls of money. Behind her a giant ham-faced rogue presided. The director, the room's overseer. Not a man to cross.

Mary ambled past rows of card tables and games of Hazard mildly disappointed. If Madame Bedwell spared no expense in the ballroom, she was flinty in here. Carpet was thin, paneled walls were scratched, and the harlots' silk stays were beyond the first gleam. None of those women gave her a second look. They were too busy draping themselves on men. Sea captains, portly bankers, men of quality. None who cried *secret society*.

She scrunched her nose. The art of paying attention was not so appealing in here.

Both hands resting in her silk panniers, she slowed her steps and forced herself to absorb the room.

Tables and chairs crammed together. The clamor vulgar. Dice clattering, men guffawing. Paintings of dubious quality covered the walls. A bland repetition of nude women. Her gaze traveled from one painting to the next. All of them were the same—plump limbs and vacant eyes—except the painting at the end of the room.

Goose bumps pricked her skin. A modestly covered woman lounged in a chair, a red flower in her outstretched palm. She squinted at the flower. Was it a tartan rosette? It was hard to tell with smoke fogging the low-ceilinged room. *Men and their cheroots.*

But the woman in the painting . . .

She marched forward until her nose was inches from the red knot. It was a plaid with thin black-and-yellow lines flanking a wider black weave. One had to be close to see the pattern and the small key underneath the rosette. She searched the plain wooden frame.

The scratched brass plate nailed to the wood read BETTY BURKE AT REST.

A thrill spiked in her veins. Betty Burke, the identity Charles Stuart took when he dressed like an Irish maid and fled Scotland. One could even say the maid's features were strikingly masculine, even similar to the pretender.

Someone has a sense of humor.

And she found her first clue.

Chin up, she took a triumphant half step back. At least the woman wore a shift and stays, which was more than the other paintings in the room.

Another step and—

"Shouldn't you have less clothes on?" a beer-drenched voice called out.

She spun around. A bald sailor was leering at her across a square table.

A white-bearded sea captain close to her hip turned in his chair. "'Course not," he said. "A man'd miss the pleasure of undressing her."

Men snickered. Her pannier was bumping the captain's chair. She brushed the silken mass aside.

"I seem to have disturbed your game. Please forgive me, sir."

He manacled her wrist with one hand. "You're a fine piece." The captain slapped his thigh. "Come join me."

She was horrified. "On your lap?"

"Best seat in the house."

She gagged on his whisky-imbued chuckle, but fine manners forbade her from pointing out he had no lap. His belly sagged over most of it.

"Thank you, but I am not interested in a game of cards."

A smirking harlot sauntered by. "Stumbled into the wrong room, have you?"

Her esteem for those women rose a notch. How did they manage this night after night? Cooing, flirting, laughing, the women in Madame Bedwell's employ never stopped, and she was too irked to *smile, be friendly, and listen.* A useless strategy when a man's sweaty hand clamped her wrist.

She tried to pull free. "Unhand me, sir."

The florid-faced captain laughed and jerked her closer as if they played a game. Angry heat gathered behind her mask.

"What a despicable man." She yanked harder, a curl flopping over her eye. "Let. Me. Go."

His mirth fading, the captain squeezed her wrist, but pride forbade her from crying out as he hefted his bulk from the chair.

"Got a sharp tongue on you."

"You don't know the half of it."

They were nearly toe to toe, his bushy white nose hairs visible. Perspiration sprang from his temples, and his eyes had shrunk to cruel, dark spots. *What an abominable oaf.* Shoulders set, she speared him with a haughty stare.

"My first night in this establishment and I have come to a conclusion."

The captain leaned in menacingly. "What might that be?"

Not to be put off, she leaned in too. "That London's finest actresses live here. They'd have to be to feign ardor for one such as you."

A harlot lounging against the wall clapped a hand over her mouth. Another turned away, giggling. Unfortunately, those two didn't rush to help. Mary was alone in this fight—an adventurous spinster's misfortune.

"Think you're too good for the likes of me?" the captain asked.

Fury sharpened her syllables. "*I am* too good for you."

His face turned claret and she swayed backward into a wall.

"Let her go, Culpepper," said a deep-timbred voice.

Tension shot to her toes. Not a wall, a man. Firm, tall, and solid as brick.

A possessive hand slipped around her waist. She swallowed hard, owned by the man behind her. There were layers of silk and linen and sturdy boned stays between them, but the shock stuck to her skin.

The captain glared above her head. "I saw her first."

"Doesn't matter. She's here to meet me." A hint of

dockside toughness seeped into her rescuer's vowels. "All night, if you must know."

All night? There was no mistaking his inference, a point made clear when warm fingers caressed her neck.

She was breathing faster, and his scent was . . . distracting.

But the captain still had a vise grip on her arm. At nearby tables men were lowering their cards, and the director's glower reached across the long room. His stance shifted as if he might leave the faro table to investigate the goings-on. She frowned, a bit desperate. To be tossed out her first night here would be most inglorious—she, who'd never been tossed from anything.

"If you don't mind, I would like to leave with a minimum of fuss." To Culpepper she offered a hasty, "There are plenty of women here. I'm sure one of them would enjoy the pleasure of your company."

"As I shall enjoy yours," the man behind her said for benefit of all.

He was toying with her choker's gold medallion. Soft, featherlight touches chased by sweet, irksome tingles sliding down her neck. The *thud-thud-thud* of her pulse in her ears drowned out conversation. Culpepper might've said something, but the man at her back consumed her.

Who is he?

His hand on her stomacher applied masterful pressure, enough to keep her in place, let her know he was in charge. She covered his hand with her own and explored. Large, warm, rough knuckles. A man who labored, yet his consonants were a gentleman's, clean and round. Definitely educated.

Long fingers linked with hers.

"Are you satisfied?" he whispered above her ear.

Their clasped hands tugged a thread inside her. This was the first time a man held her hand, albeit from an awkward angle. More grasp than hand-holding, she decided, yet potent enough to make her thoughts watery and vague.

From three tables away, a black-haired gentleman preoccupied with his cards spoke up.

"Let her go, Culpepper. This is not a Wapping Wall brothel. Women in masks pay for their entertainment, and women without masks *are* the entertainment." His glance sliced the captain. "Know the rules or you're gone."

Culpepper grumbled under his breath and released her. "My mistake, milord. I meant no harm."

She rubbed her sore wrist, a reminder that she was the insulted party on the tip of her tongue. Wisdom made her swallow it. *Men.* They had the finesse of mongrels. One fact was certain; the black-haired gentleman held court at his table. Equally notewor-thy was a tall blonde woman in leather breeches and jackboots standing by as if she had his lordship's back.

Quite an establishment, was Madame Bedwell's. London's oddest creatures gathered here.

A droopy-eyed man at the captain's table sniffed loudly.

"Captain, are you in? Or out?"

Culpepper looked sourly at Mary and the man be-hind her. "Deal me in," he grumbled and dropped into his chair.

Relieved, she sank against her brawny rescuer. Liq-uid pliancy lingered in her veins. The din resumed.

Men talking, women laughing, cards shuffling. She tried to spin around but a strong arm lashed her waist.

"We're not done," was the murmur at her ear.

"No?"

"Culpepper's had too much to drink," he said. "And he doesn't take kindly to slights."

"Don't worry. I wasn't going to let his table of cut-throats hurt you."

His low laugh vibrated along her back. "A good tongue-lashing doesn't work on that sort."

Her exhale stirred the curl hanging over her nose. "You, I collect, are skilled at keeping *that sort* in line."

"I do well enough."

She angled her head, catching a hint of cedarwood and musk. "And now you're volunteering your services to see me safely away."

"For a price."

His scandalous warmth seeped into her like a cozy blanket. She didn't want to leave. If she pushed an inch off her toes, his lips would graze her ear, and her bottom would brush his baubles.

Eyes glazing, she was sorely tempted to test the symmetry of his body with hers.

"I'm sorry to disappoint," she said. "But unlike other masked women here, I am neither titled nor wealthy."

"Which makes your presence at Madame Bedwell's all the more interesting—Miss Fletcher."

She stiffened. "You have the advantage, sir."

She slipped her hand behind her and dug her fingernails into the gentleman's wool-covered thigh. He was big and unyielding. Definitely a laborer.

"Move your hand a few more inches," he said

quietly. "And you'll find a more telling part of my anatomy."

Heat rippled through her. She breathed more of his cedarwood musk.

He smelled like an expensive mistake.

"Sheathe your claws," he said. "Then, you and I can continue our conversation in a safer place."

"Why should I? When I can simply walk away from you?"

His breath tickled her when he whispered, "Are you not the least bit curious?"

Heaven help her, she was. His voice alone poured sweet goose bumps down her back.

"Of a man threatening blackmail?" she whispered back, peevish.

"A harsh word, *blackmail.* You've trusted me in the past, Miss Fletcher. It's in your best interest to trust me again."

Peals of laughter expanded in the gaming room, the noise enough to scramble one's mind. Or was the chaos inside her entirely because of the gentleman at her back? His confident arms slid across her stomacher, and just like that, she was free.

She touched where his hand had been on her neck and turned, stunned.

Dazzling aquamarine eyes clashed with hers. Like pieces of polished glass, those eyes. They belonged to Mr. Thomas West, owner of a whaling concern. A strapping man with a piratical scar on his cheek, he embodied rough refinement. Sun had streaked gold in brown hair clubbed at his nape. His jaw was shaved and his cravat starched, a sign of his civility. But she wasn't fooled. The rugged shipmaster carried a bit of salt air and rigging wherever he went.

A sea wolf to be sure.

"Mr. West." She was cool, her hand dropping to her side.

"Miss Fletcher."

He took in the silk mask and her hair piled on her head, sparks searing her wherever his gaze wandered—especially when it landed on her bosom. The shipmaster's mouth quirked as if he couldn't believe his fortune at being the sole recipient of an up-close, magnanimous display of flesh.

She wanted badly to regain her composure, but a curl still hung over her eyes from her tangle with Culpepper. She brushed the lock off her face with all the hauteur a spinster in a brothel could muster.

"I daresay you have some questions," she said.

His attention climbed to her face.

"A few."

"Then you will be pleased to know I won't answer them. So don't bother asking."

He grinned and shook his head. "Not one question?"

"No."

The memory of his hands on her body unsettled her. They were business acquaintances after all. During the autumn season she purchased whalebones and baleen from West and Sons Shipping for her shop, and oil for her lamps. And she was always properly garbed. Neckerchiefs, mobcaps, practical wool.

Once she'd visited his shipyard at Howland Great Wet Dock to forge a key, an arrangement brokered by Will MacDonald, a friend of her league's. She was pleased Mr. West didn't mention that.

She was equally pleased *not* to receive a lecture about the damaging effects of being in a brothel. The latitude given to noblewomen did not trickle down to shopkeepers. At almost thirty years old, she'd lived too long and seen too much to care. Perhaps the same was true of Mr. West? There was a rawness about him. A man who'd tamed the sea, whispered to mermaids, and lived to tell the tale. He was a gentleman, of course, but that scar and his tantalizing scent—dangerous.

She pulled out her fan to blow cool air on hot skin. "I'd prefer you simply walked away and forgot that you saw me."

"Liar," he said in a silken voice.

She balked, but skin crinkling at the outer corners of his eyes softened her ruffled feathers.

"Admit it, Miss Fletcher. You're just as surprised at finding me here as I am at finding you in this unlikely place."

She pursed her lips. "Perhaps."

His unblinking gaze was backlit with enough admiration to send fresh warmth up and down her body.

"Considering your encounter with Culpepper, it's advisable that we keep up our ruse." He checked the room and dropped his voice, "It gets lively in the wee hours here."

Lively was a kind description for the room full of raucous, glossy-eyed men. Servants were scurrying in with frothy pints, ensuring patrons would stay deep in their cups.

"By our ruse, you mean that I'm here for an assignation," she said.

"Yes."

She touched her mask like a talisman. The brothel teemed with life, its own cosmos. Sensual currents floated as free as the haze of smoke from men puffing their cheroots. Women threaded the room, their strides fluid, but none were masked. Earlier in the evening, plans for finding the information about the secret society had dominated her conversation with Cecelia, leaving her sparse on the particulars of Madame Bedwell's house rules.

"Do women of means come here often?" she asked, entranced by the interplay of men and harlots.

"I'm not aware of their frequency, but, yes, a small number do."

She lifted her face to his, intent, curious.

"Do women come here to meet you?"

Aquamarine eyes flared with astonishment until a dark primitive flame overtook their depths.

"Answering that would be . . . indelicate."

"Yet, you didn't hesitate to say that I'm here for an assignation."

"For the greater good of helping you."

She leaned close, almost touching him. "But you imagined it. My assignation . . . with you."

His mouth tugged beguilingly. "I did."

Her heels were sinking in a sea of possibilities, a delightful metaphor for the forbidden mire in which she found herself and the tall, scarred shipmaster. The black fire in his eyes expanded, and his voice changed, low and grained, the more they talked.

Intriguing.

She cocked her head, perusing him through her lashes. "And in this imaginary assignation, did we agree to meet here? Or did I pay handsomely for you?"

His laugh had a primal quality. "You paid, and we had no regrets."

She worked her fan, loose curls teasing her hot skin. They were teetering on an impossible precipice.

"Once a woman procures a room of her own, how does she go about inviting a gentleman to join her?" she asked.

An enchanted Mr. West studied her, the effect dizzying.

"She informs him directly."

"An interesting approach." She shrugged, indifferent, but it was an act, and they both knew it. "Where's the mystery? The seduction?"

His was a sea wolf's smile. And she, the morsel he wanted.

"Forthrightness *is* seductive—in the right measure."

She contemplated that. "Are you suggesting that men prefer to be the hunters? And women, their prey?"

"It is the rules of nature, Miss Fletcher."

She touched her fan to his chest and whispered, "Sometimes nature likes to be played with."

Mr. West sucked in a fast breath. The inferno in his eyes threatened to char her. She dragged her fan lightly over his waistcoat's top buttons, wringing one last tantalizing ounce from their conversation.

"I wonder, if deep down, sir, you wish to be played with."

His sculpted mouth curved, mysterious and beautiful. "That is something to ponder."

The air taut, they considered each other. The noise, the crowded room vanished, such was the buzz in her ears. Interminable seconds passed with Mr. West's gaze flickering over her. She took a safe half step back, a reprieve from flirtation's crackling heat.

His smile eased, polite and congenial, and their talk steered to safer topics: the room's abominable air, the growing crowds, and the lack of seating unless one wanted to gamble. She was thankful for Mr. West's tacit agreement to cease their carnal conversation, yet his focused, lively eyes assured her no one else existed. In a brothel, of all places, where the other women in attendance were meant to lure men.

Looking into his eyes, she almost felt time stop.

One taste of him. That's all I want.

What defiance, her flesh. It needed to be squashed.

In her side vision, another woman smiled benignly at her. The artist's rendering of Betty Burke. Her shoulders sank: duty was calling. The league, her clan, the gold—her reasons for venturing into Maison Bedwell in the first place.

Her gaze dropped to the painted rosette. She'd seen enough.

She swayed closer to Mr. West, careful not to touch him. "Perhaps now would be a good time for you to escort me away from here."

"Agreed."

His hand was on her elbow, and she soaked up everything about him. His touch, his resolute profile, the cedarwood and musk clouding him. She smiled privately as they walked. How primitive, her scenting a man. She knew his eyes, his mouth, the angle of his scar, but she couldn't say what Mr. West was wearing beyond his cravat and the wool she touched on his thigh—rather flummoxing for a woman who earned her coin with a needle and thread.

She was about to rectify that with a side glance when a voice intruded.

"Didn't think you liked them so glacial."

The dark-haired lord had spoken while perusing the cards in his hand.

"Lord Ranleigh." Mr. West stopped their progress. "You know as well as I do, the cooler the woman, the hotter she burns . . . given the right touch, of course."

Smug male laughter cascaded across the tables. A retort wanted out but she stifled it.

Did all men lose their manners in a brothel?

His lordship's stare roamed over her, intense and interested.

She stared back.

With an arrow-straight nose, hair like polished jet, there was an air of worldly grace about him. His clothes, she noticed. Cream-colored figured silk made on a draw loom stretched across his shoulders. The costly weave was a creation from Milan or Vienna, she guessed. Privileged and insolent he might be, but his lordship had, of a sort, come to her aide.

A frisson scraped her skin when his gaze joined hers.

Elegant and deadly came to mind. Not a man to cross.

Lord Ranleigh's onyx stare sent a message, but she

was too new to subterfuge to grasp the meaning. Or her senses were too swamped.

His lordship flicked a dismissive lace-covered wrist. "Enjoy your evening."

She was glad to leave, yet, when she passed through the doorway, a ghost of a chill chased her. She peered over her shoulder. Lord Ranleigh fiddled with his cards while the blonde in jackboots bent low to whisper in his ear. Her razor-sharp eyes tracked Mary.

Definitely not a woman to cross.

Chapter Three

As they reached the entry hall nearly a dozen noblemen poured into Maison Bedwell, rain spitting at their backsides. They paid the attendant and began shedding greatcoats and hats into the arms of waiting footmen. Miss Fletcher broke away from Thomas and folded her fan, the very polite and very icy version of her back in place.

"Thank you, Mr. West. Your assistance was invaluable."

"It was my pleasure."

The Scotswoman was distracted, drifting toward the newcomers.

Had he been dismissed? Arms crossed, he waited.

She circled the crowd, searching for someone. He'd keep her in sight but he wouldn't follow. Pride, certainly, and he had fair knowledge of her. Miss Fletcher might look like a confection in white silk, but her beauty came with a bite. London's whaling trade was small, and the corset maker had a reputation for being cool and headstrong. She had to be. The business of corsets and stays was largely the province of men.

Which gave him pause—Miss Fletcher might've come here with a man.

He rested a shoulder on the wall.

Competition was inevitable.

He'd wait and see who it was. The men in the entry were gaping at her, their heads whipping left to right when she passed by.

"Fools," he said under his breath.

They missed the better part of her. The callouses and scars on her fingers. Her blunt nails and red knuckles. Their quizzical glances were an attempt to size her up. He pitied them. Miss Fletcher wasn't of their ilk. Her gait too brisk, her gaze too direct, and her nature too focused. Their way of life would bore her to tears.

Which begged the question—why was she here?

His jaw had nearly unhinged when he spied her across the gaming room. He'd left a promising game of Hazard to see what she was about. Their conversation which followed, illuminating.

Miss Fletcher was an enigma. Her skin, pearlescent under chandeliers. Her lips, lush and pillowy. The *other* pillowy parts on full display had stunned him. Such largesse considering the corset maker was usually prim and proper.

A footman stopped to speak to her, pointing at the front door. She bestowed a smile on him, and the sod practically melted on the spot. Yet, Miss Fletcher was not a purposeful seductress. She seemed not to care about her effect on men, all but ignoring the newcomers. Her polite rebuffs sent that gaggle of men to the ballroom. Revelry dimmed when a footman shut the ballroom doors behind them.

Finally, some peace and quiet.

Miss Fletcher waited in the heart of the room, her head and neck craning at the ceiling.

"Rather deceptive," she muttered.

He looked up. Frescoes covered the high-arched entry. "What's deceptive?"

Her chin dropped. "You're still here," she said, mildly surprised.

"Where else would I be? I did say I'd see you safely out."

A gentle smile creased her lips. "What an honorable man you are, Mr. West, but that's not necessary."

She stayed put. He did the same, his shoulder stuck to the wall. *So that's how she's going to play it.* Despite their extraordinary night, Miss Fletcher wanted to put them both back on the neat shelf of merchant and shopkeeper as if this interlude never happened.

He wasn't having it.

"What's wrong with the frescoes?" he asked.

She waved vaguely at the vaulted ceiling, each section a vignette.

"You don't see it? Nude women lolling on the grass. Nude women laughing on swings. And nude women riding on . . ." She huffed and grumbled, "Never mind," when a servant delivered her cloak.

"Please," Thomas said. "Do go on."

The Scotswoman whirled black velvet over her shoulders. "I really must go. My friend is waiting for me."

Friend, is it?

"But you haven't finished." He pointed at the frescoes. "We are in a brothel, Miss Fletcher. Unclothed women are part of the transaction."

Gleaming beads encircled knowing eyes while

she tied a bow under her chin. "Indeed, we are in a brothel, but those painted women are an overly cheerful lot."

"Why wouldn't they be?"

"Their cheer *is* the deceit."

"Then it's not their nakedness which bothers you," he said. "It's their demeanor."

Miss Fletcher was migrating closer to him. Her bow finished, a small frown showed above it. He grinned, delighted at having ruffled her feathers.

"Have I struck an uncomfortable note?" he asked.

"Not . . . quite."

He canted his head. "Explain yourself."

Miss Fletcher studied him as if she played a bigger conversational game and he, the unwitting opponent.

"It is not an appropriate topic of conversation."

"What about our conversation in the gaming room?" he goaded. "Was that appropriate?"

She rewarded him with an amiable smile. "Fair logic, Mr. West, but I am trying to be delicate."

"I don't need delicate."

"Ah, that's right," she said, drawing near. "You have a taste for forthrightness."

"Most men do."

The Scotswoman pinned him with an artful gaze. "Then you'll appreciate my *indelicate* summation that you, like most men, think the sun rises and sets on your John Thomas."

He grunted. *What a saucy piece.* With black velvet draping luscious curves, she made an enchanting picture until her pretty mouth spilled more sacrilege.

"And like most men, you believe women bask in the glory of your virality. The truth is most women do not."

He tried to be casual, arms crossed and all. "Never had a woman complain."

Miss Fletcher hooked a finger through a buttonhole on his coat, and a carnal earthquake rocked him.

"Oh, I'm sure the stars shimmered, and the moon shined brighter," she said teasingly soft.

A grin broke despite an effort to quash it. "Never said I inspired poetry."

Her answering smile told him he'd brought a pistol to a cannon fight.

"I tried to warn you."

Her gentle tug on his coat ran a plumb line, hot and fast, south of his navel.

Bloody hell—this woman would make a monk cry.

He was mildly affronted, highly curious, and vexingly aroused. A strange effect. The Scotswoman disassembled him, piece by piece, yet the more she talked, the more transfixed he was by her and her genteel Edinburgh accent. There was an educated back-of-the-mouth treatment Miss Fletcher gave to her words. Definitely a voice to warm his cockles on a cold winter's night.

This was a first, a woman's voice inciting lust.

What was next? Worshipping her knees?

"You sound confident," he said, a touch surly.

Her shrug slight, Miss Fletcher let go of his coat.

"I am. As the only female corset and stays maker in London, women confide in me. Lots of women, and I've found their stories remarkably similar."

He shifted off the wall, missing her hand on his coat.

"What do they say?"

Noise burst from the ballroom. A doe-eyed harlot and a barrel-chested man, his cravat fluttering loose, traipsed through the entry. A footman scurried from the shadows and shut the ballroom's gilt-trimmed doors as though he could dam revelry's tide.

Miss Fletcher watched the footman, raising her hood and hiding her glorious hair.

"Every day women come and go to my shop. None of them have any idea what others have told me. But mark me, sir. They're honest. About half the women tell me they feign enthusiasm in bed, while others confess to lying limp as yesterday's fish. The number who do find pleasure in the act is quite small, I'm afraid."

He could feel a scowl growing.

"You're telling me most women in London find no pleasure in bed sport?"

Her answer was a long-suffering exhale. "You're a smart man, Mr. West. Do the math. Most of the wives who visit my shop say it's their marital duty." She eyed the frescoes almost bored. "You and I both know, for harlots, it's a job."

He glanced at the painted ceiling, irritated. Those frolicking women. Their smiles were overbright.

"What about your pleasure?"

The gruff question popped out. It bordered on too much, but this was an evening of excess. Miss Fletcher merely brushed back a blasted curl, which kept falling on her cheek.

"I really must go," she said. "My friend is waiting."

He tensed like a predator. "Your friend?"

She started walking backward, confident. There'd be no more womanly secrets, and no utterance on who waited for her.

"Promise me you will forget this night," was her request.

"Our flirtation?" He advanced on her. "Not a chance."

Her silk petticoats shushed prettily.

"It cannot happen again," she said.

"Why not?"

The footman in pink-and-white livery whisked open the front door, doing his best to blend into the woodwork. The rain had stopped, a dense mist replacing it. Miss Fletcher swept into the night, and he joined her on the front step.

"Please, don't follow me," she said.

"You don't want me to see you safely to your carriage?"

"I'm a capable woman, Mr. West. I've spent years seeing myself in and out of carriages."

Therein was the problem—the corset maker didn't need a man.

Years of good breeding and gentlemanly fiber demanded that he see her safely away. He searched the damp square for clues as to where she was going. Candle lamps hung from trees in the center garden. Carriages clustered the road outside Maison Bedwell, their lamps chips of light. Cloaked in black, Miss Fletcher would disappear into that darkness.

But his feet and hers weren't moving.

She tipped her face to his. "Let me go."

"I'm not stopping you," he said.

Silver spectral eyes beguiled him. He'd seen the color once in nature, north of the North Sea where storm clouds sank into the water. Deep mysteries lived there. So did elusive creatures barely known to man. The same could be said of the dark-haired siren from Scotland. Standing with her was a taste of the exquisite, an unseen tether binding them.

Night blurred, a serene watercolor. Neither wanted this to end. He knew that. Miss Fletcher did, too, clutching the bow under her chin, a sable curl floating free—the moment ripe for a kiss.

Except they were on the doorstep of a brothel where men paid easy quid for a great deal more. What irony this was, him working hard for a kiss that would not happen.

"Please, go inside," she said as though she needed him to walk away.

Despite the cold, damp air, he was stubborn.

"Give me your right hand."

She balked. "My—"

Bewildered, Miss Fletcher offered him her ungloved appendage.

Water dripping down his cheeks, he folded his hands around her work-worn hand. Racked with something more powerful than lust, he caressed her palm. Crystalline droplets anointed her hood, drawing the eye to her beautiful face. But Miss Fletcher's hands were her story. Her fingers which he touched. The small white scars which he traced. And the tip of her middle finger stained green from a brass thimble, which he kissed tenderly. Sweetly.

Her lips parted on a fragile gasp.

The sound rang inside him.

Laborers at Howland Great Wet Dock would box a man's ears for attaching *tender* and *sweet* to anything he did. But it was the truth, and the innocent kiss worth it. She had amused, enlightened, irked, insulted, and surprised him—all in one hour.

What would happen if she gave him the night?

Possibly heaving breasts, hot kisses, and lively conversation with the too-smart-for-her-own-good corset maker. He'd have her spouting poetry. Shite, he'd spout some too.

But tonight, he would let her go.

"Good night, Miss Fletcher." His voice rumbled in the dark.

She hid her hand in velvet folds. "Good night, Mr. West."

Despite the Herculean resistance inside him, he forced himself to walk back inside as requested. What he did next was a secret between him and those smiling frescoes.

Chapter Four

Slim, structured waists and plump, overflowing breasts were her stock-in-trade. An illusion that she, Mary Fletcher, propagated, and she was quite good at it. Women flocked to her rose-scented shop on White Cross Street to edit what filled their gowns. The journey to fashionable perfection began in a wharf-side warehouse packed with men smelling of brine and tar, and it ended in the back of her shop where she wrangled bones and baleen into practical linen and occasionally decadent silk creations.

Transforming silhouettes was one reason for Fletcher's House of Corsets and Stays's success. Mary's patient listening ear was the other. Thus, her workroom was her sanctuary.

Sometimes a woman needed a little peace and quiet.

She found it in her bolts of rainbow-colored cloth and rows of spindled threads. Her pins and needles, the sturdy worktable, and plain brick walls warmed by a small iron stove—heaven to her. Patrons were rarely admitted to her inner sanctum, except Mrs. Rimsby. The gossipy matron wormed her way into everything. At present, she was peeking past the thin opening between the curtain and the door frame, which led to the shop.

"Miss Fletcher, I don't wish to alarm you," Mrs. Rimsby said. "But there's a man in your shop."

Mary snipped cloth, not bothering to look up.

"Men do, on occasion, bring their custom to me."

A White Cross Street merchant had recently visited her with concerns about his expanding waistline. Short, well-starched baleen stays were her solution.

Mrs. Rimsby harrumphed. "I daresay *that* gentleman does not need a corset."

"No?"

Mary inspected the linen she'd just cut, but it was hard to concentrate with visions of a scarred pirate in her head. Early that morning, when all was still, she'd searched her spindles for the exact shade of blue-green (or perhaps more green than blue?) to match his eyes. It was the kind of thing a moon-struck maid would do, not a woman on the cusp of her thirtieth birthday. Yet, her gaze often wandered to the vibrant thread perched prominently on the shelf.

Mrs. Rimsby pivoted to Mary like a bloodhound on the scent. "He's talking to your sister."

Mary set down the cloth. A man sniffing around Margaret alarmed her more than it should. Nineteen and pretty, Margaret was coming into her own—and becoming more of a challenge with each passing day.

"Now she's laughing," Mrs. Rimsby reported.

Mary walked to the doorway. "If that sly butcher boy has come calling again . . ."

She peeked past the curtain. Candlelight touched sun-streaked hair neatly clubbed, broad shoulders, and a confident stance. Short hairs on her nape prickled. The gentleman was listening politely to Margaret until her sister pointed at the workroom. The gentleman turned.

Mary jerked back, her ears ringing.

Mr. West was here. In her shop!

"Why is a man like that visiting a corset shop?" Mrs. Rimsby asked, careless with the gap between the curtain and the door frame.

Mr. West spied them, his mouth curling with amusement. He dominated her humble shop, a scarred pirate playing nice with the merchants of White Cross Street.

Had he come to do some plundering?

Mary looked away, her insides vibrating like a twice-plucked harp string.

"His name is Mr. West. A man of sterling reputation and London's finest purveyor of bones and baleen."

"Well, if he's here on business, you shouldn't keep him waiting." Mrs. Rimsby's eyes twinkled. "I wouldn't."

Mary smoothed her apron and her rattled nerves. She knocked aside the curtain and entered the rose-scented fray of Fletcher's House of Corsets and Stays. Her perfect world. Red-and-white-striped walls trimmed with white shelves, a few of them delicately chipped. The light moderate. Feminine accoutrements everywhere. A mother and daughter were examining stockings in one corner, and a housekeeper on her half day dithered over a stream of garters in another. Harriet Dalton, their new seamstress, was wrapping linen stays in brown paper at the counter for a woman with two children in tow.

No pirate's plunder here. Mr. West's unblinking gaze said otherwise.

I've come for you was written all over it.

Mary's senses blazed. His presence threatened to burn her ordered life to the ground. And that confidence of his. It was irritating. Fletcher's House of Corsets and Stays was her little kingdom. She'd not tolerate him storming it.

Margaret scurried across the shop. "The gentleman says he is Mr. West, provisioner of our bones and baleen."

"He is."

Margaret frowned. "How do I not know this, Mary?"

"Because it's grimy business on the docks, and you don't like to get dirty." She set a protective arm around her sister's shoulders, herding her toward the workroom. "Besides, you are best with needle and thread."

Her sister's chin jutted mulishly. Their hushed conversation was in danger of going awry.

"It's time I learned more about our business."

"I will teach you. Later," she whispered. "However, Mrs. Rimsby's corset needs your attention, and we both know you excel at the gentle art of . . . people."

Margaret flounced off, but not before giving Mary a warning glare. A conversation would come. Grievances would be aired, more freedoms demanded. Mary waited patiently until her sister disappeared behind the yellow curtain.

One problem was temporarily solved. Another beckoned.

Shoulders squared, she spun around. Her tall, out-of-place visitor stood by a small white table, stirring the water in a porcelain bowl with floating candles. He grinned like a lad caught with his finger in a cake when she approached.

"What a fine shop you have," he said.

"Thank you."

"And this"   he traced the rim of the bowl—"is a beautiful piece."

Pride unfurled inside her. Made her stand taller. The table had been a source of deep satisfaction. Pink and red rose petals purchased from a Hammersmith hothouse had been scattered around the table. She sprinkled a few into the bowl.

"It goes to the feelings I want to create."

"What feelings?"

She blinked twice. No one had ever asked her to put emotions to words, especially with her business. Commerce was an unsentimental topic, judged unsuitable for women by most, yet the shop was her life.

"It's hard to explain," she hedged.

"Try me."

Mr. West was not taking the polite route and letting this go. His directness, his self-possession in facing her, gave ample opportunity to put an end to the morning's riddle, that, yes, his eyes were a vivid, weatherworn green.

She rolled a silken rose petal between her fingers; how loose and soft its feel.

"I—I suppose I want to impart a sense of splendor and elegance. Every woman deserves to feel beautiful."

"Like you."

A flutter lifted in her chest.

"Mr. West," she whisper-hissed. "This is a place of business."

"What? A man cannot flirt with a woman in a shop?"

She answered with a reproachful eye, which fed his pirate's glee.

"Not in mine."

"You set the standard of honest conversation between us, Miss Fletcher. I'm merely following your lead."

She tried holding back the nervous laugh that wanted out. "And we can't let our standards slip, can we?"

The scarred side of his mouth quirked with approval.

"There's the Scotswoman who gives as good as she gets."

Mr. West's subtle smile gave her an inkling to what he was about.

"While nothing might alarm all six feet and"—she batted a hand at him—"excess inches of you, I, however, must guard my shop's reputation."

"In that, you would be incorrect."

Eyeing him warily, she pulled a rag from her apron pocket and began to dust the spotless table.

"What do you mean?"

His chest swelled from an inhale. "Of all the women in London, you alarm me."

The tenderest shiver pooled at the base of her spine.

Was Mr. West declaring himself?

Handsome, approachable, with a hint of peril, he smelled divine. She longed to revisit last night's delicious flirtation, but Fletcher's House of Corsets and Stays wasn't fertile ground for such things, and she was too blunt to be a coquette. Or too rusty. Yet, Mr. West provoked the oddest reactions—as if her body wasn't entirely hers anymore. All the more reason to give him a polite send-off.

The door opened and three giggling women entered. Maids on their half day, browsing the shops. Mary migrated to a quiet corner with a display of silk corsets. Mr. West followed, hat in hand.

"You must admit, our evening together was revelatory," he murmured.

"With interesting entertainments."

She was equally subdued, her rag dancing merrily as she dipped to wipe a display shelf. If her shop was empty, she'd give him an earful of business opinions about the brothel's wasteful extravagance. Intuition told her the practical-minded Mr. West would listen. Even welcome it.

"You were the pinnacle," he said.

"That would be a first—my directness appreciated."

"You've many fine traits, Miss Fletcher. It would be a pleasure to discover each and every one of them."

She raised her head slowly. The shipmaster's baritone touched an unchaste chord, the sound of it like a ringing bell, which must be followed. His nearness was an invitation for her to make bad choices.

Oh, this was not good. Not good at all.

She righted a corset on display just because she needed to touch something.

"Mr. West . . ."

He held up a staying hand. "Forgive me, Miss

Fletcher. I see that you are busy and I should get to the point of my visit."

There was more?

She fiddled with a bow on the corset. Mr. West tucked his hat behind his back and took in the shop at large. Ladies were chattering. The doorbell jingled the arrival of two new shoppers, and Margaret was busy bundling Mrs. Rimsby's latest purchase at the counter.

"Is there someplace we can talk freely?" he asked.

Her heart flip-flopped. "You mean *alone*?"

"We could take a walk outside."

"It's October."

He steepled a brow. "What? Your legs don't work in October?"

She dusted a new shelf vigorously. "They work just fine, but like the rest of me, they doubt the wisdom of carrying on with you."

He grinned. "Carrying on, is it? Then, how about a pint in a public room? I know for a fact your mouth works."

Brazen man. She was assembling an appropriate retort when Mr. West rested his oversized shoulder against the shelf—close enough that she bumped his biceps while dusting. Under her lashes, she studied the contoured swell covered by dark wool. What did he do to get arms like that? Careen ships singlehandedly?

"If your visit is about last season's bones and baleen, you don't need to worry. I'm quite pleased with your goods."

Wicked humor glinted in his eyes. "I'm glad you find them . . . satisfactory."

Which told her all she needed to know. The man

had come to torment her. And if she wasn't careful, she'd wipe the paint off her pretty shelves.

"Then I can't imagine why you're in my shop," she whispered as if they were conspirators planning to steal the crown jewels.

"I'm here, Miss Fletcher, to discuss a business arrangement."

She froze mid-swipe. "An *arrangement*?"

Carnal thoughts splashed in her head, vivid enough to warm her skin. When a man came round, talking like that on White Cross Street, he was seeking a domestic to clean his house or a discreet partner for sexual pleasure. Did Mr. West decide she was fit for the latter? After last night's escapade, he might. He certainly hadn't come to her for waist-cinching stays. His midsection was flat as a board.

"For Neville Warehouse," he said.

He wanted that kind of business arrangement? Last night, in the gaming room, Mr. West had whispered something about helping her for a price.

She fixed her neckerchief, disappointed. How quickly she'd assumed sensual intent.

Because she wanted it. Badly. She eyed him, guilt pinching her lusty soul.

"Last August," he said, "you and Mrs. Neville offered the use of Neville Warehouse on Gun Wharf."

"You've come to collect on our promise."

He nodded. "My first thought was to contact Mrs. Neville, but I understand she fled London."

"She did. With Mr. MacDonald."

"I thought as much. With the selling season upon us, I was going to write to you, but after last night . . ."

Well, that took the starch out of her. Mr. West didn't want to compromise her body. He wanted a building. She winced. How mortifying. She was the one with lust-fueled notions, not him. Mr. West had always conducted himself as a perfect gentleman since the moment they'd met three years ago. Their conversations were always proper.

Until last night.

"I need the warehouse for the rest of this month." He carried on, very businesslike. "Rent-free, of course."

"Of course."

She jammed the dust rag into her apron pocket. Rent-free was a fair trade for what he had done last August. Mr. West had also set a clear boundary. There was no need for her to spend long days with him, acting as an agent, factoring his goods as was typical when renting a warehouse to a merchant.

"You were incredibly generous to my league," she said. "How could we not do the same for you?"

"I appreciate your understanding."

She smiled weakly, defeat washing over her.

"I'll have the key delivered to your shipyard tomorrow."

He donned his tricorn. "Tomorrow, then."

But neither moved. They faced each other, their silence buffeted by babbling shoppers and the rattle of passing carriages beyond her window. Mary fidgeted, dispirited. There'd be no going back to shopkeeper and merchant, but she was hard-pressed on how to go forward.

Mr. West, however, was not tongue-tied.

His bold eyes spoke volumes.

"Your hair is a thing of beauty," he said gruffly. "You should leave it uncovered."

She touched her mobcap.

They were, by design, overbearing. Anything to hide her hair. She opened her mouth to say as much, except a talkative gray-haired matron and her friend sidled up to the display. Mr. West murmured a pleasantry and gave them ample room. Mary stepped back, wanting to snap at the women for the invasion. Excellent, ingrained manners and a shopkeeper's need for coin, however, prevailed.

She pasted on a smile while they peppered her with questions.

"I visited your shop . . . oh, some time ago," said the shorter woman. "I believe you sold gloves."

Sweet relief. She could shush them out the door.

"Not anymore, ma'am. But there is an excellent glover's shop on Chiswell Street."

"I'm certain I purchased a pretty blue pair in this very shop, though the seams . . ."

Mary dug impatient hands into her petticoats. Precious time with Mr. West was slipping away. Couldn't the verbose woman see that? Her restless feet seemed to know it. Mr. West had come out of his way to see *her*, if only for business.

Nodding solicitously, she inched backward as if she might flee her own shop. A powerful need seized her. To be anywhere but here. She could tell Mr. West about the rusted cog in Neville Warehouse's tread wheel. Perhaps arrange a time to show it to him.

Whirling around, she would accept his offer for a walk and a pint—why not both?

But her shop's doorbell jingled shut on Mr. West's back. Disappointment landed like an anvil on her heart. She rushed to her shop window and looked south. Mr. West's head and fine shoulders were already melting into the hive that was White Cross Street. There'd be no more conversations with her scarred pirate.

He was gone.

Chapter Five

The league met in Cecelia's bedchamber, vinegar's tang in the air. Mary, Margaret, Aunt Flora, and Aunt Maude were cramped together with their new accidental member, Mr. Alexander Sloane. Jenny slipped in with tea, saying nary a word, which should have been Mary's first clue—something was amiss. The other clue was a porcelain bowl full of vinegar by the window.

She eyed it warily.

The bedchamber was tomb-like, the aunts sipping tea and Cecelia cocooned in bed, her fluffy white counterpane tucked under her chin and a cloth draped over her forehead. Cecelia abed wasn't unusual. The woman loved her creature comforts and she was prone to rest all day when her courses came. But this was different.

Cecelia stared morosely at the ceiling, imparting indelicate news.

"I've retched much of the day."

Margaret stopped pouring her tea. "How horrid for you. Should we postpone our meeting?"

"No," Cecelia groaned. "It's been two hours since my last bout."

Aunt Flora eyed the window. "That explains the vinegar."

Vinegar—an old remedy for absorbing bad smells.

Mr. Sloane took the cloth from Cecelia's forehead and dipped it in a pitcher of water on the bedside table.

"You might as well tell them," he said, wringing the cloth. "They'll know soon enough."

Cecelia grumbled and burrowed deeper under the bed covers.

"I am with child."

Stunned silence followed her bald announcement. Mary touched her mouth.

A babe . . .

Mr. Sloane was a patrician profile to the room, quiet, attentive. He brushed a damp curl off Cecelia's forehead, his mouth curving with aching tenderness. Cecelia's lashes drifted up, her eyes adoring him. Their love was palpable and bright, the glow robbing Mary of speech.

Owl-eyed Margaret spoke first.

"But you're not . . ."

"Married?" Cecelia nabbed her with a world-weary gaze. "You do know how babes are made, don't you?"

Margaret's cheeks bloomed a ferocious red.

"Y-yes, but I—I thought . . ."

Margaret snatched a biscuit from the tray and crunched it loudly. The older women of the league honed their scowls on Mr. Sloane. He stood by Cecelia and turned to them as one might face a judge and jury.

"What matters is the well-being of Cecelia and her babe." Aunt Flora spoke to the group at large before directing her attention to Mr. Sloane. "But I suspect you have something tae say about this."

His bronze eyes solemn, he addressed the room.

"I'd marry her today, if she'd have me."

Cecelia reached for him. "You know I love you."

His mouth tugging with emotion, he held her hand lovingly. There was a small squeeze, a wealth of words passing in that minute movement. A unity that would not break.

Mary dropped into a chair, air thin in her chest.

Mr. Sloane spoke to the others, but he was all eyes for Cecelia.

"From the moment she threatened to shoot me in the arse, I knew she was the one for me. But she's a willful woman, our Cecelia. She'll marry me when she's good and ready."

Mary pinched a pleat in her petticoat. Cecelia and her tall barrister were a sight, fingers interlocked as if holding hands was second nature. As if they craved each other's touch and couldn't go another minute without it. The tableau was transcendent. The beauty painful to watch, like a painting of a bright and glorious land she'd never get to visit.

No, what passed between Cecelia and Mr. Sloane was more than love. It shimmered.

She had to look away.

The rest of the room did the same. Chins dipped and the floor was studiously examined. They bore witness to something sublime—something none of them had. But Cecelia . . . a mother. The first of the women in their league. What a surprise.

Motherhood. She couldn't fathom it.

Eventually, the bed ropes creaked as though announcing the transfiguration ended and they should all get down to business. Mary quit her careful study of the vinegar bowl to find Cecelia sitting up and Mr. Sloane plumping a pillow behind her back.

"I can't decide on a rushed wedding—very soon, of course," Cecelia said. "Or do I confirm my reputation as a wicked woman, bear my child, and wed Alexander next spring?"

Aunt Flora splashed fresh tea into her cup. "That's for you tae decide, dear. But one thing is certain. You canna be gadding about. Not in your condition."

Aunt Maude got up and helped herself to a biscuit. "Our thinning numbers make searching for the gold a wee bit difficult."

"While I'm all for recovering as much of the treasure as possible, we have a bigger problem to consider." Cecelia paused, eyeing each woman. "The Countess of Denton."

Collective groans followed the mention of that woman's name.

"A pox on her." Aunt Maude sank into a chair brought up from the kitchen. "She was brazen enough tae shoot Mr. MacLeod. She'll be coming for us next."

Rory MacLeod, another Highlander who came into their league by accident. The Countess of Denton had shot him in the back late at night on London Bridge. Why, exactly, no one could say. For a brief time he'd been her ladyship's *private footman*, the title given to men she hired for a lusty connection.

"Lady Denton is still in Scotland, and she doesn't know Mr. MacLeod survived," Aunt Flora said, between sips of tea. "But I canna say I want tae keep hunting for the gold, not with Cecelia with a bairn on the way."

Cecelia set a protective hand on her midsection. "I'm afraid we have a narrow margin of time to decide our fate. The countess must return before month's end because she's selling one of her business concerns."

Mary shifted in her chair. "Which one?"

"The Chelsea Porcelain Works. Nothing of import."

"Then we have two or three weeks," Mary said to the room. "For one last hunt."

But faces were long. Chasing the gold had taken its toll.

"Ladies," Mary implored the room. "We need the last of the treasure to purchase sheep. Remember? We did promise to replenish Clanranald MacDonald's herds. Our final task."

Aunt Maude bit into her biscuit and chewed fast. "But who will search for the gold with you?"

"I'll go with her," Margaret said brightly.

"Certainly not," Mary shot back.

"I'm not a child, Mary. I know what happens in brothels."

Her sister's *I know what happens in brothels* set her teeth on edge. "I'll not ask how you've come by this knowledge, but you in a brothel is out of the question."

Margaret eyed her, indignant. "But it's perfectly acceptable for you?"

"I didn't say that."

"But it's what you meant." Margaret sat taller. "Must I be a dull spinster like you before I get to do anything?"

A chorus of gasps spilled, but Mary wrapped

herself in cool silence. Inwardly, she smarted as much from the insult as Mr. Sloane witnessing their squabble. The barrister, at least, had the grace to busy himself wringing a new cloth.

Margaret swallowed hard and lowered her ink-dark lashes. "Forgive me," she mumbled. "I—I didn't mean to be cruel."

"Thank you."

Mary was rigid and armored and not fooled one bit. A layer of rebellion simmered under Margaret's contrition. She couldn't blame Margaret, nor could she let go of the deep tie binding them. No guidebook existed for a sister raising a sibling. In the highlands, their life had been comfortable. An easy cadence marked by one season flowing into the next—until the war. Coming to London upset the natural order, especially when Margaret turned eighteen. Since then, the two of them were increasingly at loggerheads.

Aunt Flora crossed the room and checked beyond the curtain, a gentle reminder that they faced bigger troubles than sisterly quarrels.

Nighttime meetings augured risks of men waiting in the shadows.

"Mr. MacLeod can go with Mary," Aunt Flora said, letting the curtain drop. "He's handy with his fists. He'd protect her should trouble arise."

"He's proven his loyalty tae us," Aunt Maude chimed in.

Nods of agreement circled their gathering, but the room's fire flared hotly at Mary's back. Mr. Thomas West came to mind even though Mr. MacLeod was the reasonable replacement for Cecelia.

"I'll speak to Mr. MacLeod," Mary said.

Despite visions of the scarred pirate dancing in her

head, she was sensible, informing the women of Mr. West's request to use their warehouse in Southwark— and the Betty Burke painting in Madame Bedwell's gaming room, which raised eyebrows. Who were the members of this secret society? And why did they operate in London?

Each question sent furtive glances that yes, they were onto something. But like a poorly made wooden puzzle box, not all the pieces fit.

Aunt Flora scrunched her nose. "I canna believe these people are true Jacobites."

"Neither can I," Aunt Maude said, swiping another biscuit.

Mary shot a covert *Tell them* glance at Cecelia, who was toying with the lace trim on her wrist. This was the burden of secrets—what to reveal and when.

Cecelia cleared her throat. "The Countess of Denton is part of the secret society that meets, or used to meet, at Maison Bedwell." All eyes were on her, shocked. She snorted indelicately. "But we can all agree Lady Denton is *not* a Jacobite."

"I'd like tae see her try and claim herself as one," Aunt Maude grumbled. "Highlanders would toss her out like bad fish . . . the grubby woman."

The women tittered softly, their chairs creaking. Mary checked the room. Question marks could very well have sprouted from Aunt Flora, Aunt Maude, and Margaret's heads, such was the weight of this latest news.

Aunt Flora pinned Cecelia with a grandmotherly stare.

"How do you know this? Is this something your spies shared?"

Cecelia's shrug was small and guilt laden. "It's a recent discovery. But I dare not say any more."

"You don't need tae protect us, lass," was Aunt Flora's gentle admonishment. "We're here tae help."

But this was what Mary, Cecelia, and Anne had done since their first days in Arisaig. They'd looked after the older aunts and they'd looked after little Margaret, who wasn't so little anymore. Their league was unraveling in unexpected ways. With Anne gone and now learning Lady Denton had entrenched herself in a Jacobite society . . . well, Aunt Maude said it best.

The older woman slapped the side table. "It's a world gone mad. That's what it is."

"And we must decide what to do about it." Mary injected this wisdom, which met with mute stares. The fireplace crackling cheerily, she nudged the conversation. "Cecelia, do you have anything to report from our night at Bedwell's?"

Cecelia shared that she'd found nothing, a cleaned-up tale, omitting what floor of the brothel she'd searched. She finished with frothy gossip about a pompous duke whose wig had caught on a sconce.

Cecelia giggled. "So deep in his cups he was. The old sod didn't know what was happening until it twisted sideways and the sausage curls hit his nose."

Knees cracking, Aunt Maude got up from her chair with the evening's final bit. "Flora and I plan tae take more food tae the poor souls at Tenter's Ground."

Chairs scraped, a sign their meeting was coming to an end. Dishes *clinked* as Aunt Maude set about tidying up.

"You know," Aunt Flora began, "we could use an

extra pair of hands at Tenter's Ground. What do you say, Margaret? Can you lend a hand?"

Aunt Maude beamed. "That's a fine idea."

Margaret picked up the plate of half-eaten biscuits. "I don't know . . . We're so busy at the shop."

"Our shop will be fine." Mary added her cup to the tray, her smile an olive branch. "Wouldn't you like a week of freedom?"

Margaret was doe-eyed and contrite.

"Oh, Mary . . ."

"Go on. Have fun," Mary said.

Aunt Flora's blue eyes twinkled over her stack of dishes. "We'll have a splendid time of it. Excursions on Tooley Street. A little tea and gossip with friends. Why, even Mr. MacLeod has taken tae reading aloud the *Gentleman's Monthly Intelligencer* at night."

The aunts herded Margaret out of the bedchamber, their chatter trailing cheerfully as they headed to the kitchen where Jenny was packing food for the poor Scots and Irish who made their homes in Tenter's Grounds.

"Quite a day for our little league," Cecelia said from the comfort of her bed.

Mary turned around, weary. "Months of boring nothingness, and suddenly, we're beset with drama."

"You mean the Countess of Denton revealed as Lady Pink?" Cecelia asked archly. "Or the sisterly variety?"

"Don't . . ."

"Margaret is nineteen. When I think of what I was doing at her age . . ."

"Which is precisely why I keep a careful eye on her."

Cecelia's provocative spark faded. She smoothed

the counterpane once, twice. "There are times I forget the roles you have played—mother, sister, and shopkeeper—while I've gadded freely about."

Mary folded her hands together.

"Careful, Cecelia. You're on the verge of complimenting me."

Which nursed kindly smiles between them.

"Perhaps you're owed one or two. Margaret is a credit to your steadfast care, but we both know she won't set foot in brothels anytime soon. Which reminds me"—Cecelia reached behind the pitcher on her bedside table, her blond curls falling forward—"you'll need this when you return to Maison Bedwell."

She held up a large coin. Mary crossed the room and took it.

"I should've returned it to you last night," Cecelia said.

Mary traced Charles Stuart's profile on polished metal. Only forty tokens had been commissioned, but this was the forty-first, a forgery done in an alcove behind her workroom.

"I made his nose too big."

Mr. Sloane spoke up from his seat at the edge of the mattress. "Your work is frighteningly excellent, Miss Fletcher."

Eyeing him warily, she pocketed the token.

"I appreciate the compliment, sir, but I'm still not entirely comfortable with your involvement in our league. You are—or were—a servant of the crown."

"Relax, Mary. Alexander knows everything. He is the one who gave me the rubbing of the secret society's coin."

"Did he?"

Mary angled her face to Mr. Sloane. Arms wide, he bowed silent acknowledgment.

She shot a reproving glance at Cecelia. "We keep too many secrets from each other."

"That's my fault," Mr. Sloane said. "I asked Cecelia to keep certain facts to herself."

"I see."

Though truthfully, Mary didn't. Secrets sent fissures through their league. So did the gentleman who required Cecelia's allegiance to him. It augured another break in their little family, and she was still smarting from the loss of Anne Neville. To a man, of course—Will MacDonald.

Men—they were often at the heart of what went wrong in her life.

"Because of recent events, Alexander's given me leave to share those facts with you." Cecelia shined with admiration for the man sitting on her bed. "He's the reason we know about the secret society, not one of my spies. Alexander found their names and a rubbing of the coin in that coded ledger, which the Duke of Newcastle had asked him to investigate."

Mary bit back the urge to say that Alexander had also been tasked to investigate Cecelia. But times were changing, and they needed to focus on weightier matters such as the last of the lost treasure. The secret society, Charles Stuart's supporters, must have it. The same group that smuggled Charles Stuart into London in 1750. She rubbed the token, its burden heavy in her pocket. *Why did they keep the treasure?*

Cecelia fussed with her night-robe. "Did anything else happen last night? Aside from you finding the Betty Burke painting?"

A scarred sea wolf came to mind.

"No. My venture into the gaming room was uneventful."

"Then how did you come by those bruises on your wrist?"

Mary cuffed the mottled spots with her hand.

"A misunderstanding."

"That's quite a misunderstanding." Cecelia's brows rose a doubtful half inch and she gave Mr. Sloane a speaking glance. "Would you be a dear and fetch some bread for me?"

He stood up, his bronze eyes discerning. "Of course." A wise man, Mr. Sloane would dally in the kitchen to give Cecelia all the time she needed. Mary had learned that much about him.

When the stairs creaked his descent, Cecelia confessed, "I go positively weak-kneed for bread hot from the pan, slathered with butter. Of late, I crave it more than a good tup."

Mary cracked a smile. "Don't let Mr. Sloane know."

Cecelia laughed, color returning to her cheeks. Last night they would've chewed on every detail of Maison Bedwell on the ride home, except when Mary had climbed into the carriage, Cecelia had already dozed off.

"Come." Cecelia patted the bed. "Have a seat."

Mary settled on the plush edge with a rueful, "Now the real meeting begins."

Arms folding under her bosom, Cecelia was all business. "I don't like how things are unfolding."

"Because of the countess."

"Stopping her may require drastic measures."

Mary shifted uncomfortably. "We're not violent women."

"Lady Denton is." Iron laced Cecelia's tone. Though exhaustion painted dark circles under her eyes, she was regal and decided. "You and I must agree—one week and one week only to find the gold."

"And then?"

"Then we decide what to do about the countess."

An ugly shiver drifted down Mary's spine. "I don't like what that infers. It is foul and unworthy of us."

Cecelia's white shift dripped with virginal lace, but her hazel eyes glinted fiercely.

"Lady Denton is foul. And don't forget, *we* are her next targets."

"Still, I cannot accept what you're suggesting. The war . . ." She swallowed hard. "The war was enough."

Cecelia reached for Mary's hand, her fingertips light and reassuring. "Ours has not been an easy life. Just look at the bruises on your wrist."

This time Mary didn't bother to cover them. "Time for my confessional?"

Cecelia's warm hand retreated.

"Tell me how you got them. And *do not* edit your tale."

The bed creaked, the fire crackled, and the silence crawled. Just how much would she tell? Her unchaste confessional to a certain scarred hero came to mind. What a saucebox she'd been. She'd not share *that*.

"You'll be pleased to know," she began, "last night taught me that I am not as skilled as you at subterfuge."

"Learned that, did you?"

Mary's place had always been a supportive role in their league. Arranging for a dray to haul barrels of gold, waiting in the shadows dressed as a man to hide the barrels, and later melting those gold coins little by little behind her shop's workroom. Common, needful duties done patiently, efficiently, in the background, as was her way.

"Don't let my fine praise go to your head," Mary said. "You failed to mention the distinction between masked and unmasked women at Maison Bedwell."

"But you managed all the same."

"I did."

Cecelia flopped back against her mound of pillows. "What's your plan for returning to Bedwell's? Will you play the masked spinster seeking adventure?"

"I was thinking about renting a room in Maison Bedwell."

Cecelia's eyes rounded.

"You, renting a room for an assignation? My, how far you've fallen, Miss Fletcher."

She touched her lips as if to hide her smile. "It does feel wanton."

"Because it is, but a sound idea all the same."

"I'll have to use the last of our French livres. A purse full . . . that's what's left of our league funds."

Cecelia's mouth curved a knowing smile. Pale blond wisps fell around her cheeks, carefree and girlish on the worldly Scotswoman.

"The more interesting question is do you plan to use the room?"

"As a meeting place only."

"Well, I'm sure Mr. MacLeod—"

"Stop," Mary said firmly. "Our priority is to find the gold, and oh, by the way, decide what to do about a bloodthirsty countess."

Which sounded overly prim to her ears.

"Silly of me to consider pleasures of the flesh at a time like this." Cecelia spoke in such even tones it was clear she didn't think it silly at all. "Though I can't countenance why you're so determined to hunt down the last of the gold."

"Because we should leave no stone unturned."

Cecelia wasn't sold on the explanation. The blonde drummed her fingers on the pillowy counterpane with the softest *tap tap tap* until she closed the conversational gap.

"Tell me how you came by those bruises."

Mary glanced down, relieved. Anything to steer Cecelia away from talking about rented rooms and lust-fueled assignations.

"A man named Culpepper. He was sotted and, like me, unaware of the house rules regarding masked women."

"Yet, you managed to get rid of him."

"After two men intervened on my behalf."

"Who were these men?" Cecelia asked.

Mary hesitated, a terrible mistake.

"Mr. Thomas West was one of them."

Cecelia's eyes narrowed. "The same gentleman who arrived in your shop today, requesting the key to Neville Warehouse."

Mary averted her eyes. She couldn't deny the unfolding events were peculiar.

"Mary," Cecelia groaned. "You are intelligent enough to know this is an odd coincidence."

"Possibly. But he did help us last August. As to needing the warehouse, October *is* the selling season for bones, baleen, and oil. Nothing coincidental about that."

Cecelia shook her head, unconvinced. "And the other man?"

"A Lord Ranleigh, I believe."

"Lord Julian Ranleigh?"

"He didn't announce his Christian name."

Cecelia stared at the wall as one does when cyphering a troubling equation. "As I recall, the Ranleighs are all the same. Black-haired, handsome devils, except Lord Julian's missing part of a finger on his left hand."

"I didn't notice his hands, but the Lord Ranleigh who intervened was well dressed and handsome . . . if one finds arrogance appealing."

Cecelia's brow pinched. "We must be careful. The Countess of Denton shares a distant family connection with them."

"Which is true of all England's aristocracy," Mary said dryly. "The lot of them are inbred."

Cecelia looked at her with a *stick to the matter at hand* message.

"Did it appear to you that Mr. West and Lord Ranleigh knew each other?"

Mary rose from the bed, restless. "Well enough for Lord Ranleigh to comment on Mr. West's taste in women."

Cecelia sighed. "This is an interesting turn."

"Why?"

"Because the ship which smuggled Charles Stuart into London three years ago was owned by the Countess of Denton, her brother, and the Duchess of Aldridge."

Mary tensed. Cecelia had shared this information with her last month after Cecelia and Mr. Sloane had broken into the Countess of Denton's warehouse off Arundel Stairs. They'd called it a hunt for the gold, but she suspected Cecelia and the clever barrister-cum-government man had hunted for proof of Lady Denton's illegal activities.

"And this signifies because?"

"Because the Duchess of Aldridge is Lord Julian Ranleigh's mother," Cecelia said.

"Oh." Mary nibbled her lower lip.

"Poor woman. Her sons are terrors and her husband was worse. Ranleigh's a crafty one. Trouble always seems to find him. He was quietly removed from Eton years ago—a feat considering the family name. The dukedom goes all the way back to King Edward I."

"Hammer of the Scots. Ironic, isn't it? Ranleigh's ancestors winning their title by pounding our ancestors into the ground?"

Fear shaded Cecelia's eyes. "You must watch your back."

"You've not to worry," Mary said, forcing brightness. "I can be crafty too."

"Then you ought to find out why Mr. West was at Maison Bedwell. It can't bode well for us."

Instead of replying, Mary applied herself to righting the room, blowing out extra candles and setting them in a neat array on the mantel for Jenny to collect. She needed a reprieve from Cecelia's all-too-perceptive eyes—and the inconvenient facts concerning Mr. West.

He knew she'd forged a key last August.

Had he learned what the key was for?

Standing at the mantel, her blurred reflection

showed above a damp handprint on a brass candle-
stick holder. Her lips were moving in fervent prayer:
Please may he not be involved.

"Mary," Cecelia beckoned gently.

"Yes?"

"In the gaming room last night, did you see a tall
blonde woman in jackboots and leather stays?"

Mary turned around.

"I did."

"That is Ilsa Thelen, a Swedish bare-knuckle
brawler. She is to Lord Ranleigh what Mr. Wortley is
to the Countess of Denton." Cecelia grimaced, sinking deeper into her pillows. "Don't be fooled by her
slender frame. I've witnessed her toppling men twice
her size."

Mary rubbed her nape but the chill camped there
wouldn't leave.

"Consider me forewarned."

Cecelia's eyes softened at the corners as if she understood Mary's heart and the dilemma of unstop-
pable attraction to a questionable man.

"And today Mr. West visited your shop," Cecelia
said. "An intriguing chain of events, don't you think?"

Chapter Six

There was something about going to a gentleman's place of business in the morning. Invigorating, certainly. Mary fed on her determination and charged the outside stairs of West and Sons Shipping. Seagulls perched on weathered treads squawked and flew away, while a hoary-haired clerk gaped at her through the ground-floor window as she ascended the stairs.

Hers would be a *take no prisoners* interview in Mr. West's private office. She *would* get to the bottom of his intent—how, exactly, she couldn't say.

Demand to know why he was at Maison Bedwell? A mortifying question.

Withhold the warehouse key until he explained himself? A churlish move.

Flirt boldly with Mr. West? A dangerous plan—though it was her favorite.

It was better than Cecelia's advice to *smile, be friendly, and listen.*

Cresting the landing, she frowned mutinously. Of course, she *could* smile, nor was friendliness out of the question. It was the listening part that bothered her, as though she should stifle independent thought. As to the best methods of subterfuge, she knocked on the office door, determined to find her own.

"Enter," was the brusque command from within.

She turned the latch and the sun-grayed door swung wide. The thrumming, pounding noise in her ears must be from bounding up the stairs, definitely not from Mr. West seated at his desk, a quill in hand.

"Miss Fletcher." He set down his quill.

"Mr. West."

Despite the hammering in her chest, her voice was as mellow as the autumn breeze batting her mob-cap's frilled edge. She'd worn her worst, a regrettable piece with a wide chinstrap. For the first time she wanted to be the poised, elegant creature Cecelia was. To parley witty quips. But no; her tongue was pasted to the roof of her mouth.

Her *take no prisoners* plan stalled.

A chair scraped the floor. Mr. West stood up, his mouth quirking as if her presence on his doorstep was inevitable.

"How nice to see you," he said. "Please come in."

She didn't budge. She couldn't.

Mr. West was rounding his desk when an orange tabby trotted out of the shadows, leaped up, and plopped down on a pile of papers in the middle of the desk. Mr. West stopped to pet the cat.

"This is Mr. Fisk. He requires my attention in the morning." He added a heartwarming, "The old cat likes to think he owns the place."

His quip was the perfect opportunity for polite excuses and a hasty exit, but the sight of him, stroking the orange tabby, glued her feet to the floor.

"Do you like cats?" he asked.

"I do."

A silly flutter invaded her chest. She was ensor-celled by his long fingers ruffling, then smoothing the cat's fur. Judging by the rumbling purr, Mr. Fisk approved. She wouldn't mind Mr. West ruffling and smoothing her.

"Independent creatures, cats." Mr. West lifted his head, his green-blue eyes incandescent in sunlight. "One must be patient to earn their devotion."

Her stomach flip-flopped.

"Yes, patience. A true virtue."

"And one must proceed with caution. Other-wise, they dart off—especially from doorsteps late at night."

She was dry-mouthed and snared by his potent stare. "They are quick . . . cats."

"Very quick."

Mr. West's smile was gently wicked. *The ruinous man.* He was stringing her along flirtation's path.

"But when coupled with time and the right touch," he said, "anything can happen."

He illustrated this with more tender strokes. *Oh, to be that cat.* Her own back twitched, her senses muddling. Morning light flooded her, but the office seemed to transform itself before her eyes. Mr. West could've pulled back the curtain on a life she didn't know existed. The scene filling her mind, startling. Something to make her breath catch. A hazy, domes-tic future—the two of them by a cozy fire with a cat curled up on a pillow. Their conversation was light. The mood, sweet. The contentment, devasting.

The sea wolf tamed, as it were.

She put a hand on the door frame to steady herself.

"Aren't you coming in?" he asked.

Wistful seconds passed before she found her voice.

"I—I can't. A wherry is waiting for me." She fished for the key and held it up to ward off his enchanting appeal. "I brought the key to Neville Warehouse."

"I see."

Mr. West advanced on her, bringing his devastating musk and cedarwood scent with him.

Why was she such a ninny about the scent of his skin?

Eyes like weatherworn glass studied her. Humor glinted in their depths, she suspected, as much for her delivering the key as for himself at being profoundly pleased that she had.

"Thank you." He took the proffered key, and she wished she were gloveless today.

To feel his skin on hers . . .

Lust arrowed hotly inside her.

She wetted her lips, rattled.

"Unfortunately, I cannot take the time for a social call. As you might imagine, I must return to my shop. I've orders to attend, and Mr. Baines, the wherryman who is waiting for me, has urgent business near Tower Wharf. At least I think it's Tower Wharf, and one never knows what the currents will be like or the river's traffic. And you, I suspect, must tend your—"

She froze midsentence. Mr. West braced a forearm against the door frame, his body inches from hers.

"—your business, that is," she finished on a whisper.

Sighing deeply, she averted her eyes. They both

knew she could've paid the wherryman to deliver the key. Instead, she was barely on Mr. West's doorstep and already explaining her retreat.

"I abhor mindless chatter," she said, miserable.

"It's understandable. The hour is early."

"You are too kind." She looked up at him, at the width of his shoulders and his rugged features. "No matter the hour, when I'm around you, I say whatever comes to mind."

His smile was heart-achingly beautiful.

"Freeing, isn't it?"

This wasn't freeing. She was tangled and bothered and . . . wanting.

"More like verbal dysentery."

A shot of laughter, and Mr. West was shaking his head, a charmed man.

"See what I mean? With most men I am pleasantly detached, if not arctic. Once I'm around you"—she gestured vaguely at him—"and one would think I was raised by wolves."

His smile expanded such that his eyes crinkled at the outer corners.

"I have a great appreciation for arctic climes, Miss Fletcher. They're stark and beautiful."

Basking in his smile calmed her.

"I, for one," he added, "welcome any conversation with you."

"Be careful what you wish for, sir. Highlanders are known for speaking their minds—especially the women."

Mr. West reached out and folded back her mobcap's frill.

"Only one Highland woman interests me."

She held her breath as morning sun splashed her

cheek. The scarred shipmaster began stroking the hair at her temple. Diabolically soft, his touch. No wonder the cat came around.

"As a matter of fact," Mr. West said, "I recently had the most revealing conversation with a masked Scotswoman."

"Masked Scotswomen are the worst." Her voice was drowsy and tame.

"She put me and all of London's men in their place."

"This woman sounds like a saucebox."

He was fascinated by a wisp of her hair. The more he toyed with it, the more weak-kneed she became.

"A little impudence is good for the soul, Miss Fletcher. It leads to honesty for those brave enough to seek it, and ours was a thoroughly honest conversation."

"You speak of you and this . . . masked Scotswoman."

His mouth hooked sideways, and she was caught in a magnetic pull.

"You appreciate directness, I collect," she said.

He looked into her eyes.

"All the better to know her heart."

His voice was so intimate and low she doubted that she'd heard him right. It took several sensual-fogged seconds for her brain to catch up.

Mr. West wanted to know her heart.

"And this masked Scotswoman . . . you wish to see her again?" she asked, breathless.

"I do."

"Why?"

Mr. West stopped touching her cheek.

This was a stake in the ground, her desperate need

to know his intent. *Was he aligned with Lord Ranleigh?* was one question. Yet, it faded under the deeper, soul-quenching need: *Why her?* London was riddled with beautiful women, plenty of them warmer-natured than she.

Of the two questions, she knew which one she cared about.

Mr. West squinted at the river, pensive. Solitary. Ships passed, their sails white patches on the fabric of London's scenery. Mr. West shifted his feet, nodding slowly to no one in particular.

"I've spent half my life on the North Sea, racing her wind, riding her waves. As a younger man, I yearned for her. Her excitement, her beauty. But don't be fooled. She's a brutal mistress. She kills without a second thought," he said bitterly. "Men arrogantly believe they can conquer her and steal her treasures. It'll never happen. Share a pint with the old sailors at Wapping Wall, and they'll tell you, life is fleeting. And the idea of control, laughable. Be it land or sea, we are mere sojourners in a place where nothing lasts forever. This day, this moment, *is* the treasure."

His gaze sought hers, honest and radiant.

"That is my *why*, Miss Fletcher."

She tried to swallow. He wanted her, but for how long?

A day? A month? A lifetime?

The lump in her throat was her throbbing heart. Aching, fearful, and deeply thrilled. In short, a chaotic mess. When she did find her voice, it was scratchy and tormented.

"I—I don't know what to say."

"Say yes. For however long."

His last three words were a sad, sad revelation.

"Because nothing lasts forever," she said, subdued.

This was life distilled. The blessing and the curse of a woman approaching her thirtieth year, facing a man five or six years older. Their youthful promises had been spent. Experience was their currency, and time no longer an ally.

Wind batting his cravat, Mr. West clasped both hands behind his back. "It is forward of me, I know, but after our interlude at Bedwell's . . ."

She nodded sagely.

"I understand. You thought catching me in a brothel presented an opportunity."

Mr. West checked the river again, mildly chastened. "I don't wish to be overbold, but circumstances have forced my hand."

Head tipping back, she studied him. This was the chink in her scarred pirate's armor.

"Should you trust me, I would like to hear them."

His mouth firmed. "Perhaps, in due time."

His deflection didn't put her off in the slightest.

"We are a direct pair, aren't we?"

His gaze wandered back to her. "Like with like, as my father used to say."

Brows knitting, she considered that. Were they alike? Mr. West was a sea wolf with a patina of dockside roughness, a man unafraid to use his fists . . . if one listened to rumors. His hands showed the wear and tear of a person unafraid to use them. The same was true of her. He was also a respected merchant and a ship's master, a sober gentleman given to hard work and heart-melting kisses on unusual body parts.

In quiet moments she'd caress her brass-stained fingertip—the same spot he'd kissed on the front steps of Maison Bedwell.

To feel his lips again . . .

Five years was the whisper in her head. Her last passionate kiss. She'd give anything for Mr. West to be the one to change this unfortunate fact. He was close. Less than an arm's length from her, and him with his mouth parting tenderly, his head dipping.

A soft shudder teased her.

If she pushed up on her toes—which she did— and tilted her body just so . . .

A loud cough ripped them apart.

Her heels dropped and she snapped to attention better than a new recruit. There, at the bottom of the stairs, the hoary-haired clerk waited. With him was a beefy man wearing a leather apron, his face grimed with soot.

"Mr. West, sir, there's a problem with the *Mary Jane*," the old clerk said.

"Thank you, Mr. Anstruther."

Mr. West eyed her apologetically. They'd been inches from a kiss both of them desperately wanted.

"Begging your pardon, sir, but it's serious trouble." The aproned man jabbed a thumb in the direction of the dry dock. "The cinch holding up the *Mary Jane*'s bow has cracked, nearly in two."

The clerk was emphatic. "She won't hold much longer."

Mr. West stepped onto the landing. "Put the men to work on the *Lucretia*. Make sure everyone is out of harm's way, and I'll be down shortly."

The clerk and his beefy companion stalked off, and the astonishing moment was gone. Mary touched her stomacher, the contact needful as though she might float away. She was scrambled and lost, the glow of a near kiss sadly fading.

Mr. West grimaced. "Duty calls, I'm afraid."

He dipped into his office and reappeared, donning his tricorn. They were silent, going down the stairs. Her befuddled body was taking its own sweet time recovering. Her mind, however, was reassembling and posing prudent questions.

Was she any closer to uncovering Mr. West's reason for being at Bedwell's? No.

Did she find out anything about his connection to Lord Ranleigh? No.

Did she hand over her sole bargaining piece, the key to Neville Warehouse? Yes.

Not a promising morning.

Crossing the docks, she pinched her petticoats to save her hems. It was time to admit, when it came to subterfuge, Cecelia was a goddess among women. With information gathering, with men, and with the aftermath of a missed kiss.

But that lost kiss hurt most of all.

"Miss Fletcher." Mr. Baines hailed her from his wherry.

She waved to him. The business of life called.

Mr. West grabbed her hand midair. "I'll guide her down to you, Mr. Baines."

"Very good, sir."

She locked on to their joined hands. The shipmaster's grip was fraught with messages.

Mr. West's eyes were bemused when he whispered to her, "You won't deny me this final pleasure, will you?"

"Of you witnessing my landlubber's climb into a boat?" she whispered back, grabbing the ladder.

To which he laughed, a wonderful sound winding around her heart. It made the inglorious end of their meeting almost bearable. Mr. West went down on bended knee, helping her as she made the awkward descent from the dock to the ladder. Even when she was steady with both feet in the wherry, her gloved fingers were fused with his, the warmth and yearning palpable.

She looked up at him.

Please, hold me . . . always.

A stunning want. It sucked the air out of her lungs.

Mr. West's eyes burned ardently. "You will have an answer for me soon?"

Business demands and her treasure hunt popped up like noisy children in her head. If only she was a woman of leisure . . .

She squeezed his hand, and they broke apart. "Yes, soon."

"I'll be on tenterhooks."

Mr. West had made his decision.

Had she made hers?

Sunlight bleached the scar on his tanned face. A shipmaster, a sea wolf, a man not to be taken lightly. She took her seat, her gaze fastened to his. Mr. Baines drove his pole into the river, and the narrow boat slid forward. The tide was low, the mud sticky and smelly. Mr. West stood up, his stance wide in tar-spattered jackboots. The brim of his hat shadowed his eyes. He was distant, watching her slip away.

Until his lips parted, vulnerable and wanting.

His need shook her to the marrow of her bones.

Thirsty for the sight of him, she scooted forward on the narrow seat. But her foot banged a coin purse full of French livres on the floor. Her next errand. Her duty. She toed it aside and drank in Mr. West, her tenderhearted pirate.

Visiting him, she'd done what she had no business doing.

She'd given him a breadcrumb of hope.

Chapter Seven

$\mathcal{M}$ary walked toward Maison Bedwell, her next
bad decision. Twenty polished windows shined
down on her, yet not a single curtain was drawn.
Rather sleepy for half past ten. Carriages were rolling
by, and a breeze carried a polyglot of foreign tongues,
families and merchants going about their day.

Three quick raps on the brass door knocker announced her. She was outwardly confident, though
her nerves weren't playing well with her breakfast,
a matter made worse by the lurid Grub Street news-
paper captions teasing her brain:

**CORSET MAKER RUNS AFOUL OF THE LAW
SPINSTER CAUGHT IN A HOUSE OF RUIN
SCOTSWOMAN DANCES WITH THE DEVIL**

It was just her luck; pungent smoke started curling
up through the iron railing to her left. She peered
over it. A cheroot-puffing servant was lounging by
the basement entrance.

"Dance with the devil it is," she said under her
breath.

She banged the brass ring again, hard enough to jingle the purse in her petticoat pocket. When the door cracked open, a charwoman with ash on her nose stood in the gap.

"May I help you, miss?"

"Yes, I'm here on a matter of business."

The charwoman squinted in disbelief.

"We don't open for custom until one o'clock, miss. The footmen need their sleep. Same for the harlots, if that's your fancy."

Mary stepped closer and set her gloved hand on the door.

"I'm not here for *that*. I seek an interview with Madame Bedwell."

The charwoman rolled her eyes. "Why didn't you say so in the first place?"

The door swung wide and Mary crossed the threshold into what appeared to be the scene of a crime. A fern had been upended, its porcelain vase shattered. Footprints salted the dirt fanning the white marble floor, and stockings laced the grand staircase like bunting. No blood, thankfully.

"You had quite an evening."

The maid shut the door, giggling. "This is nothing. You should see what happens when the Russians pay a visit."

Mary was about to remove her gloves when a long, tortured moan ripped through the entry hall. Alarmed, she pinched the glove's fingertip, her attention bouncing from the stairs to empty hallways. The ruckus came again, followed by hearty grunts. Definitely from the ballroom, yet the charwoman scratched her cheek, unconcerned.

"Want me to take your cloak, miss?"

Light and shadows flickered under the ballroom's closed doors.

"I'll keep it on, thank you. My business should be quick."

"Suit yourself." The charwoman picked up a red ash pail. "Wait here."

The maid crossed the dirt-spattered marble floor. Male voices, rich with laughter, echoed just before she closed the ballroom doors behind her.

Under her cloak, Mary worried a seam on her stomacher.

What madness is this?

Overhead, those frolicking women painted in the Baroque style smiled down at her. A few, she imagined, were smirking as if they weren't surprised to see her again. She stared at them. The frescoes did catch the eye. Light and gaiety filtered the artist's imagined meadow, filling each slice of the vaulted ceiling. A lovely distortion, but she knew the truth. Excess came with a price, and there weren't enough ceilings in all of London to paint *that*.

When the ballroom doors burst open, she got a taste of the madness.

A devil in stockinged feet and wrinkled breeches charged her. His pink velvet banyan fluttered like a tail, and a smoky scent came with him.

"What fool comes to call at half past ten?" he boomed.

She gaped. "Lord Ranleigh?"

He glared at her through tangled black hair. "And you are?"

"Miss Mary Fletcher of White Cross Street." She curtseyed. An excellent one. "This morning's fool, apparently."

Fraught seconds passed, enough for her to notice water pasted his shirt to his chest and his nipples poked the fabric. Head cocked, she stared at both dark points and the spectacular pectoral display on which his nipples sat.

"You are wet, my lord."

"An excellent observation."

A lesser woman would've crumbled. She had to admit this was not a banner day for her and men. Excellent manners were the only way to recover.

Hands folded, she stood tall and proper. "There seems to be a mistake, my lord. You are not the person I'm seeking. So whatever . . . mischief you were engaged in, please do carry on."

"Dismissed, am I?"

An incredible specimen, Lord Ranleigh. Magnificent in his dishabille. She would've taken further note, except behind him, seven men—three of them shirtless, their chests heaving—were in the ballroom.

"What are they doing?" She walked around Lord Ranleigh for a better view.

A blond man, his finger circling the air called out, "Gather round, lads. Time for another go."

Each man found a spot around the fountain and took hold. Backs strained, groans chorused, and water sloshed. The fountain inched along toward open doors which led to the garden. A fine effort until horrid screeching pierced her ears.

Mary was aghast. "They're ruining the ballroom floor."

His lordship padded to her side. "The fountain must go."

"Surely, Madame Bedwell will be angry about the damage done." She turned to him. "I'm upset on her behalf and this isn't even my home."

"The old woman will recover, I'm sure," he said dryly.

The bawd must owe money for the fountain, and Lord Ranleigh had come to collect. Or the arrogant man had an affinity for fountains. Who could say when it came to sons of dukes? Grub Street devoted rivers of ink to their excess—gossipy articles she'd grudgingly admit to reading on occasion.

Another awful ear-splitting scrape and she bolted into the ballroom.

"Stop!"

Lord Ranleigh followed. "Miss Fletcher . . ."

She ignored him and went straight to the fountain. The bewildered footmen unbent themselves, panting from their efforts. In the corner, the freckled charwoman ceased her sweeping.

Mary called to her, "You there. Bring me your broom, and fetch every broom in this house." The servant gawked, frozen in place. Mary clapped her hands. "Quickly, I say."

"Go on, Nettie," Lord Ranleigh said. "Do as she says."

The charwoman scurried forward and handed Mary the broom. She dashed out, her heel strikes echoing. The ballroom floor was lushly patterned wood trimmed with stone on the perimeter. A work of art. Mary crouched down on black-and-white marble cut in a swirling design, the pieces interlocked. The sheer number of craftsmen and the hours of careful labor it must've taken to create this floor boggled the mind. With a gloved finger, she rubbed a faint mark on the stone. *What Philistine could be so uncaring?*

Lord Ranleigh's dirty, silk-covered toes came into view.

Him, of course.

"Do you mean to sweep the fountain into the garden?" he asked.

She sat back on her heels and looked up. "No, but I shall save you from Madame Bedwell's wrath."

"Will you, now?"

His lordship might be amused; she was not. In fact, she was rather fascinated.

Water soaking her knees, she put her cheek to the floor and checked the fountain's base, testing the bottom of its three-tiered structure. Thick plaster over a wooden frame. A long hose with a small billow at the end stuck out like a tail. She sat up, smiling. *So that's how it works. A foot pump.* Any one of the half-dressed footmen nearby could've worked it. Fresh-faced men, all of them broad-backed and handsome. None looked a day over twenty-two. She felt a blush rising. One of them was the auburn-haired footman who'd winked at her.

Lord Ranleigh went down on one knee beside her. "Care to tell me why you've summoned every broom in the house?"

"I assure you, it's not because I'm a witch."

Three footmen laughed.

"I'm glad to hear it," Ranleigh said. "You'd be a prolific flyer if you were."

The footmen used the respite to don shirts and button their waistcoats, an odd formality she appreciated. Others were shaking their coats and retying messy queues as if a vicar's wife had come to call. With her chinstrap mobcap, she'd garbed herself like one.

"We are going to put the brooms here"—she pointed to the floor in front of the fountain—"and roll the fountain over them."

"What if they aren't long enough?"

"We'll have to improvise." She ran her hand up and down the broom handle, checking for cracks. "Though I'm afraid this one is too short."

Ranleigh's brows arched. "Are you saying my broom is . . . inadequate?"

A bloom tingled her cheeks. "My lord, if it's too early in the morning for visitors, then it's too early for innuendo."

"Oh, Miss Fletcher, it's never too early for verbal indiscretion. It's the second best of its kind."

Her mouth quirked. "I can only imagine what you deem first best."

His mouth quirked too. "I'm sure you do. Despite your puritanical headwear, you were curious about what was going on in here."

His was a quiet challenge. She'd not back down from it.

"Fortunately for you, my lord, I was."

He grunted, amused.

Never in her life did she expect to sit on the floor and flirt with the disheveled son of a duke. They were an exotic specimen. But this was a brothel, which served up all things unique, and was apparently Lord Ranleigh's favorite haunt. Cecelia had called him a devil; Mary decided he was a delight. Dark, surly, and imperious, yes. Also, handsome, humored, and indulgent.

She set the broom on the floor between them, a small message. A boundary.

A spark lit Lord Ranleigh's eyes. No doubt the debauched lord considered it a challenge.

She, however, carried on. "We'll stagger the brooms, my lord. One on this side, one on the other. Keep them close together, and it should work." She scrambled up and dusted off her gloves. "As the fountain rolls forward, brooms from the back are placed in front. It will be easier to push and kinder to the floor."

Lord Ranleigh stood up, a slow nod coming.

"Well-done, Miss Fletcher. I recall a tale about an invading army moving siege machines over logs just like this."

"It is the same principle."

"Hopefully, you're not planning to invade."

"Not at half past ten."

Ranleigh's laugh was rough from smoke and a lack of sleep. An oddly appealing sound from a man she ought not to like. The moment was a small victory, she decided, having diverted his lordship from further innuendo. Nonetheless, a soft spot for the privileged lord was blossoming. He, in turn, watched her, curious. She circled the fountain, checking for loose chunks of plaster on the ground, and tossing any she found into the half-empty bottom pool.

At his quizzical look, she explained, "It's the little things that cause the biggest problems, my lord."

He studied her keenly, apparently not giving another thought to the glorious floor or the hours it took an army of craftsmen to create.

"Your accent. Do you hail from Scotland?" he asked.

"I was born in Edinburgh."

"And . . . were you here two nights past?"

She stopped collecting the plaster bits. A tiny frisson warned her—for what, exactly, she couldn't say.

"I was."

"The woman in white. I remember you."

"I believe *glacial* was your sobriquet for me."

His mouth curved a close-lipped smile.

"I should mind my manners," he said in a tone that left no doubt he'd do nothing of the sort.

The charwoman and another maid bustled in with arms full of brooms, saving her. Under his lordship's watchful eye, Mary directed the women to make a path with the brooms to the open doors. The footmen clustered around as she explained how the fountain would roll over the brooms.

"You heard her, lads," the blond footman said. "Time to put our backs to it."

They did, and the behemoth fountain rolled along with greater ease and no visible damage to the floor. Lord Ranleigh nodded his approval.

"I think this deserves a morning refreshment," he said to Mary.

"Thank you, but I'd prefer to see Madame Bedwell—unless she is asleep."

"The old battle-ax hardly sleeps. Come with me. I'll make sure you have an audience."

Lord Ranleigh turned and strode away rather quickly for a man who'd indulged in a night of excess. She walked fast after him, coins jingling in her pocket. Ranleigh padded down the wide passage near the gaming room and pushed open a door on the left. When she caught up, he was already at the window, checking the world outside.

"Always good to know the goings-on in the square," he said absently.

Her footsteps dragged, weighed down by the vast room's opulence. The intricate ceiling medallion alone was the size of her shop. The entire room dripped with elegance. The satinwood furniture, blinding silver sconces, and fine portraits that must've cost a fortune. With the beauty came an air of nonchalance—a wrinkled shirt and breeches draped a settee; a pair of shoes caked with mud sat in a brocade chair. She could only imagine the hours it took to clean this room.

Ranleigh let the curtain drop. "Maison Bedwell does have the most interesting neighbors."

"Neighbors?"

"Envoys from Russia, Poland, Bavaria, Genoa, to name a few."

He spoke to her while slipping out of his banyan. She took a seat before the desk, agog at the explosion of money all over it. Spires of gold and silver coins. Too many to count. Lord Ranleigh didn't seem to care. He tugged off his shirt and tossed it on the floor with a soggy *slap*. Sinew rippled across his pale back when he opened a cabinet built into the wall and retrieved a shirt. *Awful man.* He wanted to shock her.

Once the new shirt and banyan were donned, he dropped into a chair and lifted a porcelain pot from a small serving tray on the desk.

"Coffee, Miss Fletcher? It's not fresh, but it is passably hot."

"No, thank you. I'd rather speak to Madame Bedwell."

His eyes gleamed, dark as the coffee he poured. The dish filled, Lord Ranleigh propped dirty, stockinged feet on wrinkled banknotes on the desk. She shrank in her seat like a dull student. The servants, the money. His dishabille and devil-may-care attitude.

"You're Madame Bedwell," she said.

Ranleigh saluted her with his cup. "I'm surprised a woman with your striking intelligence didn't realize that in the ballroom."

"My intellect works better with things, my lord, not people."

"Interesting." He sipped his coffee, appearing to mull over that nugget of information.

"If you don't mind my saying so, my lord, you're a—a . . . man."

"Kind of you to notice."

"Why the fiction?"

Brows slashing, he hesitated. "Out of respect for my mother."

Of all the things the dissolute lord could say . . .

There was a thread here. If she was careful, she might find it and give it a good tug and find more of this familial tale.

"Mrs. Bedwell came with this pile of bricks when I purchased it four years ago. She stays mostly belowstairs," Lord Ranleigh said between sips of coffee. "She keeps the troops in line and was most agreeable about me using her name. I paid her a nice sum, which helped."

How did Cecelia not know this? Maison Bedwell— owned by the dissolute lord facing her—harbored a secret society, *and* his mother, the Duchess of Aldridge, was part owner of a ship that smuggled Charles Stuart into London.

An astounding connection.

When Lord Ranleigh poured more coffee for

himself, she spied the small finger on his left hand. The tip was missing and the scar capping it, thick and white. An old scar.

His obsidian gaze wandered over her. "Since you've covered yourself like a Puritan, I assume you're not seeking employment."

"As a harlot? Certainly not."

"Come now, Miss Fletcher, surely you see the allure in"— he twirled a finger at her—"removing all those layers. A man can only wonder if you burn hotly underneath."

"I imagine you see the allure in every petticoat."

"But I'm asking about you."

Why did those words tease her skin?

"My petticoats are none of your business."

His smoky laugh floated across the desk. He wasn't chastened. Any other time or place and the man speaking so impertinently would've received a tongue-lashing, if not a pint tossed in his face should they be in a public house. But this was Lord Ranleigh's house of ill repute, and she, the one hunting Jacobite treasure.

"So, Miss Fletcher, are you going to tell me why you're here?"

"Yes, of course." She dug into her pocket. "I wish to do business with you."

She stuck out her card. Lord Ranleigh took it and read the large print aloud.

"Fletcher's House of Corsets and Stays." His eyes rounded with mild surprise. "It says that you're the proprietress."

"Indeed, I am."

He checked the card again. No doubt Lord Ranleigh was approached often by men of business wanting a sliver of the wealth displayed gluttonously on his desk.

She cleared her throat. "I've sought this meeting, my lord, because you have a problem."

"A problem?"

"Yes. Shabby silk stays."

He barked a laugh. "What a delight you are, Miss Fletcher. You've almost made this ungodly hour bearable."

Not to be put off, she soldiered on.

"My first night here I noticed stretched seams, frayed ribbons, and the silk having lost its luster."

"We can't have that," he said in mock horror.

"It's not a trifling matter."

"No? What you see as well-worn stays, I see as good business."

"Which could be improved."

He cocked his head and uncombed hair fell about his face. "You know, I can't decide what I find most intriguing about you—the earnest woman of business or the attractive spinster who tries to hide herself." His eyes narrowed a fraction. "It'd be fun to find the answer."

The provocative man. "This is a serious matter, my lord." She scooted forward, her fingertips touching his desk. "Why would a man who hosts extravagant entertainments ignore what I'd hazard to guess is his most profitable room?"

"You mean the gaming room."

"Yes."

He rubbed the card, thoughtful but not convinced.

"Did you not just speak to me of the allure of my own clothes?" she asked. "An important detail, don't you think?"

"And you sought this audience because you wish to improve the allure of my gaming room and thereby fatten my purse?"

His monotone bordered on mockery. She answered with pitch-perfect ennui.

"Do distracted men count their money, my lord?"

Silence followed—it was the sound of her verbal arrow hitting a bull's-eye.

Lord Ranleigh studied her business card. "Very well, Miss Fletcher. What do you propose I should do about all those shabby silk stays?"

"Purchase new stays from my shop, of course. About twenty-five?"

A genuine smile wreathed his unshaved face, showing perfect teeth. Lord Ranleigh no doubt left a trail of broken hearts among society's upper ranks when he graced them with his presence.

"What a bold woman you are." He tossed aside her business card and swung his feet to the floor. "You've surprised me, twice in one day." His gaze roamed appreciatively over her. "I was beginning to lose faith in the fair sex and your ability to capture my interest, but you, Miss Fletcher, have it despite your puritanical headwear."

"Perhaps if *you* worked harder to capture *our* interest, you might find an abundance of scintillating companionship."

Her voice cut with precision. Lord Ranleigh's smile was stuck as if his considerable arsenal—family name and wealth, his looks, and sardonic charm—had hit an impenetrable wall.

"Fractious words from the corset maker seeking my custom," he reminded her.

"As you said, I am a bold woman, my lord."

Lord Ranleigh angled his head as though to see her better. "And you think I need lessons on how to appeal to women."

He addressed her in a lordly monotone, while captivation danced unabashed in his eyes. A parry to her verbal thrust. Intriguing. She was spine straight, her posture perfect, just as her mother had taught her.

"No, my lord. I think you forgot that we all come into the world the same way. It's who you become afterward that matters."

"Trying to reform me?"

She laughed, mostly to steady nerves threatening to snap in two. "Hardly. But know this: I'm not your entertainment, my lord. Should we conduct business, it will be on equal footing."

Regrouping, he made a noncommittal noise. She took note of him, really a first. Something more than skin deep. True, even unwashed, he was perfection. His unshaved jaw a chiaroscuro, his nose an arrow, but his eyes were terribly intelligent. This frightened her. His constant keen assessment.

He offered the barest nod. "Make it thirty stays, Miss Fletcher, and we have a deal."

"At twenty shillings each?"

"Eighteen apiece. That is the going rate for silk stays. Ten, if we're talking about linen."

She couldn't help but smile. "Why am I not surprised that you know the market value of women's undergarments?"

If this was a fencing match, it'd be a draw. Yet, victory's rush surged inside her. She had to tamp it down to keep from leaping up like a twelve-year-old lass who'd bested the village bully.

"As you say, my lord, eighteen apiece. Have you a color preference?"

He shook his head, bored. "Do what you will. I'm sure your taste is impeccable."

"I shall do my best."

Lord Ranleigh fixed his gaze on her as though he was recalculating the sum of her parts. He was more sober-minded than the glib, self-important man she'd seen earlier. It was possible his mask had slipped and she was just now seeing him.

"Are you sure I can't entice you with coffee or tea? We could sit more comfortably" —he gestured to a settee which faced a wide, marbled fireplace— "and you could instruct me on the finer points of becoming a better man."

Her throat went dry. She dared not push her luck with a powerful man, who, she was sure, played the deepest of all games. As owner of Maison Bedwell, he had to have knowledge of the secret society. He might even be in the coded ledger, which sent a warning down her spine.

But a Jacobite sympathizer? She couldn't fathom it.

"Unfortunately, I must decline your kind offer. My shop . . . Duty calls."

"Of course, business and all that."

His dark stare would not release her. There was a force in his eyes, a man sifting through layers of decision-making—about her. She shifted in her chair, aware that she was about to add more complexity to this interview.

"Before I take my leave, I do have another request, my lord."

His eyes rounded, incredulous. "There's more?"

She was stalwart, squaring her shoulders. From

her pocket, she retrieved a purse bulging with coins and dropped it on the desk like a bold gambler increasing the stakes.

"I want to rent a room."

Lord Ranleigh's features faded to bland perfection. The same mask he wore the first night she saw him in the gaming room. He picked up the purse and gave it a small toss.

"For how long?"

"A month."

His lordship didn't bat an eye. To her racing, militant heart a month of nights sounded like forever. Lord Ranleigh bent low behind the desk, the slide of wood on wood sounding. A niggling voice in her head questioned why he didn't bother to count her purse. Was it because he was drenched in money?

"I'll give you the Red Rose room," he said, upright again.

Two keys were in his hand, both with red silk ribbons knotted on the bow heads. He offered them to her.

"One for you, and one for the gentleman meeting you." She reached for the keys, but he kept them inches from her fingers. "Unless you don't have a gentleman in mind."

With her arm out and her heart beating fast, the oddest feeling swamped her. It was the same sensation as dreaming she'd suddenly found herself standing naked in a public square with onlookers pointing at her and whispering. Knowledge as old as time danced in Lord Ranleigh's eyes. He'd found an astonishing crack in her foundation: the corset maker, embarking on a sensual journey. The league might believe she was here for the gold, but the dark lord knew the truth. She sought debasement. To feed a clawing hunger.

Her skin pebbled, everywhere.

"And if I don't have a gentleman in mind . . ."

"I am at your service."

A sweet prickle raced up her arm when he dropped the keys in her palm. His mouth curved a seductive promise: she'd not regret a moment spent with him—for conversation or for pleasure.

She curled her fingers around the iron keys.

"I'll keep that in mind, my lord."

She pocketed the keys, her gaze falling on banknotes wrinkled and dirty from Ranleigh's foot. The top note snared her: a draft in the amount of one hundred fifteen pounds, the payer West and Sons Shipping. There was another West and Sons Shipping banknote, set at an angle underneath the first one, its amount hidden. She blinked at the floor, stunned, but not before she caught Lord Ranleigh following her sight line to those wrinkled banknotes.

Frowning, he shuffled papers and tucked the banknotes into a neat pile. A dismissal.

"About the stays . . ." he said. "I'll send someone to your shop to attend the details."

"Of course, my lord."

She stood up and curtseyed, but the genuflection was lost on him. Lord Ranleigh was focusing on the papers fisted in both hands.

Marveling at what she'd learned, she exited the cavernous room a little drunk on her victories. Beauty was not the coin she'd spent this morning; her intellect was, and it rewarded her tenfold. But with that knowledge came Cecelia's warning about an inconvenient chain of events. She cheerfully shoved those thoughts away. The clock hadn't struck noon, yet she'd already gleaned a wealth of information.

At the top was what should matter the least. Two Englishmen wanted her—Mr. West and Lord Ranleigh. A sea wolf and an arrogant lord.

Walking through the marbled entry, her stride was languorous and her spirit light. She gave those Baroque frescoes a daring glance before letting herself out. They knew what was happening. The corset maker from White Cross Street was becoming a sensualist. This could be a problem—if the matter got out of control.

Blending into King's Square, she was confident.

It never would.

Chapter Eight

*P*aper lanterns, a festive red, dotted the ballroom. Their haze bled into Mary's velvet gown of the same shade. She stretched out her arm. Her skin tinted vermillion. It was hard to know where the light ended and she began. Everything drenched red. Jugglers roamed, tossing colorful balls. Nimble tumblers performed to *oohs* and *ahhs*. Harlots, costumed as exotic animals, roved in and out. Lionesses and leopards, parrots and peacocks mostly.

A mesmerizing circus. Mary feasted on it.

Her companion for the night's adventure was the league-approved Mr. Rory MacLeod. He'd cleaned up nicely in a gray coat, the wide cuffs unembellished. Despite the night's trappings, MacLeod was not impressed.

"Why do nobs need entertainments like this to do the featherbed jig?" he asked.

She sipped champagne, standing in a forest of ferns and potted trees.

"It gives a certain feel."

Not unlike her shop. *Clever man, Lord Ranleigh.* He understood the lure of setting and stage. With his piles of money, his lordship could host lavish entertainments at the cost of men like Mr. West.

But how—or on whom—the shipmaster spent his hard-earned coin was not her business. He might very well fancy a Bedwell nymph.

Which left a burning twinge in her belly.

Less than an hour ago she'd spied Mr. West's arrival through lush greenery. She'd pushed aside a palm frond and watched him hand over his greatcoat and hat to a servant, but no entry coins were paid. Interesting, that. Mr. West had taken a direct path to the gaming room, wearing a scowl and his tar-spattered jackboots. Had he come straight from Howland Great Wet Dock? By all appearances, he had. Most unusual, working this late.

She shouldn't follow him and find out why.

Tell that to your thrumming pulse.

MacLeod was oblivious, thank goodness. He nudged his pint at the room, his Western Isles brogue unaffected by the drink.

"A bare-knuckle brawl. Now that'd be entertainment."

"Because nothing says romance like a bloody drubbing."

He jerked a thumb to the room at large. "You think this speaks to romance? Even a rough sod like me knows the difference between lust and romance."

The glass to her lips, she hesitated. Exuberant bubbles popped under her nose. The gruff Highlander was full of surprises.

"It is the illusion of it," she said.

"So why not spice it up with a few bouts?" MacLeod was wistful, eyeing the room. "All these fat culls . . . One fight and I'd be flush in the pocket."

"Assuming you'd win."

His blue eyes slanted at her. "I'd win."

She shook her head, his confidence, stunning. "Beneficial for you, I collect, but hardly a segue to the business abovestairs. One needs a certain mood."

Legions of women had confessed as much in her shop.

MacLeod snorted. "Women might. Not men."

She sipped champagne, trying not to wonder if the scarred shipmaster preferred the illusion of romance or a straightforward tup to achieve his satisfaction. She eyed MacLeod, curious.

"Are you saying men don't crave the fantasy? Ever?"

The Highlander took his time, swallowing ale.

"A little tenderness isn't out of order. But it doesna take much. One crook of a woman's finger, and a man's lying bread and butter fashion with her."

She grimaced. "Such colorful cant."

Teasing sparked in his eyes. "Was I improper?"

"Don't let tonight's setting embolden you, sir. We are compatriots in a perilous venture. Outside of these walls, you and I return to polite discourse."

He laughed and said what was on his mind anyway. "Polite discourse. You talk like a Puritan, Miss Fletcher, but," he drawled, "you don't look like one."

"A Puritan—so I've been told."

She poured more champagne down her throat, its liquid eloquence blurring her edges. The red velvet was simple elegance and her carmine lips were of the same hue. A passable appearance for any of London's nighttime entertainments. But her hair sent another message. Strewn curls washing her back. Wanton tresses an eye-catching mahogany, begging to be fully undone.

Across the ballroom, the tumblers added fire to their show. Twirling flames ensorcelled, their fiery lights flashing like quick fireworks. A new torch, burning at both ends, was thrown high, sending amber and gold light bouncing off the ballroom's mirrors. A man tossed a woman above his head. Mary held her breath. The tossed-up woman caught the torch midair and landed artfully in her partner's arms.

Thunderous applause exploded. Mary gusted her amazement. The excess, stunning.

Sensual currents assaulted her. She buried a hand in her pannier and rubbed soft velvet. The touch, needful. Her gown was a fantasy. Nothing like her shop uniform's striped petticoats and plain neckerchief, which was hardly puritanical, but hardly seductive.

Mr. Thomas West's eyes light up no matter what you wear.

A sweet tingle flared behind her breastbone. It was true. She could be wearing her ugliest mobcap secured with a chinstrap, and Mr. West's mouth twitched a smile.

She rubbed more velvet, fraying inside.

Why did he have such a hold on her? Now, of all times, when she had a job to do?

There was one way to erase him from her soul. Grab MacLeod and take him to the Red Rose room, a substitute for her lustful itch.

She pinched her glass. What a lie that was.

MacLeod's blue eyes narrowed. "Is something wrong? You seem . . . off."

"I'm perfectly fine, thank you."

Her backside rested against the wall with an utter

lack of decorum. Mr. West was on the other side. She could saunter into the gaming room just to see his reaction to her gowned in red velvet. What a rebellion that would be. Her feet shifted as though she'd go. But no. She huffed, more hot and bothered than a woman her age ought to be. Tonight was about the mission—her duty to the clan who'd taken in her and Margaret years ago. She couldn't forget that.

"You don't seem fine," MacLeod said.

"Well, I am."

She pushed off the wall and drained her glass. MacLeod had become a quick disciple to the league's cause, which gave him a soft spot on her heart. Unfortunately, he had no effect on her *other* parts. It seemed the other women present felt differently. Scarred on his eyebrow and chin, he was a rough sort, a bare-knuckle brawler with a military past. Feminine heads kept turning his way, but MacLeod was all business. It was time she was too.

She set her glass on a small table with a firm *clunk*.

"Let's get to work, shall we?"

"Agreed." MacLeod added his tankard to the table. "I'll go belowstairs."

"Taking the kitchens first?"

He nodded. "Two footmen have a look about them—brothers of the blade. I'll get them to share a pint in the mews, swap army stories, and see what I can find."

The night's strategy had already been set: she would search the upper floors while MacLeod would take the outer perimeter of Bedwell House, including belowstairs. Theirs had been a detailed plan, unlike Cecelia's fluid approach. At least they would go home in style. Cecelia had loaned them her infamous robin's egg blue carriage trimmed with gold, a recent purchase from a friend drowning in debt.

MacLeod checked his pocket watch. "Nearly ten o'clock. Meet me at the carriage at midnight."

"Yes. Midnight."

She adjusted her mask, a silk creation trimmed with black feathers. Her eyelids were heavy. The buzz under her skin, constant. Layers of reserve were melting off her. Her chin tipped as she watched MacLeod fade into the ballroom with a loose-limbed stride. A laughing harlot swished her tail feathers against him. MacLeod spun her around, ending their circle with a playful kiss by glass doors which led to the garden. He produced a cheroot from his pocket and angled his head at the garden as if he'd take himself outside for a smoke.

The pouting bird slinked away, and MacLeod slipped off into the night.

The Highlander had thought of everything. His clothes, his cheroot, his blending in. Even his light-hearted kiss.

"Lost another man, did you?"

Mary turned, her limbs more fluid than they should be.

The taunt came from a tawny-haired harlot drawing near. She was garbed as a lioness, the same woman who'd smirked at her for being in the wrong room two nights past.

"He's not mine to lose."

The harlot's laugh was throaty and lax. "Ease up, love, and you might find what you're looking for."

Mary blinked. What was she looking for? Excitement?

Treasure?

Or something better than gold?

The lioness strode boldly on and linked arms with a bewigged gentleman. Drawn-on whiskers and a long, tufted tail were her costume's convincing objects. Mary had a few of her own. A treasonous coin nestled between her breasts, certainly. And keys to the Red Rose room. She shouldn't have brought them with her.

But she had.

She reached into her pocket and found those keys, warm against her hip.

Five years since you kissed a man.

Her heart cratered, a horrible shudder from years of keeping herself in check. Of near-perfect restraint, always composed. Couldn't she take what she wanted . . . just this once?

Across the ballroom, another torch was tossed high, the flames spinning. The fire controlled. No one was harmed, and the entertainment, pure joy.

Eyes shut, she touched the keys. Years of loneliness stretched so far behind her that she'd lost count how many there were. Before her were two free hours. She could spend them any way she pleased. Looking at the ballroom again, she was decided.

It was time to play with fire.

Chapter Nine

Ranleigh's faux circus was a headache in motion. The noise abominable, the crowd bloated, the costumes garish. A sickening effect, the same as gorging on nothing but sugared sweets. Thomas had made that mistake once as a boy and paid the price.

Why was he doing it again?

The gaming room, at least, was less affected by the flagrant excess. Fewer costumes to be found. Whatever Ranleigh spent in the rest of Maison Bedwell, he more than made up for in here. And he'd corralled his best and most distracting dealer to service Thomas's table. Miss Trevethan, lovely as always. She dealt two cards to each gambler with an elegant hand. *Vingt-et-un* was the game. At stake was a pile of guineas and Thomas's pride.

At twilight a messenger bearing a note had arrived at West and Sons Shipping. Ranleigh's missive had practically demanded his presence at Maison Bedwell and that alone irked him. He'd dashed off a terse answer. *This evening is doubtful.*

The ink had barely dried when he knew—no matter how late the hour, he'd go.

His father had raised no fool. A riskier game was in motion. A clash of wills between the son of a whaler and the son of a duke. Thomas tugged his cravat. An untangling was required. More money might be lost.

Miss Trevethan laid her second card face up. The queen of spades.

"Gentlemen, do you wish to increase your bets?" was her purr.

Thomas pinched his cards. A pair of nines. A capricious hand.

Across the table, Lord Ranleigh tossed in ten guineas. An exorbitant sum.

"I'll bite."

Count Aleksei Novikov, the morally ambiguous Russian envoy, discarded a six and a seven of hearts.

"You can take the risk, my friend, because you are both a player and the bank." To the dealer, he flirted. "My dear, you must give me better cards, or I shall leave a pauper."

Her smile was graceful. "I'll do my best, my lord count." She gathered his discards in one smooth swipe. "What about you, Mr. West?"

Heat pricked Thomas's scalp. Miss Trevethan waited, impassive and pretty, her gray eyes measuring him. Saying his name was a nice touch. He should've known trouble was brewing when Ranleigh pulled her from the faro table to deal their game of *vingt-et-un*. Miss Trevethan had an honest talent for taking men's money.

In front of him were exactly ten guineas—the last of his funds. It was no accident that Ranleigh's bet matched his coins. The cur.

"Come now, West. You've money to bet," Ranleigh said.

"Which I'm rather fond of, these guineas."

Novikov chuckled. "Money and women. They come and go, my friend."

"Especially when a man visits Maison Bedwell."

A scowling Ranleigh fiddled with a stack of coins. "We both know you've vast sums to wager."

Thomas drummed his fingers on the baize. Bone tired and longing for his bed, he was not in the best frame of mind for patient disentanglements. Especially with surly nobles. When he'd arrived an hour past, the servant who took his coat warned him, "His lordship is in a black mood."

"That makes two of us," Thomas had muttered.

Eyes at half-mast, his jaw clenched, and the lethal Miss Thelen nowhere in sight, Lord Ranleigh was a puzzle. Their business dealings were all but finished. West and Sons Shipping was not for sale. But the canny lord was up to something, which was perfect timing for Thomas to pave the way for a friendly exit.

"Forgive my indecision," he said to the table. "I've had a devil of a time wrestling a woman today. She wore me out."

Ranleigh's brows slashed. "What woman?"

Quite the surly edge in the dark lord's voice. Interesting, that.

"You've never cared about who I keep company with." Thomas made a show of studying his cards. "Or has a pretty piece finally gotten under your skin?" Going home with lighter pockets would be worth it if he learned the woman's name. He nudged the last of his money forward. "My wager, Miss Trevethan."

She reached for her facedown card, but Ranleigh's arm shot out to stop her.

"The woman—what is her name?"

Thomas eyed his opponent. If syllables were swords, Ranleigh would've cut him in two. Thomas welcomed the sharpness, and the power coming ever so subtly to his side of the table. Shifting in his seat, he decided to play with it.

"The *Mary Jane*. I've mentioned her in the past."

Ranleigh's scowl deepened. "Mary?"

"The *Mary Jane*." Thomas grinned, emphasizing *the* like a tutor helping a daft ward. "You saw her when you visited my shipyard. She has the prettiest pair of . . . masts."

Novikov laughed.

Ranleigh's arm sank onto the table. "You speak of a ship."

Thomas tucked his cards together, savoring the small victory. "Indeed. Don't you recall her? The schooner I acquired from a Spitsbergen whaler. Her cinch broke this morning. It took all day and some hours into the night, but we saved her."

"Such devotion," the count said. "I think you must be an excellent shipmaster."

"When it comes to women and ships, my lord count, a man does not take either one for granted."

Novikov picked up his brandy. "Of late, ships consume me."

Thomas heard dismal notes in the count's voice. West and Sons Shipping was near the Royal Naval Yard at Deptford—the King's Yard to those who earned their coin on the docks. There'd been a day of pomp and ceremony when the Russians had visited the King's Yard. His majesty counted them an ally. For the moment anyway.

But Thomas recognized hunger when he saw it. The Russians wanted a naval force to rival England's.

If Novikov wanted ships, why did he spend so much time in a brothel?

A passing footman stopped and poured more of the amber elixir into the count's glass.

"Do you know the mysterious woman who has Ranleigh's smalls in a knot?" Thomas asked, his gaze traveling from the Russian to Ranleigh. "Or has she knotted his heart?"

The count shook his head. "No woman can do that. No matter how alluring."

Ranleigh's mouth pinched a harsh line. "We've a game, gentlemen. Or have both of you forgotten that money is at stake?" He gave Miss Trevethan the barest nod, and she flipped over a six of diamonds.

"The house has sixteen, gentlemen. Please show your cards."

Ranleigh's black stare reached across the table, a challenge. He laid down a king and a queen. Frowning, Thomas flipped two nines onto the baize.

"Twenty for Lord Ranleigh. Eighteen for Mr. West. Lord Ranleigh wins," Miss Trevethan announced.

She collected the cards and Ranleigh scooped his winnings with both hands. Thomas ground his molars. The gold sliding away was a lesson learned: power was best served evenly. Never again would he attempt to do business with a man of dubious reputation and ridiculous wealth.

He pushed back from the table.

"Thank you for the evening's entertainment, but it's time I seek the comforts of home."

"So soon?" Ranleigh stopped sifting his coins. "Miss Trevethan, extend a note of credit to Mr. West. One hundred pounds should suffice. No—make it two hundred."

Ranleigh was glib, tossing out credit like candy. The cold creep up Thomas's spine was awareness and the threat of defeat. He'd felt the same years ago when he'd nearly drowned in the North Sea.

"I must decline your generous offer," he said.

Ranleigh began to stack his winnings. "We could reduce the amount."

"Which would be a debt all the same."

"Not if you reconsider my business proposition." The dark lord's eyes were unreadable above all that shiny gold.

Thomas curled both hands into fists, coaxing patience.

"I thought I made myself clear at our last two meetings. West and Sons Shipping is not for sale. Not now. Not ever."

Miss Trevethan scooted a polite inch back as though arrows were about to fly.

"Then why come here tonight?" Ranleigh asked, lethal and quiet.

"As a gesture of goodwill among gentlemen."

Ranleigh toyed with a stack of coins. "What about the matter of insurance?"

Thomas smiled harshly and threw caution to the wind. "Your concern is touching. Truly. But I'm considering other options."

Animosity was already swirling thicker than smoke at the once friendly table. Even the verbose

Russian politely studied the baize. Ranleigh cocked his head as if he'd inquire about those plans. Thomas wouldn't tell him. He had no doubt Ranleigh would use family name and influence to slam doors on West and Sons Shipping.

"What a fool you are, West. English whalers are a dying breed." Ranleigh's smile was a rapacious twist. "Haven't you heard? The Dutch won."

"Yet, you continue to fight so very hard to buy my ships and take my docks." Thomas stood up. "One might think you an overeager suitor."

Ranleigh's jaw ticked. The odds for a friendly, gentlemanly exit were dwindling when a footman garbed in pink velvet livery approached the table, a gleaming silver tray in hand.

"Mr. West. I've been requested to deliver this to you."

In the middle of the tray was a key with a red ribbon. The gaming room was crowded and noisy. The footman couldn't know he'd interrupted his employer's attempt to crush Thomas. The eager servant went on.

"You'll find the lady in the Red Rose room, sir. Down the hall to the right."

"I know the room." Thomas stared at the key.

Is this one of Ranleigh's tricks?

Ranleigh rose from his chair, irritated. "Are you certain the key is for Mr. West?"

The footman blanched. "Yes, my lord."

"What exactly did the lady say?" Ranleigh asked in a tone dripping with precision.

The servant's Adam's apple bobbed up and down. "Well, the lady stopped me in the hall and showed me her key. I informed her that I was new, about a month in service, but that I understood what the key meant."

The nervous footman checked Ranleigh and Thomas as one might survey an unlit road littered with steaming piles. The poor sod had no idea what he'd stepped into.

"Go on," Ranleigh said. "And make certain you leave nothing out."

"I—I asked her to describe the man she was looking for. She told me to find a tall gentleman in jackboots with a scar on his cheek. I said, 'You mean Mr. West? He's a big bastar—'" The footman froze, his skin turning claret from the neck up. "Begging your pardon, Mr. West. I meant no offense."

He shook his head. "Finish your story, lad. This is the best entertainment I've had in a long time."

Sweat sheening his forehead, the servant went on.

"The lady and I had a laugh, we did. She told me Mr. West was the man she wanted. I told her I knew where to find him since he was something of a regular." A small shrug and, "I would've been here sooner, sir, but I was pulled into the kitchen to move casks and such." The footman cleared his throat and spoke to Ranleigh. "After that, I came straightaway, my lord."

The tale given, the footman waited, the shiny tray in hand.

Novikov pecked at the key. "What an intoxicating turn."

"Feminine companionship can be arranged, if that's what you crave." Ranleigh opened his arms in a show of peace. "Consider it an offer from a friend."

Thomas snorted. "We're not friends."

Arms falling to his sides, Ranleigh tipped his head. "No. We are not. We are competitive, you and I. We like to win, which is why you need to reconsider my exceedingly excellent offer."

Thomas wouldn't, despite the exorbitant sum. Family pride was intangible and the legacy of West and Sons Shipping too dear. There was no explaining the powerful bond between father and son to a man who couldn't understand it.

"The only offer I'll entertain is the comfort of my own bed." He eyed the footman. "Do you know who this lady is?"

The servant shook his head. "She didn't give her name, sir, and she was wearing a mask."

Novikov picked up his brandy, shivering as if he'd tasted sour fruit. "The mask augurs a warning. The woman is probably as hideous as a gargoyle, and all the brandy in London cannot fix that."

Ranleigh waved off the footman. "Take it away. He's not interested."

"Wait." Thomas swiped the key. "I'll deliver the message myself." To the footman, "Thank you."

The nervous lad gave a jerky nod and sped off, but the night was more unsettled than before. Ranleigh sat down again, his mood worse.

"You are aware that I can crush you," Ranleigh said matter-of-fact.

Thomas gripped the key until its teeth bit his flesh.

"Is that a threat?" he asked softly, menacingly. "Do you really think I'd be afraid of a man who lets a woman do his dirty work for him?"

Ranleigh's face drained, a livid white. The reference to Ilsa Thelen hit its mark, and any trepidation

Thomas had for the noble and his ancient family fled.

"Whalers cut their teeth on fools like you," he said.

His nod for the table was quick. "Miss Trevethan, my lord count." A dismissive second and, "Ranleigh."

He stalked off. It'd be a cold day in hell before he *my lord*-ed Ranleigh—*if* they crossed paths. He'd not darken Maison Bedwell's door again. Not for all the gold in London. But the die was cast and a new enemy made. He had a few, and he wore the scars to prove it.

Chapter Ten

Mary batted a gold-tasseled pillow like a restless cat. There was an abundance of tasseled pillows in the Red Rose room: piled before a cheery fire, wedged along the wall, stacked strategically on shelves, which she found after her eyes had adjusted to the dimly lit room.

She craned her neck at those shelves.

"A new fashion, is it? Sexual congress in elevated places?"

There were enough curiosities in the bedchamber to keep her guessing. One candle flickered on a table filled with fascinating accoutrements. A bottle of wine with two glasses was to be expected. The other items were not. Feathers, riding crops, willow branch switches, coiled silken ropes (with tassels at both ends), and a short-handled birch broom, which looked oddly familiar.

She picked it up, aghast.

The handle smelled of freshly cut wood. Light laughter bubbled. "Lord Ranleigh, you are a rogue of the first order."

The broom had to be one of the many used to move his fountain this morning.

She traced the handle's cut end. Had there been a deeper intent when he offered to join her? Emboldened, she set the broom down and selected the willow branch. Long and slender, it fit her palm.

How many infamous bottoms has this switch spanked?

She sliced air with it, the *whoosh* an amusing distraction. The monstrosity of a bed spoke volumes. Five people could sleep comfortably side by side. Six, if they squeezed together. A medieval tapestry covered the wall behind it. Harts and roses surrounded a chivalrous lord on bended knee, holding the hand of his lady fair.

Lord Ranleigh was to be congratulated. A woman embarking on a romantic assignation would appreciate the tapestry.

But this wasn't a romantic pursuit.

It was carnal. Her thready pulse wouldn't let her forget that.

She was tracing the willow's length when the door swung open. Mr. West filled the portal, a phantom in tar-spattered jackboots.

Every nerve in her body singed.

His head cocked. "Miss Fletcher, are you . . . petting a switch?"

Heat flared behind her feathered mask, and her gaze dropped to the branch she held lovingly.

"It would appear that I am."

Mr. West kicked the door shut and advanced on her with a rangy stride. She stood her ground, tiny flames of anticipation licking her everywhere—until he was inches from her and those little fires blazed.

The balance of power shifted.

Darkness didn't help.

Piercing green eyes gleamed like bright gemstones set in black, his focus raking her from head to hem. Her mouth went dry.

The sea wolf had answered her call.

Chin up, she was proud. She'd invited this, but nothing prepared her for the delicious shock of being the object of a man's leisured stare. The vitality of it. Mr. West's mouth curled with pleasure when he examined the frippery hiding half her face, as if she was his new plaything.

He drew a finger through the mask's feathers. "Very pretty."

"I'm glad you like it."

Arousal stuck to her skin. She began to feel the weight of her circumstances when Mr. West didn't ask to untie the bow at the back of her head, and she didn't stop him when he reached behind her. His was a gentle claiming. His sleeve grazing her hair. His scent melting her. The wood, the leather. The hint of tar and iron, which clung to his clothes.

If Mr. West was a mistake, she'd gladly pay the price.

When the mask slipped, she gripped the switch as one might hang on to the top of a teetering ladder.

He tossed the mask onto the bed and thumbed her cheek with aching tenderness.

"Much better."

His scarred smile was a mystery. It belonged to a man who plundered hearts, a man for whom mermaids would forsake the sea and sirens their song. He was a tale of enchantment come to life. A sculpted bottom lip, a wide chest, perfect for nestling. His baritone, soul-deep and reassuring. Mr.

West, she decided, was a lethal blend of wicked and mannered.

Even a peevish nun would blush if he touched her.

He gathered her unpinned hair with excruciating care and brought it forward over her shoulder. She shivered, his light touch to her hair so gentle and alluring. Curls spilled down the front of her, the room's vague light finding a hint of auburn hidden in their depths. He ran his fingers lightly over them.

"Beautiful," he murmured.

"I won't tell you the hours it took to create this effect."

"You are a work of art, no matter how you array yourself."

She smiled. "Why, Mr. West, that was almost poetic."

Noise, faint and festive, reached into the room, the only sign of the world outside. He plied her with tender touches, blackness pooling in his eyes. Looking into them, she felt every inch of her sluggish limbs. But something was amiss.

Giving Mr. West the key wasn't enough. He was waiting for her to make the next move.

Her confidence slipped a notch. She was swimming in new depths without a chart.

"Would you like some wine?" she asked.

"I'm not thirsty for wine."

But I'm thirsty for you lit his eyes. It was hard to think. With each stroke of his hand, waves of gooseflesh pebbled her skin and messed with her mind. She was as enthralled with him as the cat, Mr. Fisk.

"What about this?" She held up the switch, mischief lurking in her smile.

His mouth dented handsomely.

"Definitely not."

She glanced at the table. "Do you fancy any of those things?"

He traced a curl over her collarbone to her breast. "Not tonight."

Her heart stuttered and her nipples went stiff. Control was slipping like water through her fingers.

"Does that mean another night you *would* fancy those things on the table?" Her voice was a thin wisp.

He shrugged. "Anything could happen."

Her eyes flared wider. Fear and fascination danced inside her and, strangely, the two emotions didn't feel far apart.

"Three simple words, Mr. West, and suddenly my imagination runs amok."

"I could say the same of you, Miss Fletcher. When you walk into a room, my senses spin like a top."

Her lips parted. Air was growing scarce. They were provocative, keeping a small aching distance between their bodies, yet not touching. The divide was driving her mad, the sea wolf working his magic on her. Overwhelmed, she had to avert her eyes. How would she get to what came next when she was swamped with pleasure at him playing with her hair?

"Those tools are for men and women seeking another form of excitement," he went on. "They're not a requirement."

"I'm glad to hear you say that," she said, a little breathless.

"You didn't request them?"

She tipped her face to him.

"I only requested you."

Shadows and light carved Mr. West's predacious

features, an ancient marauder come to life. His silence was loud and his hunger obvious. She swallowed the arid lump in her throat. Her hands itched. Her gaze roamed his jaw, his mouth.

"Mr. West, I—"

She dropped the willow branch and collided into him. Strong hands grabbed her waist. Mr. West absorbed their imperfect joining. Looking into his eyes, she slid reckless, shaking hands inside his coat.

"I can do better."

"This isn't a competition."

Wind and sea had grained his voice. A scarred and perfect sound, like him.

She pushed up on her toes until his mouth was half an inch from hers.

"Kiss me."

Mr. West inhaled and finally, finally, they closed the gap. He covered her mouth, a long, cataclysmic caress. The shock stunned her until her sea wolf softened his kiss, tender and unhurried. Her fingers curled against his chest, exultant.

She'd waited years for this.

He lashed his arm around her waist and held her tightly—enough for her to feel hardness growing behind his placket. She rubbed against it.

Flesh pebbled up and down her body. Desire radiated from her breastbone. Her breasts tingled. His body was firm. His lips, silk. Mr. West tasted of sin and whisky. She kissed the corner of his mouth, quaking in her soul as arousal slid through her veins. Gentle noises teased her. Velvet *shushing* seductively. The whisper of skin on skin.

Mr. West was hiking up her pannier, her petticoat and underskirts, his kisses going on and on. The softness was strange and desperate. To have waited this long for a kiss . . .

He groaned in her mouth when his hand found her naked hip, tracing that curve, teasing and light. Breath shuddered in and out of her.

She was the sea wolf's plunder.

She rubbed against him, the friction sweet. Pleasure flared . . . more infernos, burning everywhere. Her abdomen, her mons, her thighs. Her mouth joined hotly with his until his tongue brushed her lower lip.

Mr. West was tasting her.

His gem-hard eyes were inches from hers, an intimate mystery. A claiming.

Waistcoat buttons dragged her bodice. Her hair clung to heated flesh. She raised her knee, stroking his thigh with hers, daring him to do more.

Heat abraded her inner thigh; cool air teased flesh between her legs.

Wetness trickled there.

But this was . . . agony.

Mr. West was iron. His breath, jagged and sultry. She moaned and ground her mons against him. London vanished. The league, Scotland, her past, her future . . . all gone.

Her first kiss in five years—she prayed it wouldn't end.

The sea wolf's hand on her hip was insistent. Kneading. Holding. Soothing. His fingers were aching inches from her hot little cleft.

She squeezed his muscled chest and found his radically thumping heart.

He answered by reaching around and squeezing her bottom cheek.

She yelped, stumbling back. She touched her

kiss-swollen lips reverently, but five fingertips branded the skin on one half of her bottom. Her sea wolf was no less affected. He cuffed his mouth with the back of his hand, panting as if he'd sprinted all the way from London Bridge.

"Miss Fletcher." His voice was craggy and heated, and his eyes amused, predatory slits taking in her bodice.

She looked down. A pinkish nipple jutted over red velvet. The other was hidden by her hair. Both her breasts were in danger of popping free of her gown. She let them be. Mr. West's eyes feasted on them, his face a fierce mask. She dragged her hair back to improve his view.

"Is this better?"

Sensualists everywhere would approve.

His nostrils flared. "You're killing me."

The feeling was mutual, and this was only one passionate kiss.

One fact was undeniable: the staid corset maker of White Cross Street had broken free.

She was breathing hard, overwarm, and off-kilter. And suddenly detesting all her layers of clothes. What was she to do about this messy, nearly sweating fervor which had overtaken her? Seduction ought to be savored, not a calamitous mess. It was horrible, this wanting an ordered existence. Arms falling to her sides, she tried to clear her head, but organizing her thoughts was like swimming in a vat of honey.

"I meant this to go differently."

"Yours was an excellent greeting."

"I should like to try again," she said.

Mr. West's laugh was low and carnal. "I've no complaints with your last effort."

She paced the room like a restless cat. This explosive craving was a new development. Tonight was supposed to be about scratching an itch with a desirable man. Lusty, yes. But . . . manageable.

Tell that to the flesh between her legs. It throbbed. Full, slippery. *Demanding*.

She curled a hand against her abdomen. Nothing in her scant experience with men prepared her for—for *him*.

A rapacious sea wolf.

"Is something wrong?" Mr. West asked.

"No."

Everything was much too right, except for the clock on the mantel showing the dreaded hour. She squeezed her eyes shut.

Ten minutes. That was all she had until the stroke of midnight.

If only Mr. West had come earlier . . .

A quick coupling wouldn't do, and there was Mr. MacLeod. She dared not risk him pounding on the door.

When she opened her eyes, Mr. West was against the bedpost, smoldering.

She shivered.

His presence was palpable and his scent on her skin.

A man like that deserved ten hours, not ten minutes. Her decision made, she collected her cloak, which had been tossed carelessly over a chair. She took comfort in a sliver of truth: she could manage this inferno. Control it within set hours before returning to the rest of her life.

Her sea wolf might think differently. He was silently tracking her every move.

She began to wrap herself in wool, not bothering to tuck her breasts back where they belonged.

"This morning you propositioned me."

Mr. West's brow furrowed. "Is this your answer? One kiss and we're done?"

"Far from it."

The furrow between his eyes deepened. "Then what is your intent?"

A thoroughly vexed Mr. West studied her as she donned her mask. The stubborn man didn't budge from his place by the bed, which suited her purpose. He didn't look like he was in the mood to follow her and drop a devastating kiss on her brass-stained fingertip, and that suited her purpose too. Tender intimacy was dangerous. Lusty intrigues, however, could be contained when and where she dictated.

She walked to him and slid her hand inside his coat. His heart was skipping fast and he smelled like everything she shouldn't want.

Green-blue eyes narrowed, blade sharp.

She pushed up on her toes and kissed his scowling mouth softly.

"Meet me here at nine o'clock tomorrow night, and I'll make clear my intent. All night."

Chapter Eleven

Thomas pinched the candle flames one by one. He preferred to recover in the dark, thank you very much. Flesh inside his smalls ached. Badly. A white-hot-forget-about-walking-straight kind of pain. The assault, however, reached beyond his placket.

His soul was shaken and his heart stirred.

It was the corset maker's doing. Her and her passionate kisses.

He opened his right hand, his flesh still tingling from the feel of Miss Fletcher's bottom cheek. Firm and full. Perfectly curved. Soft skin which had never seen the sun pebbling against his palm—until she ended their embrace as suddenly as she'd started it.

He fisted his hand. It was safe to say her soul hadn't been pillaged. *Bloody siren.*

She was up to something. Beautiful spinsters were a rare breed. Women who could snare any man they wanted. No doubt Miss Fletcher could waggle her finger and win a titled scoundrel if she tried. But the proper shopkeeper had come to a brothel.

Why?

Tonight had been to consummate her invitation. If only the footman hadn't been detained . . .

But their first meeting, two nights past, was most assuredly her first night at Bedwell's. The incident with Culpepper proved that. He went to the window and dragged the curtain aside. His ragged reflection set him back. A bedraggled queue. His cravat, flagging. His lips, perverse lines, kiss-smeared with carmine, as it were.

He swiped two fingers over the corner of his red-smudged mouth. "What are you about, Miss Fletcher?"

Instinct told him she had an appointment to keep. The corset maker was true to her word. A man could set his watch by her timeliness.

Something stopped their progress—otherwise they would've progressed as nature intended.

After opening the window, he searched King's Square, cold air slapping his face. London's rogues were exiting carriages, cheerful men on their way to Bedwell's. Parked vehicles wrapped around the square's garden. He scanned each one.

Who was she meeting?

He didn't have to wait long. A woman wreathed in black crossed the road, her stride familiar.

An ugly twist burned his belly, and he stepped back into the shadows.

A large man in gray velvet was waiting for Miss Fletcher by a blue carriage trimmed with gold paint not more than ten or twelve paces from the Red Rose room window. Miss Fletcher scurried to meet the man in gray.

Thomas watched her, touching her feathered mask and checking her surroundings. Furtive and careful.

Their muffled conversation seemed businesslike . . . but the man was with her. Miss Fletcher's Edinburgh accent carried, the lilt pretty and her words questionable before she stepped into the unlikely carriage.

She'd said something about a secret society.

Thomas rubbed his bristling nape. *Bloody siren.* What kind of shite was she mixed up in?

Chapter Twelve

*M*ary pinned the last curl in place. The mirror reflected a well-kissed spinster. Her mobcap a linen crown (her smallest), its black bow trailing to her collarbone. She shook her head. Jet earbobs danced, and a wisp landed prettily on her temple. The effect, tasteful. Morning light slanted over gray eyes glowing diamond white. Despite a firm chin and angled cheeks, she was amorphous. A woman on the verge . . .

Of what?

She touched her lips as butterflies invaded her stomach. Come nightfall, Mr. West would do much more than kiss her.

Will I look different tomorrow morning?

Her lashes drooped. With all the salacious adventures she had in mind, yes. Yes, she would. Eyes opening slowly, she grinned at her reflection. The talented Mr. West wouldn't disappoint.

"We've custom in the shop," was Margaret's call, coming up the garret stairs.

She took a quick breath. Responsibility called.

"This early?"

Mary plucked her thin black velvet choker off the washstand. Light glinted on the gold piece gracing her neck. She was in the act of tying her choker when her sister crested the stairs.

"Miss Dalton is attending them." Margaret stopped abruptly, a steaming mug of coffee in hand. The mirror showed her suspicious gaze.

"Aren't you going to bring me my coffee?" Mary asked.

Margaret approached, studying her gravely.

"You look . . . different."

"I'm exactly the same." She took the proffered mug with both hands. "Last year's apron over last year's petticoat, but you look pretty in that shade of midnight blue. Is this the gown you hemmed last week?"

Arms folding, Margaret would not be diverted. "Your hair is showing, and you're wearing earbobs."

Which sounded like an accusation.

"Minor changes."

"For most women, yes. But if your name is Mary Fletcher, those are major changes."

She laughed and sipped heavenly coffee treated with a dollop of cream. Perhaps a little change was good for the soul.

A patina of dismay spread over Margaret's face. "And you dusted your cheeks with almond powder. I can smell it."

"And you are starting to sound like Aunt Maude." Mary sauntered to the garret's lone street-side window and Margaret followed.

"There is something different about you. Could it be your evening jaunts to a certain establishment?"

"It's league work, nothing more," she said, nursing her coffee.

Margaret stacked empty breakfast bowls and dirty spoons in the wash bucket, her ink-dark hair spilling forward. The garret was quiet save softly clinking dishes and her sister's shifting mood. An empty dray rumbled by on the street below. The driver yawned and scrubbed a beefy hand over his face.

"Did Miss Dalton stay late?" Mary asked.

"She did, 'til ten o'clock. Then I packed her into a hack and sent her home."

Mary rested her shoulder against the window frame, her thoughts drifting to the Red Rose room. Thirteen hours until she saw Mr. West. What would she wear? Not her red velvet, certainly. The salacious gown sprawled on her bench. Boned panniers and wrinkled underskirts in the heap, the casual discards of a wanton woman who'd undressed in the dark. The secret society token nestled somewhere in the mess. She'd hunt for it later.

Margaret wiped her hands on her apron, her uneasy gaze landing on the red velvet.

"You've never been hurly-burly with your gowns."

"Don't worry. I'll clean it up."

"It's not only that," Margaret said. "You're cavalier about coming home so late."

"A few more nights and my work will be done."

Margaret nibbled her lip. "What about the Countess of Denton?"

Mary set a cautioning finger to her lips. "Have a care," she whispered. "We cannot afford to have the wrong person overhear us. Besides, this is the wrong time to discuss league business."

"It's always the wrong time when *I'm* the one asking," Margaret whispered brusquely. "And don't you dare tell me not to worry."

Which was exactly what Mary was about to do. Contrite, she clamped her mouth shut.

"We're *all* afraid of what the countess will do next," Margaret went on in a low voice. "Especially after she shot Mr. MacLeod. Aunt Maude marks the days in her housekeeping journal when she thinks the countess will return."

Mary felt a frown forming. "I didn't know that."

"She's tracking the time it takes a well-equipped carriage to travel from Arisaig to London. And Jenny," Margaret huffed. "She hasn't been able to sleep through the night."

Fierceness swelled in Mary's chest. The need to protect.

But . . . how?

Brisk morning air seeped from the humble window. Across the street the chandler shop was dark, but next door the cobbler's wife was sweeping the walk outside her family shop. An industrious woman, Mrs. Brown. She was one thread in the fabric of White Cross Street. A kindly neighbor, she'd repaired Margaret's shoe last month. Last week Mrs. Brown had purchased linen stays for their twelve-year-old daughter, a sweet girl with a talent for embroidery.

A cozy place, White Cross Street. Home.

What was she going to do to keep it that way?

"Lady Denton is part of the puzzle to which I have no answer," she said, subdued. "I'm sure I'll figure it out."

Margaret's brow arched with exquisite wryness. "It must be very hard to admit when you don't have an answer to a problem. Especially one that only *you* can figure out."

Mary pulled her mug to her chest as if crockery

could fend off verbal shots. Why did her sister's words carry such a sting? Margaret, however, fired one opinion after another.

"I, for one, think hunting for whatever *might* be left of the gold is a fool's errand. An utter waste of time, when we should develop a plan for what's next."

"*What's next?*" Mary echoed.

"Yes. Do we stay in London? Or return to Scotland, the same as Will and Anne?" Margaret dropped her voice like a conspirator. "This is our home, certainly, but Lady Denton is out for blood. A powerful woman like that." She shuddered. "Jenny told me Cecelia wants to get rid of the countess—"

Mary gasped. "Stop," she whisper-hissed. "I forbid you to speak of such things. We are not violent women."

Margaret backed away, her mouth pinching white. Blue hems swaying, she swung around and sought the door.

"Wait . . . please." Mary set her mug on the table.

Margaret tarried in the doorway, her back a ramrod. They heard the shop's doorbell jingle, and footsteps cluttering below. Needful commerce tugged on Mary; the sooner she tended it, the sooner evening would come and she could slip away for a night with Mr. West.

But her sister was on a gentle boil, and the tension, wearying.

"Please," Mary implored. "I thought we were making progress."

Margaret turned slightly toward her. "I thought we were, too, but I'm not sure I can make you see what's right in front of you."

Oh, she was exasperated. "See what, exactly?"

"That you always know what's best." Margaret smirked. "Miss Mary Fletcher of White Cross Street responsible for everything. Me included."

Mary stood stiffly, smarting from that verbal blow.

"You'll never acknowledge me as a capable person," Margaret said. "Much less ask me for help."

"I ask for help."

Eyes to ceiling, Margaret might've sent a silent prayer for patience.

"No, you don't. You direct. You order. You opine—strongly I might add. But dear sister, being vulnerable is not a skill you own." Margaret's mouth slid in a semblance of a tolerant smile. "And once your mind is set, heaven help the poor soul who disagrees with you. Aunt Maude and Aunt Flora jest about how persuasive Anne had to be with you when she led our league, and I won't repeat what Jenny says. Her language is too salty by far." Margaret paused, huffing softly. "As for Cecelia, she simply doesn't care."

Mary blinked like a soldier who'd survived a volley of cannon fire. The smoke had barely parted when Miss Dalton's call came from below.

"Miss Fletcher, are you coming down?"

Margaret answered, "In a moment," though it was unclear which Miss Fletcher their seamstress sought. Margaret faced her, sadness etching her eyes. "We've custom to attend."

She trotted down the stairs, taking Mary's peace of mind with her.

MARY WAS AT the counter, measuring ribbon—her third attempt—when the shop's doorbell jingled. A knobby-kneed lad rushed forward and stuck a crumpled missive on the ribbon.

"A message for you, Miss Fletcher."

A soft sigh and her shoulders dropped. A fourth count would be necessary.

"Thank you." She took the note, distracted.

With a steady stream of shoppers, there'd been no chance to talk to Margaret. They'd navigated the last hour orbiting each other with cautious glances.

Mary reached into her apron pocket for a ha'penny to pay the boy.

"Keep the coin, miss. I'm not an errand boy. Mr. West pays me."

She looked up fast.

"Do you mean Mr. West of West and Sons Shipping?"

"Yes, miss. I'm Jimmy Brown. We met last August at the docks." He jammed his hat on, flattening a dark blond forelock over his eyes.

The sight of him was sheer joy. Unless Mr. West was canceling this evening?

Disappointment stabbed her.

"Don't leave. I haven't read the note. What if Mr. West expects an answer?"

Young Mr. Brown shook his head, emphatic. "He said there wouldn't be one, but that I was to watch you read his note and warn you to be ready at ten o'clock."

"Tonight?"

"No, miss. This morning."

She checked the clock. "But that's less than an hour from now."

Perplexed, she broke the wax seal. The missive's lines were orderly, the handwriting moderately slanted, and the message, a delight.

Dear Miss Fletcher,

Last night with you was illuminating. One kiss and the stars shimmered and the moon shined brighter.

To which she smiled so hard, her cheeks hurt. *Such impertinence.*

Since I don't have a poetic bone in my body, I'll get to the point. I cannot stop thinking of you. A terrible thing, isn't it? A man losing the upper hand with a woman. Something tells me you are wise to the games of men and directness suits you. In that vein, I request the honor of your gentle companionship today. I want to see you in the light of day as much as I want to do unspeakable things to you at night (things I dare not put on paper).

Do not refuse us this small pleasure. We work hard, you and I. Haven't we earned this one day?

Prepare yourself, and dress warmly, Miss Fletcher. A hack will arrive at your shop on White Cross Street at ten o'clock this morning.

*With tender regards,
Thomas*

She stared at the note, twirling a lock of hair like a moonstruck lass. Her green-eyed sea wolf was sweetly plundering her with the written word. He was willing to show his soft underbelly. Was she willing to show hers?

A daytime rendezvous meant conversation. Kisses were optional.

The greedy thrill coursing her veins was her body's answer. *Have a care* was the warning in her head. She carefully refolded the note because later she would read it again and again simply for the pleasure of it.

"Thank you, Mr. Brown."

The lad backed up, touching the brim of his hat. "Remember, miss. Ten o'clock."

"I won't forget."

She stuffed the missive into her apron pocket and set about coiling the ribbon. Her vision hazed over white silk slipping through her fingers. Meeting Mr. West was doubtful—but *if* she did meet him, her green wool gown would do. Worn with green silk stockings. A decadent choice. Should Mr. West find a private corner and put his hand under her—

"Lost something again, did you?"

Mary's cheer shriveled. A pretty woman in a flowered day gown and Bergère hat sauntered up to the counter, a cunning *Remember me?* smile on her face.

Maison Bedwell's tawny-haired harlot.

Lord Ranleigh had said he'd send someone to attend the details of his order. She expected to finally meet Mrs. Bedwell or the young charwoman who'd answered the door.

"Why, Miss Fletcher, yours is not a friendly shopkeeper's greeting," was the harlot's purr.

Mary set both hands on the counter, summoning polished manners.

"Mine was as welcoming as your greeting for me in another place of business . . ." She looked at her, askance. "Miss . . ."

"Mitchell. Miss Rebecca Mitchell, and I suppose I

deserved that." The proud harlot straightened lace at her elbow, the corners of her mouth curving with confidence. "It's just that women like you rarely darken our door."

Mary pursed her mouth, her eyes flashing a warning.

"I imagine you're here about the stays." She bent over, searching for a battered old ledger, her design book, and hoping her equilibrium would come with it. The morning had already thrown too many surprises at her. "I was thinking of using twice the usual baleen for a more structured silhouette," she said, riffling through the lower shelf where, alas, the ledger rested. Upon finding it, she straightened, head down, and began flipping the pages. "I have two designs in mind. Starched linen interlining works for—"

A metallic *clunk*, ever so chilling, sounded.

Mary clutched the open book to her chest, fear's unkind fingers running up and down her spine. On the counter was a gray coin—Charles Stuart with his nose a fraction too large.

Her secret society token.

"As I was saying, Miss Fletcher, women like you rarely darken our door."

Chapter Thirteen

$\mathcal{M}$ary reached for the token but Miss Mitchell's white-gloved hand closed around it.

"Not so fast, Miss Fletcher."

At least the woman had the wherewithal to lower her voice. Mary could feel blood draining from her cheeks. Last night with Mr. West, the coin must've fallen out when her breasts had almost done the same.

"You've been spying on me?"

"Spying? You left the door wide open." Miss Mitchell tsk-tsked. "But the willow switch? Now, that surprised me."

Mary smiled, tight-lipped and embarrassed. Mr. West left the Red Rose room wide open, had he? She'd have a word with him about locking up. Privacy was paramount.

"What's this?" Miss Mitchell asked. "You've nothing to say?"

Mary pinched the design book to stop her trembling hands. When Cumberland's men descended after Culloden, she'd calmly rounded up the children and hid them. The day her alcove (and her hem) caught fire, she'd steadily put it out. This ambush would be no different —every problem, if given careful thought, could be contained.

She looked past Miss Mitchell. "Margaret, I must go to the workroom."

Margaret glanced up from dismantling the window display. "Yes, of course."

After they passed through to the workroom, Mary checked for British soldiers outside her shop window. *The lobsterbacks*. She didn't see any soldiers loitering on White Cross Street. Nor was it logical to believe Miss Mitchell would've brought them. But logic couldn't stop her mind from ricocheting from one frantic thought to another.

Mary snapped the curtain shut, her heart climbing into her throat. This was what happened to a woman who worked a shade outside the law. She wasn't a violent woman, but she had done illegal things. Treasonous things. She had coin molds in her alcove, the storage room where she'd melted French coins into English guineas and half guineas. Passing too many French coins would've drawn attention to the league.

But a secret society token in her shop? That drew attention to her.

Mary folded trembling hands in her apron. Why had the harlot been watching her?

She turned and found Miss Mitchell skimming a bolt of painted silk with her fingertips. Rivers of pink and blue-gray silks had been spread out earlier for Mary to inspect.

"This is quite lovely," Miss Mitchell said. "I imagine you and your sister must have the prettiest corsets."

"Let us not pretend this is a friendly visit."

Miss Mitchell feigned mock horror. "Well, aren't you—what did Lord Ranleigh call you?"

"Glacial."

"Indeed, you are." Miss Mitchell picked up a tray of bodkin needles, examining the neat row set in linen. "I am here at Lord Ranleigh's behest."

"To discuss the stays he purchased, I collect."

Miss Mitchell hummed agreement and put down the tray.

"But the important business is mine."

Mary jammed both hands into her pockets, assembling quick facts. Miss Mitchell was a smart woman, but there wasn't enough silk in London to hide her coarse edges. She prowled the shop, ambition glittering in her eyes.

"Don't wait for me to put out the tea and biscuits," Mary said.

Miss Mitchell flashed a knowing smile while dragging a gloved finger across the spindles. "Do you know what happens to harlots when they're no longer useful?"

"No."

Miss Mitchell wrinkled her nose. "It's not pretty. Most women in my chosen commerce can't think beyond today, much less plan for tomorrow." She lingered on a display of spooled ribbons. "I, on the other hand, am ready to leave Bedwell's, and you, I've decided, will be my way out."

"How's that?"

"You will teach me the business of corsets and stays, Thursday next. Then I'll hie off to some place lovely like Bath and set up my own shop."

Mary laughed in disbelief. "You can't learn how to make corsets and stays in one day."

"You misunderstood me. I want basic instructions, not an apprenticeship. I'll find a desperate seamstress and get her to do the hard work." Miss Mitchell returned to the painted silk on the table. "Of course, you'll gift me with thread, cloth, supplies, and such . . . like this bit of prettiness."

She held up the glossy blue-gray cloth, light sheening on its painted-on birds and flowers.

"You want me to simply give you all my goods?" Mary asked.

"Not all your goods. One chest full will do."

"And I'm to do this," Mary scoffed, "because of a token you found on the floor?"

Miss Mitchell dropped the silk and dug into her petticoat pocket. "No, you'll do it because of the valuable information I am going to give you."

The harlot set the Charles Stuart token on the worktable, her jaw set and her eyes shards of determination.

"I *can* help you," Miss Mitchell said in an exacting tone. "But only if you help me."

Mary exhaled as though she'd been holding her breath for years. Seven years, in fact, since the Uprising ended—perhaps longer. She needed the coin. Miss Mitchell had to know this. The harlot, however, was not so forthcoming with what else she knew. This interview required a deft hand. Mary began to pace the room slowly. When it came to the league, she'd made her share of independent decisions, but this arrangement pushed a dodgy boundary. A harlot bargaining for a new life was just short of desperate.

Miss Mitchell planted half her bottom on the worktable, dangling a foot and a tempting question.

"Would it help if I told you what I know about the Jacobite treasure?"

Mary stopped, a dangerous thrill jumping in her veins.

"The treasure?"

"The one the French left on a beach in Scotland. Grub Street writes about it now and then." Miss Mitchell sniffed. "I can read, you know."

Mary eyed her suspiciously. Finding the last of the gold was an act of devotion for the clan that took her and Margaret in years ago. If she could deliver it . . .

"And you've somehow connected that treasure with me? On the basis of a common token?"

Miss Mitchell examined a seam on her glove, bored. "Miss Fletcher, are you really going to play coy with me? We both know that coin gets you into certain clandestine meetings."

Mary pinched a bow on her stomacher. She worked the edge of the fabric, twisting it. Playing coy had crossed her mind, but she wasn't very good at it. Not when well-aimed directness sliced through needless shilly-shallying.

"You, I collect, have knowledge of these particular meetings."

"I am the only harlot who's worked every one of their gatherings." Her moue was worthy of a Frenchwoman. "I hear things. About Charles Stuart, and the gold, who moved it from place to place, and who got paid for their efforts." She glanced at Mary, cool and casual. "Lord Ranleigh keeps two ledgers. One for tracking the society's tasks, and the other, an account book for the gold. That one'll tell you where your Jacobite treasure is hidden."

Mary blinked at the floor, appreciating Miss

Mitchell's silence. The harlot understood information like this was a shock that needed sorting—in particular, knowledge of Lord Ranleigh. The dark lord, a Jacobite sympathizer? It defied logic. In the stillness, she categorized explosive facts to the background of women laughing and talking in her shop beyond her doorway curtain.

One fact poked at her logical mind.

She narrowed her vision on Miss Mitchell. "If you know where the ledger is, why haven't you taken it? Taking the gold would set you up nicely."

"Because those are people I choose not to cross." Miss Mitchell was deadly serious.

"But you'll throw me to the lions?"

"They can't bite if they don't catch you."

Which told Mary this wasn't the first time the harlot had flirted with danger.

"What if something goes wrong? Someone could make a connection to you."

"I'll be long gone by the time they figure that out." Miss Mitchell stood up, plumping her panniers. "Besides . . . they'd have you."

Mary shivered. At least Miss Mitchell was honest, but the harlot wasn't the only woman to be wary of. Mary took a deep breath, a nasty picture forming. The Countess of Denton once had Cecelia tossed into Gate House prison on flimsy charges. Lord Ranleigh might be inclined to do the same to her.

If she was caught . . .

She paced the room, exhilarated and scared all at once. Four years the league had hunted for the gold. Four years!

Why not seize this chance?

Miss Mitchell was checking a faux heart-shaped

mole on her cheek in a small mirror on the wall. "I wouldn't dally if I were you. The Betty Burke painting was changed this morning." She glanced sideways at Mary. "That's how they communicate. When the painting of her on a bed is hung in the gaming room, the secret society meets a week later."

Mary fisted a hand in victory. *That painting.* "I knew it."

Miss Mitchell's smile spread, feline and satisfied.

"Does this mean you and I have an understanding?"

"Yes, yes." Mary batted the air. "A trunk's worth of supplies and a rudimentary education in corset making."

"Good. Meet me at midnight at the alcove beside the Red Rose room."

"Tonight?"

"Yes, tonight. You want the treasure, don't you?"

Hands clasped tightly at her waist, Mary nodded. "I do."

"Then it must be tonight. I'll show you where Lord Ranleigh hides his ledgers and such." Miss Mitchell dragged the doorway curtain aside. "After that, you're on your own."

Chapter Fourteen

$\mathcal{M}$ary tidied her workroom, all the possibilities simmering. It was smart of the secret society to separate the treasure. Smoothing the painted silk, she tried to think like them. If she belonged to this nameless society, where would she hide the gold? A worthy question, yet another nettled her.

Why hold on to the gold this long?

It'd been seven years since France left the treasure on Scottish shores. She fixated on the silk's floral design, answers eluding her. This particular point was something to—

"There's a hack for you."

Mary nearly jumped out of her skin. Margaret stood in the doorway, perplexed.

"Forgive me. I didn't mean to frighten you, but there's a hack parked in front of our shop window," Margaret said, the yellow curtain falling behind her. "I tried to send him away, but the driver informed me that he cannot leave without you."

She touched her apron pocket. Mr. West's note.

"I'll send him away."

Margaret cocked her head. "You're not at all surprised by this."

"No."

She tried to duck back into her thoughts but determined heel strikes approached. Margaret would not let this rest.

"What aren't you telling me?"

"Whatever do you mean?" Mary flipped the silk, one fold, then two.

"Mary . . ."

She flipped the silk into a third fold and set it on the table. It wouldn't hurt to share the astonishing invitation. "Mr. West has asked that I join him today."

"Mr. West . . . Isn't he the tall whaler?"

"He is." Mary lifted pink silk off the table and snapped it straight. "He wants me to meet him for, what I presume, is fun and frivolity."

Margaret gasped in mock horror. "We can't have that, now, can we?"

A tiny laugh burst from Mary.

"Mr. West hasn't been out to sea for some time. The demands of having to manage the shipyard at Howland Great Wet Dock, I imagine."

"Know that, do you?"

Mary could feel a tell-tale flush heating her cheeks. "Mr. West and I have . . . talked."

"I'd wager you want to do more than talk. You want to kiss him."

"Margaret!" She snapped the silk straight, mortified.

"Oh, don't *Margaret* me. Why wouldn't you want to kiss him? He's a fine figure of a man."

"That's hardly acceptable conversation for a young woman."

And her blush singed her. Margaret's jaw dropped.

"No! You've already kissed him, haven't you?" She advanced on Mary, her countenance gleeful. She was teasing and scandalized, sauntering forward. "I'd wager all my pin money that you want more than kisses from the handsome Mr. West, don't you?"

Mary checked the curtain dividing the workroom from the shop. Saucy conversations under naughty frescoes were best served in a brothel, not in her place of business, and certainly not from her gloating sister.

"You don't have to answer that. I already know the answer," Margaret said. "Though I am a little surprised."

"At what?" Mary held the silk close to her chest. She couldn't deny the powerful urge to chew on her favorite topic—Mr. West.

"With your heart's choice." Margaret's moue was practiced and artful. "I never imagined a rugged gentleman of the sea would make your blood run hot."

A sweet rush got the best of her. She'd not debate the finer points of her heart versus a lustful dalliance with Margaret. Not when decorum was of the utmost importance. Still, curiosity nipped her.

"And what kind of gentleman did you imagine would make my blood run hot?"

"Smart, definitely. Well dressed, but not these London peacocks you read about in the newspapers."

Which made her laugh. "I should hope not."

"Cecelia and I thought you needed an older man. Someone you could manage easily. Perhaps a merchant since commerce runs in your veins." Margaret shook her head, intrigued. "Not once did I think you'd be blushing and breathless over a braw man."

She dipped her lashes. Embers spangled across

her bottom cheek, a reminder just how strong and capable her sea wolf was.

"When Mr. West visited our shop," Margaret said, "he looked like he wanted to have his way with you."

"Which is why I shouldn't spend the day with him." Mary gave the silk a vigorous shake and gave Margaret an admonishing stare, as one does to a younger sister spouting salacious words.

Margaret grinned and reached for the silk. "Let me take that before you snap the pink dye right out of it."

Fabric slipped out of Mary's hands, all of her weightless and frothy. She was being managed and they both knew it.

Margaret rolled the silk carefully. "You're not setting a bad example if you leave the shop for one day. Everyone deserves a little fun now and then— even the sainted Mary Fletcher."

She set a hand on her cheek. Sainted? Hardly. Hot images of her with the tall shipmaster tempted her. Naked bodies, sheened with sweat, hands roaming. These visions didn't plague her; she sought them, often. An undeniable fever was building, akin to a cauldron brimming with steamy, bubbling water.

If she wasn't careful, it would spill over.

"Your notions about men worry me," she said, trying to keep her wits about her. "I want you to—to have a better life. To marry well."

"Yet, you haven't—married, that is." Skin around Margaret's eyes pinched. "Because of me."

Mary stilled, but inside her heart thumped a painful rapid beat. She watched her sister set the pink silk aside with cautious hands. When Margaret looked up, her mouth wobbled.

"You have spent your whole life looking after me. We both know I wouldn't be alive if it weren't for you."

A day seven years past glossed between them when smoke and screams signaled Cumberland's men were coming. Mary had frantically gathered Margaret and nearly a dozen small children into a fisherman's boat. Bloodthirsty soldiers had chased them, bayonets flashing, into the water.

Mary licked her lips, tasting fear and sea spray all over again.

Three days they'd hid on a tiny island in the bay, eating dandelions and seaweed. They'd hauled the boat ashore and tipped it over. At night the ragged group huddled together under the boat's shelter and slept. Once the smoke cleared from the horizon, they'd rowed back to the charred remains of Arisaig.

"That day when Cumberland's men attacked was not the only day you saved me. From the time I was a babe, you have been the one to care for me. I know this." Margaret's voice was a tender wisp.

"I'd gladly do it all again. I've no regrets," she said softly.

The shop door jingled background music. More custom in their bustling shop. Before her, half-sewn linen corsets waited on the worktable like butterflies. Mary touched one of them.

"Miss Dalton must be overwhelmed and there's so much work to do. I'll tell the driver to send my regrets."

"You'll do nothing of the sort." Margaret strode to the wall where a serviceable gray cloak hung on a hook. "Pinch some color into your cheeks, Mary Fletcher, because you are going to have fun."

"I can't. These corsets won't assemble themselves. And—and there's the scissors to consider."

Margaret snorted. "The scissors?"

"They need sharpening."

"I understand," Margaret said sagely. "You are the only one who speaks the language of tinkers and scissors."

"That's not what I meant."

"I can take care of the scissors," Margaret chided. "Prepare yourself, sister dear, because you are about to indulge in a day of entertainments with Mr. West."

"What about you?"

"What about me?" Margaret set the cloak on Mary's shoulders and came around to face her.

"Your week with Aunt Maude and Aunt Flora starts today, and you haven't even packed."

"My week in Southwark will begin at twilight after I close the shop, which we both know I can manage just as well as you." Margaret was almost motherly, unpinning Mary's apron.

It was sweet, her little sister taking care of her.

"But how will you get to Southwark?"

"I have two legs." The last pin removed, Margaret folded Mary's apron in two. "Who knows? I might even hire a hack."

Mary's feet rooted to the floor. Dithering was hardly her nature, but meeting a man midday was decadent. Something a sensualist would do.

Margaret set the pins on the worktable. "You know, I think this day will set you right, like a purgative."

"We're not resetting my bowels."

Margaret giggled. "Aim higher and you have the right organ."

Mary touched her bodice, her heart beating comfortingly underneath. Margaret was busy, plucking the workday's loose threads off her stomacher and fluffing her faded red panniers under the cloak as if she were a life-sized doll. The cosseting was kind. She surrendered to it.

"You look just like her," Margaret said, a little melancholy. "At least what I remember."

Between them, there was only one *her* spoken of in wistful tones.

Their beautiful, adventurous mother.

Margaret's eyes burned an emphatic blue. "But you are nothing like her."

Mary breathed in, raw and bruised. Morning was still upon them, yet days, if not years, seemed to have flown by. Life had been moving forward, and in this moment she'd looked up and noticed how far behind she was.

A very grown up Margaret ambled to a cabinet and withdrew gray gloves from its drawer.

"You are going to have a wonderful day with Mr. West and not give a single thought to the league, the shop . . . to anything."

Even the gold, she decided, nibbling her lower lip. The hunt wouldn't begin until midnight, and this might be her only chance for a daytime frolic with Mr. West.

"Me, a woman of leisure," Mary said. "I'm not sure I'll know what to do with myself."

"I'm sure Mr. West has a few ideas." Margaret winked at her and handed her the gloves.

"I think you've spent too much time with Cecelia."

Margaret laughed. "You say too much. I say not enough."

Mary took her time donning her gloves. *Why was a*

clandestine night with Mr. West perfectly acceptable? But cavorting with him in daylight, nerve-racking?

A nighttime assignation was secretive. Deceptive. Did that make a daytime interlude frighteningly honest?

Margaret linked arms with Mary and began steering her toward the curtain. "Let's get you into the hack, shall we?"

There'd be no fighting this. Mary let her sister lead her out of the workroom. They passed through their crammed shop. Even White Cross Street was well trafficked. The hack was mere steps outside their door. A morning breeze riffled her hair before she climbed into it. They deserved this, she and Mr. West. Some fun, some lightness in their workaday lives. Looking at Margaret's cheery face, she realized her dear little sister did too.

"Enjoy your week in Southwark," Mary said.

"And you enjoy your day with Mr. West. The shop will be fine." Margaret reached in and hugged her goodbye, whispering, "You've nothing to worry about."

The hack door was shut and the driver nudged the horse into the bustle of White Cross Street. Margaret's hand lifted in gentle farewell. Mary watched her sister grow smaller and smaller until she was no more.

Chapter Fifteen

Thomas paced All Hallows Wharf. The enamel face of his pocket watch read eleven o'clock, a mere two minutes later than when he'd last checked. *Bloody little clock.* He jammed it into his pocket.

Where is she?

The *she* in question was the gray-eyed corset maker. The woman who'd kissed him senseless in a brothel, only to leave him aching and angry. A ruinous combination. Even his hand in his smalls last night couldn't satisfy him. He'd leaned against the wall, thinking of their cataclysmic kiss. His release had been lackluster. A dull imitation. Only Miss Fletcher would do.

He would have her.

His mouth twisted wryly. Or she would have him.

The dark-haired siren had been very decided about what she'd wanted last night—except she left with another man.

Thomas scowled. In public, Miss Fletcher was all that was polite; and in private, she promised to be all that was wanton. Trouble was getting through all her layers. *Bloody complex woman.* He'd worn a path on the wharf waiting for her when he should be in Southwark, preparing goods for tomorrow's sale.

Miss Fletcher and her saucy kiss.

"Mr. West, sir. Do you know how much longer?" The question came from Mr. Winston, climbing the wharf stairs. "It's the oarsmen, sir, sitting at the ready all this time."

Thomas scanned the pleasure barge, an impressive design of the shallop class. A scarlet pennant trimmed in saffron whipped smartly above the ship's tent. Oarsmen resplendent in scarlet livery waited, their backs as broad as a barn. Six men, spines straight, gripping twelve-foot oars, the paddles pointing skyward. Royal pleasure barges did the same when they waited for Princess Caroline.

He, however, was not royalty.

"Tell the men they can rest easy."

"Thank you, sir." Mr. Winston set two fingers to his mouth and sent a piercing whistle through the air.

Oarsmen groaned their relief. Tall paddles collapsed in an orderly fashion, and men shifted on their seats, withdrawing pewter flasks from their coats.

"Are you thirsty?" Mr. Winston asked. "I keep a cask of small beer under my bench."

Hands clamped at the small of his back, Thomas maintained his vigil of the river. "Thank you, but no. I'll wait here."

His pride was taking a drubbing. *Women . . .*

At least one in particular.

Miss Fletcher might cloak herself as an ordinary shopkeeper. She was anything but. And this fed an inborn need—his hunter's instinct.

Whalers were, by nature, patient in their pursuit.

"Waiting is the hardest part," Mr. Winston said, standing beside Thomas. "The tension, you know."

Wind frolicked with a tuft of hair on the older man's pate. The master bargeman was a friendly sort. He'd come to West and Sons Shipping last spring for repairs to his vessel after a storm took chunks of it. Since the barge master had been light in the purse, Thomas did a favor of expedient repairs for very little coin. Today was his benevolence returned.

The barge master's advice, however, was free.

"Back in my courting days, I waited hours at a country rout for a woman." Mr. Winston sniffed. "Made a fool of myself, I did."

Thomas was tempted to say he wasn't actually courting Miss Fletcher. Instead, he said a polite, "But eventually, she did come."

"She did."

"And you promptly made her Mrs. Winston."

"I did nothing of the sort. I was already dancing with the future Mrs. Winston."

Thomas eyed him, surprised. "An unexpected tale."

Mr. Winston donned his thrum cap. "I suppose some women are worth the wait. Only you can know that, sir."

Thomas looked to the river. Miss Fletcher was a mere half an hour late from his expected arrival time. What was half an hour compared to a lifetime?

Seagulls squabbled on pilings. A bargeman regaled his shipmates with a jest, their laughter rolling easy as the tide. The master bargeman ambled back to his vessel in pursuit of small beer, while Thomas humorously considered his options.

How would he unearth Miss Fletcher's various layers?

Reciting poetry was a possibility. Writing his own verse wasn't out of the question. The only poetry he remembered (after a torturous educational indoctrination) was a sonnet he'd been forced to memorize as a lad. Something by Shakespeare . . . which he could shamelessly alter.

The *clip-clop-clip* of horse hooves saved him from the onerous chore.

"Mr. West! Mr. West, I'm here."

He closed his eyes, a hallelujah rising at Miss Fletcher's fair accent reaching across the wharf. He turned in time to see her jump from the hack.

"Forgive my lateness."

She raced toward him, hems swinging fast. The wonder at seeing her melted his irritation. At her lateness this morning. At her leaving last night. At . . . everything.

An arm's length from him, she stopped and set a hand to her brow, shading her eyes. The October skies were an unusual crisp, clear, brilliant blue.

"I must confess. I almost didn't come."

"I'm glad you did," he said softly.

He positioned himself to block the sun for her, but really it was for the greedy pleasure of standing close to stare at her winged brows, her fine-grained skin, and stunning, otherworldly eyes.

"While waiting for you, I composed some words in your honor," he said.

Her laugh was incandescent.

"You did not."

"I did. Something about the moon and the stars— all the appropriate drivel to set your pulse racing."

Miss Fletcher tilted her head just so. A delectable angle, exposing her neck, her collarbone, telling him she was his for the taking.

"You already make my heart run at breakneck speed, Mr. West. Poetry is not required."

His mouth slanted sideways. What a delight she was. A sweet flirt by day, a saucy piece by night.

"I'd planned to borrow from Shakespeare and hope you wouldn't notice," he said, astounding himself with the frank admission.

"A shameless tactic."

"A man does what he must. Love and war are the same, are they not?"

Which caused her eyes to widen. *Bloody L word.* He should strike it from his vocabulary. At least her mild panic melted to studied amusement. Hers was a gentle consideration as though he'd given her a nugget of gold.

"You quoted Don Quixote. He suits you more than Shakespeare, I think." Her hand shading her eyes drifted to his greatcoat. "And since we're being honest, I, too, have something to share."

He braced himself.

"My sister compared you to a purgative."

Laughter rumbled in his chest. "Rest assured, I taste better than a medicinal."

Sensuality glimmered in her smile. "I already know what you taste like, Mr. West."

A thrill crested inside him. The sides of her mouth curled, a barely there turn of her lips yet wonderfully salacious. The corset maker was toying with him—with words, no less—sending exciting messages to all the right places under his clothes.

She was deceptively innocent, her face tipped to his.

"Margaret, my sister, advised me to kiss you. So there's that," she said conversationally.

He nodded as if they negotiated the price of this season's goods. "That can be arranged."

"Is it one of today's entertainments? Kissing?"

He sucked in a quick breath. "One of many."

"Then I am yours to command."

He liked the sound of that as much as he liked her Edinburgh accent pouring over him. The woman could make him weak-kneed whispering a market-day list in his ear.

He twined her arm with his. "Then let's get to it, shall we?"

Which didn't sound romantic, but somehow, he knew flowery, effusive conduct wouldn't win the fair corset maker. Problem was, he couldn't say with confidence what would.

He led her on a slow walk to the wharf stairs immensely satisfied. Joy came from their arms joined and their hips bumping. From the cadence of their matching strides as if they had all the time in the world. A breeze carried her scent—linen and warmth. A comforting smell, very domestic and kind. On their approach, Mr. Winston boomed a command. Oarsmen snapped to attention, their scarlet livery impressive. Tendrils batting her cheek, Miss Fletcher took in the vessel and its private tent puffing an invitation.

Enigmatic gray eyes drew a line from the tent to him.

"Are you seducing me, Mr. West?"

"Yes."

His voice had gone husky and his stare intense. Lust would have its due, but Miss Fletcher was more than hot flirtation and sweet seduction. She was the light at the end of a long tunnel. His light. It was only a matter of time before the corset maker understood this.

She tucked herself close to him. "I can't wait to see what happens."

Chapter Sixteen

*T*he oars' rhythm was an opiate. The river ahead, picturesque. Almost empty. The view was miles of water, rippling with deceptive calm. London was giving way to green fields, to trees, and the sudden impetuously placed manse facing the river. The vessel heaved against the tide, the effort barely noticed in their little heaven.

Gauzy light inside the tent set the mood. Scarlet and saffron billowed as joyful as a woman's underskirts from a frolic on a swing. Miss Fletcher was half-reclined on a couch, a fur-trimmed blanket tossed over her legs.

She was staring ahead, tucking a wayward wisp behind her ear. "Is this when you're supposed to feed me grapes or some such nonsense?"

He grimaced. He should've thought of that. Food and wine inevitably played a role in seduction, even if not much was consumed.

"No grapes. But I can offer you Cognac as consolation," he said offhandedly.

"Is it French? Because I won't drink what the Dutch make."

Now, that was a line in the sand if he'd ever heard one. He turned to her, intrigued. The corset maker's profile reflected serious intent.

"Everyone knows Dutch cognac is cat piss," he said, amused.

She matched his intimacy, drawing her knees to her chest. "French Limousin oak. That's the secret."

"The barrel is everything."

He offered this arrogant summation because he knew it to be true and because it was the kind of detail the commerce-minded Scotswoman would appreciate. Miss Fletcher rewarded him with a gentle gaze as though she'd left all her cares behind and was truly present with him.

He reached inside his coat and offered her his flask. "Direct from the village of Cognac."

She hummed her approval and uncorked the flask with a soft *pop*. Air burst with aromas of caramel and French oak. The flask under her nose, she sniffed.

"Most impressive."

Sharing the drink opened another window in which he could examine her world. With exorbitant excise taxes, only the finest homes in London would have this kind of Cognac. Or had she consumed her Cognac in Scotland? Highlanders and the French were bosom friends in their mutual distaste for the English.

Miss Fletcher thumbed his initials etched in metal. "How do you come by it? The Cognac?"

"A smuggler gifted me with a cask. I keep it in the chamber behind my office."

She put the flask to her lips and tipped her head back, drinking like a thirsty sailor. He watched, awestruck. Miss Fletcher would be a formidable partner in tavern drinking games.

Sated, she licked her lips and handed over the flask. "An excellent refreshment. Thank you."

"You're welcome."

He needed a swig. Confidence was never an issue; delicacy, however, was. Miss Fletcher was a carefully constructed blend of fine manners and calloused fingers. A fascinating woman. She hugged her knees, a mahogany curl slouching against her temple. The heave and sway of the vessel lulled them, but her face was a study of determination—brows like bird's wings, slanting downward, the cogs and wheels of her mind ticking fiercely behind the beautiful mask that was her face.

"I'm surprised—you having smuggled Cognac," she said. "Do you meet your smuggler at Maison Bedwell?"

Another swig and, "No."

Miss Fletcher was fishing for information. Good. He was on something of a fishing expedition himself.

She canted her head. "You've nothing more to say?"

"He's a friend. A former shipmaster for West and Sons Shipping. We share a pint now and then when he's in London."

Miss Fletcher huffed and picked at the blanket warming her legs. "I don't want to know about your smuggler friend. I want to know about Maison Bedwell."

Ah, now they were getting somewhere.

"A capital establishment," he said vaguely enough.

She studied him, shrewd but impatient. He tucked the flask into his pocket, a provocative light in his eyes. He all but dared her to ask the questions plaguing her. It could be the corset maker was less enthusiastic to shed her inhibitions midday. He knew she had no problem shedding them at night. This very fact showed on her face, a veritable war playing out in their cozy tent.

"You're a coy one, Mr. West. Whisking me away on a pleasure barge and plying me with excellent Cognac." Her chin tipped a jaunty angle. "Are you spiriting me off to parts unknown? Possibly selling me to Barbary pirates?"

A wicked grin creased his lips. Did she read lurid romantic novels? The woman had a vivid imagination.

"I don't whisk, Miss Fletcher, I invite. Granted, mine was a firm invitation—"

"Demanding, certainly."

"But couched with humor. As to plying you with Cognac, you asked for refreshments and I offered what I have, which you guzzled like a Wapping Wall sailor."

Miss Fletcher's jaw unhinged. Her astonishment was priceless. Had no one given the Scotswoman *her* comeuppance? She was overdue, then. The woman excelled at putting others in their place. And from this encounter, another fact was clear. They'd have to break through her uniquely constructed wall.

Goading was in order.

"Be assured, we are not going to parts unknown," he said. "We're going to Chelsea Physic Garden, which was meant to be a surprise. And Miss Fletcher . . ." He paused to capture her gaze, which had wandered off. "I'd never sell you to Barbary pirates because I plan to keep you for myself."

She gasped.

"Any English pirate worth his salt would do the same," he said.

Air swatted the tent. Miss Fletcher was a statue slowly coming to life. The first sign was her mouth twitching as though she battled a smile and was about to lose.

"A pirate." Faint amusement laced her voice.

"A romantic notion. Lots of women have them about men who take to the sea."

She considered this, the smile still playing about her lips. He decided to spare her the truth about life on ships and let her believe the fantasy. Angling his body toward her, he stretched his arm along the back of the couch, in effect, cocooning them.

"I might've presumed overmuch, Miss Fletcher, but your giving me the keys to Neville Warehouse and a certain room at Maison Bedwell led me to believe you'd welcome not only my companionship, but my candor as well." A wisp of silence, and, "Do you?"

She nodded, the mahogany curl slipping free.

"I do."

Hers was the softest admission. So tender and vulnerable, it sent cracks rippling through his tough exterior. He took a deep breath, needing to recover. Miss Fletcher was disassembling him again, piece by piece.

She scooted closer.

"Were you ever . . . a pirate?"

His lips parted at her disarming question. He ought to wave the white flag of surrender and let her know she'd won. Miss Fletcher was gently storming the wall around his heart and stripping him bare. *Women and their fanciful minds.* The truth was he'd be whatever the corset maker wanted him to be.

"I am the proprietor of an honest, but struggling, whaling concern," he said quietly. "Nothing more."

She traced the scar on his cheek.

"You did say you planned to keep me for yourself."

"I suppose I did."

Her otherworldly eyes locked with his.

"What would you do with me?"

He groaned. Miss Fletcher was ruining him. She craved the fantasy, and damn his eyes, he wanted to give it to her. He shifted on his seat, heaviness expanding in his smalls. This excursion was meant to make her comfortable for sensual adventures to come. Women, even the bold ones, needed a certain amount of trust. But true to form, Miss Fletcher was flipping nature on its head.

The woman was a siren; that's what she was.

"The average pirate," he said, "would put a siren in a tower and surround her with the finest silks and velvets. All the luxuries to please a woman. That, however, would be a mistake with you."

Delight lit her face. "Did you say *siren*?"

"I did."

"But I'm not—"

"*Shhhh*." He touched her mouth. "It's my answer. I'll say what I want."

She smiled against his finger.

"The siren of White Cross Street—the rarest of sirens—needs adventures and cosseting in equal measure." He traced her mouth. Her lower lip hinting at passion; her upper lip hinting at intellect. "Only a fool would enshrine her in a tower."

She was a little breathless. "That was better than poetry."

He and Miss Fletcher stared at each other, an

invisible string connecting them, pulling him, pulling her, winding them ever closer. Their breaths mingled. The draw was powerful. Addictive. He couldn't stop. Her face tipped to his. Submissive, desirable.

Until at last, their lips touched.

Miss Fletcher hummed a blissful little sound. Her mouth, so, so soft. Velvet and warmth.

A shudder broke him.

His eyelids closed, their weight too much.

He couldn't think or maneuver. There was only this tender joining. Their long, sweet kiss. A treasure to hoard. Miss Fletcher's lips parted under his, guiding and giving. Adrift on a sea of pleasure, he was hapless, the tide of emotions changing him. She inched into the shelter of his body as though this gentle storm overwhelmed her and she needed the protection only he could give.

Her breath grazed his jaw. Her breast brushed his arm. He dug his hands into her hair, the silk slipping through his fingers. He kissed her deeply, his comely siren. She was everything supple and sweet, her contented sighs music to his soul. Her clean scent a comfort. Fragile and strong was Miss Fletcher . . . and she was giving herself to him.

Age-old mysteries whispered. If their first kiss was carnal, this, their second kiss, was exquisite. Something perfect. It should never end.

Except the world lurched.

It might've been Thomas's heart, or it might've been the pleasure barge. He couldn't tell the difference.

"Cheyne Walk, Chelsea," a voice announced.

The untouching of Thomas's mouth to hers left him wanting. A loss. He curled a hand at his side.

Tacit separation came, infinitesimal yet enough to steal Miss Fletcher's warmth from him.

She watched him under sable lashes, her eyes glossy, black erotic orbs. He scrubbed a hand over his mouth, trying to hold himself together. They were both ruined by this kiss, while life went on outside the saffron tent. Oars were stacked. Ropes were tossed, and two men jumped onto the dock to moor the vessel. Mr. Winston's portly profile became a silhouette beyond their tent.

The master bargeman cleared his throat. "We've arrived, Mr. West."

"A minute, if you please." Thomas hardly recognized his lust-thick voice.

Miss Fletcher folded her body into his, her eyes imploring him. Even desperate.

She was too shaken to move. He was too devastated to let her go.

"The pleasure barge is yours, sir," Mr. Winston said. "Find us at the Black Boar when you're ready to depart."

Oarsmen averted their gazes to the river, to the sky, to the vessel floor, anywhere but the tent's opening. Footsteps pounded, and the barge listed until those fine Englishmen took their leave.

All that remained were two souls too shattered to move.

Chapter Seventeen

*W*ho would've thought heaven was near a boat-house, west of London? Specifically, in Mr. West's lap, which she enjoyed while resting nose deep in his cravat. The linen was of middling quality, a summation she couldn't help; it was her nature to assess fabric. But the man who wore it—splendid.

She nudged her face an inch higher into his warm neck. If she was inclined to make a list of what she liked about Mr. West, his talent with whimsical tales would rank high. *Wretched man with his sirens and pirates.* She clutched a handful of his coat, wrecked.

He was figuring out how her mind worked.

Who knew sea wolves could do that? Or make a woman feel utterly safe? Mr. West was a riddle, holding her, his chin resting on her head, both of them staring at the river, waiting for their kiss-born fog to lift.

She was content.

It wouldn't last. This kind of marrow-deep happiness never did.

The handsome shipmaster belonged to her nights, not her days. He was a passing fancy. Their outing a rarity. She'd negotiated a month of nights at Maison Bedwell, and she'd gladly give each one to Mr. West. Blame sensuality's powerful draw for that.

But this?

Whatever *this* was, it wouldn't do to let certain emotions get out of hand.

Uncoiling herself from the safety of his arms took colossal effort, the undertaking as Herculean as striding a vertical mountain. She forced herself forward, stretching off the couch and pushing up on her toes like a dancer. Blood rushed in her veins. Sensations skittered across her limbs. Everything was magnified. Underskirts skimming her thighs, hair tickling her neck, Mr. West's cedarwood musk clinging to her skin.

If she wasn't careful, she'd flop back down and finish what their kiss started.

Giving her attention to the river might quash that craving.

"It's already past noon. We should proceed, shouldn't we?" Her voice was drowsy and resentful.

"One kiss and you're running away?" was the enticing drawl behind her.

She turned, riveted.

Mr. West was in a majestic sprawl. Legs spread, arms wide and casual, his chest impossibly broad. Victorious kings of old had done the same. Rode pleasure barges as if they ruled the world. Except she faced a hungry sea wolf, a man who got his hands dirty and did the actual conquering. If he'd lived in times past, matters of state would bore him. The man before her would be the king's best pirate. A hunter of goods and treasure.

And sirens.

She shivered from her nape to her toes. *Mr. West and his glinting eyes . . .* He looked like he wanted a sensual bite of her.

The move was hers.

"Our kiss was excellent," she admitted.

His smile was lazy. "We need not limit ourselves to one."

Air crackled. If tinder was on hand, the pleasure barge would spontaneously ignite. There was lust, certainly. Heady and undeniable, yet different. She'd indulged her sexual curiosity not long after the war. With a Highlander, in fact, with middling results. This business unfolding with Mr. West was more than a womanly itch that needed scratching. To save herself, she went to the tent's opening, fixing a pin in her hair.

"Shouldn't we partake of the day's entertainment?"

"I am."

She shivered again, temptation nipping her fiercely. His lust-grained voice would be her undoing. It'd be easy to close the tent and straddle his lap right here, right now. This pleasure barge . . . It was a scourge to clear thinking. Mr. West was scarred and dangerous, not a man to trifle with—except between the hours of nine o'clock and midnight in Maison Bedwell's Red Rose room. Then, much trifling would be done.

If she could make it 'til then. Really, the man could unprude a prude.

But another want niggled her. A taste for excitement and diversion beyond White Cross Street. She gusted a soft sigh because of it.

"The truth is, Mr. West, I have this one day for leisure."

She walked into the sunshine, struggling to contain

a vulnerability that wanted out. She was so confused. One would think a woman approaching her thirtieth birthday would have such matters sorted.

One would think . . .

A man who'd visited foreign ports might not understand how cramped her world had become.

The deck creaked with footfalls behind her. Mr. West came to her side, donning his tricorn, a breeze whipping the hem of his blue wool coat. He offered his arm, a little bearish.

"I am yours to command."

To which she snorted a laugh and curled her arm with his. "Why don't I believe that?"

"Because you are a confident woman who says what she thinks."

"Bluntly so, I'm afraid."

Mr. West squinted at the sun and led the way.

"Do not hesitate to speak your mind with me, Miss Fletcher." His sidelong assurance came with a handsome, crooked smile. "Especially this day, which is devoted to your pleasure."

She eyed their wooden path and let his words sink in. When was the last time she'd spent an entire day devoted to her own pleasure? She couldn't recall, but this day with Mr. West wouldn't be wasted. It would be her little adventure.

The dock took them to a row of brightly painted boathouses. Reds and blues mostly, the trim clean and white. Amiable voices spilled from a nearby public house. The botanical gardens, hedged by trees and a low fence, consumed a vast lot to their right, but it was a sign with an arrow pointing to the left that snared her. VILLAGE OF CHELSEA, it read.

Of course. Chelsea Physic Botanical Gardens would

be near the village—where the Countess of Denton's Chelsea Porcelain Works was. If she hadn't been so addled with lust, she would've connected this obvious fact earlier.

She tugged free of Mr. West for a better view of rambling structures clumped together. Brick and flintstone, wattle and daub. A decent-sized village, but nothing impressive.

Why did the vile woman have a business here? Lady Denton thrived on wealth and the appearance of wealth. She owned the best brick warehouses, which stored the best wallpaper, fabrics, and other luxury goods—all in London.

The porcelain works was the only business lacking a fine address. She pointed in the general direction of it.

"Mr. West, would you mind if we strolled that way?"

"Not the garden?" His intrigued glance bounced from her to the village and back to her.

"It would be a short visit," she said. "Then we can go to the gardens."

Emboldened by the empty docks, she pushed up on her toes, rubbing against him.

His pupils blackened.

"I'll do my best to make our village jaunt worthwhile," she whispered before kissing him softly on the mouth.

The sultry kiss didn't have the desired effect. Mr. West's lust-dark eyes narrowed a wary fraction when she laced her arm with his. The tiniest unease descended on her as he led the way to Cheyne Walk. The stamped-earth path was shaded by a few trees.

The air was infinitely sweeter, and the water free of questionable matter. Orderly buildings faced the river with lanes in between them. Lawrence Street was the one she looked for until Mr. West fired a cannonball of a question at her.

"I noticed you left with a man last night. Who was he?"

He'd watched her leaving Bedwell's? This was not good.

A tendril of hair floated across her eyes. She brushed it back, nonchalant. "I'm not sure what you mean."

His profile was grim. "I thought we were making great progress, learning about each other."

"You said I drink Cognac like a Wapping Wall sailor," she said, trying for lightness.

"But very telling."

"Ah, then, should I wax long about my favorite flower? Or my preference for coffee or tea?"

"Don't be evasive, Miss Fletcher. I won't tolerate another man."

There was a bite in his tone as deliberate and even as a knife swipe.

She clamped her lips in a hard line. Questioning her was a shot across the bow, but this? This was him staking a flag in sacred territory—her independence.

"Forgive me, Mr. West, but I'm still quite taken by your excellent claim that this day is devoted entirely to my pleasure." When he said nothing, she spoke to his flinty profile. "Who I come and go with is not your concern."

"I'm sure it is."

She pulled away, speechless.

"You require our assignations be at a time and place suitable to you. For a duration · suitable to you . . . for as much as I can tell." His voice firmed. "I'll allow it—"

"You will allow it?" She laughed, harsh and abrupt. Thankfully, they were alone on Cheyne Walk, the benefit of being near the less-than-fashionable village.

"You want me for an indiscretion? I'm happy to oblige, but I won't share."

Her nerves tingled—his body for her pleasure. A concise explanation, as it were.

She tipped her head back to make eye contact. The brim of his hat shadowed his face, but there was no mistaking his menacing eyes. The sea wolf, staking his claim. Crawling into his lap on the pleasure barge might've been a mistake.

This, she supposed, is what happened to the sensualist seeking adventure.

Raising her hood, she sought precious seconds to think.

"Why wait to ask now? Why didn't you ask me as soon as I exited the hack at All Hollows Wharf?"

His stare impaled her.

"Because I don't think straight when I'm with you."

Her stomach did a silly flip-flop. She could say the same of Mr. West. Talking to him stirred her. And touching him? Incendiary. Yet, his question, framed as a demand, drove a sledgehammer through her peace. Mr. West wanted her body and her secrets. Blasted man.

She faced the shushing river. Air soughed through the trees, carrying a risky idea: *it wouldn't hurt to give him something.* Mr. West already knew she'd forged a Wilkes-Lock key at his shipyard last August. No lobsterbacks had hauled her off to prison for it.

"The man you saw is a business acquaintance and nothing more."

"A corset maker, is he?"

She winced. Mr. West's irony was merciless. "He's not that kind of acquaintance."

"Is he a suitor?"

"Of course not." She angled her face to his. "I don't keep suitors. They're boring and needy and entirely unnecessary because I'll not marry."

"Never?"

"Yes, never."

Judging by the expanded whites of his eyes, Mr. West was stunned. But they weren't any closer to Chelsea Porcelain Works, and if she was honest, serving the needs of the league rated just above serving the needs of Mr. West. If only just. The league was her true family, and they'd survived a war together.

But, with her startling revelation shared, the genie was out of the bottle. There was no putting it back in.

Mr. West searched her face. "Do you believe in love?"

A simple but devastating question. Though perfectly still, she was floundering. Mr. West might as well ask her to explain the universe or map the tides.

She plucked a low-hanging leaf, one of the few on the branch. "Your question implies that love and marriage are synonymous, but we both know they are not."

"Sometimes they are," was his gentle reply.

Which put salt on an unseen wound. She ripped the dry leaf in half, bits of it crumbling to the ground.

"Aren't you the man who told me nothing lasts forever?"

"Lives end, Miss Fletcher, but love, in its purest form, has no end."

Her throat was raw and her thoughts muddled. *No end?* How fanciful, her shipmaster. Mr. West was being diabolically kind. His focus a dandelion-soft stroke to her soul, and she wanted more. *Wretched man.* She was no better than Mr. Fisk, Mr. West's shipyard cat, craving his tender attention.

"Love is not enough," was her whispered rebellion—a belief she'd hold 'til her dying day.

Mr. West's eyes took on a peculiar light, dawning with understanding, and she simply couldn't bear it. She had to look away. The ache inside her was untenable. It was her heart squashing itself into a stony thing.

"We both know practically every unmarried woman wants to snare an excellent husband. It's the same as winning a lottery," she said.

"The business of marriage." He was judicious in saying so. "I won't deny that aspect exists."

"Nor will I. And just like London's lotteries, marriage is a sham."

"Or it builds dynasties, fills nations, and provides the foundation for happy families."

"Not all of them are happy." She was stronger now, tossing away the torn leaf and doing what she knew best. "Let's carry on, shall we?"

Hems swinging and chin up, she tried to carry on. A pinch invaded her chest. Her private pain. She'd not share it. Shouldn't it be possible to enjoy Mr.

West's companionship sans difficult conversations? This was a day for entertainments—at least it was supposed to be. Perhaps they should've stayed on the pleasure barge. Sensual pursuits were fun, and conversation was not required.

Determined footsteps crunched the ground beside her. *Mr. West and his long legs.*

"This non-suitor of yours—does he know you'll never marry?"

She slanted her eyes at him and found a handsome profile etched by daylight as they walked. "Why would he? I've never kissed him nor has he asked such impertinent questions." Two brisk steps and she added, "Not that I would answer him."

"You answered me." There was a note of triumph in his voice.

"I did."

"Do you want to kiss him?"

"No."

Impatient, she picked up the pace and turned onto Lawrence Street. The porcelain works shingle was ahead. The gold to buy the sheep. This is what she should be about, not the delirious distraction of a tall Englishman bent on doling out questions and kisses.

"The man you saw, Mr. MacLeod, is helping my kinswomen. We have a league . . . of sorts."

"What does your league do?"

"We help Highlanders." A tight but truthful summation.

She stopped under a black shingle, its wood gleaming as though it had been freshly painted.

CHELSEA PORCELAIN WORKS, ESTABLISHED 1749.

Mr. West checked the sign overhead, his gaze

landing slowly on her. If she didn't know any better, she'd say the scarred shipmaster was making sense of conversational bits and pieces.

"Mr. MacLeod—is he part of your league?"

There was something deliberate and parsing in his tone.

"Of a sort. You'll see him at Neville Warehouse. Fixing things, and the like."

Questions lit Mr. West's sharp eyes. They both knew it was a leap of logic, warehouse work to brothel visits. Before he could unleash more questions, she ran her fingers lightly over the button flash of his greatcoat.

"There is only one man I want to kiss," she said softly. "A sea wolf who happens to possess an unfounded jealous streak."

"A sea wolf?" His baritone rumbled with surprise.

"Appropriate, considering his behavior of late."

A breeze tapped his properly knotted cravat and the half smile tugging his mouth. She might be onto something with tender touches and colorful monikers.

"I do enjoy him. Thoroughly, in fact."

His gaze sharpened. "Your sea wolf? Or your non-suitor?"

She explored a buttonhole on his greatcoat.

"There is only one non-suitor for me."

"Indeed."

His eyes were a brilliant shade of green-blue. A woman could lose herself in them.

"As it happens, I have plans to further my acquaintance with him in the most delightful ways, as long as he understands one unwavering fact."

"And that is?"

"That everything ends when the month is out," she said, gently and carefully.

A strange stiffness came over Mr. West.

"As it happens, a month suits me."

Which was veiled and stoic all at once. Her hand fell to her side, useless. She regretted her bluntness and cast her attention to the lane where a young girl in clogs was shushing along five geese. She was at a loss, her usual confidence vanished.

Cecelia would have something witty to say, and Margaret, something kind.

"I don't wish to be—to be . . ."

She was floundering, her emotions a quagmire.

Mr. West tucked a wisp of hair behind her ear. "We both agreed to this unusual arrangement. No further explanation is needed."

She tipped her chin high. "Thank you."

Birds chirped and a door was opened and shut on Lawrence Street. Inside the porcelain works shop, workmen bantered about a tavern wench. Laughter hung in the air. Pottery clattered as though someone was stacking dishes. Yet, she of the forward charge couldn't make her feet obey and enter the shop.

"We're both charting new waters, Miss Fletcher. Patience is in order. For both of us."

She swallowed the lump in her throat.

"Yes, patience."

Mr. West was sage and his eyes tender. He'd stormed her ramparts and was giving her an olive branch. Was this what it was like to be understood? This genuine, starry perfection in which she could soar with happiness one minute and express anger the next? In the space of a few hours, Mr. West managed to learn more about her than most did in months or years, if not a lifetime.

Bloody Englishman. Her sea wolf was a master of ships and a master of sirens.

Or one siren, she hoped.

And that was a dangerous wish.

Chapter Eighteen

Thomas entered the pottery works, bemused. Miss Fletcher had called him a sea wolf. The name fit. His years at sea had been full of fierce adventures. Leading men on hunts through the North Sea was not for the faint of heart. Engaging the attentions of Mary Fletcher was proving to be a similar challenge.

Pirates and whalers had a taste for fast living. Both professions preferred sleek schooners for their speed and maneuverability in the face of peril.

Rather like the glossy-haired Miss Fletcher, a woman rife with mysteries.

A woman who never wanted love or marriage?

Her claim was the strangest thing.

She lowered her hood and browsed Chelsea Pottery Works, which was more manufactory than shop. Straw crunched underfoot and earthy smells of clay and freshly cut wood met the nose. A man was nailing crates with an exuberant hammer, while another worker in a leather apron inspected a platter. It was this man who crossed the room and welcomed them.

"Good afternoon," he said, pushing spectacles up his nose.

Miss Fletcher's fingertips grazed a pretty painted shepherdess clock. "Good afternoon, sir. Your shop has some lovely pieces."

His chin dipped affably. "You're too kind, but what you see here . . ." He gestured at the shelves. "These are the flawed pieces. My better work can be found at Melton's Curiosity Shop on Pall Mall."

"Changing your business name, are you?"

"Goodness, no. The Countess of Denton owns the manufactory. Her ladyship is in the process of selling the entire inventory to Mr. Melton."

"But not the manufactory?" Miss Fletcher browsed a stack of plates.

"Chelsea Porcelain Works will soon close its doors." He grimaced. "I'm afraid we were never able to make a suitable profit."

"What a shame . . . all these pretty things." She traced the rim of a bowl. "Just look at this glaze."

Thomas stood back and watched. Miss Fletcher was artful, drawing in the porcelain master who was rightfully proud of his work. Heads bent, they discussed a platter painted with Bristol blue.

Miss Fletcher scowled prettily. "If these are your flawed pieces, I find it hard to believe this manufactory couldn't turn a profit."

"One would think so," the man grumbled. "But I was never allowed to bring in apprentices or given the funds to hire workers."

"Really?"

"I'm afraid it's just me and my wife, who is out at the moment. I work the clay. She paints. Despite our best efforts, we couldn't create enough goods in a timely fashion."

"How awful. You and your wife are obviously a talented pair."

The blushing porcelain master peered at her over his spectacles.

"Thank you, Miss . . . ?"

"I—" Miss Fletcher blinked fast. "I am Mrs. West, and this is my husband, Mr. West."

Her moonstone gaze implored Thomas.

His brows shot up. What was the *I'll never marry* corset maker about? Undaunted, he ambled forward and made sure to stand close to her.

"Forgive my surprise," he said a touch droll to the porcelain master. "Sometimes I forget that I'm a married man."

"We've only recently wed." Miss Fletcher added this quick note.

Thomas let his hand wander intimately down her back.

"Yes. Very, *very* recently."

The porcelain master beamed at them. "Ah, felicitations are in order."

Introductions were made, and the conversational dam broke wide open. The porcelain master was Mr. Clabberhorn, long in the employ of Lady Denton, a woman who, according to the long-suffering Clabberhorn, lacked a head for business. A fact which made no sense: everyone with a ship knew the countess collected prime warehouses the way other ladies of her station collected *à bric et à brac*. Or handsome men to keep as her private footmen.

None of this was adding up correctly.

Hearing Lady Denton had no head for business was as astonishing as suddenly finding himself a married man. Nevertheless, the porcelain master was in a bind and about to lose his income.

"My sympathies to you and Mrs. Clabberhorn at having to leave this fine manufactory," he said. "Have you found new employment?"

"We're returning to Kent. My wife has family in Maidstone where we shall open our own manufactory." Mr. Clabberhorn was solemn. "Closing this manufactory is both a blessing and a curse, I collect."

"The countess doesn't mind?" the newly styled Mrs. West asked. "You and Mrs. Clabberhorn opening your own porcelain works . . . it seems rather sudden."

"Goodness, no. Her ladyship is most happy to be rid of us."

"Oh?"

The porcelain master leaned in like a conspirator. "Come, let me show you something."

Thomas followed Miss Fletcher, who followed Mr. Clabberhorn. What a merry line. Thomas couldn't help but think he was walking into a deeper mystery than a simple jaunt to a porcelain works. Miss Fletcher was hanging on Mr. Clabberhorn's words as if she would nurse every last ounce of information from the hapless man.

The manufactory had gone quiet. The laborer assembling crates was presently in the alley, smoking a pipe. Mr. Clabberhorn led a winding path to a barrel of broken pottery. At the top was the bust of a woman, the clay rough and unfired.

Mr. Clabberhorn tilted the piece for their inspection. "Look at this."

The sculpture was distinct. Cloth-draped shoulders, a crescent moon tiara, and a quiver of arrows strapped to her back. The face, however, was vaguely familiar.

"Is that . . . Lady Denton?" Miss Fletcher asked.

"Styled as the Roman goddess Diana," Clabberhorn said.

Miss Fletcher tapped the nose, which had lost its tip. "I thought the nobility commissioned marble busts."

"I thought the very same." Mr. Clabberhorn eyed her over the rim of his spectacles. "This is a useless vanity."

Miss Fletcher checked the barrel. "And you have quite a collection of them."

Thomas looked over her shoulder. The barrel brimmed with unfired busts of Lady Denton fashioned as the Roman goddess, all of them flawed. Cracks, chips, some split in two. The bottom half of the barrel appeared to be the sandy remains of earlier attempts of the same artwork.

"Lady Denton insisted I devote myself to creating this particular bust. And look here . . ." He turned over the ruined piece, revealing a jagged hole. "This was her oddest request. She insisted I make a hollow bust with a hole in the back."

Miss Fletcher's gloved finger circumnavigated an opening about three inches in diameter.

"A hollow bust."

The porcelain master snorted. "An inexplicably difficult process to sculpt a hollow piece of this magnitude—as you can see by all my failed attempts."

"It must've taken a great deal of time to create these," Thomas said.

"Indeed, four years of work is in this barrel." Clabberhorn, his brow furrowing, laid the flawed bust to rest. "It is not false flattery when I say only the most skilled craftsman can sculpt a hollow piece of this detail and of this size."

"How frustrating."

Miss Fletcher was the voice of compassion. Mr. Clabberhorn smiled wearily.

"Indeed, it was for a time. But I did manage to create a bust as per her ladyship's instructions."

"Where is the piece now?" she asked.

"In Lady Denton's Grosvenor Square home. I delivered it last winter. Shortly afterward, her ladyship announced that she would sell the manufactory." He dragged clay-dusted hands down his leather apron. "She left us alone until summer. Since then, there's been a great urgency to shut the manufactory's doors."

"When exactly this summer?" Miss Fletcher asked.

The porcelain master studied the floor. "August, I believe."

Thomas's ears prickled at the hitch in the corset maker's breath. Her posture stiffened, a minute change most wouldn't catch. He had, and it clanged a warning—*how quick you are to notice every little thing about her.*

He brushed that aside. She'd come to his shipyard in August to forge a key. This couldn't be a coincidence.

"Thank you, Mr. Clabberhorn. Thank you very much," she said. "You've been so kind, showing us your work. We won't take up another minute of your time."

Thomas touched the small of her back. "Yes, thank

you, sir. Next time Mrs. West and I visit Kent, we'll look for your new shop in Maidstone."

Miss Fletcher's body was shaking against his hand as though she was stifling a laugh.

The porcelain master grinned from ear to ear. "It would be my pleasure to show you and Mrs. West our new manufactory."

The trio migrated to the front of the shop and said their goodbyes.

Outside, a rumple of clouds hid the sun and traffic had picked up on Lawrence Street. Thomas tucked Miss Fletcher's arm with his for their walk to the gardens, but inside he was dancing a jig. The air tasted like victory.

"Thank you for that." Her glance was quick and coded.

"You're welcome."

They traversed Lawrence Street, but Miss Fletcher was nose forward, her pretty profile a watery replica in passing windows. *Enigmatic woman.* London was full of prattle-baskets; it was just his luck to find the city's only tight-lipped beauty.

Clearly, the upstanding corset maker was up to something. She had dropped certain clues today. He wasn't worried. Intimate knowledge would come. Given the right circumstances, the Siren of White Cross Street would spill her truths.

No hunter won his reward without ample patience—and she was the prize he wanted.

When the Chelsea Physic Gardens were in view, he set his first trap.

"Why the keen interest in Chelsea Porcelain Works . . . *Mrs. West?*"

Chapter Nineteen

A smile flirted with the corner of her mouth. Their gaits matched and neither missed a beat when she slanted her eyes at him.

"What piques your curiosity more? The unplanned visit to the porcelain works? Or my temporary use of your name?"

"As it happens, both."

"Rather greedy of you," she teased. "Pillaging my secrets."

"This day, by design, is entirely mercenary."

"For whose benefit?"

He flashed a wolfish smile. "Mine, of course."

"And we wouldn't want to deny you your rightful reward, now, would we?"

She was a little breathless saying that. Mr. West grinned his approval.

"Alas, rules of the sea prevail, Miss Fletcher. The first to stake a claim, wins."

"Obviously, I need to work on my pirate skills. I'm quite out of my depth."

His laugh was rich and lovely. "To the contrary, you are very adept."

Excitement drove them toward the garden gate, their hips practically glued together. One might think they were in a rush because a kiss would happen upon entering the garden. The air was crisp, and every inch of her was electric. Soft earth yielded underfoot as they reached the wrought iron gate. She grasped the open sides of his greatcoat and pressed into his warmth.

"As the victor, how will you celebrate?"

Mr. West's eyes were like polished pieces of green-blue glass. "You have it backward. I am not the victor here."

"How so?"

"You claimed me when you stole my name."

And there it was, more champagne giddiness filling her. A breeze tossing her hair against her cheek was a fair reminder she was not lighter than air. The teasing strands tickled her skin, the same as his baritone. He'd played the part with ease when she claimed to be his wife. One might say the ruse was fun.

"It wasn't stealing," she said. "I temporarily borrowed it."

"At sea, we'd call you a pirate."

"Except we are on land."

"A fair point. For that reason"—he folded a hand over hers and brought their joined hands to his mouth—"I'll call you a siren."

"Dangerous women, sirens."

She hardly recognized the sensual creature she'd become. Lips parting, breasts thrusting, her legs tangling with his as they leaned against the gate. At this rate a passionate kiss might happen on the village side of the garden for any passerby to see.

"A man must be vigilant or he'll fall prey to their charms." Mr. West was just as snared, planting featherlight kisses on pale flesh below her wrist. "An interesting fact—sirens are very busy in the month of August."

Intelligence glittered in his eyes. She coaxed herself not to react. To be utterly still, which under Mr. West's perusal was a road sign, guiding his way. *The bloody man.* Mr. West paid attention to every little thing about her. He'd made a connection between her forging a key in his shipyard to the Countess of Denton urgently deciding to sell her shop. Both done last August.

"Have you nothing to say?" he asked.

She shrugged, elegant and oblique. "Summer . . . It's a maddening season."

Under his coat, she found his heartbeat. Steady and reassuring, its thud. The touch, her bid for a reprieve. She'd spilled much of her heart today and was almost wearied by it.

He had to know this.

Leaves from trees lining the wall drifted around them. Yellows, ambers, and reds floating like colorful gifts. The same breeze tossing those leaves toyed with his cravat. How handsome and imposing, her sea wolf.

"This is our day for adventure, is it not?" she reminded him.

Mr. West studied her, another breeze kicking his queue. He offered the barest nod, a truce, though she had no doubt they'd revisit today's discoveries. Then he opened the iron gate with a flourish.

"Your secret garden awaits."

She brushed a leaf off his shoulder. "The only gardens I've known are the practical vegetable variety."

His mouth gentled. "Every woman needs something magical now and then."

She passed him, doubting a physic garden had the power to enchant. How wrong she was.

Her breath caught and her steps slowed.

Espaliered apple trees lined a garden wall. Ruby-red fruit dressed their lattice-work branches. Rows of stunted pear trees, wine-red Anjou, and a green varietal grew from large pots. Their foliage had been cut into playful shapes—balls and twirling spires mostly. But the artistic espaliered trees drew the eye. She'd seen pictures of them in books. Very French, very sophisticated. Yet, nothing compared to witnessing nature bent in intricate patterns. The unnatural made fascinating.

A wide path led to a glass house where exotic leaves pressed steamy windows like the green-gloved hands of a woman in a passionate tryst. There was something illicit and endearing, a secluded land that needed exploring.

Iron creaked behind her, Mr. West shutting the gate.

"I always thought garden walks were so . . . overdone," she said as he joined her.

"English gardens, yes."

Her eyes rounded. "Not exactly loyal to your own kind."

Tall and proud, Mr. West surveyed the landscape. On the pleasure barge, he'd been every inch the conquering sea wolf; alone with him like this was the victor's private celebration.

"English cottage gardens are the same as consuming a chop house dinner. Satisfying, giving one a sturdy sense of home, but French designs are effervescent." He cocked his head, a connoisseur. "Beauty for beauty's sake."

This revelation left her mildly dazed.

"How does an English whaler come by this knowledge?"

"By his very French mother." He hesitated. "When I was a boy, she dragged my sisters and me here more times than I can count."

She leaned closer, hearing a treasured childhood in his voice. Mr. West had done more than open a garden gate for her. He'd opened a door to his heart.

"Aren't you full of surprises with a French maman and a youth spent on garden walks." She tipped her head just so. "I can almost picture you as a lad digging in your heels."

His laugh was graveled and his eyes distant. Even the cadence of his voice changed.

"My poor mother. I was a handful. When summer came, we would picnic here. She would wipe jelly off my cheek and scold me in French."

"Your childhood, it sounds lovely."

"It was. My mother kept us busy, all to divert our fears—and hers—that my father's ship might not return. But he always came home."

"What a quaint family history."

His green-blue gaze pinned her with a message. *Time to pay the piper.* "As it happens, I'm plagued with history—recent history, in fact."

Mr. West twined their arms and led them on a meander fraught with a small dose of tension. He'd shared a piece of himself; it was time she shared hers.

She angled her face to his. "If you want to know something, ask me. But fair warning, my life is rather dull."

"Then why not begin with the dull explanation of why we visited the pottery works, and why you told Mr. Clabberhorn that you were my wife."

They walked on, pebbles crunching underfoot. Crows were gathering, lining the garden wall like eavesdroppers.

"My mother collected porcelain pieces. Dishes mostly."

Concise but true. Still, his mouth twisted with disappointment.

"You're trying to tell me our visit was paying homage to your mother."

His monotone bordered on mockery. She pinched her brows together. *Lud*, it actually hurt to disappoint him.

"And it had nothing to do with the Countess of Denton?" he asked. Another heavy silence and he squinted at the path ahead. "Perhaps you're not ready for candor after all."

Yet, she was ready to remove every last stitch of clothing and explore carnal delights with him? She studied the ground, facing a vexing fact. This was— *she* was—diving into profound waters.

"I know you're flirting when you call me a siren, but you're closer to the truth than you think," she said, which snared his interest. "Any candor from me could cause you great harm."

"I'll take my chances."

She stopped their progress, desperate.

"You don't know what you're saying."

He tucked loose strands of hair behind her ear. So

tender and thoughtful. Something a lover would do. "I'll take the risk, if you're the prize."

Her knees puddled. *Drat the man!* If Mr. West was a marauding pirate, he'd just scaled her walls and won the day.

Somehow, this left her both miserable and happy—an exhausting combination.

"Mr. West . . ."

"Thomas," he corrected gingerly.

Which was an arrow, striking her heart. She didn't deserve his kindness.

There was a bench conveniently facing the espaliered trees. She nudged them toward it. Once on the wooden seat, she melted into him. Rattled. And weak. Her courage evaporating. Thomas wrapped his arm around her back as though he understood. He'd give her the time she needed to unwind her fears. They sat, holding each other for the longest time. Their breathing matched; their bodies fit. Pure heaven.

Her eyes fluttered shut. Was it possible he knew how to unwind a woman's heart? Holding her and waiting? Birds chirped and in the distance she heard voices, possibly from the village. But Thomas drew her in. His warmth and the contentment of being held by him.

In this state, words began to pour out of her.

Small bits came first. The Uprising, the league, and their four-year hunt for the lost Jacobite gold. Her diction sharpened, a fast-slicing sword when she spoke of the countess and her violent watchdog, Mr. Wortley. Those parts were surprisingly easy. Other parts, not so much.

She eventually reached back to her childhood in Edinburgh. Her mother's infidelities, her father's indifference, and the joys and sorrows of raising her sister, Margaret. All bittersweet memories. Thomas was very good at shepherding her through each one—especially disappointment's deep, deep scars.

He stroked her hair gently and said a word she'd not been able to utter. "Abandonment . . . it is a hard thing to survive."

She sucked in a needle-sharp breath, ready to defend her mother, but Thomas anticipated her.

"It doesn't matter if abandonment comes by death or by decision," he said comfortingly, "those left behind feel the same."

She burrowed her cheek into his coat. "But I loved her so much."

How fragile her voice was. Thomas hugged her closer and kissed the crown of her head.

"Sometimes we love people who at heart are good, yet they make awful decisions."

Love. How staunchly her sea wolf defended it.

Bemused, she removed her gloves and showed him the most damning part of her.

The little scars on her hands.

"When I was twelve, my mother stayed home a long while. One day she asked me to deliver a midday luncheon to my father's shop on High Street. For some reason I asked my father about his work. That was the day he began to teach me silversmithing. Nothing serious, of course, because I was a girl." She sat up, wanting to look him in the eye. "But I became good at it. Very good." She splayed a *this is important* hand on Thomas's chest. "I melted a portion of the

Jacobite treasure and turned them into guineas and half guineas. All done in the back of my shop on White Cross Street."

Anvil hardness crept into his eyes. "Counterfeiting."

She squirmed. A harsh word, *counterfeiting*.

"Passing too many French coins in London would draw attention to us. The league needed English money to occasionally . . . purchase information."

She winced. This honesty business wasn't putting her in a good light. Hooking an elbow on the back of the bench, Thomas considered the far wall.

"Let me see if I have this right. I'm enthralled by a counterfeiting Jacobite housebreaker who bribes people."

"Well, I'm not quite a counterfeiter."

"Either one is or one isn't," he said.

"I did try to warn you off." A fire was growing in her belly. She'd not give up without a fight. "And if you must know, I do not insert tin discs in my coins." A common trick of counterfeiters. "I merely transform one currency for another." Which earned her a dubious look. "Nor are we housebreakers. The Countess of Denton invited members of our league to her house for an art salon the night we took the gold—*our* gold, mind you, which she stole from us—and *bribing* is such a . . . a callous word. I prefer to call it a business transaction."

"That's quite a list. You might be splitting hairs with it, but I appreciate your honesty." He brushed his knuckles across her cheek. "Do you know what I find amusing about it?"

"What?"

"It's coming from a woman with an unwavering sense of absolutes, yet she just argued for ambiguity."

She narrowed her eyes. He was like a dog with a bone, her sea wolf. "You're talking about love, while I'm talking about justice."

Thomas laughed in good humor. "The crown would take a different view."

"Hang the crown."

She slumped against the back rest, recalcitrant. Why did the good opinion of Mr. Thomas West matter? He caressed her nape and for the life of her, she couldn't move. She was just like the cat, Mr. Fisk—ensorcelled by the shipmaster's stroking hand. Leaves skittered past their feet, and more crows descended. Gardeners were coming as well. One of them hailed Thomas, and he waved back.

"By the by, there's a tea or luncheon waiting for us. Might be cold by now. I was supposed to lead you to the main building some time ago."

Thomas, however, thought it more important to listen to her. His kindness again, so unexpected from the rugged man of the sea. Now people were coming, and their interlude was over. Mary corrected her posture and pasted a smile on her face.

"Refreshments sound wonderful." She started to rise, but Thomas caught her wrist.

Green, green eyes held her captive.

"Tell me. Am I falling for a Jacobite rebel?"

The shipmaster's stare was backlit with dangerous messages. Lust she understood. The others left her shaky.

Falling for her was dangerous.

"Aren't you going to answer me?" he asked.

"No."

A subtle battle was launched. The warfare between two hearts, one English, another Scots. She'd given Thomas West enough ammunition to sink her. But the greater war was of the heart, and this, their first real skirmish. His hand still cuffed her forearm, bare skin to bare skin. Her breasts, her belly, and her thighs tingled joyously, ready to surrender. This was perilous ground—desire and affections braiding with hazardous secrets. Mostly hers.

Lips clamping, she'd say no more. In the distance gardeners stopped their progress. Two men, armed with rakes and shovels, were listening to an older gentleman in a fine frock coat. The head gardener, she assumed, wishing he would make haste and join Thomas and her.

Thomas stood up and eyed those men as though calculating how much time he had left in this treasonous conversation.

"About your list," he said in hushed tones. "You failed to mention whether or not you're done with your treasure hunt." He pulled her close, a patina of worry on his face. "Are you? Done?"

Clever man. The shipmaster was navigating treacherous waters—and her confessional had been just the invitation to guide him there.

"Our question-and-answer time is done." She put a hand over his until he let go.

"But we were just getting started."

She felt a feline smile growing. Her sea wolf was racing ahead. Someone ought to put a leash on him.

"Aren't there rules to how fast ships can travel the Thames?" she asked.

He cocked his head, curious at this conversational turn. "The king's harbor master likes to think so."

"Then let this be a warning, *Mr. West.* You've exceeded it."

"Gone too fast, have I?"

"Yes."

His mouth dented handsomely. "What if I ignore your warning?"

"Then you do so at your own peril."

Thomas West loomed, his presence sending a delicious shiver across her limbs. "Pirates ignore the rules, *Miss Fletcher*. Especially when they're hunting sirens."

Chapter Twenty

ℳr. West's siren hunt had been cut short when Mr. Philip Miller, chief gardener, approached. A Scotsman, as it were, long in residence with a passion for collecting and nurturing plants and trees from around the world. Mr. Miller's guided tour couldn't cool the heated waters between her and Thomas.

Mary wished she had a fan. She needed one to counter Thomas's hot gaze. He was irked and unsatisfied. A deadly combination.

"Careful, Mr. West," she murmured upon entering the Bermuda Glasshouse. "Or you'll burn the house down with that stare of yours."

"Just wait until I get you alone tonight," he whispered behind her ear.

Excitement was the fuel in her veins. It was in the air she breathed, in the quick glances with Thomas. Wide green leaves brushed her seductively. She paused to admire one, holding it up to the light.

"And what will you do," she whispered, "when we're alone? Kiss me? Or question me?"

Thomas admired the leaf, his finger teasing hers.

"Only kisses and questions, Miss Fletcher? Is that all you think I'll do to you?" He tsk-tsked. "Your imagination needs fewer rules."

Which dried her mouth.

"I'll help you break them all." His grin was positively piratical.

Thomas wandered after Mr. Miller, who was blathering on, unaware a subtle siege was taking place behind him. Mary tried to collect herself. Bermuda Glasshouse was sultry, the banana trees exotic, and her limbs sluggish. And she was getting so, so . . . hot. She slipped free of her cloak.

Mr. Miller was rocking on his toes, waiting. "Miss Fletcher, have you had a banana fruit?"

"No. I'm afraid mine is a limited existence." She eyed Thomas. "Too much restraint, I think."

The master gardener's brow looked puzzled. "With fruit?"

"With everything," Thomas intoned.

She was airy, brushing past him. "A man can't always get what he wants, now, can he?"

Mr. Miller trailed after her, puzzled. "I suppose not. Bananas are a costly fruit."

A table with silver and fine dishes had been laid out. She went to it and draped her cloak over the back of a seat.

"Indeed, too costly." This was, she hoped, her final salvo, delivered with a pointed look at Thomas.

He helped her settle into her chair. "Tell that to men who risk life and limb at sea."

"Doing what? Hunting sirens?" she teased under her breath.

"No. Just me, hunting you," Thomas murmured above her ear.

She dug her fingernails into her serviette to stop from quivering. It didn't work.

"Some treasures are worth the risk," her scarred pirate said before taking his seat. To Mr. Miller, "Earlier, you mentioned the gardens have several first editions of Mr. John Gerard's *The Herbal or General History of Plants*. I'd like to purchase a copy for my mother."

Mr. Miller snapped his serviette straight. "Consider it done."

How did Mr. West manage to reassemble himself so easily? Her nerves sparked like popping embers.

Her lashes heavy, she fought to recover. Steady breathing helped. So did conversation on tamer topics, though it took her long minutes to find her equilibrium.

Mr. Miller regaled them with stories of various plants and their healthful benefits. He stayed with her and Thomas for the entire visit—to the chagrin of her scarred pirate. Mr. Miller was so enthusiastic that he insisted on seeing them safely returned to the pleasure barge, where Mr. Winston and company awaited them.

The chief gardener was escorting Mary as Thomas trailed behind. "It was a pleasure to host another Scot."

She patted his velvet sleeve. "Thank you for a wonderful afternoon, sir. It was very generous of you to devote yourself to our visit."

"It was a delight." He tipped his head to hers. "Though I confess, Mr. West's generous donation of whale bones helped."

"Whale bones?"

He nodded vigorously. "Mr. West, like his father

before him, grinds whale bones and sells them to us. Fodder for the plants."

They stopped beside the pleasure barge and she raised her hood against the chill.

"I had no idea."

She glanced at Mr. West. Who would have thought? A beauty-loving, garden-souled pirate lived in his tall frame. Mr. Miller handed her over to Mr. West fairly beaming.

"This year, however, I received a most astonishing letter. Mr. West offered to deliver his goods, free of charge if I would but close the gardens to the public and offer a private tour."

She glanced at Thomas. Maneuvered that, had he?

"That is exceedingly generous. I, too, have found he has a talent for writing the most astonishing letters," she said to Mr. Miller. "Quite persuasive, our Mr. West."

Thomas was stoic under the shower of such fine praise.

"Indeed." The chief gardener clicked his heels and executed an elegant bow. "Please do come again, Miss Fletcher. Mr. West."

She curtseyed, Thomas bowed, and the sight of Mr. Miller speeding off was Mr. Winston's cue to rush forward.

"Ready, Mr. West?" The barge master was on the vessel. "I lit two braziers for you. Should warm up the tent."

Daylight was all but gone. Torches flickered along the rail, and sturdy oarsmen sat at the ready. Thomas turned a keen eye on the river.

"A lively current, I see. We should make good time."

Cool air nipping her face, Mary ducked into the

tent. She bundled up with the same blanket she'd used before and waited. Outside, torches infused the tent with vermillion and amber light. Silhouettes passed back and forth. Thomas was helping Mr. Winston unmoor the pleasure barge. She knew his tall profile and watched it. The cut of his tricorn, the breadth of his shoulders. He seemed quite anxious to depart. But who would join her in the tent?

The pirate? Or the gentlemanly shipmaster?

The better question might be who would join her later tonight?

She tucked the blanket under her chin as the creaking pleasure barge heaved forward. Thomas entered the tent, shadows carving his face. He let the panels close behind him, a mantle of calm authority dressing him. But there was something else. A predacious air, perhaps.

Her pulse quickened. This would be a private ride home.

Thomas stood confident and sure, withdrawing his flask from his coat. Purposeful, methodical. He was unaffected by the swaying vessel.

She let the blanket fall to her waist. "Thank you for today."

"You're welcome." He swigged Cognac, his eyes peculiar and bright. "Current's picking up. A storm's coming."

"I like storms. They come on fast, but the next morning I wake up so . . . refreshed." She gave a feline smile. "Provided I'm safe and warm in bed when they come."

"Any sailor will tell you there's no sleeping on fast seas. A force of nature, storms."

She angled her chin high. "Fast ships, fast waters. They don't scare me."

He took another drink of Cognac, his eyes primal. "What about fast men, Miss Fletcher?"

"They don't frighten me in the slightest."

His grin was crooked. "Think you can keep up?"

"The question is can *you* keep up with me?"

He laughed and raised his flask in salute. "I'll do my best."

Skin pebbled her bottom. They were hurling at breakneck speed toward the inevitable. What began on their journey to Chelsea would conclude in a dimly lit room in a brothel—something ravenous and exquisite. Or had their journey started long before this morning? Watching Thomas sink into the couch beside her, a sense of the undeniable struck her. Today changed them. There was rampant anticipation, certainly. There was also a sharing of souls. She'd painted a clear picture of her life, her choices—enough to send brave men running.

Danger camped around her. In the haze of kisses and conversation, she hadn't forgotten tonight's *other* meeting—Miss Mitchell at midnight. The evening would be a balancing act. Thomas West's eyes sparkled as though he welcomed whatever Mary had to offer.

He offered his flask to her and she shook her head, another topic bubbling up.

"Why do you go to Maison Bedwell?"

Thomas was deliberate, corking his flask and returning it to his coat pocket. The corners of his mouth curled with amusement.

"I've wondered when you would ask."

"Funny that. I've wondered when you would tell me."

He touched the brim of his hat, a touché. Arms folded and eyes forward, Thomas settled back against the seat.

"My first visit was for a business arrangement with Ranleigh. For insurance. My usual insurer, Lloyds, sent a polite letter the first of September, informing me they could no longer insure a whaling concern." He glanced sideways at her. "Parliament announced they will no longer underwrite English whalers."

"I read about that in the papers."

Thomas squinted at the tent flaps.

"At first, all went well. Ranleigh visited the shipyard. He combed through the account books with Mr. Anstruther. He seemed interested."

"You, in turn, visited Maison Bedwell."

"I did. As a gesture of goodwill. And the gambling was an amiable pastime. Most nights I left with a fat purse." His mouth tugged at one corner. "Never discount the power of distracted men when gambling."

"You mean the harlots."

"Good brandy and bad women. An irresistible combination."

"Because men don't go to Bedwell's looking for good women," she said dryly.

The brazier's amber light colored the rugged angles of his face and made the scar a stern line across his cheek.

"I didn't sample Bedwell's harlots, if that's what you're wondering," he said as dryly as she did. Her scarred pirate stroked strands of hair on her temple. "I didn't know what I was looking for—until I saw you."

HER EYES WERE bright moonstones. They belonged to a woman who was inordinately pleased with what he'd said. It was gratifying, saying something right. Miss Fletcher inched closer, and he breathed in her plain soap and clean starch scent. For the rest of his days he would remember this. Her lush curves bumping him and the auburn in her dark hair, glinting in the brazier's light, each strand a super-fine thread. Brown seemed insignificant. Sable, or mahogany? Deep sienna, or a rich mink?

He was intent on a pretty curl when she asked, "Will Lord Ranleigh insure West and Sons Shipping?"

He let go of her hair, false assurances coming to mind. Men like him were defined by success or the lack of it. To say anything less would reveal a chink in his armor.

Miss Fletcher put a guarded inch between them and he instantly regretted his male pride.

"I apologize. That was forward of me," she said.

"No, claiming to be my wife was forward."

She dipped her head against his shoulder, the intimate gesture taking him down a notch. The simple act was rife with messages he wanted to decipher: acceptance, comfort, womanly respect. He wrapped his arm around her back, and truth's bitter medicine wasn't so awful.

"Ranleigh smelled blood in the water. Conversations turned from insurance to buying the ships and, in particular, the dockyard lease, which makes no sense. Ranleigh wouldn't know a bowsprit if it poked him in the arse."

Her giggle was sweet. "I must admit, neither do I."

"Long pole. Front of the ship."

She hummed thoughtfully. "I can see I'll get quite an education with you."

Which made his salty whaler's heart sing.

He squeezed her close. "As the weeks went by, Ranleigh became a determined suitor, if you will. I politely refused. The last time was over a game of *vingt-et-un*, which didn't end well."

"Is the matter with Lord Ranleigh done?"

"Quite done."

"There must be others willing to insure West and Sons Shipping."

"Possibly." But his tone was doubtful even to his own ears.

She smoothed the front of his coat. "I believe you are a man of many talents. You'll figure this out."

He liked the weight of her hand on his chest and the earnest belief in her eyes as though he could slay dragons.

"Aside from rope climbing and storytelling, I'm a man of few talents."

Her finger was circumnavigating a buttonhole on his coat. Was she applying her considerable talent in commerce to solving his problems? Male pride wanted to brush feminine suggestions aside, but wisdom got the better of him. Miss Fletcher had become something of a success; listening to her would be worthwhile. She'd built her business out of nothing, while he had inherited his.

"Thinking of ways to save West and Sons Shipping?" he asked.

Miss Fletcher scooted back to look at him, her face awash in gentleness. "No," she said solemnly. "I wouldn't dream of intruding."

He glanced at her brass-stained fingertip resting

on him. "I've discovered you say the most astonishing things when touching me."

Which earned him a light laugh.

"I was surprised to hear you list storytelling as a talent. Now that intrigues me."

"A necessary skill. Months at sea can be very dull." Her lashes fluttered low then rose slowly.

"Did you whisper stories to mermaids?"

Miss Fletcher's eyes shadowed with uncertainty. Gravity expanded in the small tent, spinning a tangled web.

"No mermaids," he said softly.

"Any sirens? I hear sailors keep one in every port."

"There is only one siren, and she hails from Edinburgh."

Miss Fletcher's spectral stare absorbed him. She traced his scar to his mouth, her touch featherlight.

"Sirens are beautifully horrid."

Embers of need shot to his smalls. She kissed him where her finger had been on the corner of his mouth. So much hope and thoughtfulness in the simple act. He kissed her back, tasting almond, the powder warm and sweet on her skin. This was a reconnection from their first hot, blundering kiss at Bedwell's to their stunning sensual kiss this morning.

How many varieties of kisses would they share? The answer pounded behind his breastbone. He could spend a lifetime finding the answer.

"This particular siren," he murmured against her cheek, "has sharp claws and a cool tongue."

"Hardly enticing."

"There is plenty to recommend her."

"Such as?" She kissed his chin, his jaw, the lobe of his ear. A tender torture. He couldn't touch her. If he did, it'd be his undoing, but he wouldn't tell her to stop.

Arms spread wide, he submitted to her attentions.

"She lures me with her polished Edinburgh accent."

He shivered as Miss Fletcher beaded a soft-mouthed trail down the side of his neck. Fists clenching, he forced himself not to touch her. This exploration would escalate if he did.

"As you lure her with your voice. It's not bad, for an Englishman's."

Nimble fingers untied his cravat. Cloth whispered. Waistcoat buttons were undone and the top of his shirt opened. Ragged breaths came. His, of course. Miss Fletcher was calm seduction in the flesh. She explored his neck, her enticing caresses dripping to his breastbone.

Thomas glued his gaze to the tent ceiling, his voice straining. "This siren of whom we speak is not for the Union, I collect."

"She is of the Jacobite variety," she said between kisses.

He was English to the bone, and he'd long suspected the corset maker favored Scotland's independence. Her garden confession today confirmed it.

But the rebellion ended seven years ago.

It was time for all and sundry to move on. He'd hired Scots straight off the prison hulks when most wouldn't. Nothing bonded men better than working toward a common goal—if they avoided tetchy topics. It was best he and the corset maker aired this. A surprising development, actually. It had taken months before he and the Scots who labored for him broached the Uprising.

He and Miss Fletcher had already talked intimately of sex. Why not add the powder keg of politics?

Unfortunately, the topic caused Miss Fletcher's hand to stop its delightful exploration of his body.

"I presume your heart belongs to the crown," she said.

He gusted an exhale and met her gaze. Intent, focused, trying hard to think straight.

"The realm has my loyalty, not my heart." He twitched a taut smile. "My heart is another matter entirely."

Her brows slanted with disapproval.

"The Uprising doesn't matter to you? At all?"

Miss Fletcher's sharpness carved a moat around his heart. There was a message here. The corset maker welcomed their expanding lust, but it came with a warning: tender emotions would have to scale the walls of her staunch beliefs.

Very well.

"I don't give a shite about a war that ended seven years ago."

It was a blunt but salty answer—as a man does when his placket argues for brevity. He loved England, and his loyalty was true, but the Government manufactured enemies like cloth—one long roll after another. His French mother made sure he'd learned that.

"We don't have to speak of anything that divides us," Miss Fletcher said. "I've already decided that I shall enjoy you . . . for however long we last."

He flinched, deep in his solar plexus.

"Decided that, have you?"

Her gentle declaration pummeled him. Hand flexing against the cushion, he wanted the enigmatic

Scotswoman. Not piecemeal kisses and conversations. *Her.* Underneath them, the pleasure barge creaked in the swollen current racing them back to London and their first night together. He should be overjoyed. An evening of lust sated.

It wasn't enough.

Miss Fletcher shocked him by nestling her head in his lap.

"Let us not waste a splendid day on such things, Mr. West." Her moonstone eyes glimmered. "I'd much rather test your storytelling skills."

The Scotswoman was beautiful. A wild thing, her face half-shadowed, hair spilling wantonly, her mouth a rosy smudge. A little lower, her ever-present medallion choker gleamed. It was the first time he noticed the number nine etched in the metal—the symbol of a stouthearted Jacobite.

Sobered, he touched the gold piece resting in the well of her neck. No. They'd not waste a moment together.

"What kind of story would you like?"

"Something with adventure and intrigue," she cooed. "A romance, definitely."

"Do you favor them? Romances?"

She stretched like a contented cat and linked a hand with his.

"On occasion."

He liked this, the two of them holding hands.

"We had a tradition on our ships. Whoever could spin an interesting tale over the most nights won a half guinea when we returned home. We tracked it with a tally chart."

"It sounds like a wonderful tradition."

"My father started it, and I've kept it going."

"A nice reward, a half guinea."

"You should know I won three summers in a row."
She gaped in mock wonder. "That good, are you?"

"I am."

"Please, do regale me, sir. If your story pleases me,
you shall have your reward."

"If I can sustain my tale . . ."

"We've a month of nights ahead of us." She
squeezed his hand. "I've no doubt you shall dazzle
me, sir."

He ached to say he wanted her days too. To spend
them in common places. Leadenhall's Market, a
promenade around St. James, visiting public houses
to decide which one served the best beef stew. Instead, he buried those unsafe declarations. His corset
maker wasn't ready to hear them, and if he knew anything about hunting, patience was a worthy weapon.

A small nod and, "You start the tale by giving me
a place or a character. It's West and Sons tradition."

A hush filled the tent. He was stroking bare skin
on her forearm. So, so soft was this small real estate
of flesh. He contented himself with the slight touch
even though he wanted much more. More than her
body, more than her heart, more than her soul—all of
her. To spend his nights writhing in passion with the
corset maker and his days discovering the mundane.
This was life, exotic and pure, finding perfection in
how she dressed, how she threaded a needle, or enjoyed her soup. Simple wants, each one.

They chipped away at his heart.

Enigmatic light reflected in her eyes. She was bold,
dragging their clasped hands over her heart.

"Tell me the story of the scarred shipmaster and
the siren."

Chapter Twenty-One

Hours later . . .

To prepare for an assignation in a brothel, the adventurous spinster must carefully arm herself with rouged cheeks, carmined lips, and artfully pinned hair. Delicate weapons, each one. They'd be smeared or removed, but were necessary accoutrements, nonetheless. Their purpose: to engage a rugged gentleman in the sensual art of war.

And she did adore Mr. West's dockside edge. Hewn from the sea, burnished by the sun, he was rough refinement. No doubt he'd lent his smile to women in other ports.

Tonight he was hers alone.

Velvet slipping off her shoulders, Mary welcomed the coming battle. Tender goose bumps peppered her skin. Her nipples peaked. She'd never felt so alive, crossing Maison Bedwell's threshold as though an undiscovered world awaited her. The frescoed nymphs looking down approved. She was entering the evening fray without a mask. A bold move. Very bold.

The footman taking her cloak blinked twice. "Miss . . . Fletcher."

His fingers brushing hers stoked excitement. So did the flirtatious slide of his mouth.

"Connor's my name, miss." A polite cough and, "We didn't meet directly, but you helped the lot of us with the fountain." Azure eyes sparkled above a smattering of freckles. "The lads and I are most grateful."

Her pulse quickened. Visions of Connor, water sluicing his braw shirtless chest, sprang to mind. This could be dangerous, being known in a brothel.

"I am glad I could be of service."

He was careful, draping her cloak over his arm. "Are you here for a particular entertainment?"

Friendly fire banked in azure eyes. Genuine, thrilling, and a touch solicitous as to put the power in her hands. The feeling was delicious. Smiling warmly, she tipped her head a degree, the rust on her feminine wiles sliding off.

"As it happens, I am."

The footman cocked his head, curious. "Is there a chance I might help you, miss?"

Connor's Irish brogue was playing nicely on her ears. He held her gaze and stood, a gentleman at the ready. Her wish would be his command. An intoxicating premise. If it wasn't for a certain sea wolf, she'd cave. Or worse, she'd come here every week and hand over all her shop's profits for the drug Connor was selling.

Did Lord Ranleigh give tutorials on how to seduce

a woman? The average man fresh from the country-side couldn't be this nuanced.

Or am I a little desperate for intimacy? A leveling thought.

She touched Connor's velvet sleeve. "Yours is a kind offer, but another gentleman will . . . help me."

Help? Lud. She sounded like a maiden aunt in need of a tup.

Entertain, seduce, enthrall—these would be more honest.

"My loss, miss." Connor sketched a bow and glanced at the hallway. "But if your gentleman dis-appoints, please find me."

Newcomers crested the front door, laughing, chattering, the men dropping good coin into Con-nor's outstretched palm. She took the chance to fade into the hubbub that filled the entry, but at the hallway's turn she looked back. Connor wasn't watching her. She was a transaction. A means to his livelihood's end.

Crestfallen, she'd been duped. A sea wolf's hot kisses by day, and a footman's flirtatious touch by night. Her footfalls landed on thick carpet, the hall-way awash in light and noise. The Red Rose room waited at the end. A quiet place. The door closed. Pleasure waiting to happen. Digging for the key in her pocket, she wouldn't play the fool. A vow ex-tracted nearly fifteen years ago rang in her head.

Do not let men turn your head. Ever.

They never would.

Chapter Twenty-Two

$\mathcal{T}$homas waited by the fireplace, a patient man. Years of hunting on the North Sea left him battered but strong, and his thirst for life steady—pleasures of the flesh included. But this was peculiar, him close to bedding a beautiful woman, yet he couldn't stop thinking about her heart. He was equally certain her heart was the one treasure she'd never give away. The corset maker would come to him in body but keep her emotions safely hidden. Like a treasure.

He drew in a long, taut breath. Her body was a most desirable treasure, and he was base enough to admit they would indulge each other's whim.

Eyes closing, he verged on reckless.

He'd have no peace. Every part of him, inside and out, was amplified. Distant noises intruded, Maison Bedwell's usual antics reaching his ears. Behind his eyelids, he could see Mary's face curving to his. Their quick, stolen kisses in a steamy glasshouse, the leaves of the banana tree hiding them. Her moonstone eyes imploring him to tell her a story while she'd rested her head in his lap. What sweet torture.

Hairs on his nape stirred. When he opened his eyes, hall light traced Mary Fletcher's silhouette.

"You're early," she said, shutting the door on the rest of the world.

He tried to be casual, checking the clock. Nine o'clock it read. "You're on time, per usual."

She strode forward, petticoats swaying seductively. He gripped the mantel, her swishing silks mild torture. Their time together on the pleasure barge lingered like the dregs of potent wine.

His pretty corset maker cupped his shaved jaw with aching gentleness. "You smell like . . . heaven."

Pleasure rippled through his legs. He was about to be used for her pleasure.

"I visited Neville Warehouse. A cleanup was necessary."

"Your visit to Neville Warehouse—to prepare for tomorrow's sale, I presume."

"Yes."

Tension increased under his skin. Mary drew a delicate circle on his chin, the beginning of her campaign. She was focused, his corset maker. Her nimble hands outlining his shoulders and finding the shape of his chest, molding the wide curve of his pectoral muscles. Arousal marched just under his flesh, slow and steady.

Pale otherworldly eyes sought his.

"You will let me have my way with you, won't you? To explore you and to . . ." She hesitated, a womanly smile growing in the shadows. "Well, you understand."

"I do."

His voice was lust-scratched, and they were both still properly dressed. Miss Fletcher was intent on changing that. He submitted to her questing hands, untying his cravat in her unhurried way. A careful tug, one hand, then two. Tender sounds followed. Skin brushing cloth and linen slipping free, all of it dispatching a crackle of electricity down the length of his spine.

She sent his neckwear fluttering to the floor.

"Why, Mr. West, I believe I must inspect the goods."

He grunted. *Saucy wench.*

He stared hungrily at her. "Will I see you tomorrow?"

Shite. He had it bad. They'd barely begun this assignation and he was already planning the next one.

Her hand slithered artfully to his placket. "As it happens, I do need more bones and baleen."

Her eyes sparkled, vivid and playful.

She reached up and spread his shirt wider at the neck and buried her nose against him. He'd not touch her . . . not yet. Her butterfly kisses teased his chest. His eyelids were heavy. His head too. He wanted all her days and nights but he couldn't think about that now. Blood moved, steamy and sluggish, in his veins, no part of him wishing to rush carnal delights. Clever hands freed buttons on his waistcoat. Mary was adept, plundering his neck, his earlobes, his collarbones, with her hot mouth.

He stood still and took her sweet attack.

A tender quake shook him. Mary had dressed herself in confident fashion.

"That first night, when you stood behind me," she whispered, "I thought you smelled like an expensive mistake."

Spectral gray eyes peered up at him. Open, feline,

ready for anything and daring him to be the same. Mary reached for his placket and tugged, gently. The jolt shot to his penis. His ballocks ached and his pulse roared.

She flicked the first button like an expert tavern wench. "Ever since that night I've wondered what's in your soap?"

Another button slipped free, and both her hands were on an expedition over his placket.

His grip on the mantel tightened, the stone edge digging into his palm. He was holding on with all his might.

"Aren't you going to tell me?" she asked archly.

"Tell y—"

He inhaled like a dying man when her hand slipped inside his breeches. His John Thomas was quite happy. That part told him he was alive. Blood-engorged and anxious to be petted. Mary stroked him, her hand outside his smalls.

Air heaved in and out of his lungs. The more she explored, the more heightened his sensations—one rush after another. His legs shook, and he was rogue enough to admit he lived for what was going on in his smalls. The linen caressing his flesh. The rustle of cloth. Mary's warm hand playing with him.

She was quite creative.

"Your soap . . ." She popped another button from its hole. "An intoxicating potion."

His breeches slouched. His knees trembled. *Shite.* He reached for her, weak as a newborn lamb.

Gray eyes glittered with mischief. He hooked his fingers in Mary's bodice and hauled her to him. She laughed, her hand flattening in his placket and her mouth inches from his.

"Sure you want to talk about soap?" He barely finished before devouring her mouth.

Feral urges swamped him, so primal, he couldn't think straight. He yanked hard on her bodice. Pins tumbled. Her stomacher sagged. Mary's eyes rounded as the robe à la française slackened off her shoulders. Fire glowed softly on her shoulders. He shoved her gown lower and they kissed. Hard. Frantic. Desperate kisses. Wet and imperfect.

He bit, sucked, and pulled.

Mary's carnal kisses were her answer.

What torment, her passionate mouth on his, her fingers exploring his ballocks, cupping and rolling them like a practiced harlot. Lust arrowed through him. So sharp and hot and nearly painful.

Shite. He was about to spend himself inside his smalls.

Clutching her arms, he broke away.

They were panting hard.

Firelight painted Mary in orange and yellow. Her high cheeks, her linen-covered breasts. She tipped her chin, a haughty angle. The same as when the corset maker won an argument on the docks.

One sight wrecked him—round nipples jutting against her shift. The light caressing them, molding their shape.

The image burned him.

He bent over her cleavage, his breath stirring her shift's little bow. Her sweet curves pebbled. Little goose bumps disappeared into the prettiest cleavage he'd ever seen. How mysterious that shadowed line. He set his mouth on it, open and hot. She hissed and cupped the back of his head, encouraging him. He took the bow between his teeth and yanked it.

Linen ripping was a satisfying sound. A small tear, two inches. He could've done worse.

Mary's breath skittered when he looked her in the eye.

He was none too gentle, dragging down her shift. Her breasts spilled, their fullness perfection. Pearlescent and swaying. He stared, awed. Reverent. His jaw slack. Moments slipped by. Time was nothing until he forced his gaze upward.

Her soft-lipped smile said *I've conquered you.*

Shite. She had.

"You like it rough, do you?" he growled.

"I like you." She was nonchalant. A natural at this.

Teeth clenching, he was irritated at her power to turn him into a base animal. Like a starving man too weak to fight nature's need, he stared at her breasts. Round and soft, the tips more russet than pink.

Impertinent nipples.

He touched the end of one with the pad of his thumb. Barely there circles, so light. So erotic. She moaned, her body twitching from sheer pleasure. He peacocked, glad to give as good as he got.

"Now do you want to talk about soap?" His ragged voice shredded his words.

Mary's laugh was husky, her body melting into his. He could count their heartbeats, standing this close. Better was the intimacy in her little laugh—an admission, power belonged to him too. But this would be an evocative night-long battle. The possibilities . . . endless. As though confirming this, Mary slid her hand inside his smalls with a *take that* smile.

White-hot pleasure shocked him. He wheezed when the heel of her palm rubbed him.

"I'd rather you tell me a story," she said.

The confident woman. Her eyes glittered darkly.

"A story—that is a surprise."

"Your voice, it calms me," she confessed.

Arousal seeped through his abdomen. His thighs were taut. Her clever hand busy. Small noises were magnified. Rasping cloth, her studied breaths. Wispy curls falling on her neck. The fire's leaping flames were witnessing an excellent seduction. If the enterprising corset maker kept this up, he would spend himself in his smalls.

A corner of his mouth hitched. "Have a care, or you'll have a mess on your hands."

She stopped, her forehead dipping beguilingly against his chest. Dark curls shimmered on her back. He cosseted their silkiness, the strands dripping through his fingers. Reluctantly, he brought her playful hand to his mouth and kissed her palm. Smelling himself on her hand was primal. She'd leave tonight, wearing his scent.

"Do you know what's wrong here?" he asked.

"No." Her eyes fixed on him. "I thought this was going rather well."

"What's wrong is you're talking in complete sentences." He kissed her wrist, lingering on her skin. "Which means I've not done my job . . ." He kissed her pale forearm. "Because if I had, you'd be lust-addled"—he kissed the crook of her elbow—"and speechless."

She swallowed hard. "What do you propose?"

Chapter Twenty-Three

*et me do whatever I want to you." Thomas was pensive, focused.

"For a story?" Her voice pitched higher.

She was, after all, standing, breasts bared, negotiating wanton acts.

Her mouth dried as flesh between her legs trickled wetness. Behind those persuasive green eyes her sea wolf was hatching a plan. This turn shouldn't come as a surprise, him thinking about tonight, anticipating it. She knew why they were here—she'd planned this, for goodness' sake. But nothing prepared her for the primeval rush. For everything magnified. The heightened scent of his skin or the smell of whatever soap his laundress must use. The feel of his clothes, his skin, his body.

Easing into this would've been preferable. Five years had made her rusty, and the clock's *tick-tock* was conspicuously loud. She checked it. *Two and a half hours 'til midnight.* It wouldn't do to miss her meeting with Miss Mitchell, but she feared she might.

Thomas West was the drug she couldn't refuse.

He followed her sight line to the clock. "Got some-where else to be?"

His question lit a match. *Why not play along?* was the fire flaring inside her.

She flirted with the open button flash of his waist-coat. "No. Nowhere else but with you." Like a proper sensualist, she strolled to the bed, an impudent hand on her hip. "Want me here?"

Gem-hard eyes sharpened in the shadows.

"I want you on the bed, naked."

Her blood was liquid fuel set aflame. Thomas was backlit by fire, his smile ruthless.

"Undress for me," he said.

She felt her lips part, velvety and slow. If their rough play lit a match, his telling her what to do scorched her. The longer he watched, the more her mind surrendered to a haze. She could be an odal-isque serving the conquering sea wolf. His danger-ous scar only added to her excitement.

Flooded and sensual, she worked her front-laced stays. The ties slid through her fingers like water, slipping this way and that, until the useless garment fell. It was heady, this undressing while Thomas's uncivilized stare ravaged her.

Reaching behind her back, she couldn't take her eyes off him.

The things he would do. The places he would touch . . .

Her breasts jostled, supple and heavy, and her nipples poked forward. Cold air pinched them. Thomas's predatory smile faded. His visage be-came stark and destroyed.

Her breasts were his weakness.

Arms still behind her back, she thrusted them forward. "The story . . . or I stop."

Thomas's eyes became green slits.

"Always seeking the most advantageous terms."

"Nothing wrong with a woman asking for what she wants."

Which tasted foreign on her tongue. A fine sentiment in commerce, but this was her gloriously letting go.

The corner of his mouth curled with approval. "A tale, then," he said softly.

She waited, her fingers snagging on the tapes of her petticoat. His voice really did things to her. Its cadence, smooth and jagged in perfect measure. His occasional dockside accent.

And so he began, "There once was a fair ship. Bold, beautiful, her lines sleek. She ruled the North Sea, but make no mistake, she was a saucy piece, this ship, with the prettiest pair of . . . masts."

Mary giggled. "Masts are not pretty."

He arched a wicked brow. "These two are. And I'll bid you to remember this is my story."

"Consider me duly chastised."

She was buoyant and pleased, undoing her petticoat. The tapes were flimsy but agreeable. Thomas began to undo more waistcoat buttons, his long, agile fingers careful, adroit. She watched them until her gaze found his eyes sparkling with humor as though he understood the tempo of their assignation must strike a perfect balance. Not too fast and not too slow.

Thomas let his waistcoat fall to his feet. Her fingers got clumsy when she noticed his open placket. Brown curls sprang above his smalls—the part of him she'd touched but hadn't seen.

"Her masts were a remarkable sight, curving high and proud," he went on. "The foresail and the mainsail, as it happens. An indispensable pair."

Her red-and-white-striped petticoat drifted down her legs. "On a ship, these would be?"

"Why, the largest pair."

"Of course."

She was certain she dimpled. Thomas delighted in spinning this story. He was a sight, his waistcoat loose and shirt half-untucked.

"She was finely curved," he said. "Her contours elegant. As well crafted as any ship could be."

Chin to chest, Mary set to work on her underskirt and panniers, aware that he might end with a laugh and a naughty limerick.

Humor, however, would not be his lure. His deliberate heel strikes were.

Like a startled doe, she raised her head. He was coming for her.

Air stirred against her skin. Her pannier and underskirt puddled around her feet. She clutched her shift to her belly, challenging his hungry stare until he drifted behind her and brushed aside her hair. Precious seconds were spent waiting, the back of her ablaze.

Thomas drew a worshipful line in the furrow of her spine.

Tiny quakes erupted. Everywhere. Intense shocks of pleasure falling from the crown of her head to her bottom.

Her sea wolf's hand tarried at the small of her back. "She was capable of riding any storm."

His humor was a Trojan horse. She'd remember that when Thomas let her have her body back.

"Fierce storms, calm seas," he murmured, stroking her again and again. "She soared through them all."

He traced her ribs, her shoulder blades. Innocuous bones. She was heavy eyed and grateful Thomas found them. An artful sculptor, he adored each one.

"Finely curved, indeed," he whispered.

He touched her as though her torso was the rarest treasure. Tracing her ribs, memorizing the dip of her waist, her hip still covered with cloth. Her hold on her shift was feeble. The linen too much. Fabric falling down her thighs was met by a warm caress on her bottom.

Her eyes flew open.

Not a hand, a feather!

One of the implements from the bedside table. She blinked fast, the room's fire, piercing and bright to her lust-blurred eyes. Thomas was using the frippery to sketch a line through her bottom's crevice to the backs of her knees.

"On the bow of this ship was a womanly figurehead. Beautifully carved, beautifully painted." Thomas kissed the ball of her shoulder. "Her eyes were the color of North Sea lightning."

His mouth lingered on her shoulder, her shoulder blade, places she'd never thought erotic.

She was grateful for them now.

Her lashes were heavy. Her limbs like quicksilver. She turned her face to his, tried to see him, but he eluded her, busy as he was, feathering her backside. She couldn't move. Carnal shivers had taken over. Her head lolled sideways, its weight too much. Thomas was stroking her hips with his hand and the feather, the contrast a delight.

"Sailors claimed she was a North Sea siren punished by Poseidon."

"Punished?"

She tried to be coherent. Thomas's laugh was a diabolical rumble.

"Poseidon forced her to live untouched on the bow."

A ticklish sensation stopped her from asking why. She looked down. Light played on something blue-green and dandelion-soft poking between her thighs. The eye of the peacock feather.

Would Thomas drag it up? Or down?

She pressed a hand against her abdomen. The ache, palpable.

Thomas's face was in her side vision. Amber light smudged his features and turned the tips of his lashes golden. His smile creased blade-sharp.

"What'll it be? The story? Or the feather?"

A dangerous taunt.

Her mouth opened but her tongue refused to answer. She was as shimmery and lithesome as the iridescent feather between her legs. Thomas decided for her, stroking her inner thighs with the feathery tip. Sweet waves skittered across her skin. Air hissed past her lips.

"Like that, do you?" he asked hoarsely.

Small, tender brushes went on and on and on. Down her stocking-covered calves. Across her bottom, her back, her shoulders. Until the feather slipped between her legs. Watching it was torture. The blue-green eye rose, inch by agonizing inch, almost touching her quim.

She swayed, waiting for it. Wanting it.

"On the bed." Thomas was gruff and the story forgotten.

She didn't question him. Her sea wolf obviously knew what he was doing. She only hoped the feather was part of whatever came next. She wasn't above begging for it.

Raising a knee, she navigated the mattress. She was arms and legs, striving. Awkward. Coolness shocked delicate, wet flesh between her legs. Years she'd climbed into bed. She should do it competently. But Thomas watched her. Protective and sensual, his hand on her bottom. She could be his most treasured war prize—or she spent too many evenings reading salacious stories.

Her heart galloped. Her labia slicked. And she tingled deliciously from head to toe.

A new tremor was building. A quickening.

Sinking into the plush mattress, she felt it. Watching Thomas undo the last buttons on his placket, she felt it. Spreading her legs while he stretched out beside her, she felt it. This gnawing, slamming sensation.

This was the bargain they'd struck.

She grabbed his hand and guided it to the apex of her legs. "Touch me."

His lust-dark eyes flared in surprise.

"I'm not wasting another minute with you," she whispered, desperate.

His ravenous mouth swooped onto hers, and she eagerly dug both hands through his hair.

Thomas's fingers were tender and imaginative, stroking her curls, parting her cleft, while he kissed her. His tongue was velvet on hers. When he drew a line through her inner folds of skin, she bowed off the bed, need shocking her.

Wet snicks matched the sweltering heat inside her. Thomas strummed her flesh—so, so thoughtful.

Her head was heavy, falling back. Her legs spreading wide. How could he be this intimately acquainted with her?

Her moans increased. She was writhing against him. Soft touches vanished. The beauty was gone. Their kisses were fierce. Imperfect. She couldn't get enough.

Thomas grunted when she grabbed his shoulders and held on tight. The storm's fury expanded, tightening her spine until she groaned an animal sound.

"Please!" she cried.

Her legs were shaking. Her skin sheened. Thomas rolled onto her, growling unintelligible words. He was heavy, but not forceful enough. She had to have him. *Now.* Brass buttons pressed her thighs. The bed squeaked and rattled. Her needy hips were rocking against him.

She was breathless. "I need you inside me."

Thomas unleashed salty words, bracing a forearm on the bed and reaching frantically inside his breeches.

"Doing my best." His voice was as ragged as his smile.

Knuckles and fingers grazed her slippery flesh. Thomas and his urgent fingers. There was smooth pressure between her legs. Thomas was panting, touching his forehead to hers. The crown of his penis slipped against her.

And then—sweet heaven—he pushed.

"Yes!" She arched into him.

He slid deep inside her. Eyes wide open, she whimpered. Him filling her was exquisite. She understood the savagery queens would commit for their kings. To sate this craving. To chase it ruthlessly and gorge on it. Thomas buried his face in her shoulder, his body shaking as though he, too, couldn't fathom the depths of their joining.

Euphoric stillness didn't last.

Mutual hunger demanded to be fed, a hot base pursuit with Thomas leading the way. They were desperate and fast. Skin slapping skin, she met his fervor, her hands reaching for terra firma. She found the bed linens, scratching and clawing them. Forgetting herself.

Her hoarse groans escalated. Her peak was coming. The force of it stunning.

Thomas's hands bracketed her face. "Remember what this feels like."

Memory had no hold on her. She was soaring through erotic clouds. Beautifully lost yet found. London and Scotland, the past and present blurred. Feeling was all she could do—the utter cleaving of body and soul. She was vivid and burning. A sensualist to the bone. And Thomas—handsome, brutal, and wrecked—fixated on her. His impossible green eyes searing her.

He was part of her. He always would be. This was the ferocious message in his eyes.

Mary tipped her head and let go. There was nothing else but to ride the brutal freedom ripping through her.

Chapter Twenty-Four

*M*ary tiptoed to the door after dressing hastily. She'd fought the drug of sleep, barely. Thomas, however, slept like the dead, sprawled naked as one does after a sound tupping. Two of them, actually. Near the end the tenderest bed sport took place. Gentle games, sweet touches, and explorations as though both knew they had to ride the rough storm before finding tranquil seas.

She looked at him fondly. Half his face in a pillow, sun-streaked hair falling. Firelight painted his arse gold, the taut muscle scooped at the side—the sea wolf transformed to a sea god at rest. All of him was golden.

There'd never be another night like this.

She pinched her medallion, the metal warm. Some treasures could only be touched once. This night was one of them. During their time together, Thomas had removed every stitch of clothing except her choker. He'd said a woman dressed in nothing but jewelry was alluring, which had her wondering.

Had Thomas courted a wealthy woman?

Chewing her bottom lip, she turned the door latch

with the softest click. *No need to go melancholy.* She had a month of nights with Thomas. Confidences shared were optional.

Exiting the Red Rose room, she winced at noise and light blasting her.

"You're late." A surly Miss Mitchell emerged from an alcove.

The harlot was garbed as a bird of paradise. Maison Bedwell hosted another faux circus. Smoke and thunderous applause came from the ballroom. Very disorienting. Mary touched her head.

"Forgive me. I lost track of time."

"Three hours with a man like Mr. West'll do that, I suppose. Not that I'd know, mind you." Miss Mitchell tilted her head at the empty end of the hallway. "Shall we?"

There'd be no easing into this, not with the harlot speeding down the hallway and Mary trotting to keep up with her. They neared the end when Miss Mitchell pressed a floral plaster medallion on the wall. The medallion sank into the wall and beside it, the wall clicked a half inch open. The harlot stood in front of it and checked the brothel's hallway. A footman was leading three gentlemen into the gaming room. None took note of the opposite end of the hall.

"Keep up with me," the harlot whisper-hissed. "I'm in no mood to rescue you should you lose your way."

Miss Mitchell pulled open the door and they quickly entered a dark passage. They headed down a short stack of stairs, the harlot calling back, "If anyone crosses our path, I'm taking you to meet Mrs. Bedwell. Got it?"

"Yes." Mary gulped air. The sensual fog in her head wasn't helping.

They scurried along an unlit hallway. Limestone walls captured moonlight from a small window at the far end of the passage, but they weren't going that way. The harlot turned abruptly and opened a door to a musty storage room—at least, this was Mary's guess while she waited for her eyes to adjust. Damp air chilled her. She rubbed her arms for warmth, bumping into barrels and crates in the cramped room. Thudding and scraping sounded. Miss Mitchell was shoving and stacking crates until a rough-planked wall was visible.

The harlot jammed the heel of her hand against a plank. Warped wood gave way. Gray light crept in, forming a path from Mary's feet to a rich chamber beyond.

Miss Mitchell beckoned. "This way."

Swiping dust from her petticoats, Mary followed the harlot's bouncing tail feathers. She nabbed a quick study of the mysterious door. Warped planks on one side, a bookcase on the other. To a library, possibly. She couldn't be sure since Miss Mitchell was hell-bent on racing out of the unfurnished room. Mary tried to keep up.

The entire house appeared to be unlit. No sconce burning for the master coming home late. Every ten steps Mary glanced back to memorize the way they'd come. No wonder Lord Ranleigh preferred the brothel. This house was polished but cold. Scant furnishings. No art on the wall. The chandeliers entombed in cloth. What a lonely place.

"Fortunate for you," the harlot said over her shoulder, "the footman who watches the house has it bad for my friend Molly. I've promised her a half guinea to keep him occupied in the mews for an hour. That ought to give you plenty of time to search the premises."

They turned down a carpeted hall and stopped at the first wide door.

Miss Mitchell blocked the entrance. "Of course, if you don't have a half guinea on your person, that gold piece you're wearing works."

Mary's hand flew to her medallion tied to her neck. Each woman in her league had one.

"You want payment now?"

"Now is as good a time as any."

"You should've told me."

The harlot was disdainful. "You think I can plan for every little thing that *might* go wrong."

Mary squared her shoulders. She wouldn't argue the merits of thinking ahead.

"You'll have your half guinea when you come to my shop."

Miss Mitchell gusted a sigh. "I suppose that'll do." She swung the door open and let Mary pass. "You'll find what you're looking for in here."

Moonlight flooded the chamber, its curtainless window facing King's Square. Mary swept deeper inside, marveling at moonbeams cutting diamond-bright prisms on a chandelier left uncovered.

She took two more steps, drawn to a row of paintings propped against the wall. One of them was the seated Betty Burke, the artwork she saw in the gaming room her first night at Maison Bedwell. Miss Mitchell had said the seated Betty Burke had been replaced by a portrait of Betty Burke reclining in bed—the secret society's message to meet the following week.

She would search the cabinets behind the paintings, except whining hinges sent a chill up her spine. She spun around.

Miss Mitchell was closing the door.

Mary ran toward it. "Wait! How do I get out of here?"

Through the crack, the harlot's eyes pitied her.

"That's the thing, miss. You're not leaving."

Chapter Twenty-Five

*O*nce the door was shut, Julian casually crossed one leg over another. He'd been sitting in the dark for half an hour, which was twenty-nine minutes too long. He didn't wait for women. They waited for him. This newfound patience intrigued his henchwoman, Ilsa. She called this phenomenon the corset-maker effect. An untidy theorem. His was simpler. Miss Fletcher was an objective—his, of course.

Unfortunately, she was running helter-skelter toward a closing door.

He traced the braided trim on his coat. Minor chaos was to be expected.

"Miss Fletcher," he called out.

She twisted around so fast her hems whipped her legs. She might've paled, though it was hard to tell in the cavernous room.

"We've got to stop meeting like this," he said. "Otherwise, the good folk of King's Square will gossip."

"You!"

Miss Fletcher charged him like a Fury. Hair in disarray, rage on her face, yet beautiful enough to steal his breath. She was two paces from accosting him when a pistol cocked. His late-night guest froze, searching for the source of that deadly *click*.

Ilsa emerged from the shadows, her pistol drawn. "To think you called her *glacial*."

His henchwoman's accent gave an up-and-down treatment of the king's English. *Swedes* . . .

Miss Fletcher stiffened as one does when a lethal weapon is aimed at one's heart.

"An accurate assessment. I stand by it. Catching her unawares like this must be off-putting. Some feathers will need smoothing, I collect."

"I don't think so." Ilsa honed her aim on the corset maker. "Miss Fletcher is made of . . . What is it you English say? Sterner stuff?"

"An adequate description," he said.

"Nevertheless, you should be careful," Ilsa warned. "Your brain is in your breeches when it comes to this woman."

Amused, he fixed a lace cuff. "You say that about all the pretty brunette corset makers with plump . . . cheeks."

He ignored Ilsa's stern side-eye and soaked up his wrathful guest and her lovely heaving bosom.

"Is it necessary to talk so rudely about me?" Miss Fletcher interjected with the hauteur of a disapproving Scottish nurse. "I am within earshot."

He laughed. "If you only knew what I've said about you when you weren't in earshot."

His attempt to lighten the mood didn't work. Miss Fletcher glared at Ilsa.

"Unless you're ordering me to stand and deliver, that pistol is unnecessary. I am unarmed and light in the purse."

"Ranleigh said you like to take charge."

Miss Fletcher shifted, uneasy. He waved off the pistol.

"Put it down before our guest flays us with her scolding tongue."

Ilsa obeyed with militaristic precision, tucking the pistol into a leather holster tied to her thigh. A terse flick of blond ringlets was her small rebellion. He welcomed it. The Swede was keenly perceptive. Men were blunt tools, heavy-handed and rarely nuanced. Women, on the other hand, were precision instruments capable of great subtlety.

He gestured to the chair facing his. "Please, have a seat."

"Do I have a choice?" Miss Fletcher asked.

"Of course you do. Stay standing, if that's your preference. My offer stems from excellent manners drubbed into me as a wayward boy. And if that doesn't entice you, there's this." He picked up a small ledger off the chess table and offered it to her.

"What is it?"

"Information about the Jacobite gold you've hunted. In particular, proof that it's all gone."

Miss Fletcher eyed him like a viper bearing gifts. "And you're just going to hand it over."

"That is the idea."

Her doubtful huff was to be expected. This was a lot to absorb, and if he were in her shoes, he'd be wary of an enemy's sudden generosity, and the disappointment coming with it. She'd devoted four years to finding the Lost Treasure of Arkaig. He couldn't help but admire her for it. Her spirit, her tenacity. And if that wasn't enough, he'd happily spend the night admiring her extraordinary face. Her eyes in the dark were ethereal.

And so damned silver.

Ilsa snorted, irritated. "Sit down and read the ledger."

Miss Fletcher snatched the book, seated herself in the opposite chair, and started riffling the pages.

"I can't read it. The light is inadequate."

He snapped his fingers. "Ilsa. The candles."

While Ilsa was striking tinder at the mantel, Miss Fletcher angled the ledger in moonlight. She wore the signs of a woman who'd indulged her passion and dressed in haste. Her unfettered hair. A bruised, well-kissed mouth. Her stomacher askew and her shift puckering, its white linen tie sadly torn and hanging over her bodice.

She might as well announce *I just had a life-altering tup.*

He brushed his silk sleeve, vexed. "Would you like me to summarize? It would help us get to the point."

"I'm at a disadvantage, my lord."

A page was turned slowly as though she wanted to string him along. *The minx.*

"Here I am, caught sneaking around your home. You could call for Bow Street and have me hauled off. Instead, you've offered me a seat in an exceedingly comfortable chair and handed over, what I imagine, is a treasonous ledger." Looking up from the pages, she speared him with an acerbic stare. "So why don't *you* get to the point?"

Ilsa set the candelabra on the table. "I like her."

"She can be entertaining when her claws are sheathed."

"The evening's far from over, my lord," was Miss Fletcher's retort.

Light from the candelabra glinted on her choker's gold medallion. The corset maker was a dark-haired lioness. Beautiful, yes. But she'd operated in London for some years—without his notice. And that made her dangerous.

He planted both elbows on the chair's arms, his fingers steepling. "You're here for two reasons. The first is the Treasure of Arkaig."

Her eyes rounded. "Are you giving it to me?"

"I can't," he said, summoning patience. "It's gone."

"Why should I believe you?"

"You shouldn't. That ledger, however, supports my claim."

"And you're sharing it out of the goodness of your heart?"

There was a bite in her voice. She ought to be careful, or he'd bite back. Clamping his molars, he coaxed himself. Patience was necessary, and he was so close to the ultimate prize.

Mellow light drew his eye to the black knight on the table between them. He picked up the chess piece. His favorite, damaged yet polished. Like him.

"I don't have a heart. And your quips, however warranted, are wearing thin."

He was deadly serious.

His guest sat up, alert, her troubled gaze shooting between him and Ilsa blowing gently on tinder flaring to life in the fireplace. If he took Miss Fletcher's pulse, it'd bang hard at the intrusion of his testing finger. He had himself to thank for that. But to woo her to his purpose, certain explanations were inevitable.

"I can give a loose accounting of the gold once it crossed the border," he said. "It's all right there."

"I recognize some of the names." She propped the open book on the table's edge. "It says here Donald Macpherson of Breachachie moved the gold to the Scottish border for the sum of six hundred pounds."

"A grubby Jacobite."

By her pinched smile, she agreed. "From there it was stored in a barn belonging to the Selby family."

"English Catholics sympathetic to the Stuart cause," he confirmed. "They refused payment."

"But you don't say how much gold crossed the border. For an accounting book, the entries are deplorable."

He stroked the trim on his wide cuff. "Accounting—not one of my strengths."

She skimmed the page with a hurried finger. "There's only a column of payments. A small amount to a Major Kennedy, seventeen hundred gold livres to a shipping partnership of which Lady Denton is the receiver, and the last entry"—her breath snagged—"paid to Charles Stuart, September, 1750."

"Major Kennedy took the money from the Selby's barn and delivered it to Lady Pink here in London. You know her as the Countess of Denton, my cousin. She brought the gold to Charles Selby's bank where it remained in safe keeping."

Miss Fletcher massaged her forehead. "You're telling me six thousand pounds . . . that's the last of the treasure?"

"Evidence points to this. My cousin, however, has a different opinion."

Miss Fletcher glanced up from the book. "That's why she's in Scotland, chasing rumors of gold."

His cousin, the Countess of Denton to the world, Lady Pink to the secret society, was the foul fish in this stew.

He was pensive, thumbing the chess piece. "Of all people, she's the one you have to watch out for."

Miss Fletcher cocked her head. "Warning me off?"

"For you and your kin? Yes. Exacting vengeance is her pastime."

"But the gold," she insisted.

"Forget the gold," he said, fisting the chess piece.

Outside, rain pattered the window, pleasant enough to chase London's finest citizens indoors. Custom would thrive tonight at Maison Bedwell. Only one visitor mattered—the corset maker who'd stumbled on a hornet's nest. She had to understand this.

He held up his damaged finger.

"Ancilla—my cousin—did this years ago at my family's country home. I was on my knees, hunting insects by the garden stairs. My hand was on the edge of the middle step." He leaned forward all the better for her to see the twisted scar. "My cousin appeared out of nowhere and ground her heel onto my finger. I've no doubt she stalked me. Of course, I screamed and passed out from horrendous pain. When I awoke later, the tip of my finger was gone. The physician told my mother the damage was too severe. He couldn't save it."

Miss Fletcher's jaw dropped. "But . . . you must've been a little boy."

"I was five," he said, cold and precise. "And my dear cousin was twelve or thirteen. After the shock wore off, I told my mother what Ancilla said before I passed out. 'That's what you get for being a tattle.' My mother begged me not to say a word to anyone."

"Why?"

"Because she wanted to protect me. She always has.

Ancilla is abominable and her father, more so. There would've been retribution—from Ancilla, I'm sure."

"I don't understand." Miss Fletcher was wispy voiced. "She was cruel for—for the sake of being cruel?"

"No. She is calculating in everything she does. My crime, as it turned out, occurred months earlier when I had innocently mentioned to my nurse that I'd seen my cousin in my father's study. Ancilla and her family had been visiting. The adults had gone shooting. When they returned, my father found his favorite crystal decanter broken. He'd rounded up the servants to investigate. My nurse, unbeknownst to me, shared what I had told her. Ancilla was given a lashing. Two months later . . ." He spiked the air with his stunted finger. "This happened."

Miss Fletcher set the ledger on the table, the ebb and flow of her breath noticeable. Her fear was his focus and whatever he could do to mold it to his purpose.

"You brought me here because you wanted me to know how vile your cousin is?"

"In part, yes."

She rose from the chair, terse and bothered. "If that was your aim, my lord, you could've come to my shop and told me. No need to send Miss Mitchell with a manufactured tale."

"Miss Mitchell bought me an extra day to confirm certain facts." He smiled grimly. "Considering what I do, it was a necessity."

His guest rubbed her forehead.

She was, no doubt, tired, confused, and defeated. He'd disappointed her search for the gold and dumped a pile of ugliness at her feet.

"I want to go home," she said.

"Tell her," Ilsa snapped.

Miss Fletcher's forehead-rubbing hand fell to her side. "Tell me what?"

The time for niceties was over.

"I want you to break into my cousin's home," he said. "The same as you and your league did last August."

There was nothing quite like the power of a blunt request. When her eyes flared wide, he tipped his head. An acknowledgment.

"You forged the key to Ancilla's Wilkes-Lock safe to steal her share of the Jacobite gold, and I know you forged it at the shipyard of our mutual friend, Mr. Thomas West."

He let that knowledge sink in before delivering a soft but lethal thrust.

"Do you think West and Sons Shipping could survive the crown's scrutiny? Probably not. The harbor master is a thorough public servant. Likes to put ships in dry dock for a year if he suspects malfeasance."

Rain pounded harder outside. His dark-haired lioness stood, unflinching. Steeliness was a quality he admired. She'd need it for what was coming.

"Using Thomas as leverage . . ." She was scornful. "What do you want?"

"Isn't it obvious? I want you." He stood up, unrelenting, forceful, hooking a finger under her chin. "Come work for me. You won't regret it."

Chapter Twenty-Six

*T*hreats, my lord, are a strange form of persuasion," Mary said.

Shadows and light wavered on Lord Ranleigh's blade-straight nose. His queue was stygian perfection. Styled in a cream silk coat, everything about him was lavish. Assured and wealthy, Lord Julian Ranleigh was one of England's chosen sons. A praetorium guard ascending. Looking into his onyx eyes was her only clue. A ferocious drive camped there, and he wore it well.

Lord save her—she was intrigued. Even the devil himself appealed to the eye.

He stroked her jaw. "You're not frightened, are you?"

"No." She angled her chin higher. "But I don't appreciate you threatening my . . . friend."

"Friend?"

His mocking tone left no doubt he thought otherwise.

"Do you want to go on about Mr. West? Or should we talk about you?" She smiled, tight-lipped and cool. "Something tells me *you* are your favorite subject."

Ilsa giggle-snorted, and Lord Ranleigh's hand fell to his side. It was a small victory. Mary would take it.

"Who are you?" she asked.

Fire's molten shadows carved Lord Ranleigh's face. He was pensive, opening his palm, the horse head game piece still there.

"I am the Dark Knight. I keep chaos at bay."

Her vision narrowed. What a cryptic answer. "A code name, is it?"

His lordship rolled his shoulder and kept his focus on the game piece in hand. Mary suspected he wasn't keen on painting vivid details nor was he bothered by false impressions. Was he a bawd? A libertine? A common thief? A leader of thieves?

Lines of tension circled his mouth. "Ilsa, give us the room."

Flames shined on the Swede's guinea-gold ringlets. She was gold and iron. Lots and lots of polished iron . . . on the butt of her pistol, on her knives (one visible in each sleeve), and a small, oiled ax tied to her left thigh. The woman was a walking arsenal.

"Are you sure?" Ilsa asked.

"Quite."

The henchwoman checked Mary a split second before her long, leather-clad legs took her swiftly across the room. If she was upset, she hid it well, shutting the door ever so carefully behind her.

"She's headstrong, but I trust her with my life," he mused.

"If you consider that headstrong, my lord, then you'll find me positively ungovernable."

His short laugh was comforting. "Such directness. It is one of the reasons why I like you, Miss Fletcher."

"Thank you, my lord, but . . . I'm not so sure that I like you."

Lord Ranleigh was a guarded creature. A twinge in her chest warned her to pay attention to every facet of the man. They were burning dross from gold in their conversation and finally getting to why she was alone with him in an empty house. Yet, these flares of attraction—his mostly—would only get in the way.

"You don't have to like me for an assignation," he said gingerly.

"You didn't bring me here for a night of swiving."

He was rubbing the chess piece in his hand. "No, I didn't. I brought you here for something far better."

"And that would be?"

"Power."

Lord Ranleigh shifted to the table, its chessboard painted on the surface. He set about arranging pieces in a very un-chess-like array as though a tutoring session was in progress.

"You asked who I am." He set the king in the middle of the board. "What you ought to ask is what do I do?"

A hand fisted behind his back, Lord Ranleigh bent to his task, quietly moving pawns. Tucking hair behind her ear, she focused. There was an object lesson here. His offer, his veiled threat, the slim ledger on the table, and its contents all came into play.

Power is better than money kept running through her head.

She swiveled around to the rain-drenched window. All those stately homes.

King's Square hosted foreign envoys.

The charwoman's quip about the Russians. His

lordship's casual watch on his neighbors when he took her to Maison Bedwell's study. *Poland, Bavaria, Genoa, to name a few . . .* That's what he'd said.

How many dignitaries visited this well-placed brothel?

She huffed softly. *Of course.* Money, power, and passion were currencies exchanged all under one roof. She turned to face him.

"Are you a spy?"

His lordship put another chess piece in place. "I am many things in service to the crown. A soldier of fortune. A messenger." He glanced at her. "A man who finds answers to the realm's difficult questions."

"The secret society—is that your creation?"

His nod was regal. "Well-done, Miss Fletcher. Now follow that vein of gold, and ask yourself *why*."

This was too much. She rubbed a dull throb at her temple. Fragments were sliding into place with the comfort of glass shards. Everything gleamed, painful and sharp. Her joyful day with Thomas was the tender note in her soul. The pleasure barge, kissing him, his impossible green-blue eyes. Her night with him ought to be enshrined. Her body would never forget. And their day together? Her heart would never forget that, either.

But Thomas's livelihood had been threatened in this cold, dark room. Because of his connection to her.

She had to protect Thomas, yet Lord Ranleigh wanted her to follow a bread-crumb trail about himself. On the table was the well-used ledger. *The dratted book.* In it was just enough information to keep her on a hook.

Six thousand pounds paid to a man who would never be king.

Why didn't the English keep the treasure?

"Six thousand pounds. Six thousand—" She gasped and dropped onto tufted leather. "You *wanted* him to have the money. It was your plan all along."

Lord Ranleigh beamed like a proud tutor. "Better to keep Charles Stuart drunk on wine and foolishness," he said. "Selby, however, thought he was serving Stuart."

"And you let him believe it."

"Because it served my purpose."

And this was the heart of the matter—Lord Ranleigh cultivated useful people.

"Selby's an English Jacobite," he said. "The man blusters about the Union and the Stuart lineage from the comfort of his excellent London home, but he has no stomach for war."

"Unlike those Scottish Jacobites in petticoats . . . Those are the ones you have to watch out for."

His grin expanded. "You're all of a piece."

She let her spine hit the backrest. Like Selby, she, too, had no stomach for war, but puzzles fascinated her, and this midnight meeting with Lord Ranleigh was a complex one.

She blinked slowly, trying to assimilate this stunning news. "Charles Stuart had no idea the crown was behind it, did he?"

"None at all."

She folded her arms under her bosom. More parts were falling into place. "You needed true Jacobites in your fold to make your secret group believable." A slight nod to that. "Your intrigue ran deep."

"A necessity, I'm afraid. The realm couldn't afford another war." His mouth curled disdainfully. "I gave the pretender enough money to keep him on the continent, enough to drink himself silly so that no sovereign would take him seriously."

"You must've been at this for quite some time."

His lordship sank down in the opposite chair. "Chaos is the mistress who can't take no for an answer."

"Women . . . of course."

"Chess is my preferred pastime." He was detached saying so, picking up a pawn and putting it down. "Do you play?"

"Barely."

"I could teach you," he said, which sounded like flirting.

She leaned forward, her red-and-white-striped petticoats rustling. The only way to protect Thomas was to have as much knowledge as possible.

"I'd rather you explain exactly what you do."

Being alone with him was intimate. The empty house. The sparkling moonlit chandelier and the stunning secrets shared under it. Lord Ranleigh was lustrous and refined, his silk coat glowing in candlelight, his cravat mercilessly starched. Despite the trappings of wealth and station, he leaned in, cozying to her.

"Kings need three things to stay in power." With his open hand, he swept a wall of pawns forward. "An army, a navy. That's your brute force." He put a finger on the castle already by the king. "The rook is money. Necessary for any king to survive. If that ruler has secret funds, even better."

"Like stolen Jacobite gold. No one has to account for it."

He smiled. "Exactly."

She rested her chin on her hand, watching him scoot another game piece in the king's vicinity.

"Now, the bishop is information. Also necessary."

"Force, money, and information." She picked up the chipped knight he had cradled in his hand a moment ago. "And the horse?"

Skin around Lord Ranleigh's eyes softened. He closed his hand around hers, and her skin tingled at his touch.

"The dark knight does what is necessary to bring all the parts together."

Intimacy couched them. He was luring her just so with his confession, his voice a little craggy when she tipped forward as though a kiss might happen.

"I could use someone like you," he said. "A beautiful commoner with rare intelligence."

"Unlike beautiful noblewomen. They're as numerous as leaves on trees but not nearly as smart."

His mouth quirked, and she let the knight fall into his hand. Outside the window a carriage parked, rudely blocking the moonlight when she needed every bit of light to see the libertine-cum-soldier of intrigue.

A fist pounded the chamber door.

"The carriage is ready, my lord," was the booming voice on the other side. His lordship smiled unevenly.

"That would be Ilsa's doing." He unfolded himself from the chair. "Come. I'll see you out."

For a woman who wanted her bed, she was awfully sluggish getting out of her chair. Crossing the room, she looked beyond the window. The waiting carriage boasted brass candle lamps and matching white horses.

"That's not your typical hack, my lord."

"The carriage is mine." He opened the door for her.

"Planning to torment more corset makers tonight?"

"Only one has caught my interest," he said when she brushed by.

She touched her nape, glad for the dark. Her skin was pebbling there.

Lord Ranleigh led her to his front door, where a pink-liveried footman stood at attention with her gray cloak draped over his arm. His lordship settled the cloak on her shoulders, and the footman opened the door to a growing storm. She was about to dart into the elements, in search of a hack, when Lord Ranleigh put a hand to her elbow and scuttled into the rain with her. They huddled close, rushing to his carriage. Another servant, gripping his great-coat against blustery wind, swung the carriage door wide.

Confused, she asked, "The carriage is for me?"

Lord Ranleigh spoke above pounding rain. "You need a ride home."

"Please convey my appreciation to Miss Thelen."

Which made his mouth quirk. "My carriage—using of it is one of the many benefits, should you join me."

She climbed inside. The interior was masculine browns. More tufted leather with hints of expensive cheroot smoke. She was unfolding the waiting wool blanket when Lord Ranleigh leaned past the open door. Rain plastered his back and droplets clung to his lashes.

He reached for her, his cold, damaged hand covering hers.

"You are an astonishing woman. You've been hunting the gold, yet you've managed to elude anyone's notice. Mine, in particular." Dismay slanted his mouth. "You and your league also managed to find my cousin's Wilkes-Lock key, something I could never do. That's a feat, Miss Fletcher."

His onyx eyes told her he'd just offered his truest compliment.

"Thank you, my lord."

He let go of her hands and straightened like a military man. "I want you with me, and we both want my cousin declawed. Those papers in her Wilkes-Lock safe are what I need to do that. You are the only person who can get them, assuming you still have the key."

"I do, but has your cousin changed the lock?" In the evening's shock, she hadn't thought to ask.

"She hasn't. It takes months to manufacture a new one, and the devices are in high demand." He smirked. "Even my cousin must get in line behind foreign princes."

Lord Ranleigh was resolute, the downpour ruining his silks and his excellent queue. Of course, he'd tracked this.

"We will discuss this again," he said. "In the near future."

"Yes, my lord."

He shut the door, and she hugged the blanket to her body.

What was in those papers?

The carriage rolled forward, the lamps well set, they hardly moved. Lord Ranleigh was watching her depart outside his lovely barren home. How rigid he was, standing in the tempest. An ambitious praetorium guard—they did the dirtiest work.

She sank into the backrest, leveled. This was a

blow, but she was not crushed. Lord Ranleigh's invitation to join him was not a request. The ruthless Englishman would have his due. And Thomas? Lord Ranleigh's veiled threat could not be overlooked.

She worried the blanket's edge.

What about Thomas?

This day, this night, with him was too exquisite. She wouldn't mar the memory of it.

The memory of him might be all she'd have left.

Chapter Twenty-Seven

*T*he fine souls of White Cross Street were starting their day. An idle hack driver was scratching his arse, checking a wheel. A slouching orange girl was yawning, eyeing a shop window. Thomas crossed the street to meet her. Oranges, he decided, were the perfect gift after a night of elevating passion.

"How much?" he asked.

The orange girl turned from her window shopping. "Three for a penny."

The citrus was fragrant, perfect for Fletcher's House of Corsets and Stays. Red flashed in the shop window and his spirit soared. Feminine hands were polishing the glass. Very industrious, his Mary, with very talented hands. Flesh in his smalls agreed. He was eyes on that window, a grand gesture forming.

He reached into his waistcoat pocket. "What if I purchased the entire basket?"

"All my oranges, sir? I have at least thirty."

"I'm very hungry. So is my friend."

The maid gawked like a caught fish under her straw bonnet. Untying his purse, he took pity on her, the early hour and such.

"How about I give you two shillings for the entire basket, three if you deliver them"—he fanned three shillings and nodded at Mary's window—"to that shop?"

She followed his nod. "I know the shop, sir, but . . ." The orange girl hoisted her basket into the crook of her waist. "There's a problem, sir." Pity filled her eyes. "It's your ciphering."

"What about my ciphering?"

"It's—it's a little off."

He laughed gently. "When a man loves a woman, his entire existence is thrown off."

"In love, sir," she cooed, practically melting on the spot.

"My overpayment is a reward for your assistance."

"Of course, sir. All you had to do was tell me, if it's wooing you're about." She took his money, dropping the coins in her petticoat pocket. "Anything you want me to say on your behalf?"

How refreshing, having a young maid for an ally.

"I hadn't thought that far ahead."

The orange girl nodded sagely. "My brother, Roger, has the same problem. A laundress has his head in the clouds, she does. Of course, you're *much* older than my brother."

Apparently, his ally thought love was inconceivable among her elders.

"Not that you don't have a fine appearance to recommend you," she said hastily.

"Cupid has taken his sweet time with me," he intoned. "Fortunately, he's overlooked how long in the tooth I am."

She giggled. "Does the lady know how you feel?"

He glanced heavenward. *So many ways to answer that.*

The orange girl, who couldn't be more than fifteen, patted his sleeve. "Leave it to me, sir. I'll put in a good word. Something romantic . . ." Her youthful eyes lit up. "Maybe a gift from a mysterious but honorable gentleman. And then you can walk in and surprise her."

"Excellent."

He watched her go, her step light as she made her way into Fletcher's House of Corsets and Stays. Had he ever been that fanciful? He leaned a shoulder against the street lamp. Hunting the siren of White Cross Street was tricky business. No map existed for this journey. They'd agreed to passion-filled nights. The problem was he wanted Mary Fletcher's days.

He was becoming a reckless man. Caution was necessary. Today must be a negotiation for more time. Anything else would scare her off.

Drays passed, their harnesses jingling. A chandler stepped out and swept the sidewalk in front of his door. Foggy wisps still clung to the road. He removed his hat and smoothed his hair. A mother and her twin daughters ambled into the corset shop, the doorbell jingling merrily. A sweet sound. He brushed a speck of lint off his blue wool waistcoat, his best. West and Sons employees would think he wore it for today's commerce. He wore it for her. Ironed it himself at the crack of dawn to his housekeeper's dismay.

The doorbell jingled again. The orange girl popped out of the shop, dimpling and tucking her basket under her arm as she approached Thomas.

"She was delighted, sir. I made sure to put in a *very* good word for you."

The maid dipped a curtsey and headed off with a skip.

"Out of the mouth of babes," he said under his breath. "Courting it is."

Thomas braced himself. His first daytime visit was business. His second (this one) was obvious. The corset maker who vowed to never marry would have an inkling what he was about. Striding to her shop door, he was resolved. Whatever it took. Pleasant conversation, indulging entertainments, or scorching passion. Mary Fletcher would rethink her vow and pledge her troth to him.

He'd never been so decided in his life.

The shop door rang his entrance. Mary was at the window, daylight blessing her. Her hands slowed on whatever frippery she was arranging as if she sensed him. When she turned, his feet stalled. She was a true siren. Serene. Luminous. Her lips parting, her skin glowing, a lone curl brushing her cheek.

A twinge bloomed in his chest. Mary Fletcher was the source of his joy, filling his heart.

Her slight nod hooked him. An awareness, their time had come.

They were two souls who'd find each other, no matter what seas they had to cross. He'd never forget this moment, this pleasure rippling through him.

"Mr. West. Good morning."

He removed his hat. "Good morning, Miss Fletcher."

They both took an unwise step toward each other. The draw was magnetic. Fisting his hand into the small of his back, he faced an immutable fact—he had it bad for her.

"Thank you for the kind gift of oranges." She folded both hands demurely. "With my sister visiting kin in Southwark, I'm not sure that I'll be able to eat them all."

"I could help."

"You enjoy oranges, I collect."

"I enjoy you, and one can do very creative things with oranges," he said for her ears alone.

She tipped her head, fighting a smile. He couldn't regret making her smile. Mary's proper facade was cracking before his eyes and he would be the man to see it fracture completely. She'd already broken apart in his arms in the dark of night. Why not see what happened in the light of day?

She spoke louder and officiously, "Why don't I show you the baleen you sold me last year. Some of the fibers are fraying."

"Like the flue on a peacock feather?"

Her cheeks bloomed a ferocious red. "Perhaps if I showed you . . ."

"Excellent. I do need to see your goods, Miss Fletcher."

He didn't think it possible, but a crimson blush blazed ever brighter on her face.

"Please, follow me." She sped across her shop, saying, "Miss Dalton, I will be in the workroom."

At the counter, a brown-haired miss looked up from discussing woolen stays with a patron. "Of course, miss."

Mary darted past the yellow curtain dividing her shop from her workroom and he followed, praying Miss Dalton would treat that curtain like a portcullis and not trespass. Oranges filled a bucket in the middle of a worktable. Around them were half-formed stays with uncut baleen poking above unsewn hems. Rows of cloth and spindles of thread lined a wall, set up like the colors of the rainbow. A tidy place, her workshop. Only one color drew him. The red of Mary Fletcher's swishing gown. She swirled around, her eyes alight.

"What are you doing here?" Her voice was just above a whisper.

"Isn't it obvious?" He dropped his hat on the table. "I'm here to ensure your complete satisfaction."

"With last night?" she whispered, her eyes rounding. "Oh, you are incorrigible."

"Count me determined, delighted, and thoroughly . . . smitten." He cocked a smile. "Forgive me. I couldn't think of another word beginning with a D to describe my enthusiasm for you."

She touched her lips to suppress a giggle. "Have you lost your mind?"

"Undoubtedly. I have it on good authority that it's loose in the clouds."

"What are you talking about?"

"Blame the orange girl for that."

She canted her head, confused.

"My being here pertains to one matter and one matter alone."

"Pray tell, what is this matter?" she asked, a little breathless.

"It's you."

"Me?" Mary took a cautious step backward. He took a cautious step forward.

"I've come to expand our agreement."

She glanced nervously at the yellow curtain. "You shouldn't have. Our agreement never mentioned days."

He ignored that, though in deference to her place of business he kept his voice low.

"I'll begin by escorting you to Neville Warehouse today, which I acknowledge is not the most enticing of entertainments, but I'll remind you, I can do better."

"Can you?" Eyes sparkling, she inched backward.

He inched forward. "Need I remind you of the pleasure barge?"

"There's no need. It's fresh on my mind as are other . . . places."

The saucy wench.

"Then you'll agree our verbal contract needs further negotiation."

"Because you decided it?" She was walking backward, her lips suppressing a smile while he followed.

"You have your plans for our business arrangement. I have mine."

"I can't argue with that logic. Both parties must be *satisfied*," she said, then promptly shook her head as though she couldn't believe her own flagrant innuendo.

"I'm glad you agree, Miss Fletcher."

Their footfalls pattered faster. Mary was biting her lower lip, rounding the table backward.

"And what did you have in mind, sir?"

His steps deliberate, he honed on her lush lip which she nibbled so enticingly. "I have certain needs."

"Please explain."

Mary's bodice rose and fell, a noticeable rhythm in their careful chase around her workroom table.

"Our thirty-day contract has very stingy time allowances," he said.

"Stingy, is it?" She arched a brow, holding his gaze. "What do you suggest?"

"Spend more than the allotted three hours with me. Daytime work, if you will."

"The two of us, working together?" Her smile was splendid and bright. "Considering our respective businesses, how will our new commerce fit?"

"Oh, it fits very well, Miss Fletcher."

Though she rolled her eyes at his quip, her smile deepened. He was close to catching her. A kiss, a touch . . . something would happen.

"That's quite a lot to ask, sir," she said. "As I recall, our last meeting didn't entirely satisfy all my requirements."

"You weren't satisfied?" Now, that surprised him.

She shook her head fast, causing that blasted curl to dance prettily. "Not completely. Certain elements were missing, while I delivered splendidly."

Laughter shot out of him. "Indeed, Miss Fletcher. You did."

Mary's life vein pulsed noticeably on her neck. He'd kiss that tiny throb just to see if he could make it race faster. He knew a place in the crook of her thighs that made her pulse gallop.

She surprised him, ducking into a smaller room off her workroom. An alcove of sorts blocked by a heavier curtain. One brick wall was charred as though it had caught fire. He backed her into a corner and braced his arm on the wall near her head.

"Now, what is this about something missing."

She tipped her face to his, her eyes liquid with unspent lust.

"My story—you never finished it."

He was gentle, dipping his head to nuzzle her neck. "Is that your only complaint?"

She arched her neck and grabbed his waistcoat with desperate fingers. "Yes."

Mary speared his heart with Cupid's arrow. The ache in her voice was sweet. He nuzzled her cheek, her smell driving him mad. She was unscented soap and hints of starch, washing him clean. If Mary wanted this to end, this was the moment.

Instead, she drew him flush to her.

He brushed the softest kiss on her lips. "Then I promise to fill you with every imaginable tale. Tonight."

She raised a knee, stroking her leg on his. He gathered her petticoats, volumes of them, until he glimpsed his prize—white wool stockings gartered with red above the knee. Another tempting bow he ought to untie. He slid a hand the length of her thigh and found it.

"Thomas, I—"

Mary hissed when he caressed her bare inner thigh. Red-and-white wool billowed like colorful clouds on her hip. He was losing himself to the airy rustle of cloth, to the hitch of her breath mingling with his. Her face disappeared when his lashes dropped, all the better to unleash his other senses. To feel, smell, and taste her.

The world needed to go away. There could only be this—Mary melting into him. Gentle rubbing, his mouth on hers. Warm and wet. He kissed the thrilling corner of her mouth. He kissed her lips, her stubborn chin, her neck. He would devote hours to her pleasure—to her liking for rough, fast bed sport and her glossy-eyed surrender when he was oh so tender.

"Mary . . ." Her name was a plea from a drowning man.

His questing hands traveled up her ribs. Wool abraded his palms cresting Mary's salacious curves. He craved what was hidden. Her skin. Her nipples. Her cleavage, which he adored. His fingertips slid above her bodice. A neckerchief was in the way.

He moaned and pulled away.

Gauzy fabric tried to hide her swelling breasts. Blasted, useless cloth.

He toyed with it. "How much of your breasts does this neckerchief cover?"

Mary opened her eyes. She was like a swimmer, breaking the surface, desperate for air.

"My neckerchief?"

"Yes. This." He pinched its gossamer lightness.

Curls had come undone and her mobcap slipped. She was more wanton chambermaid than staid shopkeeper.

"It's long. I tuck the ends under each breast."

"Do you?" He tugged it lightly, deviously, and her eyes rounded. "Directly on the skin?"

Her tender nipples were undoubtedly teased by the pull.

The tip of her tongue wetted her lips. "Should I tuck it anywhere else?"

"Saucy wench. You'll pay for that."

Their legs were tangled and their breath hot. He pressed a hand under her breast to make the neckerchief's journey out of her bodice agonizingly slow. Mary's hip pumped sluggishly against his. A mutual torture. He'd make it last.

Pulling inch by inch, the neckerchief was coming free. Mary gasped long, her eyes glossy. Their gazes locked in sensual torment. Her stomacher was well used and boneless, and her stays, light and short. He raised a hallelujah for old stomachers and light stays, all the better to feel a woman.

"Now, where did I leave our tale?" he asked.

Mary thrust her charms at him, drunk on their game. "Why, I believe the siren was punished by a sea god."

He dragged the neckerchief nipple-teasing inches upward.

"Yes, punished." His lips curled inward. "For tempting the wrong shipmaster."

A flush darkened Mary's cheeks. Were her nipples changing color? A dark red? Were they distended and begging to be sucked? For all her delight in rough play, she liked her nipples treated with the utmost care.

Heat shot through him. *Chubby Cupid and his arrows.* The little god knew where to aim.

Thomas ground his back teeth. This wasn't going well for him. His placket was tenting ruthlessly at the woman pinned submissively before him.

The siren of White Cross Street was winning.

He yanked the neckerchief out of her bodice. Mary's stunned inhale was satisfying and erotic.

"She was ruining his life. The shipmaster had no satisfaction," he said.

"None at all?" she asked far too innocently.

His eyes narrowed. She was playing this to the hilt. He leaned in close, his arm braced to the wall.

"None. Or any other adjectives a man can think of when a woman drives him to distraction." He smiled tightly at her. This game was far from over. "The sea god owed this shipmaster a great debt."

"The siren was his recompense."

"Paid in full."

He lifted the sheer cloth to his face and breathed her scent. He was close to combusting. The smell of her breasts was on this cloth. He'd go mad trying to parse her essence.

"Even being with you smells good." He jammed her neckerchief into his coat pocket, the one that rested over his heart. It was sentimental; he didn't care.

Mary traced his ear, his scar, before her hands drifted to his chest. "I'm not getting my neckerchief back, am I?"

"Not until I need you to wear it again." His mouth slanted sideways. "Your skin has a certain fragrance which drives me to distraction."

She laughed softly. "You mentioned that. But we're not making progress, not with my promised story or our negotiations."

He brushed untidy wisps off her forehead. Her skin was warm silk to his touch.

"Let's agree those are bedtime stories."

She tipped her face to his. "And the other part? Your request for daytime arrangements?"

He kissed her lightly on the forehead before forcing some distance between them. She huffed and tried reaching for his coat, but he stayed a wise arm's length from her.

"If I don't put some distance between us," he said, "I'll put your petticoats under your chin and swive the daylights out of you, and this would be bad for business at Fletcher's House of Corsets and Stays."

She was coy, petting her thigh where her hem was above her garter. He gritted his teeth, madness bearing down on him.

"Mary . . ." He growled his warning. "You're loud when you reach satisfaction."

"Am I?"

Her startled look was priceless.

He nodded emphatically. "Very loud."

She shook her petticoats until her hems dropped. She smoothed her stomacher, collecting herself before brushing past him to her workroom. He followed, of course, which was becoming a bad habit. Mary went to a small mirror on the wall. She was pretty, arms raised, fixing pins and tucking curls.

"What makes you think we can carry on politely today?"

A fair question.

He adjusted rioting flesh in his breeches, grumbling. "I don't know."

It was an honest answer. Her wary gaze met his in the mirror. They were in uncharted waters. Her with her vow of no serious entanglements and him bothered in more ways than he could count. If he cared to look deeper than his own base needs, he might find what made Mary Fletcher tick. Her league, her kin, were inviolable, but he couldn't say what drove her. Duty? Responsibility? A need to protect? He dragged both hands over his head.

She turned from the mirror. "You're frustrated, and I don't mean"—she pointed to his placket—"*that*. It's something else."

His ballocks pained him but he managed to tuck his erection upward in his placket. It would do, but she'd touched a poignant nerve.

"We should not refuse ourselves this small pleasure," he said.

"The pleasure of companionship." Mary rubbed

her thimble-stained fingertip. "You wrote that in your letter yesterday."

His letter had invited her to spend one day with him. They'd indulged themselves and come out better for it, but half-formed corsets were laid out on the table. Beyond the yellow curtain, her doorbell had jingled twice. More voices, more custom, in a matter of minutes.

Responsibility beckoned.

"There are no easy answers, Mary. Our life, our choices. My father used to say life is like building a ship while trying to sail it." He hesitated. "I see the truth in it."

Her brows knit a tender line above her nose. He'd given her something of depth to consider, which made him inordinately happy. One way to Mary Fletcher's heart was through her mind. Of that, he was certain. All other ways remained a mystery; he was determined to uncover each one.

She gathered her serviceable gray cloak off a hook on the wall. "I'll agree to a daytime contract. An occasional luncheon or a pint in a public house will do."

His mouth quirked. His Mary was all business about the business of having fun.

"This is acceptable to me." He collected his hat off the table.

"We could start today if you'd like. If you don't mind escorting me to Dowgate to see a friend." She wrapped her shoulders in wool. "It'll be quick. She's not been well, so I won't stay long. Then we can go to Neville Warehouse."

"Mixing business with pleasure. A novel idea."

A smile cracked her visage. "Pleased with yourself, are you?"

"Very much. But a daytime promenade," he teased. "Are you sure your legs will work? It is October."

She tried not to laugh. "They work about as well as my nose for a good Cognac." Which made him grin from ear to ear. "So be warned, Mr. West. I also have a nose for gentlemen who cannot contain themselves as decorum requires."

He was tempted to remind her of his decorum in her alcove, but he kept that to himself. Sometimes a man had to know when to keep his mouth shut—a lesson his father had taught him.

He set his hat on his head. "Understood. Anything else?"

"Yes." She pushed up on her toes, whispering, "Please kiss me again before we walk outside and become mere business associates. Otherwise, I can't be responsible for my actions today at Neville Warehouse."

Softly parted lips inches from his won the day.

"Duly noted."

He hooked a finger under her chin and did what any smart man would do—he kissed the siren of White Cross Street and made silent plans to do much, much more.

Chapter Twenty-Eight

$\mathcal{D}$owgate was a quiet place, decently cobbled, its foggy streets anointing Mary's hems. Each step was an act of faith. She'd left Fletcher's House of Corsets and Stays twice in one week. Midmorning, no less. A risky venture. Cecelia would be proud.

After Mary had left Miss Dalton in charge of the shop, she'd crammed into a hack with Thomas, landing nearly on his lap. He didn't complain. She was sure he'd hired the smallest hack he could find, all the better to squeeze them together while he covertly caressed her bottom through yards of wool from Cheapside to Thames Street near Swan Lane.

An entire hack ride of furtive caresses—stouthearted sensualists would approve.

Once out of the hack, Thomas was vigilant as though footpads might attack. He was face forward, his profile a menacing line. She kept checking it.

"Have you a question?" he asked. "Or are you memorizing my chin?"

She ducked in closer. Their gaits matched as she looped her arm with his. "Your chin is interesting as chins go. However, there's no need to scowl. Swan Lane is harmless."

"The closer we get to the river, the closer we are to trouble."

She laughed softly. "I suppose you're right. Cecelia MacDonald's home is just above the Thames, and she is the most scandalous member of our league."

"More scandalous than you?" When he glanced at her, his eyebrows were practically in his hat.

"I'm not a woman of questionable repute."

"Of course not," he said, dipping his head to hers. "You merely redesign the realm's coins to suit your needs."

Which oddly made her laugh. She had confessed an awful lot at Chelsea Physic Gardens. And she couldn't ignore the fact that she'd stripped naked like a wanton at his command.

She bumped her hip companionably to his. "I'd rather we talk about you."

"What about me?"

Oh, he was adorably stoic.

"Well, there is a very interesting scar on the bottom of your . . . bottom."

"Why, Miss Fletcher, I do believe you're flirting with me." He waved vaguely at cobblestones stretching before them. "In public, no less."

"Shocking, isn't it?"

"It's proof—pigs do indeed fly."

"Why do you say that?"

An innocent question. But Thomas had gone a touch rigid beside her. Chirping birds poked around the front steps of a home they passed while Thomas appeared to consider how he'd answer her.

"The truth is you were a favorite topic amongst the merchants, sailors, and dockside workers at Mr. Dorrien-Smith's King Edward Street warehouse."

"I wasn't aware."

"You were focused and we were men with too much time on our hands. Usually, one of two aspects were discussed." He sucked in a chest-expanding breath. "Your charms or your chilliness."

"I see."

He brushed a fingertip across his brow. "Not very gentlemanly, I admit."

They passed a home, its lacy curtains drawn back. She tried not to look, but the scene behind wavy-paned windows drew her, nonetheless. A mother mending a shirt while two boys played with blocks on the floor. On the settee, an elderly woman, a grandmother possibly, was reading aloud to a little girl. Mary craned her neck to one side as though she could hold on to that tender scene while walking by. How quaint Dowgate was, where mums and grandmums cared for and educated their children. A graceful, timeless way of life because some things never changed—men and their ways included.

"Do you know what I think?" She posed this, humbled. "If historians had recorded ancient dockside conversations, they'd be as earthy then as they are today." She was subdued, adding, "Age to age, men never change."

"You're not upset?"

She was surprised at how fervently she wanted to spare Thomas his discomfort.

"Not at all. We're bound to discover unsavory things about each other, but if we don't shed light on them, we'll not advance our—"

"Friendship."

The corners of his eyes crinkled, causing a silly glow to blossom in her chest.

"You and I already carry on like two lechers at midnight. Why not broach delicate topics midmorning with equal enthusiasm?"

Laughter shot out of Thomas. "Indeed."

She blushed, thrilled to her toes. The proper shopkeeper she used to be would never have jested about midnight debauchery. Could be she was improving, this friendship with Thomas and all. She grinned like a village fool at nothing in particular.

Daytime promenades with Thomas—she could get used to them.

"Please, tell me about the King Edward Street warehouse," she said.

"Not much to tell. It was our primary market for years. I was in and out, more a man of the sea than commerce."

"That all changed after your father died, no?"

"It all changed once I laid eyes on you," he said in a soft, rumbly voice. "I made sure I was there when you purchased my goods from Mr. Dorrien-Smith's factor."

"I recall seeing you in the crowd."

Thomas dared a glance. "I was smitten, but too proud to test the waters with you."

Her sea wolf was baring his tender underbelly.

She nibbled her lower lip, swamped by more emotions this morning than she usually felt in an entire month. London had done the same to her when she'd first arrived. How overwhelmed she'd been. All the dockside mayhem and teeming streets, and her, trying to start a business. The journey from Arisaig to the City had been a deep dive into unknown waters. Sink or swim had been her choices—with fifteen-year-old Margaret in tow.

What woman had time to notice men in all of that?

Englishmen to boot. Still, guilt pinched her.

She pushed a tendril of hair out of her face. "I wasn't very friendly, was I?"

"The docks are a tough place, and King Edward Street is obscenely busy. Given that you're a woman in a profession dominated by men, your cool demeanor was understandable."

"I know what I was," she said, crestfallen.

Their steps filled an awkward silence. This metaphorical sharing of underbellies wasn't easy when the shoe was on the other foot. Why couldn't they just flirt? She was starting to get good at it.

Thomas cleared his throat. "Being a staunch Jacobite among so many Englishmen made you uncomfortable, I collect."

She winced. Now he was tossing salt on a wound. "It did."

"But you've learned we don't all have horns and spiked tails."

"No, but I'm sure Cumberland does," she said tartly. "He's the devil incarnate."

Thomas exhaled long. "You do know I'm not Cumberland."

Their steps slowed as the churn of London Bridge's water wheels grew louder. Cecelia's cottage was in view, its stonework tipsy to the eye. Her home sat on a wall above the river where the curving lane ended.

She knocked on Cecelia's door. "We don't need to discuss the war."

"What happened to the brave woman who said we ought to broach delicate topics?"

Thomas's eyes were a kindly green as though he understood her loss. The war, her home, her way of life. If Scotland had won, would she be here in London? With him?

Probably not.

"Speaking of delicate topics," he said, "are we presenting ourselves as Mr. and Mrs. West? Or do you expect me to be your non-suitor?"

"You are incorrigible."

"As long as I'm your *favorite* incorrigible Englishman . . ."

Footsteps inside the house *click-clacked*. Probably Jenny coming to answer the door. Mary straightened her posture. Had she been foolish, saying they could speak openly? Perhaps Thomas was proving himself wiser here. What would he do if she told him what happened *after* she'd left him sprawled naked in bed? She hadn't said a word about Lord Ranleigh's threat to West and Sons Shipping. If she had, it would surely wipe that handsome smile off his face. Better to safeguard this happiness they shared. Bearing burdens was her specialty.

It always was.

Chapter Twenty-Nine

*C*ecelia's bedchamber was a shocking scene. The polished window cracked open, the bed stripped bare, and the floor mopped clean. Shoes had been put away and not a single discarded stocking hung in view. To compensate for the chill this open-windowed cleaning frenzy had wrought, a blazing fire crackled in the fireplace. Mary settled in a chair close to it. Cecelia was a gorgeous mess, curled up in her ugly night-robe, a red scarf warming her head and a thick braid draping her shoulder.

Mary wrinkled her nose at Cecelia's uncharacteristic night-robe: brown wool outside, pea-green felt inside, and the stitching a clash of colors.

"Please, bring that abomination you're wearing to my shop," she said. "I'm sure Margaret and I can transform it."

Cecelia clutched her night-robe. "Not a chance."

Cecelia adored the robe, a playful gift from Mr. Sloane. It had been his shot across the bow as it were. Once she'd accepted it, the one-time government man was unceasing in his pursuit of Cecelia—luring her with late-night meetings, popping up in her favorite haunts, and defending her before London's staunch anti-Jacobite magistrate.

Mr. Sloane even read a romantic novel to her in bed. *What man did that?*

A determined one.

The result was a deep, abiding passion.

"Is this what happens to a woman when she falls in love?" Mary asked. "She loses her fashion sense?"

"I doubt it."

"And what happened to your bedchamber?" Mary twisted in the chair, skeptical. "Everything's in pristine order."

"It's Alexander. He likes things tidy."

Mary unwound herself and found Cecelia sipping beef tea, content.

"Never thought I'd see the day when Cecelia Mac-Donald happily accommodates a man's preferences."

Cecelia stared at nothing in particular, dreamy eyed and soft with her lips unpainted, which was a startling change. The woman always had a miniature pot of carmine on hand.

"It's love. There's nothing like it. A force to knock you down and soften brittle hearts. It seeps into the cracked places we all try to hide and blesses us with something better." Her gaze sought Mary's. "Why wouldn't I want this?"

"Of course. Why wouldn't you?" But Mary didn't sound convinced.

She looked into the fire. All this talk of love and hearts and cracked places was enough to drive a woman mad. She was happy for Cecelia. Truly. But this was how visits of late were going. Talk of unnerving changes revolving around love, babes, or Alexander.

Mary wanted to cry out, *Can we stop the starry-eyed pronouncements and get on with business?* She wisely kept her mouth shut.

Cecelia set down her beef tea and reached for her. "I've stunning news."

"Bigger than announcing you are with child?"

"Very close." Cecelia's braid swung forward in the dramatic pause. "Alexander is presently inspecting a house on South Audley Street."

"Why?"

"Because it could be our future home, you ninny. I want to see it, but I won't go out in public until I can hold down something more substantial than beef tea."

Envy took tiny bites of Mary's soul. She couldn't deny it.

"A new home . . . how wonderful."

"My cottage is fine for Alexander, Jenny, and me but"—Cecelia sat back and put a loving hand on her non-existent belly—"everything changes once our little one arrives."

"I suppose it would."

Cecelia picked up her mug. "You know, I always thought Margaret would be the first of our number to have a child."

"Why Margaret?"

"She's a natural at caring for others, and the most nurturing of our humble league, aside from Aunt Flora."

Mary could barely breathe for the sharp pain climbing through her. Why did hearing Cecelia's unvarnished assessment hurt?

"Most young women of nineteen are married with a babe or two." Cecelia sipped beef tea. "You, me,

Anne—our lives have been skewed by war. And the terrible shortage of desirable men when we were ensconced in Arisaig."

"One can't procreate without them," Mary said a little too bright.

She pressed a new wrinkle in her petticoats, the stripes dull from years of washing and ironing. Was this her fate? To fade into the background, while the rest of the league members chased new lives? Cecelia would soon wed and have a babe and possibly live in a new home near Grosvenor Square. Margaret wouldn't be far behind. Her little sister was more than ready to find a husband and start a family.

She winced. That would make her a dried-up old spinster aunt—a reasonable conclusion, considering her plan to never marry.

"I'm this close"—Cecelia pinched an inch of air between her thumb and forefinger—"to dying of curiosity about the gentleman waiting for you in my salon downstairs."

Mary shrugged, nonchalant. "His presence here means nothing. Mr. West is escorting me to Neville Warehouse. He's selling his goods today."

"I thought you were going to exercise caution with the shipmaster." Cecelia's brow arched with pitch-perfect expression. The woman could conduct entire conversations with them. "I know Mr. MacLeod wasn't with you at Maison Bedwell last night."

Mary warmed her hands over the fire. "Spying on me?"

"No. Jenny went to the Iron Bell last night and, lo and behold, Mr. MacLeod was there—the man who's supposed to look out for you."

"I do well enough on my own."

"Why the sudden aversion to sticking with our plan?" Cecelia studied her. "Or does the Englishman in my salon have something to do with this?"

Mary pivoted sharply on her seat. "It doesn't matter that Thomas is English. I'll bid you to remember, you have your Mr. Sloane."

"Divvying up the Englishmen, are we? One for you, and one for me."

Mary bit back a grimace. Why were they dithering over homes, babes, and Mr. West? There was so much serious news to share: her meeting with Lord Ranleigh, his stunning if sparse ledger, and his shocking offer to work for him. Never mind that the Jacobite gold was all gone. Yet, above it all, one matter plagued her deeply—Lord Ranleigh's threat to West and Sons Shipping.

How would she explain that?

There was a gasp in the silence, and Cecelia's jaw unhinged. "You're meeting Mr. West at Bedwell's."

Mary blinked fast. "I—"

"Don't deny it. The truth is written all over your face."

Shame scalded Mary as though Cecelia knew exactly what went on in the Red Rose room. She sat taller and tried to shake it off.

"I've never questioned your indiscretions. Please don't jest about mine. I don't think I could take it."

"Oh dear. You have it bad for him, don't you?"

The fire snapped and flared. Mary turned and lost seconds staring at it. Layers of responsibility called to her, but every fiber of her being yearned to spend all her spare minutes with the man waiting for her belowstairs. At times the drive was almost primal.

She fisted a hand against her abdomen in a futile effort to quell it.

"If by *having it bad* you mean I enjoy Mr. West, then yes. I do."

"He's your partner at Bedwell's. For the Red Rose room."

There. The unthinkable had been said aloud— Mary Fletcher of White Cross Street was indulging in passionate sexual interludes in an unseemly location. Cecelia was blasé while Mary folded her hands like a schoolgirl caught in the naughtiest infraction.

"You don't have to make it sound so sordid."

"We both know I'm not doing that." Cecelia tipped a pitcher over her empty cup and beef tea trickled into the dish.

Little goose bumps prickled Mary's skin. Cecelia's crockery reminded her of Chelsea Porcelain Works. Another item to report, yet she'd all but forgotten that news because of Thomas. How easily she'd let her duties slip from her grasp.

Man-on-the-brain disease. That was what this was.

Cecelia was kinder. "You're the good girl who's buried herself in years of responsibility, and now you're finally coming up for air. No need to feel guilty about it."

"Sometimes I do."

"Mr. West is a loose variable for me. But . . ." Cecelia's shrug was worthy of a Frenchwoman. "If you can manage your tasks, who am I to question what you do after dark?"

Mary idly traced her collarbone. Manage her passion for Thomas? Clandestine kisses under a banana tree came to mind. A sweet stolen moment, though it paled in comparison to a peacock feather stroking her skin. Yet, being with him was more than a string of randy assignations.

Words tumbled in her mind—sweet, enjoyable, a ray of happiness. Wonderful things, but not . . . love.

She rose from the chair, restless.

Cecelia watched her like a cat.

"Sooner or later, everyone faces their worst enemy. For you, Mary Fletcher, it is yourself—your own pleasure."

Fearing her own pleasure? That bordered on absurd. Mary opened her mouth with a suitable retort but voices drifted up the stairs. Aunt Maude was in the entry, speaking to Jenny.

"Are you expecting Aunt Maude?" Mary asked.

Cecelia uncurled from the chair. "No, but I suppose we ought to go down and greet her. While I'm at it, I'll give Mr. West the gimlet eye," she said with mock bravado. "And I'll tell him no one trifles with Mary Fletcher's heart."

"Oh, you'll have him shaking in his boots."

Cecelia laughed sweetly. "Of course, I will."

Mary headed downstairs with Cecelia in tow. Thomas was in the salon doorway, witnessing their hugs and greetings. Introductions were quickly made, and Aunt Maude, who'd come to deliver a tincture for Cecelia, didn't bat an eye to the whaler's presence. The curmudgeonly spinster actually beamed at him and made polite inquiries.

"I understand you're selling your goods at Neville Warehouse. Did that begin yesterday?"

"It began today, ma'am."

"Are the sales going well?" Aunt Maude asked.

"I expect so." He grinned like a man who knew

he ought to be at the warehouse rather than whiling away the morning in Dowgate. "Mr. Anstruther is in charge today, which allowed me to escort Miss Fletcher this morning."

"Mingling with the merchants, is it?" Aunt Maude winked at him.

The stout spinster swathed in black was taking a shine to Thomas. This pleased Mary. She looped her arm with his and said to the room, "Mr. West has graciously offered to help me educate Margaret on the intricacies of bones and baleen."

A tiny stretch of the truth since she hadn't asked this of him yet, but she'd meant to.

Jenny, the maid, snorted. "Eh, whale bones. A fascinating topic, I'm sure."

"I, for one, think it's an excellent idea." Aunt Maude peered into the salon. "And where is wee sweet Margaret? Is she here? Or waiting for you at the warehouse?"

Confused, Mary looked at Cecelia and then Aunt Maude. "No. She's spending this week with you at Neville House."

Aunt Maude shook her head. "Margaret's not at Neville House, dear. She sent a note last night, saying she couldn't come after all."

Mary's throat clogged, but she managed a whispery, "That can't be. Miss Dalton sent her off in a hack yesterday."

Yesterday she had enjoyed a ride on a pleasure barge with Mr. West. Yesterday she had toured a garden and sneaked kisses with Mr. West. And yesterday something happened to Margaret.

She took a step forward, white-hot fear seizing her. *Dear Margaret . . .*

The knot in her throat was growing, truth coming with it. The entry was cramped and not a soul said a word, their worried glances bouncing from one to another. Mary took another step, but nothing was stable. She slumped against a small table, the bowl on it rattling.

She clapped a hand over her mouth. "Margaret is gone."

Thomas, Cecelia, Jenny, and Aunt Maude crowded her, their frantic, fear-pitched voices spearing her with questions.

"Where could she be?" Cecelia asked.

"Do you think she ran off with a young man?" was Jenny.

"Are you sure she's not at the shop?" was Aunt Maude.

Above the fray was Thomas. His voice was the iron thread she grabbed.

"Does this have anything to do with your hunt for Jacobite gold?" which silenced the room.

He towered over everyone and stood outside the cluster of worried women crowding Mary. If they turned to him, she wouldn't know. She was cold . . . so very, very cold.

Sweet Margaret, her one responsibility in this life, was gone. Taken.

Only one name came to mind—Lord Ranleigh. The cur.

Was his threat to Thomas not enough? Did he think taking Margaret would bring her to heel? Fury reached up through her knees and made her stand straight, a steely, fortified anger, infusing her spine and setting her course. Ranleigh was messing with the wrong woman.

She looked to the maid. "Jenny, my cloak, if you please." To Cecelia, "Have you a pistol I may use?"

"No, but Alexander does. Two of them. I'll load them for you."

Mary watched her race upstairs. It was gratifying, Cecelia's quick support, no questions asked. Thomas was an obelisk in the background, his mouth grim. One message from him prevailed—*I am with you.*

She felt it in the marrow of her bones.

"Pistols?" Worry clouded Aunt Maude's face. "What are you going tae do, dear?"

"I'm going to bring Margaret home."

Chapter Thirty

Margaret is missing.

Words to prod Mary when she charged the front door of Maison Bedwell, the pistol in hand hidden in her cloak. She rued the day she crossed paths with the brothel's owner.

"Mary," Thomas soothed. "Please, exercise caution."

She turned a sharp chin at him. "I said you could accompany me as long as you stayed out of my way."

Her calm resolve formed in Cecelia's cozy entry had crumbled. She badly needed it again. The black lacquer door was her River Styx. Once she crossed it, she would become unbeatable or face her own death. Either way, there'd be no going back.

"Please give me the pistol," he said.

Thomas already had the second pistol tucked in his breeches at the small of his back. And he wanted hers?

"No." To emphasize her point, she pounded the butt on the door. "This isn't the time for half measures. Either I have your full support or none at all."

His green-blue eyes were fathomless.

"You know you have it."

Tension uncoiled a small degree. She wanted to weep. She wasn't alone. His word was as solid as oak and his presence more so. Considering Thomas's profound offer, she ought to give something in return.

"You have my word—I won't shoot to kill," she said, mollified.

"Glad to hear it. The day's too lovely for prison."

She cracked a smile. "It is . . . and you dressed so handsomely."

"I wore my best waistcoat for this promenade of ours."

A sweet jest. It wasn't lost on her. Thomas was standing in front of a brothel when he ought to be across the river in Southwark, tending his business. This entire day had been a shocking detour. Cecelia's small but luxurious robin's egg blue carriage had taken them from Dowgate. She hadn't said much on that ride. Thomas seemed to understand her need for quiet.

Now they were in noisy King's Square like two outlaws girded for plunder.

Loyal Thomas . . .

Mary was humbled, knocking on the door again, reasonably this time.

"Thank you," she whispered.

Thomas touched the brim of his hat, a gentle salute. "Anything for you."

His words settled in her heart as Maison Bedwell's door opened. The footman, Connor, blocked the entrance. He was sleepy eyed, sliding an arm into his pink velvet livery.

"Good morning, Miss Fletcher, Mr. West. What brings you to Bedwell's?"

Mary was quick to tuck her pistol into her cloak.

"Oh, Connor. Do you ask that of all the patrons? Or just me?"

The footman finger-combed unruly hair. "It's the hour, miss."

Thomas's pocket watch had just reached eleven o'clock when they'd exited Cecelia's pretty carriage.

"Does passion really care what time it is?" she asked sweetly.

"No, miss."

"Then we can agree, you need to let us in." When Connor hedged, she added, "You do know I paid handsomely for the Red Rose room. Lord Ranleigh made no mention of limited hours." To Thomas, "Did his lordship say anything to you?"

"Not that I recall."

Connor sighed and stepped aside. "Will you be needing wine in your room, miss?"

"No." She waved him off. "And I'll keep my cloak. By the by, is Lord Ranleigh up and about?"

"He's not accepting visitors, miss," was the footman's cryptic answer.

Thomas removed his hat but kept his greatcoat on. Like her, he scanned their environs. Ranleigh could be anywhere: next door, or deep in the bowels of his brothel, sleeping off his victory, or he could be scurrying through London like a cockroach in service to the crown.

She needed to draw him out.

As Connor was closing the door, she laid her trap.

"When it's convenient, please give Lord Ranleigh a message." She eyed the frescoes smiling down on her. "Tell his lordship I might have given him the French Pox."

Connor went white around the gills. "Miss?"

"Nasty business. When I last visited his lordship, we didn't use a French card, and . . ." She batted the air. "Well, a man ought to know, don't you think?"

The footman nodded emphatically. "Of course."

"Don't worry about us," she said, linking arms with Thomas. "We know the way."

They meandered through the cavernous entry. If she had her bearings right, Connor was darting off to the doorway that connected to the kitchen. MacLeod had given her an idea of the layout belowstairs. She ascertained that either Connor was exceedingly hungry or Lord Ranleigh was belowstairs.

Thomas's biceps were tense. "You and Ranleigh haven't . . ."

His unfinished question hung awkwardly. She couldn't bear that he felt the need to ask if she'd been intimate with Lord Ranleigh. She stopped their progress by the empty gaming room and tipped her face to his.

"There is only one non-suitor for me."

"I'm glad to hear it." A smile played at the corners of his mouth. "The French Pox. That was clever."

She touched a button on his waistcoat. "Thank you."

"It was forward of me asking, but you've not said much and . . ." His shrug was eloquent. "These are strange times."

Thomas's voice scraped with contained emotions. She was miserable, being the cause of his uncertainty and he a staunch ally. But he had to know, beneath her calm, emotions seethed like a kettle about to boil over.

"You are very, very dear to me, but please understand . . . I *must* get Margaret back. I'll do anything—anything to save her."

Thomas covered her hand with his. Solid, tanned from the sun, and scarred like hers and so, so strong.

"I am with you, Mary. In full measure, for whatever it takes."

Her lips parted and her throat was parched from worry. She would've soaked up more of his strength but heel strikes broke the silence. Ranleigh was crossing the entry hall.

"Miss Fletcher, back so soon and with the most interesting news about my health."

She pulled away from Thomas, the pistol still hidden from view. Miss Thelen was donning a man's black frock coat, trailing Ranleigh. Mary was relieved. The henchwoman packed only one weapon this morning, a knife tied to her thigh.

"Bad news is one way to flush out a rat," Mary shot back.

The dark lord sauntered forward, lace cuffs feathering his hands. "What's this? And here I thought you were anxious to begin our connection."

Air stirred beside her. Dear Thomas. Waves of irritation were rolling off him.

"Is there someplace we can talk discreetly?" she asked.

"In a brothel?" Ranleigh laughed. "Of course." He gestured to the empty gaming room. "This should suffice."

The dark lord was casual this morning, his shirt open at the neck and his queue plainly tied. He wore black velvet and dark circles under his eyes, the price of late hours. The four of them formed a line and went into the long chamber ripe with lingering smells of unwashed men and stale air. Miss Thelen tossed back a loose braid and stood hip-cocked against the wall. Lord Ranleigh dispensed with niceties and took the chair at a gaming table in front of her. Thomas was strategic, closing the door.

Mary swallowed hard. Fear and anger competed inside her. Both emotions could be helpful if handled properly—like the pistol in her trembling hand. To calm herself, she gripped the butt until the metal filigree bit her skin.

"Where is Margaret?"

Ranleigh linked both hands on the baize. "Margaret who?"

"Don't play coy with me." She raised her pistol and pointed it at him.

Ranleigh blanched and his henchwoman sprang off the wall as though she'd leap over the table and end this threat. Mary had no doubt she could. To make sure the henchwoman understood the gravity, Mary pointed the pistol at her heart.

"Don't. Move."

Ranleigh raised his hands in a show of peace. "Easy now. I thought you were here for friendlier reasons."

"Clearly not," she snapped. "I don't have patience for you, my lord. I've had a bad day."

Ranleigh's gaze traveled over her. "I can see that."

Her hair was loose from clutching her skull, her eyes pained with unshed tears, and her stomacher boasted a tiny rip from her fretting fingers, which would be visible where her untied cloak had parted. She didn't care.

"It's the new look for women hunting rats." She

advanced on him, frustrated and angry. "Where is Margaret?"

"Who is Margaret?" Ranleigh asked, agitated.

"My sister!"

Miss Thelen took a half step around the table. "Put that away. You're not a killer."

Thomas produced his pistol and aimed it at the henchwoman. "Back away."

The henchwoman glared at Ranleigh and said a string of angry foreign words. "Skit! När det gäller den här kvinnan har du slutat använda båda årorna."

Thomas chuckled as if he understood. "Now, now, Miss Thelen. Arms up and your back to the wall."

A scowling Miss Thelen complied, positioning herself in front of an awful brothel portrait.

Mary glared at the henchwoman and asked Thomas, "What did she say?"

"An old Swedish adage about not using both oars." Thomas glanced at her, amused. "Miss Thelen is convinced, when it comes to you, Ranleigh can't think straight."

The dark lord was rigid and steely eyed as if he could, by force of will, change this interview. Mary's blood was racing, her hands were sweating, and she might've been wild-eyed, addressing him.

"What? You've nothing to say?"

"Not with a pistol pointed at me."

Oh, he was a cool one.

"Your henchwoman might be right about me not being a killer, but a flesh wound won't stop your mouth from running." She cocked the pistol with a shaky hand. "Let's test that theory, shall we?"

"I don't have your sister," Ranleigh growled and

put his arms up like Miss Thelen. "Harming innocents is not my usual practice, but she can't be all that innocent if she's stealing Jacobite gold."

"A rich jab, sir. Thank you, but I'll remind you that I'm the woman pointing a pistol at you, and you are the very same man I met last night who told me he'd do anything for the crown." She smirked, having placed delicious emphasis on *anything*. "You can try and dress up what you do, Lord Ranleigh, but you're just a rabid dog on a leash."

Ranleigh's brows slanted tersely, and his chest was expanding under the increasing ebb and flow of aggravated breaths.

"It appears, Miss Fletcher, that you and I have a choice. We can trade insults, or we can work together to get your sister back."

Mary startled and checked Thomas. He was stoic beside her.

She stepped closer to the gaming table. "What do you mean?"

"I'd wager half my wealth that my cousin took her." Ranleigh was too definitive. She took another step.

"The Countess of Denton? She's in Scotland."

"No, I learned this morning that she returned to London two nights ago. She hasn't gone anywhere, which is unlike her."

A vein throbbed on the dark lord's temple and his nostrils flared. He was angry for being caught like this. A man in his position would say anything to escape. Mary shook her head.

"I don't believe you. It takes weeks to travel from Arisaig to London."

"If going by carriage, yes. Ancilla, however, took

a schooner. Very fast, those schooners." His near-black eyes narrowed. "If you don't believe me, ask your friend Mr. West."

She counted to ten silently in her head. She resented Ranleigh's logic, but the countess wreaking havoc made sense.

"Mary," Thomas said. "I've gambled enough with the lout to know when he's playing a sham."

"And?"

Thomas lowered his pistol. "He's telling the truth . . . at least what he believes it to be."

Mary's elbow gave way, and her arm dropped to her side. Her body didn't feel like hers anymore. Shock, fear, worry. Wave after wave of distraught was taking control. She had to grip the chair to stay standing. It was all she could do to hold back stinging tears.

She swallowed hard and sought Thomas. "For the first time in my life, I don't know what to do."

Chapter Thirty-One

"If you both put your pistols on the table, I'm prepared to offer my help." Ranleigh. His hands were down but his tone was severe.

Mary set the pistol on the baize with a heavy *clunk*. Thomas was reticent, eyeing Ranleigh. Strange details started coming into focus. Little things like how tired Ranleigh looked, and Maison Bedwell's gaming room, an ugly place by day. The stench of lost fortunes and ruined families clung to its walls.

How many nights had he gambled in this room? At this very table in front of him? Or any of the tables just like it? He'd left too much hard-earned money in the bowels of this godforsaken place. He'd almost lost his business.

Even worse, he'd almost lost his soul—to Ranleigh.

The dark lord prodded him. "West . . . put down your pistol."

Thomas studied Mr. Sloane's excellent weapon. French made, brass fittings throughout. A flintlock Holster pistol befitting a French officer and a gentleman. He smiled fondly at it.

"It's like Mary said. Your mouth still works even

if you've got a flesh wound." Thomas grunted. "Of course, a hole in your foul heart might be just the thing to make my day."

"Shooting me won't help your lady love. And it definitely won't get her sister back."

Thomas gusted a sigh. He didn't like Ranleigh being the voice of reason, but he couldn't argue with the man's logic.

"Just so we're clear. This isn't for you." He put his weapon on the table with care. "I'm doing this for the Scot's heart only."

Ranleigh's shoulder sank in relief. They were a motley foursome, gathering around the table. The baize had seen better days. Stains smudged the green, and small burn holes dotted the table where Ilsa Thelen took her seat.

Thomas took a seat and bounced his knee under the table. This was bitter medicine, working with Ranleigh. This morning he was gambling for higher stakes. They all were, with Ranleigh and his henchwoman on one side of the table, Thomas and Mary on the other, pistols in front of them.

Ranleigh steepled his fingers. "We need to know what Ancilla wants."

"I thought she was all about revenge," Mary said. "This was the crux of your late-night tale."

Under the table, Thomas squeezed his thigh. He'd come to terms with certain truths this morning: he was breaking his vow to never return to Bedwell's, and Mary left him asleep after a rousing tumble to meet with the dark turd facing them. Not an excellent morning, as it were.

He gritted his teeth, tempted to shoot the smug bastard after all.

"Forgive me for saying so, Miss Fletcher, but your sister is of no consequence," Ranleigh said. "Ergo my cousin taking her is for a greater end."

"You speak as though Margaret is a pawn on your chessboard."

"It is the game we play."

Mary was pensive. A game of chess or a game of chance, someone would win and another would lose.

"Does this have anything to do with the papers you want me to steal?" she asked.

Ranleigh's mouth twisted. "I wish you hadn't said that."

"What's the matter, Ranleigh? You look constipated." Thomas couldn't regret the jibe.

Mary reached for him under the table. "Thomas is with me. No matter what."

He clasped hands with her. Her intervention was full of bravado. He knew the truth. Her palms were damp and her hand a little shaky. She owed him an explanation about nighttime meetings and papers, and when the time came, he'd put his foot down. But this moment had its sweetness—Mary Fletcher needed him.

He gave her hand a tender squeeze. Mary's gray gaze slid to his, softer and reassured.

"The most likely reason Ancilla took your sister is she wants something from you," Ranleigh said.

"But you don't really know, do you?" Mary shook her head. "Enough of this. I need to start looking for Margaret."

Ranleigh leaned forward. "And where would you start?"

"With the hack she took yesterday at twilight,"

Mary said, rising. "Someone on White Cross Street is bound to remember the number plate on the back . . . at least part of it."

"Wait." Ranleigh stood up. "I'm willing to put my considerable resources into finding your sister."

"You're welcome to join us, my lord." Mary picked up her pistol and dropped it into her petticoat pocket. "But I'm not wasting another minute here."

Thomas got up, collected his pistol, and tucked it into the back of his breeches. He couldn't regret this short-lived parley. But Ranleigh was rounding the table, emphatic.

"Miss Fletcher. Believe me, I want your sister safely returned to you. But you and West are only two people, while I have more than a dozen men at my disposal. Men trained to ask the right questions. Men who can sniff out trouble." He extended an arm toward his henchwoman. "And if that's not enough, Ilsa's part bloodhound. She's the best tracker I know."

Mary brushed back hair from her eyes, her face troubled. Thomas stood beside her. This couldn't be an easy decision, but she alone had to make it.

Ranleigh reached for Mary but stopped short, his hand curling to a fist midair.

"I know my cousin. I know her habits and the places she goes when she steps outside of the law. Get those papers for me and I will unleash Ilsa and a team of men to find your sister. Please," he added softly. "Let me help you."

Mary's mouth wobbled from a sad, sad smile.

"That's the thing, isn't it? If you were a good man, you would help me. But your help comes with a price, which means it's not really help at all."

Ranleigh's arm dropped to his side. He took the

much-deserved verbal blow, his shoulders straight and his eyes hooded. Outside the gaming room's closed doors, footsteps pattered. The brothel was waking up. Business would soon be underway, or at least preparation for it.

Mary pinched the bridge of her nose. "Let's imagine for a moment that I'm agreeing to steal those coveted papers. What does it mean exactly?"

"Tomorrow night Ancilla is attending a ball at my brother, the duke's, home at Park Place," Ranleigh said. "That's your opportunity."

"And in return, you'll hope to find my sister by then?"

Ranleigh assured her, "We will do our utmost to make that happen."

"But you can't guarantee it."

"No."

Desperate unshed tears glittered in Mary's eyes. "I don't know." She pressed her lips together. "The time might be better served if I searched for Margaret. I—I can only imagine how awful this has been for her."

"Mary." Thomas touched the small of her back.

He'd go to hell and back for this woman, but certain truths were undeniable. Ranleigh had the resources, the knowledge, and the experience Mary needed. It pained Thomas to put in a good word for the well-shod blackguard. For Mary and her sister's sake, he would.

He was gruff, advising her. "Listen to him, Mary. He's Margaret's best hope."

If Ranleigh was surprised by the support, he didn't show it. The dark lord was focusing on Mary alone.

"When the people we love are threatened, it's natural to leap into a fight. But, Miss Fletcher, you have no idea what this fight is about. The only thing you have is your fear and your anger, and that will blind you to common sense."

"Am I supposed to do nothing?" Mary's voice was watery and indignant. "Just . . . wait?"

"The best thing you can do right now is go about your day and make plans for tomorrow night. The element of surprise is on our side."

"It's helpful for you if I fetch those papers, but not for Margaret."

Ranleigh touched her sleeve. "My cousin is blissfully unaware that the four of us know your sister is missing. Let Ancilla think she has the advantage."

Mary wavered beside Thomas. Not searching for her sister was a sound idea. And terribly distressing. Bright tears began rolling down her cheeks. Each droplet pricked Thomas like a knife. Mary sniffled when he pushed back her hood and cupped her jaw. Tears slid, salty and slow, wetting his hand until eyes as mysterious as North Sea storms met his.

"We'll face this together," he said.

"Together." Mary sniffled again and gave Ranleigh the barest nod. "I'll do it."

A partnership was forged, quick details exchanged, ending with a request from Mary.

"My lord, I need to write a note and have our coachman deliver it to my friend." Mary added, "She's the one who can get me into Lady Denton's home tomorrow night."

Ranleigh nodded. "Of course. Let's go to my study."

They were migrating to the door and near the empty faro table when Miss Thelen called Mary.

"Miss Fletcher."

Mary turned. "Yes?"

The henchwoman was alone by the table.

"I will lead the search for Margaret." She fisted a hand over her heart. "You have my word. We will find her."

Chapter Thirty-Two

*T*he carriage ride from Maison Bedwell to White Cross Street was an exercise in control. Mary's mostly. She watched passing traffic from the safe confines of their splendid carriage, while Thomas watched her. He reveled in the tender things. Her gold medallion bouncing in the well of her neck. A sacred place, that sweet slope. He would dip his finger there, trace her collarbones, her peach-soft earlobe—to comfort her, if she'd let him.

The Mary Fletcher who'd left Bedwell's was not the same woman who'd charged into it.

Could be she needed to collect her thoughts. Turning his hat over and over, he wished she'd share some of her musings. It was a bit of irony, this wanting a woman to talk, when most men of his acquaintance wanted a woman's silence.

"You look like you belong in this carriage," he said, trying to make conversation.

"Do I?" She stopped her vigil of the world outside and folded both hands in her lap.

"You do."

Her gaze traced silky, gold-tasseled ropes looped

in the corners. "I always thought this carriage was silly excess."

Those luxurious ropes did have him wondering.

He pushed down on his plush seat. Butter-smooth leather had just the right give under his hand. "You must admit, tufted leather is preferable to hacks with stingy seats."

The smallest of smiles curved her mouth. "Stingy-seated hack rides can be just the thing."

Her gaze lingered on him. A tiny flame of happiness fought for survival in her eyes. The weak flicker gouged him as severely as any harpoon, tearing his heart. The Mary Fletcher he knew and loved had vanished.

He squinted at the carriage floor.

What happened in Ranleigh's study?

He tried to make sense of it. They'd left the gaming room and gone to Ranleigh's study. Mary had dashed off her note. There'd been two minutes, possibly three, when she'd tarried at Ranleigh's desk, waiting for the ink to dry. A footman had beckoned Thomas into the hall with a message about their carriage. Behind him, voices clashed in a hushed argument. He'd checked the room. A flash of malevolence came from Ranleigh, but nothing more. Mary had left the study, present in body, but not in spirit.

She'd swept by him, murmuring, "Let's get out of here."

He'd been all too happy to oblige, but Mary had kept a polite distance. Racing off unescorted out of Bedwell's, him trotting after her.

Ranleigh had watched it all from his study window like a dark crow.

Presently, they were crossing Beech Lane, and

Mary had returned to staring at the world beyond the carriage window. It could be the farce was getting to her. He couldn't fault her for it. What happened to her sister was unthinkable and silence was her way to handle it. If anyone took his mother or sisters, he'd tear London apart looking for them. But this remoteness of Mary's niggled him. Something else was afoot.

He pinched the corner of his hat. "Mary, what happened in Ranleigh's study?"

She dragged her pained gaze to his.

"I saw what looked to be a brief argument," he said.

"It was nothing."

A blatant lie, and now Lord Ranleigh was with them, unseen poison. What hold did the man have on her? He tossed his hat on the seat and crossed his arms. He should've shot the cur when he had the chance.

"I'll go to Neville Warehouse, check on business," he said. "Mr. MacLeod will be there. I'll inform him of what we're doing and to keep Margaret's disappearance a secret."

Annoyance tightened her features. "Yes, we've gone over this. I'll have the coachman deliver my note to Cecelia."

Mary's stare went right through him, cool and remote, while he chewed on his frustration. He had no idea how to reach the woman. Or why her sudden distance. As the carriage rumbled to a stop, she looked ready to flee. Fletcher's House of Corsets and Stays was outside, her haven. Mary reached for the door, not waiting for the coachman.

Thomas followed her out. "Mary . . ."

She turned to him, wisps of hair blowing across her cheeks. "Yes?"

"I will come back and look after you."

"About that . . . It's really not necessary. I'm used to looking after myself." Mary studied the ground, misery sinking her shoulders. "Please know that I am grateful for your help . . . all of it," she whispered. "But I want you to go away."

He felt his eyes rounding. Was he dismissed?

She raised her head slowly, her eyes lifeless. "Don't come back. Not tonight. Not ever."

A bolt of shock stilled him.

"Mary . . ." He reached for her and she flinched as though his touch would scald her. "What is this?"

"I've rethought our . . . connection, and I simply can't find satisfaction in it."

He stared, dumbfounded. She didn't need him? Not for comfort and kisses? Or to help her steal the blasted papers in Ranleigh's Machiavellian trade to get her sister back? Thomas huffed, looking at nothing in particular. He was hamstrung, unable to clarify this befuddling turnabout in the middle of White Cross Street.

Then, there was his stunned pride. Behind that emotion was reason. What passed between them had burned swift and bright—perhaps too swiftly.

"I might be fooling myself, but I'm certain at our last *connection* the stars did shimmer and the moon did shine brighter. For both of us," he said pointedly.

If anything, they shared *that*.

"I shall be forever grateful, but this . . . you and I . . . are done."

"Mary . . ." Her name was a strange whisper on his lips.

Silence prevailed. Her eyes were shuttered until she curtseyed.

"Thank you, Mr. West." And she ran into her shop as though the devil nipped her heels.

His jaw dropped. She bloody curtseyed to him. He ought to move on, but his feet were glued to the ground. The road was busy. Pedestrians bumped him. Midday sunlight made everything crystal clear. Standing outside the window, he could see Miss Fletcher was a sylph inside her shop until she disappeared past the yellow curtain.

This had to be some misguided wish to protect him (not a rejection of their passion, or so his pride assured him). Seconds fled as he considered which of the two explanations was true. More time would've passed, except the coachman coughed into his balled fist.

"Sir, if it's Neville Warehouse you're wanting, we ought to go. London Bridge and all."

"Yes. To Neville Warehouse." He was too old to stand like a lovelorn swain outside her shop.

Thomas climbed back into the blue confection of a carriage. Once White Cross Street was behind him, another piece to Mary Fletcher's puzzle came back to him—her midnight meeting with Ranleigh. She'd never told him the substance of it.

Staring out the window, he dragged a knuckle over the glass. It was time to acknowledge an unpleasant fact.

His siren was keeping another secret.

MARY STIRRED THE simmering pot on her workshop stove. The glue's woodsy smells steamed her nose. Flour, water, alum, and a few drops of birch oil. Her hands trembled too much for needle and thread, and touching baleen made her cry. She hiccupped and went to the worktable where strips of linen waited. *Dear Thomas.* Losing him was almost as heartbreaking as the thought of losing her sister.

She dipped her rag in a pot of glue.

Oh, Margaret, where are you?

Was she tied up? Had she eaten? Was she hurt?

She slapped the rag on linen and began smearing it with glue. Leaning into her labor, loose hairs fell forward. She swiped them off her face with the back of her hand, sniffling and careful to keep her sticky fingers from touching her hair. More tears threatened to come. Signs of Margaret were everywhere, each kindness a stab to Mary's soul. The stairs to their garret swept clean. The bed tidy. Margaret's latest arrangement in the shop window. How talented her sister was. Colorful streamers on white fabric, the entire display like colorful candies on meringue.

Miss Dalton was at the yellow curtain, her eyes popping. "My goodness, miss. You weren't jesting when you said you were making buckram. This looks like a year's worth."

Undyed linen hung like small banners on a dozen ropes stretching back and forth in the workroom. Half of the linens were dry and half still glistened. Tomorrow they'd get a second coat, and on the third day become buckram—the stiff inner fabric for corsets and stays.

Miss Dalton threaded the maze of shoulder high ropes. "It's twilight, miss. Do you want me to stay?"

"That's kind of you, but no."

The seamstress stood in the forest of cloth. Her forehead wrinkled with worry but she was too well mannered to ask about her employer's swollen red eyes. An afternoon of solitary crying did that to a woman.

Mary smiled benignly. "Go on. I'll lock the door when I'm done with this batch."

They said their goodbyes and Mary stirred the pot again. Work was the best remedy to chase away fear and utter helplessness. Several times she'd been tempted to don her cloak and hunt for Margaret. But the notes in her pocket advised her to stay put and maintain the appearance that all was well.

Miss Thelen was making progress. She had hunted down a hack with the number plate 183—Margaret's hack. Cecelia had sent word, stating that Denton House's study window would be left open at ten o'clock tomorrow night. Lord Ranleigh had sent a missive—the search was going well. How tidy, all these arrangements, and she, unable to take charge.

This uselessness was driving her mad.

For comfort, she pulled out Lord Ranleigh's message and read it again.

Dear Miss Fletcher,

Following the hack number was an excellent idea. We've narrowed down your sister's location to one of three hamlets outside London.

A splotch of ink marred the page as though the dark lord's quill had hovered while he decided how to state his demand.

Regarding tomorrow night; deliver your package to the mews behind my home. Connor will wait for you. I'm sure you remember him. He's the Irishman who informed me I have the French Pox.

R.

P.S. Burn this note.

Everything was falling into place. Except for Thomas. She crumpled the note and jammed it into her apron pocket. His stricken face haunted her. The agony in his eyes. His mouth agape, then slowly shutting in an unforgiving line. She had done her worst. Glacial Mary Fletcher. A cold bitch.

Pain was a rock in her belly. She held on to the worktable, a sob climbing up her throat. Her eyes were hot and bleary. She dabbed them with her apron. Oh, she was a mess. When the time was right, she'd explain all to Thomas—if he'd allow her the chance.

The awful turn with Thomas had been Lord Ranleigh's doing. The scene that morning in his study was the newest wound, refusing to heal. She'd been waiting for the ink to dry on her message to Cecelia when the dark lord leaned in.

"*You need to send West packing,*" Ranleigh whisper-hissed.

"*Why?*"

"*If Ancilla finds out he's involved, she will destroy him. Then, she'll go after his family, his business.*"

"*You threatened his business,*" she shot back.

"*To get you to work for me.*" His jaw tipped an arrogant angle. "*And now you are.*"

"*Only to get Margaret safely home. Then, we're done.*"

"We most definitely are, Miss Fletcher." Tension lines bracketed his mouth. "You'll have to leave London. You, your sister, your league friends—all of you." His onyx gaze went to the door where Thomas had finished talking with a footman. "You and your league are in the thick of things. Him, you can spare. But that's up to you."

She absorbed this, keeping her back to Thomas. He had an uncanny ability to read each twitch, each smile, each frown.

"I thought these papers would spare us all from your cousin's wrath," she said.

"Ancilla made a move before me." Ranleigh shuffled papers. "Everything's going too fast, and I don't want to make a promise I can't keep."

"A fine time to tell me you're honorable, my lord, when you conveniently can't be."

She'd stalked out of Ranleigh's study and hadn't looked back. His lordship had neatly put more burdens on her. Tell Cecelia she must leave London? She dreaded that. Aunt Maude and Aunt Flora wouldn't care. Her league knew what they had gotten themselves into.

The man who'd waited for her didn't.

Thomas, her tall, scarred sea wolf. He'd fight for her. She knew this, but she needed to fight for him. She braced both arms on the table, badly wanting him back.

When her shop door jingled, her heart soared. Thomas! *He'd come after all.*

She rushed through banners of linen. "Thomas? Is that you?"

Mary knocked aside the yellow curtain and froze. Expensive silk rustled, a sublime sound drawing the ear and the eye. One would want to follow it.

The beautiful woman wearing it was meticulous perfection. Pearlescent silk, a red-raspberry shade. Unsurprisingly, her lips matched. Mary knew the meaning of swimming beyond one's depth.

If Ranleigh was a praetorium guard on the rise, the woman in her shop was the lethal, highborn widow who drank power like wine.

"Lady Denton."

$\mathscr{M}$iss Fletcher. I don't believe I've made your acquaintance," the countess said.

"We haven't, my lady."

"But I've met your sister."

Mary clutched her stomacher. "My sister?"

Per Ranleigh's instructions, she was supposed to act shocked. It wasn't hard. White-hot fear was eating her from the inside out.

"She never crossed London Bridge. But Margaret is doing well, mind you."

Mary couldn't stop herself from stepping forward, menacingly. "What have you done to her?"

"Well, she's not in Southwark, which is a blessing, don't you think? Grimy and unpleasant, Southwark is. No, your sister is tucked safely away." Lady Denton's manicured brows rose a fraction. "Which means we are alone, aren't we?"

"Yes." It was hard to talk with her heart in her throat.

Lady Denton flicked gloved fingers at someone behind her. "See if she's telling the truth."

A thick-boned redhead in a brown frock coat

stalked past Mary. He held his flintlock with a possessive hand. Definitely a man who'd shoot first, ask questions later. Lady Denton smiled thinly while her boorish henchman stomped around the workroom. Mary could hear the damage being done. Ropes snapping. Crockery smashed. A chair was overturned. Lady Denton's man emerged, knocking a scrap of linen off his shoulder.

"Looks clear, milady. Want me to check abovestairs?"

"No, I don't think that's necessary." Lady Denton was droll, fixing her gloves. "From what I hear, the elder Miss Fletcher keeps to herself." To her henchman, she said, "Leave us."

A blunt "Milady," and he exited the shop.

Lady Denton winced as the door slammed shut. "He's a rough one, but efficient."

Her soft-worded *efficient* made Mary's skin crawl. Outside, the very same henchman gave a nod to the Night Watch lighting the street lamp near Mary's shop. What a mad world this was. Lady Denton smiled, apparently thinking the same thing.

"Ironic, isn't it? You want to call for help because you're frightened of me. But if you did, there'd be the burden of proof and all the sticky questions as to how our paths crossed in the first place." The countess touched a finger to the decorative table in the heart of the shop. "The upper hand is mine, of course. The sooner you calm down and realize this, the better."

"You were direct with Anne and most direct with Cecelia. So why don't you state your wants plainly?"

The countess's eyes narrowed. "Yet, they both got away. Slippery women . . . I won't make the same mistakes with you and your sister."

Fear and fine manners disappeared. Mary was almost belligerent, folding her arms under her bosom. "What do you want?"

"I want my gold back. Return it to me Thursday next, and Margaret comes home."

"That's a week and a day," Mary said.

"You can read a calendar. Excellent."

"But—but that's impossible," she sputtered.

"Why? Because your league spent it all? Or because you've sent it to Scotland?"

What a fine trap. Mary almost snared herself in it. All the gold had gone to Scotland with Anne and Will. There'd be no getting it back. She rubbed her eyes with the back of her wrist and the countess looked askance at her.

"Have you been crying, Miss Fletcher? Your eyes are red as is the tip of your nose."

"It's the glue I made." She showed her sticky fingertips.

The countess seemed to accept this. "Well, you know my demands. Delivery of seventeen hundred gold livres to my house by noon Thursday next. If you don't have the livres, a comparable currency will suffice."

"I'm certain we'll need more time."

The countess hummed as though Mary had given her an important piece of information.

Lady Denton sauntered to the shop door and opened it. "Thursday next, Miss Fletcher. Or the man who tore through your workroom gets your sister." She rolled an elegant shoulder. "I can't say what happens after that."

Mary's breaths were shallow, and her ribs could be slowly squeezed in a vise. Fear, anger . . . both

burned inside her. The countess took a long, memorizing look. Her lips flattened as though she didn't
like what she saw. If the countess had looked lower,
to the lump in Mary's apron pocket, she would've
seen the crumpled note, which would've tipped
Ranleigh's hand.

Perhaps Mary ought to have cowered before her?
Instead, she stood tall, her chin ax-blade sharp.

Lady Denton snorted. "You don't look like you're
afraid. But you will."

Mary rushed forward, furious. "If one hair on
Margaret's head is harmed . . ."

She let the threat dissolve. Her life was unraveling, but this was one facet she could control. For the
first time since this mess began, she was looking forward to breaking into Denton House. This time for
sweet revenge.

"Good night, Miss Fletcher."

The door closed and Lady Denton swept into her
waiting carriage. Her henchman climbed onto the
back and tipped his hat at Mary. His evil grin made
her shiver in disgust. Mr. Wortley, the countess's
usual watchdog, didn't show his face. He had to be
with Margaret.

From the heart of her shop, she watched the carriage roll away, struck by a simple fact. Lady Denton
had announced her ugliest threat with the shop door
wide open.

The emboldened woman didn't care who heard her.

Chapter Thirty-Four

The hour could've been six o'clock or it could've been midnight. Determination fueled her to march into her workroom and restore order from the mess someone else made. She scrubbed her hands clean and took the glue pot off the stove; thankfully, that hadn't been upended. Cleaning glue off the floor would've been unbearable. White porcelain had been thrown down instead. She toed shards of what had been a pretty bowl for holding odds and ends.

All her hard work tossed willy-nilly.

She was on her knees, collecting linen strips and stacking them when another truth struck her: much of her life had been spent cleaning up messes made by others. Her sense of responsibility was a mile wide. There was Margaret, and the women of her league, and her clan Clanranald MacDonald.

What about her responsibility to herself?

She rose from the floor and rubbed the back of her neck, unsure. Tomorrow night she would get those papers. Then, what would she do? All this—her colorful bolts of cloth, her needles and threads, her business, her home—could be for naught.

All because Lord Ranleigh and his cousin battled each other in a larger game of chess.

"I'm done being a pawn." She blew out the work-room candles. "And I'm done being alone."

EVENING CAME, LONELY and still in her garret. The emptiness, stifling. She was at the window facing White Cross Street. Traffic had thinned. Shops had closed. Rooftops poked the sky as far as the eye could see. Somewhere out there, Margaret was held against her will. And somewhere out there, Thomas West thought the worst of her.

Both burdens were crushing. She could lose them both.

Then where would she be?

The hollow-eyed reflection staring back at her was frightening.

A sharp breath, and she decided to fight this. Work was the ideal curative for times like these. She ought to mend something. Rising from her seat, she spied a black tricorn on the street below. Her knees wavered. She leaned in, touching the glass to be sure. The tricorn's owner tipped his head to her window and offered a kind smile.

Mr. West was standing outside her shop door.

Her heart skipping in her chest, she tore out of her garret and raced to unlock her door.

"Thomas!" She launched herself into his arms.

He stumbled back the same as their awkward first kiss, his strong arms wrapping around her. She buried her nose in his chest and breathed his cedar-wood musk. Relief had never been sweeter.

"Mary." His voice was one part raw and one part surprise.

"I don't ever want to let you go."

He kissed the crown of her head. "I'm like a barnacle. Once I stick, I'm hard to scrape off."

His jest eased the butterflies taking a turn in her stomach. She wished she had the facility for words like Cecelia. Honest words would come, but for the moment a hug would do.

"I like being stuck with you," she whispered.

Soft laughter in her ear was his answer. Thomas had to know that was the closest she'd come to declaring herself. What a patient man, her sea wolf. He buried a hand in her hair, cosseting her in front of her shop, and she didn't care.

"I promised to stay by your side and not even a prickly siren can stop me." His voice was a comforting vibration.

"You are a man of your word."

"So I've heard." His hands stroked her back lovingly. "Mind you, I do a better job when my belly is full."

She tipped her head, the better to see his face. Night made his rugged features beautiful. The slopes and angles mysterious. His scar a piratical slash, leading to his kissable mouth. But his eyes snared her, tender and bright, more green-blue this time under the brim of his black hat. She caressed his jaw, her palm tickled by rasping whiskers.

"I have much to explain," she said.

"We both do."

She would've said more, except a *meowing* basket jiggled near her feet. She looked down. The whole thing rattled.

"You might be curious about that," Thomas said.

She stepped back. There were two baskets (one

of them *meowing*), a satchel, and a small cask clustered on the sidewalk. Thomas crouched down and opened the noisy basket's lid. Mr. Fisk jumped out, his tail flicking. The tabby put one graceful paw in front of the other and slipped into her shop as though he ought to inspect the place.

Thomas was on one knee, his mouth slanting a grin. "Mr. Fisk is an excellent attack cat."

She laughed, clasping both hands to her chin. "A chivalrous four-legged gentleman. I shall depend on him to defend me."

Thomas stood up, his eyes shining. "He'll have to get in line behind me."

The streetlamp showered him in a kind glow. The lump gathering behind her breastbone came with a message. *You adore this man. You always will.*

She swallowed delicately. "With a fine cat and his master slaying my dragons, I shall be the safest woman in London."

"Don't let him hear you say that," Thomas said, scooting his things into her shop. "Mr. Fisk likes to think he has charge of me."

She followed him and took her time closing the door. These profound emotions both humbled and delighted her. A wonderful chaos to sort through later. But she wouldn't have the luxury of doing that alone. After the door was locked, they loaded up their arms and carried baskets and such upstairs. Mr. Fisk was left to his devices, but a dish of cream would lure him to join them.

Once in her garret, she stoked the fire. Warmth already rolled off her. The shock of her neighbors seeing a man dip into her shop after twilight would have tongues wagging.

This was a first—being alone with a man up here. But this was her and Thomas. They . . . fit.

She set aside the poker and swiped both hands down her apron. With him, here, the chamber took on a new luster. Everything was brighter. The fire, the window, her soul.

Thomas pivoted a slow circle, a friendly smile showing on his face. "Very nice."

"You're being kind. The home of a shipmaster must be grand."

"Better to live happy in a humble place than live miserably in a palace." His eyes lit with deep affection. He removed his hat, subdued. There was a basket of mending near the fire, stacks of books on the mantel, and tidy but well-worn furniture. "Your home looks very, very happy," he said, reverent.

She stood taller and a bit awkward for his praise. "Thank you."

They stared at each other like silly youths who'd just stumbled on the wonder of love. Fireworks were going off under her skin. Her pulse banged a marching cadence loud enough her neighbors would hear.

Her bed was hard to miss. They were going to use it.

Thomas caught the direction of her gaze. His brow arched with a question. *Now?*

She blushed profusely. "I suppose you're hungry."

"Very much."

The suggestion in his voice teased her.

She opened a narrow cabinet and retrieved two bowls. "Thomas, this isn't the Red Rose room. This is my home."

He was in the act of removing his coat, wool sliding off broad shoulders, the kind a woman could count on. He grinned and tossed his coat onto his satchel.

"I'm here until Margaret returns. What comes after that is for us to decide at a better time."

She set the bowls on the table, relieved. Thomas understood the need to take life in small steps. This knowledge was as surprising as the sight of him rolling up his sleeves.

"I brought a ham and pea hachy," he announced.

"A hachy?"

"Trust me, you'll like it. If not, I have bread and beer to feed you."

She laughed. "Sustenance of the gods."

"And hungry sailors and corset makers."

Thomas was making himself at home in her makeshift kitchen, collecting spoons and serviettes. He surprised her when he poured the contents of a heavy crock into a pot hanging over the fire. She peered over his shoulder. A thick soup simmered in her small cauldron.

"You really are going to cook for me?" The very idea . . .

Thomas whisked a dishtowel from her cabinet and tossed it over his shoulder. "Isn't it time someone took care of you?"

Someone to take care of her—a foreign notion. It settled on her like an ill-fitting corset. He was more than willing to pitch in and do woman's work. Setting the table. Seeing to dinner. Thomas refused to let her lift a finger. When she mentioned this was the hour when she'd don her robe volant, the shapeless gown which freed her from her stays, Thomas herded her to the screen to change her clothes.

She unpinned her gown to pleasant aromas tickling her nose: bread's sweet, floury goodness, and the warming hachy, which she decided must be a poor man's stew. Dropping her robe volant over her head, she heard the soft *pop* of an uncorking. She rounded the screen, shaking out heavy velvet. Thomas was filling a tankard, and his shirt was open at the neck.

"Fancy a beer?" he asked.

"I'll try it." She settled at the table to sliced bread, bowls thick with peas and chunks of ham in a creamy broth, a butter crock, and an apple tart on a plate. "This looks wonderful."

Thomas set a tankard in front of her. "I do dishes too."

"You're hired. Though I don't know what to call you."

He took a seat, facing her. "Non-suitor works."

She grinned. "You are devious, plying me with dinner and thoughtful gestures."

"Deviousness—it's all part of my master plan."

They dug into their dinner with relish. Any awkwardness gone. They were not creatures of leisure. They worked. A life ingrained in them. Two cogs in the City's wheel. Being with Thomas, a partnership was forming right under her nose. He slathered bread with butter—two slices, one for her and one for him—and poured more beer when she needed it. This was strange, someone taking care of her first. Even sweet Margaret wasn't this solicitous.

Sinking her teeth in warm bread, she was happy and ready. She pulled Ranleigh's wrinkled note from her pocket and offered it to him. Thomas read it.

"Good news about Margaret. I'm sure she's safe."

He dropped the note on the table with a snort. "Looks like Ranleigh's given us our marching orders."

"But do we have to do as he says?" She dragged her spoon through the bowl. "What if we read the papers first before we hand them over? If we do at all?"

Thomas sat back, his tankard at his bottom lip. "That sounds like a dangerous game. What about Margaret?"

She scooped another spoonful of hachy. "We're in agreement. She must come first. But Ranleigh was emphatic I keep you out of this." She looked up from her bowl. "He was equally emphatic that I leave London once I've handed over the papers and Margaret is safely with me. He said the same for all the women of my league."

"If I didn't know any better, I'd say the cur is afraid."

She nodded. "Of what his cousin might do. And those papers."

He dipped his bread in his bowl and tore into it. "Which is good reason to stick to the plan and wash your hands of them."

"He also told me to send you packing."

"Ranleigh? Trying to protect me?" He swallowed more beer, then stretched out his hand for the conveniently close cask. He turned the spout and amber liquid splashed in his tankard. Above the spout, words were branded in wood: PEACOCK BREWHOUSE.

Mary gasped, humored and scandalized. "The beer . . ."

Thomas's smile split from ear to ear, and she

glimpsed the carefree man. No burdens of business or bloodthirsty countesses. It might've been the same smile he wore when he first went out to sea. She wanted to see more of it.

Was this love? Wanting glorious happiness for someone else?

"I have an affinity for peacocks of late." He eyed her over the rim of his tankard. "And the brewhouse is a quick stretch of the legs on Red Cross Street."

"We ought to visit it soon."

"We will." But his smile faded and his voice became gruff with emotion. "Let us agree, Mary Fletcher, that we'll speak to each other first and together, we'll decide our fate."

She sipped her beer. "Yes, we will."

Thomas deserved the reassurance. A comforting thing, an agreement. But her past was littered with disappointments. Life had never been easy.

It never was.

Chapter Thirty-Five

The evening sped by, and everything was done together as though there was no shop to tend or ships to careen. Dishes were washed side by side, the floor swept clean, and the fire stoked. She'd yawned once and rubbed her neck. Sleep or passion—both sounded heavenly.

When she yawned again, Thomas was gentle, coming up behind her. His thumbs worked magic, finding all the knots on her neck and shoulders.

"You're tired. Why don't we go to bed?" he murmured above her ear.

"Because I don't want this night to end. I like being with you."

He kissed the crook of her neck. "I like being with you too."

Her bed was the obvious furniture in her garret. Dark wool curtains, fluffy pillows, a practical wool counterpane, plainly stitched. No silk tassels or erotic fripperies, which made this so . . . domestic. Thomas nudged them along, pinching the candles and leaving them in the dark. He returned to her, rubbing his sooty thumb and forefinger on his breeches. *Men.*

Through the window, a three-quarter moon and scattered stars were their lights.

"This isn't the same as an exciting interlude. No one's going to make the bed or bring a bottle of wine." She snorted good-naturedly. "Nor can I boast feathers and switches. It's just me and you."

"And that's unexciting to you?" He folded her body against his and kept rubbing those knots.

"No, it's . . . normal."

His laugh was tender. "Do you crave the fantasy?"

"No."

Her only craving was his hands on her shoulders. She was sure the knots would surrender any moment now. Thomas's hands were that persuasive. The more he massaged her neck, the more she struggled to put syllables together when speaking.

Then, he whispered the most wonderful words. "Let's go to bed and be normal. I can hold you and rub your shoulders. You're very tense, you know."

"That's almost as erotic as saying you'll do the dishes."

Masculine laughter rumbled low. "I'll keep that in mind."

Thomas guided her to the bed while his calloused hands made sweet snicks on her velvet-covered back.

"Wait until tomorrow night when I show my skills with needle and thread," he teased.

"What? You sew?"

His face was beautiful above hers. "Don't get excited. I can sew a button that's fallen off. Nothing more."

She traced his scar. He'd said *tomorrow night* so easily, but tomorrow night they would sneak into the Countess of Denton's house. She made grumbly noises and scratched the roguish whiskers on his jaw. Sea wolf, shipmaster, man of business. Thomas was those things and more. His clever hands caressed her arms, her ribs. Before she could guess what he was doing, Thomas whisked the robe volant off her body, and the heavy velvet went flying over her screen.

"Mary Fletcher, you have nothing on but your shift and stockings."

"The benefit of my garret. There's not much to heat." She pulled a pin from her hair and a lock tumbled loose. "And there is you. You're exceedingly warm."

"I am."

He spoke and goose bumps flared on her skin. She loved hearing the arousal in his voice. Unlike their last time together, she would not take orders. Nor would she give them. This would be a mutual discovery. Slow and easy.

She drew a line down his button flash and started at the bottom.

He watched her fingers. "An unusual tactic."

"Yet, I'm undressing you. It feels very domestic . . . like something someone who wants to take care of you and see to your well-being would do."

"Is that's a longwinded way of saying a wife?"

Wife—a dangerous word. About as perilous as another four-letter word that began with an *L* and ended with an *E*. One should have a care when uttering them. She worked the buttons faster, daring an upward glance.

Moonlight splashed Thomas. He was stark shades of light and dark.

"You said earlier, no secrets." She stalled, her mouth open until she forced herself to finish. "After you fell asleep in the Red Rose room, I went to Ranleigh's house."

"To meet him?"

"No. To look for the last of the Jacobite gold." Buttons and cloth felt loose in her hands while she gave her awkward confessional. "We're trying to purchase a small herd of sheep—Cheviots, excellent wool, sturdy creatures," she murmured.

"You are a woman of many talents."

"Not really. Ranleigh was there. It was a trap and I walked right into it."

Thomas watched her. It was getting harder to breathe even though he was being quite reasonable as though men and women throughout the realm carried on sensible conversations about treasure and sheep and dark lords.

"We don't have to talk about him," Thomas said.

"We must." She slipped the waistcoat off his shoulders, her gaze glued to his chest. "He asked me to work for him."

Thomas put firm hands on her shoulders. His eyes were anvil-hard.

"To do what?"

"Spying, I think."

Thomas's hands dropped from her shoulders, his relief palpable. "Because you're smart. And you're beautiful. You could be anywhere and do anything. It's very possible that you could snag a baron and become a baroness. But you're here with me."

"You're infinitely better," she said in a rush. "Better than any man I've ever met."

Thomas reached up and freed a pin from her hair and a curl flopped in her side vision. He smiled.

"You just like me because of my cat."

His spoonful of humor was perfect. What followed was intimate and dear. Lovely Mr. Fisk. She hoped the cat found a cozy spot to sleep.

She climbed into bed with Thomas, drifting in and out of conversation. He closed the bed curtains and rubbed her soreness from standing at her worktable all day. His talented hands massaged her calves and skimmed the backs of her knees. Her shift's hem climbed higher. To her thighs, her hips, her navel. Thomas kissed the small dip in the middle of her belly, and he kissed the small dip at the base of her neck.

And he kissed and he kissed and he kissed, finding astonishing places to put his mouth.

She explored the texture of his skin. His crinkling masculine hairs, the slope of muscles, the abrupt lines of scars. He'd led a hard life. She had too. But this, their connection, ran deeper than the seas. There was an alchemy to it. No conjurer could explain it. For once in her practical workaday life, she'd let it be. No thinking, no wondering.

Her bed became a storm of sheets and bodies. Cloth twisting, kisses burning, fingers seeking. A slow discovery. An indolent pleasure. Conversation dwindled to grunts and cries. Tears pricked her eyes privately. This was giving and taking in perfect measure.

Nothing could break this. Nothing at all.

Chapter Thirty-Six

Morning with Thomas and Mr. Fisk was a quiet affair. She'd bathed behind her screen; Thomas had bathed naked by her washstand. It was startling, coming out from her screen and finding a man splashing water on his body, his bare feet shifting from the cold. They'd forgotten to tend the fire before slipping into bed.

"I could heat some water for you."

He grinned and lathered soap to shave with. "No, thanks. Chilly water wakes me up. Reminds me I'm alive."

She eyed her rumpled bed. "After last night, I feel plenty alive."

Which was the kind of quip Cecelia would say. While making the bed, she felt new kinship for the woman. A shirtless Thomas could make a woman forget where she was going. Little tufts of brown hair encircled his nipples. Taut skin covered slabs of muscle on his back. He was breathtaking in daylight, scraping a blade over his jaw. He flashed a smile in the mirror. She smiled back, fluffing a pillow, and almost clunked her head on a bedpost.

Mr. Fisk favored the new arrangement. He jumped up on the freshly smoothed counterpane and licked his paw. He purred when she came round and petted him.

She wanted to bottle this contentment.

But their porridge was boiling, and there were plans to make. The countess, of course. The woman was a blight on their happiness, and the reason Margaret was gone.

Mary nibbled her lower lip and made her way to the pot hanging from an iron hook over the fire. Margaret's return meant Thomas would leave. He was already gathering his things and putting them in his satchel.

Here for a short time . . . then he'd be gone.

Eyes shut, she hoarded the tenderness. The sound of his footsteps, his soap scenting the air, the tune he hummed under his breath. How dear this was. Almost sacred. When she opened her eyes, Mr. Fisk was rubbing her leg, his green eyes convincing her to part with more cream.

She scratched behind his ears, whispering, "We share the deepest affections for the same man, don't we?"

The cherished gentleman was oblivious, scrubbing a white towel over his face.

"About tonight," Thomas said. "Meet me at the Three Arrows in Nixon's Square at nine o'clock. Do you know it?"

She scooped porridge into a bowl. "I know Nixon's Square."

"Wear suitable clothes, a scarf for your face. You do have clothes for this, don't you?" Thomas said this while hiking up his breeches.

"Dark clothes, men's breeches, suitable for skulking about in the dark? Yes." She smiled and poured cream for Mr. Fisk. "I have those."

Discussing the rest of the plans went smoothly. As house breaking went, this was small and precise. In through an open window to open a locked cabinet and take papers. Hardly exciting. Yet, every part of her felt alive. Margaret not being here was upsetting, but if Margaret had been here, Thomas wouldn't be, a fact that kept niggling her as though her heart was big enough for one person or the other—not both.

She sipped her coffee. "I can't help but feel guilty about Margaret."

"If what Lady Denton told you is true, she's not been harmed. Frightened, of course, but safe." He took a seat at the table and tucked into his porridge. "I wouldn't be surprised if Miss Thelen's already found your sister."

"There is that, yes."

"Anything else?"

"Yes." She set down her coffee and looked him in the eye. "What happens afterward?"

Thomas went still. His reaction was unexpected, especially for a man who'd been so ardent.

"I meant after Margaret is safely returned and Ranleigh gets his papers." She traced a smudge on the table. "What happens to you and me?"

"What do you want to happen?"

She angled her head, unsure. Was she suddenly sitting with a different version of Thomas West?

"I want to be with . . . you."

"For how long, Mary? For a week? A day? Or thirty days?"

She flinched at his reference to the Red Rose room. Her arrangement, as it were.

"I've never met anyone like you. You've turned me upside down and made me rethink everything I've ever wanted. Consider this . . ." He opened his hand, palm up. "Tonight I'm going to break into the home of a prominent London citizen. A wretched woman who deserves it, but I'm doing it for you. I have no regrets, because you mean that much to me."

Mr. Fisk rubbed her legs, purring. She leaned down and petted him.

"Why do I feel like there's more trouble here?"

"I could say the same of you. Just yesterday you curtseyed to me as though we were strangers. Then, you told me Ranleigh informed you that you needed to leave London."

"Yesterday was a mistake."

"It was, and I came back because I want you safe."

"That's all?"

Thomas was implacable on the other side of her little table. He'd expanded somehow, larger than life. She could imagine him standing at the bow of a ship, the sun on his face, the wind whipping his hair. He'd drive the sea hunt by sheer force of will.

Why, then, did she sense something held him back?

"I want all of you, but I'm not sure that's what you want." He smiled crookedly. "You enjoy the extraordinary passion we share, as do I. But you've said from the beginning, 'love is not enough.' For you, at least."

A cold draft seemed to have crept in. She hunched over her coffee, nursing its warmth.

"I accept that marriage is many things. To build

families, start business arrangements, and on rare occasions . . . for love." Thomas studied the table for long seconds. "The truth is West and Sons Shipping is at a crossroads. To keep it alive, I must find someone to underwrite the insurance."

She was perfectly still, her hands and her feet going numb.

"As time allows, I've been looking into other possibilities." He fiddled with his bowl. "Every door has been firmly shut—except one."

She shook her head as though cobwebs needed clearing. "What are you saying?"

His gaze met hers. "That you were right. Marriage in London is a lottery."

Her throat was dry and clogged such that only a whisper could get out.

"You plan to marry a woman of means."

Tension lines bracketed his mouth. "It's what I must do if I cannot secure insurance."

"Do you have . . . a woman in mind?"

His green gaze pinned her. "There is only you."

Bittersweet words since they both knew she was not a wealthy woman.

She lost seconds while an ache bloomed in her chest.

A choice must be made—her or his family business.

Thomas, excellent hunter that he was, would easily find a wife at London's next social season. He was handsome and tall and good. Once word spread that he sought a wife, mamas and papas of the merchant class would come calling. He could have his pick of the wealthy families. She smiled, dismal and sad. He'd claimed she could've won a baron for herself.

She wouldn't be surprised if a widowed baroness with rich coffers offered herself to him.

"I want West and Sons Shipping to thrive." His voice scraped with sadness. "I want to keep my legacy alive. It's possible someday I will have sons. I want to give them something."

She swallowed hard. Hearing that was difficult.

Ancient philosophers would be proud of her stoicism. Or perhaps holding everything in was one of the lies she'd learned to live with. It felt like she'd been swimming in them and was only now coming up for air.

But this was Thomas's life. He deserved so, so much.

All this time she'd been consumed with her troubles when he had his share of burdens. She could tell him that he was the greatest gift his children could ever have. He'd make a wonderful father. He'd take them to beautiful gardens and give them thoughtful gifts of wisdom and understanding. He'd challenge them and make them laugh.

Thomas West was *the* treasure.

He'd been there all along, while she'd worked and hunted for Jacobite gold. If only she had searched for the right treasure. This was the knife twisting in her heart. No, there was something worse. His dilemma was a footnote to an undeniably bitter truth. A lesson she'd learned long ago.

Love wasn't enough.

It never was.

Chapter Thirty-Seven

Thomas guided the horse along Tiburn Lane. Taking it made sense. Hyde Park unfurled to their left and sleepy mews were on their right. Only a dray and two coaches had been their brief road companions. The empty lane emboldened Mary.

"You would've made a dashing highwayman. Your height alone is imposing."

Thomas was tight-lipped and serious about the night's business. The *clip-clop, clip-clop, clip* of horse hooves the only noise. They were west of London's west end, a veritable wild land for the City's well-shod residents. No street lamps guided the weary traveler and the stillness, unnerving for a woman about to commit a crime. But she was ready. Dressed in black, her braid properly tucked into her shirt. She looked like a slender man, with her arms around Thomas. His steadiness calmed her, but his silence she could do without.

"You're imposing in the saddle," she said. "And you're a good rider. I think your talents are wasted on the sea."

He coughed a laugh. "Life at sea is never a waste."

"Ah, he speaks."

"I still have my wits about me."

"I wouldn't know. You haven't said much."

He angled his head to her, his profile etched in the night. "Because you've been talking enough for both of us."

She set her cheek against his back. "Very unlike me. I think it's your effect."

"Mary . . ." He touched her hand under his coat. "If you're nervous, don't be."

"You're not angry with me?" she asked.

"No. Why would I be?"

She didn't have a suitable answer, mostly because she was frustrated with their impossible situation.

"I shouldn't have embroiled you in this," she said.

"I'm here with you as I should be."

No, he shouldn't.

Thomas carried the weight of his family business on his shoulders. West and Sons Shipping employed dozens of men, a number that expanded when whaling season was upon them. Everything he'd done was honest and lawful . . . until tonight. She wanted to ease his burdens, not add to them. But what could she give him? Her heart was her sole offering, and that organ was breaking, little bits at a time.

"Prepare yourself," Thomas said. "We're almost there."

Ever vigilant, he was scanning their environs. She sat up and took note when the horse turned down a new lane. Small hairs on her nape stood on end. The lane was dark, familiar. The back end of Upper Brooke Street.

"That's Denton House at the other end," she said.

"I know it. I rode by when I mapped our escape today."

Is that what he'd rushed off to do after breakfast?

"My, my, what a thorough criminal you would be."

Grosvenor Square was the bright jewel ahead, the address of London's wealthiest denizens. Candle lamps hung from well-equipped carriages crossing the square. People had other places to go. This was good, yet she couldn't shake her dread.

A white curtain showing through an open window caught her eye.

She pointed to it. "That's our window."

"I see it."

Thomas steered the horse to a nearby tree and leapt from the saddle. She followed him, landing with a soft *thud* on stamped earth. Horses nickered and a stableman's shushing soothed them. The mews were around the corner.

She froze. Had Lady Denton moved her mews?

Thomas stoically pinched the black scarf around her neck. His scarf was already up over his nose. A nod and she raised hers too. She could hear her heart banging in her ears, the stillness dreadful. Thomas passed a coiled rope to her and crept forward on stealthy feet.

Darkness cloaked them as they approached the window. She craned her neck. Had it always been that high off the ground? Or the tree, that close? Last August she'd parked a dray in this very spot. Anne and Will had climbed through the open window and took the seventeen hundred gold livres hidden in Lady Denton's study. Part of the Lost Treasure of Arkaig. But this time, they didn't have the advantage of climbing onto a tall dray to reach the window.

Thomas wasted no time leaping for the lowest tree limb. He grabbed it and scooted along, hand over hand, until he put the toe of his boot between ashlar cut stone. Levering himself, he held on to the slender end of the branch until he gripped the window's ledge.

Talented man. He could earn his coin with traveling tumblers.

Both hands on the ledge, Thomas hoisted himself up. His shoulder nudged the glass. He swung one leg over and climbed inside. Curtains outlined his dark form filling the opening. His queue was nearly undone.

She stood under the window, whispering, "You look like a male Rapunzel."

He braced both hands on the ledge. "Toss up the rope."

She did and he caught it easily "I could save some time and toss up the key."

But they both knew this was her nerves talking. Only she could manage it. Working the Wilkes-Lock was a complex instrument and the key, not your typical key.

"We do this together," he said in a low voice, unwinding the thin rope. Once undone, he dropped the knotted end. "Grab the rope and put your toe between the stones."

She started the climb, air swishing the hem of her frock coat. Hand over hand, she went. All of her was heavy. Her boots, the leather folio strapped to her back. She glanced down, sweat pricking her forehead. There was a good ten or twelve feet between her and the ground.

"Look at me," Thomas beckoned softly. "Just breathe."

The scarf covering her from the nose down billowed. She was breathing hard. Turning her face to Thomas, she found her comfort. Green eyes, gem bright and reassuring.

"Come to me, Mary."

No wonder men followed him to distant seas. Straining, she dug the toe of her boot into another crevice. Thomas reached for her. Big hands gripped her arms and hauled her up.

"I've got you," he said, pulling her through the window.

She sank against him, his solidness a necessity.

"You're safe." Thomas was hugging her, stroking the back of her head.

She held on to him and pressed her ear against his chest. His galloping heart was loud. She heard how much he was risking, being in Lady Denton's study. If she truly loved him, she'd get Thomas out of here as quickly as possible so he could get on with his life.

Taking a bracing breath, she got her bearings. "Let's finish this."

The desk was near the window as before. She went around it and searched the bookcase. The Wilkes-Locks cabinet had to be close to the floor. She dropped to her knees in thick carpet and found the brass lock.

"I've got it."

Thomas crouched beside her as she fisted the key forged last summer in his shipyard. His warmth was steady and reassuring. Without candlelight, she had to feel her way through this. Wilkes-Locks were fanciful and intricate by design—a Dutchman with movable parts etched in brass and a numbered dial to track when the lock was opened.

She pressed a small knob on the brass plate, and the Dutchman kicked up his plump leg. The key-hole was the opening where his calf had been. More whimsy for one of the best locks in all of Europe.

Her pulse banging in her ears, she inserted the key. The final step was tipping the Dutchman's hat and turning the key at the same time. She glanced at Thomas. His eyes were glittering in darkness.

There'd be no going back once she turned the key.

His nod was firm. "Do it."

One twist of the key and the dial clicked.

The cabinet door opened a fraction. She breathed a sigh of relief.

"Our work is almost done," she whispered, opening the door wider. Bending down, she examined the inside of the cabinet.

There was nothing but a stack of papers.

"There's no gold."

"You sound disappointed."

"I am." She twisted the folio around to the front of her. "After all this time, there should be a greater reward."

Thomas retrieved the papers and handed them to her. "One could say you already have it."

His face was close to hers but utterly unreadable.

"I'm not sure what you mean," she said in a low voice while jamming papers into her folio.

Thomas stiffened, alert. He turned his ear to the window and his hand stopped hers from stuffing the folio.

She could feel her eyes get bigger. The night was

stillness with nothing but her thoughts and the curtains stirring until Thomas's hand slipped off hers.

"Thought I heard something." A shake of his head and suspicion clouded his eyes. "This was too easy."

"Don't say that." She folded over the folio's leather flap, her palms dampening by the second.

Upon rising, she dropped the key onto the desk, her parting gift for the countess of Denton. It was a *take that!* arrogant thing to do. Lady Denton was a smart woman, but she was a vain one as well.

Why else would she commission the bust of a goddess to be sculpted with her face?

Mary swiveled on plush carpet, her eyes having adjusted to the unlit room. There, on a shelf, was the audacious sculpture. Lady Denton styled as a goddess. The delicate nose was a giveaway, as was the imperious angle of her face.

"Let's go." Thomas was already striding to the window.

"Wait. Look at that. It's Mr. Clabberhorn's sculpture."

"I see it. Now let's go."

"Not yet."

She was drawn to the unpainted porcelain. A magnetic pull that would not be denied. Why not examine it? They had the papers, and Denton House was as soundless as a church on Monday morning. All the servants were gone or abed.

And she was done being afraid of this woman.

Her feet seemed to agree the bust needed checking. The folio hanging in front of her, she went to the sculpture. Mr. Clabberhorn had said there was a hole in the back. An odd request. She reached around the porcelain goddess and searched for an opening. She was heavy, this Diana. More like a true marble bust than something made of dirt and clay. Mary pushed up on her toes and reached higher.

"The hole. I found it." She stuck two fingers inside and touched air. She tried harder. The hole was big enough for her hand to slip inside, but when she tried to take it out, the porcelain bust toppled over and landed with a weighty *thud* on thick carpet.

She clapped a hand over her mouth.

Coins scattered at her feet. A shiny pond of gold mixed with broken porcelain from the bust split in two.

Thomas raced around the desk. "What is this?"

Mary dropped to her knees and ran her fingers through the mass. Money trickled through her fingers, clinking as it fell. What a lovely sound. Though it was dark, she scrutinized one gold piece.

"Well, would you look at that squinting profile."

Thomas was on the ground beside her. "I'm not familiar with my squinting monarchs."

She bumped her shoulder companionably into his. "You'll like this one." She put the coin in his hand. "Meet your new friend, louis d'or." She sifted through the gold, trying to contain her excitement. "Do you know what this means?"

Thomas pocketed the coin. "It means we need to go. Someone's bound to have heard us and will come check the room."

She ignored him, caught in the glow of their find.

"These are louis d'or aux lunettes, and they are wonderful because one of these is worth twenty livres." She excitedly grabbed fistfuls of coins. "This must be the last of the Jacobite treasure." She opened the leather folio and dumped the louis d'ors into the pouch.

"A few handfuls and then we go."

"Yes, yes."

Thomas scooped up coins and poured them into the expanding folio. "With this much money, you can buy a large herd of Cheviots."

"This isn't for me. It's for you. To save West and Sons Shipping."

Thomas jerked to his feet. "I don't care about the money. We need to get out of here."

She struggled to get up, the weight of the bag unruly. So much gold spilled across the floor. They couldn't take all the coins, but they'd taken a large bite of the countess's ill-gotten gains.

Thomas reached for the bag. "Let me take that."

Light flickered in the hallway outside the study door. Footsteps were pounding, coming closer.

"Shite!" Thomas grabbed her arm. "To the window."

She rushed forward while he upended a liquor cabinet to block the door. Glass shards flew everywhere while shouts assaulted them from the hallway.

Thomas ran to her side and yanked down the curtain. "Out with you."

"No. You must go first. Then, I'll drop this down and follow."

She fisted the leather strap, a reminder.

Thomas's eyes glittered angrily. "Leave it."

"No. We need this for Margaret," she argued to the noise of someone ramming the study door.

Thomas's glare could melt ice, but he swung his leg over the window ledge. "Tie the rope to a chair and use it to climb down."

Mary was frantic, grabbing the rope off the floor.

She wound it around a sturdy leather chair, her hands jittery. More voices shouted beyond the door. Loud ramming and the sound of cracking wood filled the room. She tied a fast knot, shaking.

Bright light sliced over her. The door's gap was growing. Mr. Wortley pressed his face to the opening, his malevolent stare finding her.

Fear flooded her limbs. She tossed the rope out the window and held her breath. Thomas had already leapt off the window ledge and flung himself at the tree.

Mr. Wortley's voice rose above the din. "Grab a weapon and go to the other side of the house."

Her heart climbed into her throat. She was trapped, and the folio hung like dead weight on her chest.

"Go! Go now!" she yelled to Thomas. At least he could go free.

Wood splintered. A panel on the study door was buckling from a booted foot kicking it.

In all the noise, her ears picked out Thomas's voice. "I'm not leaving without you."

He was on the ground and reaching for her in the dark. Her frightened body seemed to know what was right. The folio hanging like an anchor, she swung a leg out the window and held onto the rope. Wortley was half through the door, his pistol aimed at Mary's heart. She was at the window, scrambling to get her other leg out, when sparks flared.

A shot rang out. Then another.

She fell backward, the rope ripping her palms. Thomas caught her, though they stumbled painfully hard, a smattering of coins rolling free.

He yanked her to her feet. "Come on!"

The horse was ready. Thomas put one foot in

the stirrup and hauled himself into the saddle. She was aware he reached down. They were graceless, her hugging the folio, and him dragging her up behind him.

The horse drove forward as though the devil was on its tail. Thomas rode boldly into Grosvenor Square. The black steed's legs pumped the ground and ran headlong at three men running out of Denton House. They fell like pins, flames flaring off their pistols when they took their shots.

Breathing hard, she dug her fingers into Thomas's waistcoat and sank against him. Excitement surged in her. They'd done it.

Lights glared, a fast blur. Grosvenor Square was behind them. Another square was ahead. Her chest hurt. Her palms stung. She was gulping midnight air, could hardly breathe. The scarf over her face wasn't helping.

Thomas's head whipped sideways. "Men are chasing us," he said above cold, piercing winds. "Dump the gold."

"I—no." Her voice was weak.

The bag *was* dreadfully heavy. Over her shoulder, three riders raced toward them. Wortley and two men. They were twenty or thirty paces out and gaining.

"Get rid of it!" Thomas yelled.

Another pistol shot rang out in the night. Women screamed. Men dove for cover behind carriages. She was light-headed, one arm around Thomas. Wind stung her eyes. Carriages and coachmen were ahead. The lights were terribly bright. An entertainment, a ball.

"Dump it now!" Thomas's voice was a ragged roar.

Her fogged mind whispered, *He's right*.

She blinked, more tired than she'd been in a long time. She struggled to open the folio. Blood was sticky on her palms, her fingers. Rope burns had slashed her skin. Her thigh nudged the bag and it tipped just so.

Streams of gold poured out. A pretty flash, those coins. They were gone forever.

Checking the road, she witnessed the wisdom of Thomas's plan. Coachmen swarmed first. Then, thirty or forty people set about scooping and shoving and grabbing unexpected wealth. Mr. Wortley and the two riders with him were on the other side of the mob and growing smaller by the second.

She rested her head on Thomas's back.

"No one's following us." It took all her might to say those words.

Thomas answered by squeezing her hand. Her eyelids were getting heavier, and her body slumped. She hugged the folio to her side. She couldn't afford to lose the papers too. Clutching the leather, she tried to get comfortable. Under her nose, an exposed corner of the papers riffled in the wind. Wine red stains were unexpected. Was it blood?

How could fresh blood be dripping on the pages?

Chapter Thirty-Eight

Morning broke slowly over Mary Fletcher. She was entombed in his bed, more fragile than his heart could take. She stirred, groaning.

"I ache," she said through cracked lips.

"Try this." Thomas held the back of her head and set a cup to her lips.

She slurped water, some of it dribbling down her chin. Once satisfied, her head fell on the pillow. He dabbed her chin and throat with a linen cloth.

"Is that better?"

"Water is good," she mumbled, "but I'd be ever so grateful if you stopped the arrows from piercing my chest. Unless you're telling me Cupid has finally struck."

Thomas felt his shoulders sink from relief. Mary's spirited humor was a good sign.

"Let me take a look."

He pulled back the covers and lowered the bodice of her thin shift. A bandage had been strapped around her chest above her heart. Gingerly, he peeked under the tightly wound cloth. The hole above her heart was the vivid wine color of congealed blood. Another positive sign. She was healing. Even better, only a small red ring encircled the wound. No infection, though it bore watching.

He'd removed the iron ball and saved it (he'd wager Mary would want to see the piece). It wasn't the first shot he'd removed; it wouldn't be the last. She'd been lucky, his Mary. Layers of leather and a gold medallion had saved her life. The shot had lodged half an inch into her body. Any deeper and she wouldn't be here to jest about her heart.

He was delicate with the bandage. "I'm sorry to say, but you've been attacked by the chubby love god."

She croaked a laugh, which ended in a wince. "Please, don't make me laugh. I can't take it."

Her bandaged hand rested on the coverlet near his. It wasn't long before they were holding hands and gazing into each other's eyes. Death breathing down one's neck could do that. Life, or the threat of losing it, rearranged priorities and clarified needs with alarming speed.

"I'll restrain myself today, if you promise that I'll be the man to make you laugh all the days of your life."

"That's quite a promise. Are you sure you can deliver?"

"Quite so."

She smiled weakly but her eyes glowed with undeniable affection. "No more standing shilly-shally for us."

"No." He brushed a wisp of hair off her forehead. "We are decided, you and I."

This was the moment his tabby cat sauntered into

354

the room, as one does when one is a cat. He leapt up on the other side of the bed and proceeded to lick one of his paws.

"It's Mr. Fisk." She was delighted to see the cat until she focused on what was behind him. "Where am I? And what time is it?"

She tried to sit up, but it was obvious every part of her ached. Thomas went to the window and drew back brown wool curtains. Subdued sunlight poured in, a reminder it was autumn and storms were coming.

"You're in my bedchamber in Southwark, not far from Vauxhall Gardens, and it's a few minutes past noon."

"I see." Miss Fletcher was curious, taking in somber browns paired with more somber browns.

He opened another curtain and went to the fireplace to stir the coals. "I suppose you'll want to redecorate."

"It's very . . . brown, but we can fix that."

Mary craned her neck this way and that, as though she was already changing the decor. He poured a coffee for himself, thrilled at her acceptance of what were profound changes. They were going from *you* and *I* to *us* and *we*. He contained his joy, so as not to frighten her too much, and held up the pot with a silent offer.

"No, thank you. I'll practice sipping water for a few hours first." She folded both hands on the coverlet, and he expected to see her do that for decades to come.

Miss Fletcher *would* eventually become Mrs. West. It was only a matter of time—and, he suspected, a matter of one carefully worded proclamation of love. His siren was cagey when it came to that four-letter word, but the time had come to be firm. To put feelings to words as a man does when he's found the woman who will share his name.

He went back to his place by the bed, the steaming cup in hand. "We keep talking around what is important to us both."

Her chest rose and fell gently. Even pale and recovering, she was pretty. Her braid a heavy rope, her mouth tender.

"We ought to say what we mean." Bold words but her voice was barely above a whisper.

"There is something sacred about love. Once given, you can't lose it or give it back. It's yours forever. And you, Mary Fletcher, have my undying love."

His voice had thickened with emotion. Questions were brimming in her eyes. The glittery tears, however, took him by surprise. With some effort, she sat up. Her lips pressed a wobbly line as though a tidal wave of words was coming, and they needed some organization.

"I may muddle this, but I want you to know—no, you deserve to know—that I have only loved one man in my life." Her watery gaze pricked him. "It's you . . . I love you, Thomas."

"And I love you," he said softer this time.

A hiss of inward breath, and she absorbed this.

"I can't begin to say all the things that—that I know are inside me, yet I don't even know what they are myself." She dabbed her eyes with her sleeve because great silvery drops had begun to flow. "Does that make me a ninny?"

"I think it makes you a woman in love."

She sniffled. "But I'd wager you are far better at expressing yourself . . . at making sense of your emotions, while I am quite ill prepared."

He set his coffee cup down. "I've been on the receiving end of your messages and . . ." He leaned forward and folded her hands with his. "We get along just fine. Why else would I devote myself to a lifetime with you?"

"Because of love." Her cheeks puffed an exhale.

Whatever Mary did, it wouldn't be done in half measure.

"What about last night?" she asked. "The gold we lost and your family's shipping legacy? And—and the countess?"

If he wasn't careful, she'd work herself into a fever and that would not be helpful to her recovery.

"The only metal I care about is the iron ball I removed from your chest." His voice had an edge. "It almost took you from me."

"But it didn't." She picked up the black ribbon on the bedside table. The medallion was concave, swinging back and forth.

"That gold piece, and the folio's thick leather, saved your life," he said.

"And what about your life and what you want? You still need a wealthy woman."

"I don't want one," he said simply enough.

"Truly?"

"For richer or for poorer, you are the only woman for me."

She wrapped her fingers around the smashed medallion. "You could've had one, you know. A wealthy woman. I tried to get a folio's worth of gold for you, but every last coin found its way into other men's pockets."

"Terrible, that."

"An imperious man on horseback ordered me to get rid of it."

He brushed his thumb over her cheek. "I'm glad he did. It saved your life."

"But what about his life? His future?"

"He has the best prize—you."

Mary sank back against the headboard, taking this all in until her eyes flew open. "My sister—"

"*Shhh.* Margaret is fine. She's safely hidden in Ranleigh's house. Miss Thelen rescued her last night."

"You consider that safe?"

"Your friend Miss MacDonald sent her maid to check on her. If that's not sufficient, I understand your aunt Maude will pay a visit later today."

"Oh, she'll set him straight." But a dark cloud of worry crossed her face. "Ranleigh's not releasing her, is he?"

"I explained our predicament." He jutted his chin at her chest. "You being shot, for example. Ranleigh was understanding—"

"Gracious of him," she muttered.

"—but the Countess of Denton? I'm not so sure. If she comes calling there are four men, each with two pistols, prepared to defend us. Three are outside and one inside by the front door. But my guess is Lady Denton doesn't know your whereabouts."

She fell back, defeated. "All those years, hunting the gold, and it's gone."

"All those years, you were hunting French livres. Last night you found louis d'ors."

"And your point?"

"You uncovered treasure that, if I'm guessing right, no one else save the countess knew about." He let that sink in before adding, "I believe you are more about the hunt than the prize."

"You might be onto something." She tucked loose hair behind her ear. "There is something about adventures big and small that appeal to me."

Her league work was all but finished. A transition was in store for her. Freedom, possibly, and he would be the man to give it to her. Now that their future as Mr. and Mrs. West was settled, another matter needed tending. He got up from the chair.

"Before we go any further, there is something you need to read."

Chapter Thirty-Nine

Two days later . . .

*G*un Wharf was a useful place to give a countess and a lord their comeuppance. Skies roiled an unfriendly gray to match weathered wood underfoot. Even the Thames matched the mood, its surface like pewter.

Thomas sidled up to the future Mrs. West, his greatcoat swirling around tar-spattered jackboots. Docks and ships were in his blood, but the sea was calling. It whispered of new adventures of love and marriage. He was keeping an eye on Mary. She was too pale, and her rich, dark hair only emphasized this.

"Everyone's in place." He fixed a bit of lace on her cloak which the wind had turned over. "Are you ready for this?"

"Very much. This marks a new beginning." Her mouth softened and tears threatened to come. "And I need to hug Margaret."

Ranleigh had dug in his heels. No papers, no sister.

"You will hug your sister today," he said.

Thomas felt a grin expanding. He was looking forward to this. At least Ranleigh had perfect timing; his carriage came jiggling over Gun Wharf. It pleased Thomas, seeing Ranleigh's head bobbing uncomfortably through the window. When the prancing bays stopped, a carriage door opened. Margaret flew out of it and ran to her sister.

"Mary!" The younger Miss Fletcher's eyes lit with joy.

They embraced, parting a few seconds, touching cheeks, shoulders, and embracing again amidst relieved laughs.

"As you can see, your sister is in excellent health." This came from Ranleigh, strolling across Gun Wharf as if it were St. James Square.

"Thank you, my lord," Mary said. To her sister, "We have a carriage if you wish to take shelter." She pointed at the West family conveyance. "It's the very brown one. You could tell the driver to take you to Neville House. Aunt Maude and Aunt Flora are waiting for you."

"That would be lovely." Margaret's brow furrowed. "But you'll come with me, won't you?"

Mary smoothed her sister's windblown hair. "I'll join you in a few minutes. There's so much I need to share."

Another hug, and sisterly whispers ensued. When they pulled apart, Margaret's eyes sparked with mischief at Thomas.

"Very well. I'll alert Aunt Maude and Aunt Flora that you're bringing a guest to Neville House." Margaret pivoted to Ranleigh and curtseyed. "My lord. Thank you for your gracious kindness these past few days. The same for Miss Thelen." Margaret waved to the henchwoman, who waved back from her perch on the coachman's seat.

Margaret darted into the West carriage and the conveyance rumbled off. Thomas was watching Miss Thelen. A mild frown played on the Swede's face. Her head tipped to subtle spots around the wharf. She would notice her surroundings, while Ranleigh was only interested in the leather folio by Mary's feet.

"Now that the exchange has been made, I'd like to take that."

Mary picked up the folio. "Not yet."

"Playing coy, Miss Fletcher?"

"No. I'm waiting for one more person."

Another carriage came creaking and swaying. Lady Denton. However, she had come with a finely curated collection of henchmen. Four of them, Mr. Wortley, her lead dog, among them. The countess wasted no time jumping from her carriage. She marched forward in breeches, her ruffians like bookends beside her, their pistols out.

"I came against my better judgment, Miss Fletcher. But your note was most enlightening."

Her attention went to the folio in Mary's hands.

"Someone with a leather folio broke into my home and took what belongs to me." Her carmine lips twisted a smile. "Oddly enough, they only took a portion of my money. Then they scattered it in the streets. Would you know anything about that?"

"I'm not interested in such fanciful tales. Insurance, however, is another matter," Mary said. "Very practical, I think."

Ranleigh widened his stance, a glower darkening his face. "I don't like the direction this is going."

Lady Denton's mouth pursed. "I'm inclined to agree with my cousin."

"I don't care about your likes or your inclinations. My kin and I have suffered under your whims long enough. We've been pawns, but not anymore." Mary was fierce, the wind batting her hems. "Our demands are simple. Leave us alone."

Lady Denton laughed. "You called me here for that?"

Mary tucked the folio under her arm and forged ahead with what would be a prickly conversation.

"Here are my terms. You will not harm any of the women in my league. Not one hair on their heads or mine. The same goes for any husbands, lovers, and children. Whoever we hold dear, you must treat them the same."

"Or?" This pertinent question came from Ranleigh.

Mary faced him. "Grub Street will publish certain true but undesirable stories about your mother." To the countess, "As for you, the crown and the governors of the East India Company will receive evidence of unflattering truths about you and your son."

Lady Denton's eyes were malevolent slits. "I could order my men to shoot you and walk away unscathed."

"Think again, Lady Denton. You're outnumbered, and you have the low ground," Thomas said. "An untenable position."

It was gratifying, seeing her henchmen twitch like children forced to sit too long. Mr. Wortley scowled at their perimeter. A beefy redhead who might've been the man who destroyed Mary's workroom was doing the same.

Iron gleamed like spots to the eyes from men

standing up on the roof of the surrounding warehouses. A mix of sailors and dock workers with nothing to lose. Each man had been carefully chosen for his toughness and unquestioning loyalty to Thomas. All of them had their weapons aimed at the countess, her men, and Ranleigh.

"Obviously, we have the high ground," Thomas said. "I recruit men from the prisons to come work for me. It turns out, my lady, when you take the time to believe in someone, to let them know they matter, this breeds profound loyalty. It works much better than money."

A muscle on Wortley's jaw ticked. The henchman shook his head. "We don't stand a chance, my lady."

She glared at him, but any argument died when he lowered his weapon. The ruffians with him did the same.

The countess turned her ire on Mary. "How do I know I can trust you?"

"Because I give you my word."

By the murderous gleam in her ladyship's eyes, this promise was difficult to digest.

The noblewoman's terse gaze bounced from roof to roof before landing on Mary. "You won't always have armed men to save you."

"But I'll always have those papers, my lady. You know their contents will destroy you."

Lady Denton pinched the ruby ring on her finger. She swallowed visibly and lifted her worried face to Wortley. An unpleasant breeze blew across Gun Wharf. Wortley arched a brow—his answer, apparently. One might believe trust passed between the countess and her vicious attack dog. After the barest nod, she turned to Mary.

"Very well. I understand your terms." Lady Denton looked as if she'd swallowed brine.

Wortley touched her elbow and, eyeing the four ruffians, he jerked his head at their carriage. The defeated countess and her men were leaving.

Ranleigh said not one word until her carriage exited Gun Wharf. "I must admit this was superbly played." He spoke to Thomas and Mary. "You don't want money, do you?"

"Freedom is sweeter than gold, my lord," Mary said. "Your cousin is controlled by greed, while you hunger for power."

"Not entirely. Love has its way." The dark lord squinted as the wind picked up.

"You are, at heart, a decent man, my lord." Mary was quite the negotiator, adjusting the empty folio under her arm. She understood the art of delivering insight with a well-timed compliment.

Ranleigh's smile was guarded. "So you read the contents of my cousin's safe?"

"Thomas and I read every word of it."

The dark lord came closer, his arms low and wide. "I told you once, I'd do anything to protect my mother, and I have."

Thomas stepped forward to shield Mary. "Easy, Ranleigh. It wouldn't bother me one bit to take you down a notch."

Mary touched Thomas's sleeve. "He won't harm me."

Ranleigh's smile curved ironically. Years he'd cultivated power. Thomas knew this, and in a matter of days, a corset maker of no consequence had done what no one else could do. She'd brought Ranleigh, metaphorically, to his knees.

"What kind of guarantee do I have? I'm not sure I can trust the word of a thief," Ranleigh said. "And Miss Fletcher, you are a thief."

"We know each other's sins, don't we? But you and I have something in common—a deep affection for our mothers. I've devoted nineteen years to honor my mother's dying wish. I'm certain you would do the same for your mother. At least she's alive. Enjoy that, my lord"—she put a firm chin forward—"and accept the terms I'm offering."

Ranleigh tipped his head, respect bright in his eyes. "Enjoy this, Miss Fletcher. You are the only woman to defeat me in this chess game I play."

"Checkmate, my lord."

Ranleigh huffed his discontent. He bowed, and upon rising, he said to Thomas, "Marry her before she gets away."

"I intend to."

Ranleigh turned on his heel and was two steps forward when Mary suddenly called to him. "Wait. There is one thing, my lord. A favor, if you please."

Ranleigh halted, his back twitching under the best great coat money could buy. The dark lord pivoted, autumn winds mussing his superbly styled queue.

"This should be good."

Mary sucked in a quick breath as though she grabbed fresh courage.

"I want you to arrange for a special dispensation for West and Sons Shipping. Guaranteed insurance. Next year only."

Thomas winced. "Mary, we didn't agree to this."

She touched his coat, her moonstone eyes tender. "You don't have to take it, but it's there, if you want it."

"A special dispensation?" Ranleigh laughed in disbelief.

"Please, my lord." Mary was bold, stepping forward. "Today has been a harsh blow to your cousin, and I gave that to you."

"Thank you for that, but I wanted those papers."

"To feed the awful revenge that keeps growing between you and your cousin." Mary hesitated, hugging the folio to her chest. "Isn't it time to be the better person? To show . . . kindness?"

"Kindness?" Ranleigh snorted. "You are a rare one, Miss Fletcher."

"Please . . ."

Thomas strode forward. He'd not have her beg on his behalf.

The dark lord's mouth firmed, but his gaze eased. "I can already hear the sphincters at Whitehall tightening. Very well. I'll seek one on your behalf, but I make no promises."

"That's all I ask," she said.

Thomas touched Mary's elbow, and watched Ranleigh depart. Miss Thelen climbed down off her perch and into the carriage.

The folio Mary held was empty. It was bait to ensure they got out of their carriage. The damning papers had been safely hidden away. Lady Denton and her cousin were in a bitter tug-of-war. The countess had uncovered proof that Ranleigh's mother had been a smuggler and had killed a man—a peer, supposedly in self-defense. The stain, however, could ruin her. Lord Julian Ranleigh would move heaven and earth to protect his mother.

Lady Denton's file was darker. Very few men

were on the board of governors of the East India Company; the Earl of Denton once had a seat at the table until he died. Lady Denton's son would take his father's place once he came of age.

Yet, her son was not an heir of the body. She'd bought him from a Scottish couple with similar coloring and features to her own and the earl's.

It had been a shock to read this. But the lady's purpose was clear. The countess could control her son—his wealth and his vote on the East India Company board of governors. If he dared to challenge her, he'd lose his title and become a pariah. This had to be why she kept such damning papers. And Ranleigh? Thomas suspected the dark lord wanted those papers to control the hapless young earl. It was possible, but he no longer cared.

Wind battered him and Mary, standing on Gun Wharf. He wrapped her cloak about her and signaled for the men to come down off the roofs. There were jovial calls to grab a pint at the Iron Bell. Thomas and Mary were invited, but for the moment he wanted her all to himself.

They watched ships gliding through the water, their bodies molded together. Mary settled her head against his chest. He lashed an arm around her waist, liking the feel of her against him.

He kissed the crown of her head, a blustery breeze knocking her curls. Though patience was a virtue, he'd not wait much longer to make her Mrs. West.

"I don't know what our future holds, but I do know that I love you," he said.

She rubbed his arm. "Promise me you will tell me stories every night."

"I will."

"You might want to finish your tale about the shipmaster and the siren."

"That one has no end."

She hummed pleasantly and turned to link arms with him. "I like the sound of that."

Mary guided him across Gun Wharf. Weathered wood creaked underfoot. Seagulls darted near and landed. Though they didn't say a word, he knew they were ambling toward the Iron Bell. They'd share a pint before they visited Neville House. Then, they'd go home—to their home—not far from Vauxhall Gardens.

After a moment she asked, "Would you consider composing poetry?"

"Poetry . . . that's a bit of a stretch."

"I was thinking something in the vein of stars shimmering and moons shining brightly."

He grinned. Stoking the carnal fires, was she?

"You want *that* kind of poetry?"

She gave him a saucy side-eye. "Think you can do that?"

"I can do anything for you."

Because love was more than enough.

Epilogue

Spring 1754

*T*he schooner was flying. Adventure was afoot. Mary rode the front of the ship like a bow head siren—which was her husband's latest endearment for her. One of many, as one does when married. Life with Thomas was excellent. Mary soared with happiness. Freedom was infinite.

At moments like these, she truly lived it. Her arms out, wind whipping her hair, sails billowing overhead—the foresail and mainsails, of course.

They were crossing the Sea of Hebrides. Their course set for Benbecula, part of Clanranald Mac-Donald lands. The humble island was a scraggy bump on the horizon, the sky behind it a painter's smeared strokes of orange, lavender, peach, and blue.

She leaned forward, tasting the Hebrides in the wind.

"Have a care, Mrs. West. There's no chancier wench than the sea. She might decide to give you the toss."

Her husband. She closed her eyes and let the setting sun kiss her face. She felt his presence beside her.

"And would you jump in to save me?" she asked.

"Of course."

Thomas's voice took on gruff tenderness. She savored it and the wind brushing past her cheeks.

"You look as beautiful as the first day I clapped eyes on you," he said.

"Let's hope you say that when I'm old."

She opened her eyes to his gentle touch on her chin. "I always will."

They huddled together, forearms braced on the rail as they watched the island grow bigger. Sea spray anointed their hands, and the sun washed their faces. This was the kind of adventure she craved—sunshine and the open sea with Thomas.

"Does this feel like you're returning to the scene of a crime?" he asked.

"Whatever do you mean?"

"The island where Flora MacDonald hid Charles Stuart."

"And then dressed him like a maid to secret him away. Yes, I'm aware of the story."

His eyes, so infinitely green, snared hers.

"Would you say it was the beginning of our story?"

She traced his very kissable scar. "A philosopher's conundrum, Mr. West. Could be you're reading too many books and not having enough adventures."

"Oh-ho, you mean hying off to France to pick up all these"—he gestured at their audience—"lovely ladies isn't adequate?'

She laughed. "They are staring at us again, aren't they?"

"I'd stare at you too."

"You do quite often." She sealed that with a slow kiss.

They turned to face the twenty-odd Cheviot sheep chewing the last of the hay, their liquid brown eyes watching them. It had been a long journey from Rochelle, but they weathered their travels well. They were pretty sheep. Fluffy and round, their wool white and their faces and hooves pitch-black. Bits of hay poked out of their mouths. Heels clicked nervously as they bleated their sorrow at being stuck on a ship.

"Landlubbers, all of them," she said.

This had been Mary's final vow to Clanranald MacDonald—to begin restoring the herds. Stroking one damp obliging ewe nose, she felt good. This was a kindness done, a promise fulfilled. She petted another ewe, who had been especially nice to Mr. Fisk.

The poor cat. He preferred home over ships, to the chagrin of Mr. West.

Thomas crouched beside her and petted the sheep too. "This is a good thing you're doing, Mary."

His praise made her heart expand and her soul lighter.

"It's only happening because of you," she said.

His offer to get the sheep and deliver them had come at an inopportune time. Whaling season had begun. It would be West and Sons's last summer of whale hunts. After this season West and Sons would turn their efforts to making deliveries: Ireland, Scotland, Holland, the Baltics, generally any seas that weren't at war with the crown. It was a hard decision, but a good one. Thomas was keeping his father's legacy of ships alive.

Margaret was in charge of Fletcher's House of

Corsets and Stays, and Mary would travel with Thomas—for new adventures.

And she couldn't get enough. Of her sea wolf especially.

Mary rested her head on Thomas's shoulder. Freedom tasted wonderful. Love tasted even better. It might've been the hardest lesson to learn but finally, finally, she'd grasped it.

Love was always enough.

Acknowledgments

Thank you, Sarah Younger, for being the best agent. We've been going strong for a decade (wow!). Thank you, Sylvan Creekmore, for helping me to truly see this story. You have a keen editorial eye. I look forward to working on the next project with you. Thank you, Avon peeps, for making this book shine: Amy Halperin (cover illustration) and Gene Mollica and Sasha Almazan, of GS Cover Design Studio. Thank you, Kathleen Mancini and Mark Burkeitt, for keeping me on my grammar-ish and etymology toes. Sometimes I play fast and loose with the rules. Thank you to the production team, marketing team, and Avon's publicity team: I hope you read these acknowledgments. You are the energy behind getting my books into the stores and into the hands of readers. Really, thank you!

Lastly, thank you readers for sticking with me. Much love to you! —Gina